"Liparulo has crafted a diabolical thrill ride of a novel that makes the roller coaster at Magic Mountain seem like a speed bump. Part serial killer procedural, part global techno-thriller, part spiritual suspense epic, *Comes a Horseman* has enough plot twists and action to decode Da Vinci! Highly recommended!"

—Jay Bonansinga, author of *Frozen, The Killer's Game,*
and *The Sinking of the Eastland*

"Prophecy and murder run roughshod through *Comes a Horseman.* From the mountain peaks of Colorado down to a labyrinth beneath Jerusalem, mystery and adventure abound in a read that will keep you up to the wee hours of the morning. Not to be missed!"

—James Rollins, *New York Times* best-selling author of
Sandstorm and *Map of Bones*

"[In *Comes a Horseman*] Robert Liparulo starts off with a bang and then lulls us momentarily with well-modeled and sympathetic characters before he drops those same totally likeable characters into a series of harrowing confrontations. Some of the fights involving razor-edged weapons manage to be excruciatingly wince-inducing while remaining truly entertaining. This is what is meant by guilty fun."

—Larry Hama, writer, Marvel Comics' *G.I. Joe* and *Wolverine*

"Read this book with the lights on! Gory and ghastly, yet with a gripping plot, these pages will literally tremble in the hands of readers! *Comes a Horseman* is a chilling ride into a horrifying possibility!"

—www.inthelibraryreviews.com

germ

ROBERT LIPARULO

THOMAS NELSON
Since 1798

NASHVILLE   DALLAS   MEXICO CITY   RIO DE JANEIRO   BEIJING

To my boys—
Matt, always thoughtful and a joy to know
and
Anthony, who keeps me young and smiling

Published in Nashville, Tennessee, by Thomas Nelson. Thomas Nelson is a
registered trademark of Thomas Nelson, Inc.

Thomas Nelson, Inc. books may be purchased in bulk for educational, business,
fund-raising, or sales promotional use. For information, please e-mail
SpecialMarkets@ThomasNelson.com.

Publisher's Note: This novel is a work of fiction. Names, characters, places,
and incidents are either products of the author's imagination or used fictitiously.
All characters are fictional, and any similarity to people living or dead is purely
coincidental.

Library of Congress Cataloging-in-Publication Data

Liparulo, Robert.
  Germ / Robert Liparulo.
    p. cm.
  ISBN 978-0-7852-6178-0 (hardcover)
  ISBN 978-1-59554-365-3 (mass market)
  1. Viruses—Fiction. 2. Biological warfare—Fiction. 3. Scientists—Fiction. 4.
Center for Disease Control—Fiction. I. Title.
  PS3612.I63G47 2006
  813'.6—dc22

                              2006026645

Printed in the United States of America
08 09 10 11 12 QW 6 5 4 3 2 1

facts

- Ebola is one of the most lethal viruses known to man.
- With each outbreak, a higher percentage of people who contract it die.
- In 1995, an airborne strain of Ebola was discovered.
- Even thirty years after the first Ebola outbreak, no one knows where it came from or where it resides when it is absent from humans or monkeys.
- The Guthrie test, also called a PKU test, was developed by Robert Guthrie in 1962. It involves drawing a sample of blood from a newborn's heel and helps diagnose certain genetic diseases, such as phenylketonuria. It is routinely administered to all babies born in industrialized nations.
- Most Guthrie cards, with these blood spots, are stored in warehouses and never destroyed.
- The blood on these cards contains DNA that identifies the donors.
- With the advent of gene splicing, scientists are capable of encoding viruses with human DNA.
- Theoretically, this gives viruses the ability to *find* specific DNA—to find *you*.

In the arts of life man invents nothing;
but in the arts of death he outdoes Nature herself,
and produces by chemistry and machinery all
the slaughter of plague, pestilence, and famine.
—George Bernard Shaw

"Let there be light!" said God, and there was light!
"Let there be blood!" says man, and there's a sea!
—Lord Byron, *Don Juan*

Courage is almost a contradiction in terms.
It means a strong desire to live taking the
form of a readiness to die.
—G. K. Chesterton

one

HARDLY RESEMBLING A MAN ANYMORE, THE THING ON THE bed jerked and thrashed like a nocturnal creature dragged into the light of day. His eyes had filled with blood and rolled back into his head, so only crimson orbs glared out from behind swollen, bleeding lids. Black flecks stained his lips, curled back from canted teeth and blistered gums. Blood poured from nostrils, ears, fingernails. Flung from the convulsing body, it streaked up curtains and walls and streamed into dark pools on the tile floor.

Despesorio Vero, clad in a white lab coat, leaned over the body, pushing an intratracheal tube down the patient's throat; his fingers were slick on the instrument. He snapped his head away from the crimson mist that marked each gasp and cough. His nostrils burned from the acidic tang of the sludge. He caught sight of greasy black mucus streaking the blood and tightened his lips. Having immersed his hands in innumerable body cavities—of the living and the dead—few things the human body could do or produce repulsed him. But *this* . . . He found himself at once steeling his stomach against the urge to expel his lunch and narrowing his attention to the mechanics of saving this man's life.

Around him, patients writhed on their beds. They howled in horror and strained against their bonds. Vero ached for them, feeling more sorrow for them than he felt for the dying man; at least his anguish would end soon. For the others, this scene would play over and over in their minds—every time an organ cramped in pain; when the fever pushed beads of perspiration, then blood, through their pores; and later, during brief moments of lucidity.

The body under him abruptly leaped into an explosive arch. Then it landed heavily and was still. One hand on the intratracheal tube, the other gripping the man's shoulder, Vero thought mercy had finally come—until he noticed the patient's skin quivering from head to toe. The man's head rotated slowly on its neck to rest those pupil-less eyes on the doctor. With stuttering movements, as if a battle of fierce wills raged inside, the eyes rolled into their normal position. The cocoa irises were difficult to distinguish from the crimson sclera.

For one nightmarish moment, Vero looked into those eyes. Gone were the insanity of a diseased brain and the madness that accompanies great pain. Deep in those bottomless eyes, he saw something much worse.

He saw the man within. A man who fully realized his circumstances, who understood with torturous clarity that his organs were liquefying and pouring out of his body. In those eyes, Vero saw a man who was pleading, pleading . . .

The skin on the patient's face began to split open. As a gurgling scream filled the ward, Vero turned, an order on his lips. But the nurses and assistants had fled. He saw a figure in the doorway at the far end of the room.

"Help me!" he called. "Morphine! On that cart . . ."

The man in the doorway would not help.

Karl Litt. He had caused this pain, this death. Of course he would not help.

Still, it shocked Vero to see the expression on Litt's face. He had heard that warriors derived no pleasure from taking life; their task was necessary but tragic. Litt was no warrior. Only a monster could look as Litt did upon the suffering of the man writhing under Vero. Only a monster could smile so broadly at the sight of all this blood.

two

thirteen months later

FOR ONE INTENSE MOMENT, SUNLIGHT BLAZED AGAINST THE windshield, making it impossible to see the traffic streaming ahead on I-75. Special Agent Goodwin Donnelley kept the accelerator floored; he could only hope he didn't plow into another vehicle. At the top of the on-ramp, the sedan took flight. Donnelley and his passenger smacked their heads against the roof; then the car crashed down in an explosion of sparks. Its front bumper crumpled the rear quarter panel of a Honda before Donnelley's frantic overcorrection slammed the car against the right-hand guardrail.

He saw a clear path in the breakdown lane and straightened the wheel to accelerate past Atlanta's lunchtime congestion. In the rearview mirror, the black Nissan Maxima pursuing them bounded onto the highway, disappeared behind a semitrailer, then reappeared in the breakdown lane.

The man beside him—Despesorio Vero, he had called himself—turned to look, blocking Donnelley's view.

"They're gaining!"

"Sit down!" Donnelley shoved him, then scanned the roadway ahead. A glint of sunlight flashed off a car stopped in the breakdown lane a half mile ahead. At eighty miles per hour, the distance would evaporate in twenty seconds. Traffic was lighter here; he could swerve into the lane on his left anytime.

Another glance at the rearview: the Maxima was almost on top of them. A figure armed with a shotgun jutted up from the passenger-side window.

If Donnelley waited until the last moment to swerve, the Maxima would crash into the stalled car. The car's hood was up, but Donnelley could not see anyone around it. If he tricked the Maxima into hitting it, he would impose a death sentence on anyone standing in front of the car.

He veered back into the traffic lane, granting the Maxima time to follow.

His pursuers crossed into the middle lane and in a burst of speed edged closer. Now the Maxima's bumper was even with Donnelley's door. Instinctively, he touched the outside of his pants pocket. It was still there—the tracking device. He had not been able to place it on Vero's clothing, but it was turned on: his partner could track them. She was back there now, somewhere behind the Maxima.

He drew his pistol from the holster under his arm, bringing it across his body to shoot. Just then, the rear driver's-side window shattered into thousands of tiny crystals that sailed across the car's interior, along with the thunderous sound of a shotgun blast from the Maxima. Vero screamed, and both men ducked.

Another blast hit Donnelley's door. He kept his head down, blind to the road ahead, letting minor collisions with the guardrail on his right and the Maxima on his left keep the vehicle relatively straight. Another blast took out the metal pillar between the front and rear side windows and most of Donnelley's headrest. His gun flew across the car and skidded around on the passenger floor mat.

Boom! Vero's window disintegrated.

"Enough of this!" Donnelley slammed his foot down on the brake for a mere instant. The car jolted, and the Maxima pulled ahead. He cranked the wheel to the left. The sedan's front corner rammed dead into the Maxima's passenger door, directly below the startled face of the shooter hanging halfway out the window.

The man's torso jerked down, as if for an enthusiastic Oriental greeting. From his position ducked behind the wheel, Donnelley didn't witness the man's face hitting the sedan's hood, but that it did was indisputable: the shotgun pinwheeled across the windshield and over the roof. A split second later the man jerked back into view, blood spewing from both nostrils. He disappeared back into the Maxima.

Donnelley sat up and cranked the wheel again. This time, the sedan nailed the Maxima just forward of the front tire. The pursuer's car shot across three lanes and fell back. Just as he was registering the decent distance he'd gained on the Maxima, the bloody-faced shooter reemerged, a new shotgun in hand. He appeared to be bellowing in rage, a warrior whose battle had become personal.

Donnelley slapped Vero in the chest and pointed to the floor. "Hand me that pistol. *Now!*"

BACK AT THE ON-RAMP THAT HAD ADMITTED THE DUELING VE-hicles onto I-75, another car, this one a chocolate brown Ford

Taurus, vaulted onto the highway. In a chorus of screeching rubber, it fishtailed across three lanes before choosing one and bulleting forward.

Inside, Julia Matheson straightened the wheel and pushed the accelerator. Her lips were pressed tightly against her teeth. Dark bangs clung to her sweaty face, despite the car's air-conditioning. Her wide eyes darted around, looking for openings in the traffic and for her partner up ahead.

The pandemonium coming through the tiny speaker nestled in her ear was maddening. Through intermittent patches of static and dead air came explosions of gunfire, ferocious commotion that could have been crunching metal or more static, screams, and shouted expletives.

Her partner, Goody Donnelley, wore a wireless microphone designed for monitoring conversations from no farther than a mile away, but she saw no signs of him.

Once again she tried reaching him on the in-car police-band radio: "Goody! Pick up. This is Julia. Goody!"

She knew the problem: he had turned it off before going into the hotel to pick up the guy they'd said was causing trouble, because it tended to interfere with the body microphone's signal.

Through the earpiece she heard Goody yell, "Hand me that pistol. *Now!*" Static followed.

She thought again of contacting the Atlanta police, Georgia state patrol, her own agency . . . *anyone;* but she trusted Goody's instincts, and when it had all hit the fan, he had told her not to call for backup.

She slapped a palm down against the wheel.

It was not supposed to have gone down like this. *Not like this.*

Okay, no duh. But an hour ago the assignment had seemed more than boring. It had seemed beneath them.

three

Goody had called her shortly after six.

"Rise and shine," he said.

She could hear his sons laughing and yelling in the background. She couldn't image that kind of energy this early.

He continued, "Our mad caller's in town. He showed up at CDC this morning."

"Vero?" Julia asked, still groggy. "He's here?"

For two days the guy had been calling, demanding to speak to the director of the CDC's National Center for Infectious Diseases. He had been only semicoherent, rambling about an old virus that was really a new virus and a threat that may or may not be related to bioterrorism. As agents of the NCID's new Law Enforcement Division, which Congress created as part of the Bioterrorism Weapons Antiterrorism Act, Julia Matheson and Goodwin Donnelley had attempted to trace the calls and find out more about the man making them. The calls had been placed from different pay phones in the DC area, and the name "Despesorio Vero" had been conspicuously absent from every database available to them.

"Showed up at Gate 1 about five, hysterical about getting in. The security guard thought he was going to ram the barricade. The guard force was about to detain him when he backed up and took off. Rental car, picked up at the airport last night."

"So we gotta find him?"

"He's meeting us at the Excelsior at nine."

"He's meeting *us*?"

"Well, *me*. He thinks I'm Sweeney." Director of NCID, John Sweeney. "Vero called right after taking off. They patched him to me."

And meeting off-site was standard operating procedure. Samples of most of the world's deadliest pathogens were housed in the CDC's labs. A candy store for terrorists. Prudence demanded knowing who wanted in and why. It was a policy that rankled CDC scientists who had invited their peers and the public relations staff who thought every taxpayer and his kids deserved access. But nobody wanted nuts roaming the halls. And Vero sounded certifiable.

"You going in wired?" Julia had special training in surveillance technology. These days, everything was recorded.

"'Course," he answered. "And bring the SATD. Molland wants this guy tagged, in case he bolts and there's something to his claims."

Edward Molland was the director of Domestic Operations, their boss.

"Give me forty-five minutes."

"How's your mom?" His voice took on a gentle tone.

"Good days, lately. She watches too much TV."

"And you don't?"

"Only *Lost* these days, Goody. You saw me at my worst."

Before her mother had gotten sick and come to live with her, Julia had spent a few months in the Donnelleys' guest bedroom. She'd just broken up with a guy and hadn't felt like socializing, so she'd spent her evenings soaking up sitcoms and docudramas. She'd gained five pounds too. Long gone now.

"Worst. Best. What are friends for? See you in thirty."

"Forty-five," she said, but he'd already hung up.

On the way out she had listened outside her mother's bedroom, then knocked softly and cracked the door. Mae Matheson was sitting on the edge of the bed, reading the label of a pill bottle.

"You all right?"

She looked up, startled. "Oh, I didn't hear you. What are you doing up so early?"

"Case came up. I'm heading out. You going to be all right?"

Mae smiled, and Julia felt a familiar dull ache in her chest. Her mother was too young to be like this. Fifty-three. Multiple sclerosis made her more like eighty-three.

She'd been diagnosed six years ago. Julia's father had decided he didn't want to spend the rest of his life taking care of an invalid, and he'd taken off. Two years ago, her mother had moved in with her. Some days she couldn't get out of bed, couldn't eat. If Julia could not stay home—more often than not—she called in a nurse or an assisted-living worker. It looked as though today she could get by on her own, already sitting up, doing things.

"Couldn't sleep," Mae replied. "What else is new? I'll be fine. Have a good day, sweetie."

Julia had held the door open a moment longer. One of these days, she'd have to stay home with her on a good day, just to do it, just for fun. She'd thought the same thing every day for two years. She smiled a good-bye and shut the door.

At their offices on the CDC compound, she had rigged her equipment and strategized with Goody and Molland. By five minutes to nine, she was sitting in her car across from the marble-and-gold Excelsior Hotel, listening.

"No sign of him yet," Goody said from inside the hotel's restaurant. He had reconnoitered the lobby, offices, and kitchen before taking a seat.

Julia heard a waitress ask him what he wanted, heard him order a large OJ.

"Oh no!" he said, panicky.

Her body tensed. "What?"

"These prices are ridiculous. Becky in accounting's going to have a stroke."

"Funny." She eyed the laptop computer in the passenger seat. Its monitor displayed a map of the area surrounding the hotel. A glowing red dot marked Goody's location inside the building.

A cable ran from the computer to a box the size of a hardback book on the floor. Another cable connected the box to a device that looked like a mobile phone antenna with a flanged tip, which was suction-cupped to the outside of the passenger window. The box and antenna, along with custom software on the laptop's hard drive, made up a unit called the Satellite-Assisted Tracking Device, or SATD. Developed by a defense contractor under the joint supervision of the FBI and the CIA, it allowed agents to locate a transmitter the size of a fingernail to within several feet from halfway around the world.

"Here we go," Goody said under his breath.

Another voice, breathy and raw: "Sweeney? Are you Sweeney?"

Goody: "Are you all right? You don't look so good."

The other voice: "Don't worry about it."

"Hold on. I am worried about it. Waitress, some water, please! Let me take you to the hospital. We can talk there."

"Look, I want to go to your office. Why did we have to meet—?"

The transmitter conveyed the piercing sound of smashing glass.

"Down! Down!" It was Goody. A volley of booming explosions followed—shotgun blasts, judging by their deep resonance. Six pistol shots rang out in quick succession: Goody's return fire.

Julia simultaneously unbuckled her seat belt and opened the door. She was about to leap out when she heard Goody address her: "Julia! Pull up—" More gunfire. "Pull up out front. I got Vero. We're coming out."

She started the car, cranked the wheel, and jammed her foot on the accelerator. Her half-opened door swung out, smashed into the corner of the car parked in front of her, and slammed shut. A car screeched to a halt inches from her. Her car vaulted across three lanes of downtown traffic toward the hotel's canopied entrance.

"Get down! Get down! Everybody down!" Goody shouted through the wireless microphone.

Two shotgun blasts, close together—too close to have come from a single weapon.

Just as Julia's car bounded onto the sidewalk directly in front of the hotel doors, valets and pedestrians leaping aside, she heard Goody.

"Can't get there, Julia! Get out of here! We're heading for my car in the parking garage. You go! *Go!*"

She cranked the wheel left to shoot back into the street. She drove two blocks, turned two corners, and pulled to the curb. She was facing the hotel again on the street that ran past the rear entrance—and the parking garage exit. The wireless conveyed mostly static now. Then: "—Julia? . . . hear me? I'm on . . . McGill . . . west . . . right on my tail!"

McGill! She was on the same street. He was driving away from her. She made a squealing U-turn.

"Listen to me," Goody said. The reception was clearer now. "I recognized one of the shooters. James something. Satratori—something like that. Almost busted him a few years back. Serpico for DEA at the time, as far as I could figure. They got him out of my custody faster than—sit down!"

He berated Vero for getting in his way.

Julia bit her lip. *Serpico* meant he was a deep-undercover agent.

"Don't call in backup," Goody continued. "Not till we figure out why a fed's on the hit team. Got it?"

There was silence and the rustling of Goody's shirt over the microphone. He was probably maneuvering through traffic. She could hear Vero rambling in the background.

"As soon as I lose these guys, we'll meet and decide on a plan," Goody said. "But for now, it's just us, okay?" More silence, then: "Gettin' on the highway. Hear me? I-75 north."

THAT WAS ONLY MINUTES AGO, TWENTY AT MOST. NOW, AS SHE barreled down I-75 somewhere behind Goody, only static filled her ear. Goody's frantic movements must have dislodged the transmitter's wires, or he had finally traveled out of range. She plucked out the earphone and glanced at the laptop. The glowing red dot indicated that her partner was about two miles ahead. Her foot muscles flexed harder against the accelerator.

Julia realized with sudden terror that the knot of cars in front of her was stopped. She slammed on the brakes. As the smell of burnt rubber washed over her, she saw the glass and bits of plastic that littered the roadway. Paint the color of Goody's car clung in long streaks to the crushed guardrail. On the SATD display, the red dot was moving away fast. She laid on the horn. From the car in front of her, a hand with an upraised finger shot out of the driver's window.

"Suit yourself," she said and stepped on the gas.

four

THE MAN IN THE PILOT'S SEAT OF THE CESSNA CJ2 WAS obsessed with serving his clients well. He believed in quick responses and promptness, so much so that he hadn't given a second thought to purchasing the jet, or the one before it or the one before that. He believed in confidentiality, so he piloted the plane himself, and he had no staff, just a series of electronic telephone relays that ultimately dumped inquiries into a voice mailbox in Amsterdam. He didn't buy the currently voguish axiom "Underpromise/overdeliver." He listened to his clients' needs; they agreed to an action plan and when that plan would be completed; and he carried it out on time. Enough said.

Take his last job. The client had been a stockbroker, entangled in an SEC investigation. His defense's weak link had been his assistant, whom he'd foolishly allowed to know more than he should have. The pilot had visited the assistant's apartment and shot the man twice in the head. Problem solved. As usual, he had charged a staggering sum for his services, but the fee had barely made a dent in the broker's annual bonus. And now the broker would be cashing next year's bonus check as well, instead of cleaning toilets at Danbury. He had made a wise investment.

One client had said he'd heard the assassin was the best in his field. He didn't know about that. He didn't care. He did his job. Period.

That's not to say he was dispassionate about it. He loved his job, which allowed him to do it without comparing his performance to others'. He loved the economics of death: hastening a person's passage into the afterlife not only provided him with a good living; it gave work to coroners, beat cops, detectives, crime scene technicians, the people who made fingerprint powder and luminol and other sundry chemicals and devices—not to mention firearm, ammunition, coffin, and tissue manufacturers—obituary writers, crime reporters, novelists. He'd spent an evening once enumerating the occupations that owed their existence, either wholly or in part, to murder—seventy-eight—and the economic impact of homicide—more than $23 billion, trumping the recording, motion picture, and video game industries.

He loved that he was able to remedy a critical life problem as quickly and easily as a plumber unclogs a drain or a mechanic tunes an engine. Who else could make that claim? Not attorneys, accountants, or doctors. Not homebuilders, psychiatrists, or priests. He'd considered hanging around after a kill to covertly watch his client happily get on with his life, to derive that extra pleasure of witnessing the benefits of his service to them. But that would be unprofessional and unwise.

He held a glass of club soda and lime in his hand and watched the autopilot gently maneuver the control stick. The sky outside was bright and blue and clear. He closed his eyes.

Another thing he loved: being part of a mysterious and fearful force of nature. The ways people personified death fascinated him—the stereotypic hooded, faceless Reaper, harvesting souls with the snap of a gleaming scythe; Hemingway's stealthy beast that consumed the ill fated adventurer in the shadow of Kilimanjaro; the beautiful woman, whose kiss bore eternal consequences, in the movie *All That Jazz*.

He felt them all dwelling within.

Even his name, the only name he had ever known, fit the lexicon of death. Atropos. The ancient Greeks depicted Fate as three stern old sisters, goddesses though they were. Clotho, the Spinner, spun the thread of life; Lachesis, the Dispenser of Lots, decided the thread's span and assigned to each person his or her destiny; and Atropos, the Inexorable, carried the dreaded shears that cut the thread of life at the proper time, which was often determined by her whim. This third sister's role was his. He gladly accepted the mantle and the name.

Death was a release from this world's problems. He had seen serenity in his victims' eyes as they focused on something invisible to the living. In his experience, all humans lived in a constant state of terror; but in death, peace engulfed them. No more fear, no more worries. Just peace. That was his gift to them.

Blessed are the peacemakers. He liked the idea of being blessed.

A drop of moisture slid down the glass and pooled on his finger. Then another and another. A single bead of cold condensation trickled over his knuckles.

His eyes flicked open.

He'd almost drifted off. He took a sip from the glass and placed it in a cup holder, then he rolled sideways out of the pilot's seat and stood, staying low to slip out of the cockpit. Even in the cabin, he walked stooped over. His six-foot-four frame was ill-suited for the cabin's five-foot height. For the thousandth time, he yearned for a Gulfstream G500. But as pricey as the Cessna was, the Gulfstream cost ten times more. He couldn't justify the expenditure. Not yet.

The Cessna's cabin had been converted to accommodate a galley, a plush chair that folded flat for sleeping, video and stereo equipment, a hanging martial arts heavy bag, and a workout bench with fastened-down weights. In the back wall, a door serviced a room with a shower, sink, and commode. For better or worse, this was home, as much as anywhere.

He bent lower to peer into a mirror. His thick black hair was cut short, but not short enough to keep it from standing up on one side and spiking on the other. He ran his fingers back through it, which failed to alter the design. He had green eyes behind thick-framed glasses that made him look like either a geek—despite his muscular build—or a trendy filmmaker. A strong, straight nose, square jaw, and—when he smiled—deep dimples that made charming the ladies relatively easy—a skill he often tapped to keep a store clerk from chasing him off as he staked out a nearby target or to get a waitress to divulge her knowledge of a target. He shaved twice a day, but still his stubble was heavy, accentuating a long hairline furrow on his left cheek where nothing grew.

Acquiring that scar had taught him to appreciate the speed at which a human could produce and use a previously undetected weapon. Prior to that incident, he had killed exclusively by hand. Well, technically, by *gauntlet*, a weapon he'd had custom-made. It allowed him to be near his targets when he released them from life's burdens, to *feel* the physicality of the release. But his own release wasn't part of the deal, so he'd also taken to using a pistol when he thought it would be prudent. Life was about adjusting, fine-tuning, and being forced to amend his killing style to include both gauntlet and gun was so perfect, it felt to him like divine guidance.

He picked up the television remote and pushed a button. Two forty-two-inch plasma screens—one at each end of the cabin—sprang to life, showing blue screens and the words LOCKING IN SATELLITE RECEPTION. Then an image appeared, a woman slapping a man . . . The image changed to a kid eating cereal . . . and changed again to a black-and-white western *Shane*, the assassin thought—then it changed again . . . and again . . .

The channel-changing button had been permanently depressed with a toothpick. It was the way the assassin liked it. Frenetic and active, never still. Flip, flip, flip . . .

". . . never thought I'd see anything like . . ."

". . . act now and we'll throw in these . . ."

[the low, grieving sound of a violin]

". . . what was it like playing an animal . . ."

[engines revving, tires screeching]

[static]

". . . because I *know* you did it. I *know* . . ."

Yeah. He felt his synapses picking up speed, trying to catch up with the information cycling past. Before long, he'd be able to start and finish the sentences whose fragments each channel spat out with blinding speed. The chances of his guesses being the actual sentences were slim, but they made sense, and that alone meant his mind was clicking, and clicking fast.

A beep sounded from the cockpit. He returned to the pilot's seat and checked the laptop strapped into the copilot's seat. His new client had fed updated coordinates into the mapping software he had provided upon retaining Atropos's services. The target was on the move. The man's current trajectory warranted a change in destination airports. He found the new airport coordinates in a GPS unit and punched them into the autopilot. The cockpit brightened as the plane banked toward the sun.

five

"WE HAVE A LOCK ON THE SATD SIGNAL."

The man who spoke did not take his eyes off the three flat-panel displays arranged before him. One showed a twenty-five-square-mile section of Atlanta, with a thick vein running diagonally through it. Small letters next to the vein identified it as I-75. A red dot moved steadily northwest along the highway.

An old man in a wheelchair turned from surveying the bucolic landscape beyond a wall of windows. The chair buzzed across an expanse of hardwood floor and edged up next to the technician.

"Can we seize the signal completely?" the old man asked.

"You mean cut the CDC agent out of the loop, so only we have it?"

"Exactly."

"Yes, sir."

"Will anybody—the FBI, CIA, CDC, anybody—be able to intercept it once we take it?"

"No, sir. Nobody."

"Will they be able to trace it back to us?"

"We are completely cloaked, sir."

"Will this CDC woman be able to reconnect or disrupt our use of it?"

"If she tries, the program itself will block her out. She'll just keep getting error messages on her computer."

"Then do it."

The technician typed a command and hit ENTER. The image flicked once. "Done."

Wheeling away, the old man said, "Now tell our men to back off."

He shook his head. You always tried to hire professionals for jobs like this, but with freelancers you never knew what you'd get: someone calm and competent or a complete nut job. These two had come highly recommended, and look: They didn't seem to care who they blew away in their quest to capture the target. They'd destroyed a restaurant and were now engaged in a high-speed gun battle with a federal agent. Not exactly the discretion he'd hoped for.

"Keep them close, but not too close," he instructed. "Let's give 'em a chance to calm down."

JULIA'S TAURUS RAMMED INTO THE SPACE BETWEEN THE CONcrete median and the car ahead. The force knocked the other car only partially out of the way; its bumper screeched along the entire length of the sedan. Then her car popped free, and Julia roared toward her partner.

The SATD showed her partner at least five miles ahead of her now, the assailants all over him, no doubt.

Hang in there, Goody. I'm coming.

As she watched, the red dot sputtered and blinked out. Then the map switched off, leaving only faint gridlines. She slammed on the brakes and stopped in the center lane of the momentarily empty highway. She stared at the screen, dumbfounded.

Her hands flashed to the keyboard. She punched in command after command. Nothing. She checked the connections at the antenna, at the box on the floor, at the back of the computer. The screen remained blank.

She snatched the radio mike and keyed the talk button. "Goody! What's happened? Goody!"

She grabbed the wire connected to the receiver for Goody's body mike and slid her hand up to the earplug. She jammed it into her ear. Static. She ripped it out again.

With a last futile look at the computer monitor, she hit the accelerator and plunged ahead, blind.

DONNELLEY WAS ABOUT TO TAKE ANOTHER SHOT AT THE MAHIMA when it swerved out of sight behind him.

Vero yelled out in surprise and pointed. "Look!"

In the rearview Donnelley saw the Maxima fly off the shoulder and down an embankment, kicking up a cloud of dust.

"You beat 'em!" Vero laughed, almost giddy.

Donnelley wasn't so sure, but he set his gun on the seat. He felt as though he'd been kicked hard in the side. He touched the pain, and his hand came back drenched in blood.

Vero stared. He gripped Donnelley's shoulder. "I should drive."

Donnelley eyed him. "I don't think so."

Vero himself looked terrible: oily sweat glistened on his face and arms and plastered his curly brown hair to his skull. His lips, cracked and bleeding, quivered constantly. His eyes bulged, held in place, it seemed, by the red vessels fanning out from each corner. Blood was crusted around the opening of his ear.

Registering Donnelley's quick assessment, he said, "I'm not as bad as I look. Not yet. Pull over."

"No. Sit back." Flicking his attention between the road ahead and the rearview mirrors, Donnelley clutched the wheel with his bloody fist. His face hardened with purpose.

six

SHE'D LOST THEM. GOODY AND VERO HAD SIMPLY VANISHED.

Julia had long ago passed the place they had been when the SATD malfunctioned. Surely they could not have continued their fierce battle with the assailants this long. One of them would have triumphed, the other beaten too hard to carry on. Yet she had not come across wreckage—of car or man—other than a periodic scattering of glass, plastic, and paint.

Three state patrol cruisers, cherry-tops blazing, had sailed by in the other direction miles ago, suggesting that the troopers had not spotted two feuding vehicles up ahead. They apparently thought the trouble lay in the stalled and battered traffic behind her. It wouldn't be long before they realized their error and started combing ahead for the culprits. She had to find Goody before they did.

She swept the hair back from her forehead and realized that tension was contracting every muscle in her body: her abs burned, her forearms bulged in crisp definition from gripping the wheel so tightly, even her face ached. She inhaled deeply through her nose, then let the air escape slowly through her mouth.

She had known Goody for six years, ever since her assignment to the FBI's Denver field office. He'd been an office hotshot with a reputation for cracking the toughest cases and collaring the most elusive criminals. Twenty-five years old and fresh from the Academy, she was consigned to grunt work and rarely had occasion to watch the great Goodwin Donnelley in action.

For eight months the Denver SAC had her handling background investigations of people applying for sensitive government jobs. This was a choice assignment in DC, where the subject might be a potential Superior Court judge or congressional aide. But in Denver it amounted to drudgery, especially for an eager young agent with a master's degree in criminology.

Whenever she could, she'd quietly sit in on Goody's case meetings, just to watch him work and learn the investigative ropes, if only vicariously. At first she was merely a curiosity, a pretty woman with a thing for criminal investigators.

But her attraction to him had nothing to do with the man's physical appearance. She conceded that his trim frame, chiseled features, and Caribbean-blue eyes were a handsome combination, but she believed his greatest asset was his ability to capture criminals.

After all, physical characteristics were simply handed to you: luck of the draw. She knew that people found her attractive. But what she admired—and wanted people to admire in her—were accomplishments, strength of character, applied logic. Things for which a person had to work.

Goody was a good investigator because he wanted to be, he tried to be. That's what she found alluring.

One day an argument had flared up between Goody and Special Agent Lou Preston, a surveillance expert, over the reason several wireless transmitters kept malfunctioning. Preston had placed the bugging devices under the tables in the visiting room of the Quincy State Correctional Facility to monitor conversations between a hood named Jimmy Gee, imprisoned there, and his brother-in-law, Mike Simon. The Bureau suspected Gee of negotiating with Simon to kill a young woman who had witnessed Gee murder a rival.

But during Simon's visits, white noise—in the form of continuous static, sudden loud pops, and high-pitched whistles—interrupted the reception for five or more minutes at a time.

The snatches of conversations that were clear had led Goody to believe he had one last chance to get the scheme recorded. White noise at the wrong moment would blow attempted-murder charges against the two and could cost the young woman her life.

"You're telling me there's *nothing* you can do?" complained Goody. He stood at the front of a small conference room. Someone had taped color pictures of the suspects on a dry-erase board. Beside them was a portrait of the intended victim, a blonde in her twenties, with girl-next-door freckles and a radiant smile. A diagram of the visiting room leaned against a tripod. Humming fluorescents bathed the room in a bluish-white glow.

Preston's anger strained his voice and got him out of his seat. "You know electronic surveillance is prone to all kinds of problems—background noise, weak signals, even electro-magnetic interference from the sun, for crying out loud! We're lucky we got what we did."

Other agents around the long table appeared to shrink in their chairs. Julia watched in fascination from the back of the room.

"So this girl's gonna die because of *solar flares*?" Goody asked, pointing at the portrait.

"I'm not saying that's what's causing the white noise. But we've considered everything." Preston began counting on his fingers. "Are we too close to the kitchen? No. The laundry? The wood shop? The metal shop? No, no, no. Could one of the guards have a device to intentionally disrupt our recep-tion? We've changed guards. Could Gee or Simon be carry-ing something? Our searches came up with zip. We've replaced the bugs and the receivers and the tape machines. What more do you want?"

"I want to get an entire conversation recorded for once."

Preston threw up his arms and turned his back on Goody.

Julia stared at the diagram on the tripod. Before realizing it, she had raised her arm.

Goody gawked at her faintly waving hand, as rare in these meetings as albino bats from Mars. "Julia, what is it?"

She cleared her throat. "Excuse me, sir, but what's in the cor-ner there?" She pointed toward the diagram. "There, where the row of tables stops? There's room for another table, but it's not on the diagram."

"Maybe they ran out of tables!" Preston blurted, obviously annoyed.

"No," said Goody. "It's a Coke machine."

Julia stood, counting on her firm posture to belie her shaky confidence. She focused on Goody's interested face, knowing that a glance at the other agents in the room would be as ruinous to her composure as a novice mountain climber's look down.

"Pop machines are *not* the problem," Preston said sharply. "We've planted bugs *in* them before."

Goody waved him off. "Julia, what's your point?"

"If the electrical contacts—the brushes—in the Coke machine's compressor motor are worn, they would spark more than usual. Electrical sparks produce broadband radio signals—white noise. Such broadband interference covers most of the usable RF spectrum, which is why replacing the bugs and receivers didn't work."

Goody's smile broadened. He looked at Preston, who just glared.

"Like a household refrigerator," she continued, walking to the front of the room. "The motor kicks on only when the temperature inside rises above a preset point. That's why the interference is sporadic. And look . . ." She tapped a spot on the diagram. "We're monitoring from this room on the other side of the wall from the Coke machine. Some motors spit out more sparks than others, even when they're working fine. The brand that goes in this machine may be that kind. I'd bet even replacing the motor won't entirely fix the problem, considering its proximity to the receiver."

She stopped, realizing she may have overstepped her bounds. She had said *we*, though she was not part of this investigation. Worse, she had flaunted her textbook understanding of electronics in front of Preston, who would find this humiliation hard to live down.

She lowered her head and said quietly, "I'm sorry."

"Don't be ridiculous," Donnelley said. He grasped her shoulder and gave it a brief shake. "There's nothing to be sorry about. It's about time we reaped the benefit of your presence." He winked.

Julia was sure only she saw it.

"Preston! What do you think of Agent Matheson's analysis?"

"Might work. We'll unplug the thing and see."

He turned back to her, satisfied. "Thank you, Julia. Feel free to interrupt anytime."

She smiled and nodded. She left the room and walked back to her cubicle. Her mouth was dry. Despite the positive outcome, she feared that the way she had imposed herself on the tight group of men would label her overeager and unprofessional.

A half hour later, Goody leaned into her cubicle. "Good job, kid," he said. "I mean it."

"Thank you, sir. I'm sorry I stepped on Agent Preston's toes like that."

"Preston needs more than his toes stepped on. Don't worry about it. He knows you're right. We all do."

"Sir? I wouldn't unplug the Coke machine."

"Oh?"

"Might tip 'em off. If it doesn't dispense pop, or the display lights are out, Gee and Simon might talk about everything but what you want them to."

"What do you suggest?"

She squared herself in her chair. "Well, clip only the compressor's wire. Do it early, or if you can't be sure when Simon will show, run the wire through the wall and disengage it only when he shows up, so the drinks will still be cold."

Goody paused. "Good idea—again." As he walked away, he called back to her, "Keep it up, and I'll think you're after my job."

I am, she thought.

Turned out she was right; the Bureau captured Gee's evil scheme on tape, helping to send him to prison for life, and Simon for five years. The incident started the department grapevine buzzing, and among other congratulations, Goody insisted on putting a letter of commendation into her personnel jacket. Julia soon found herself working alongside him, designing complicated surveillance strategies and brainstorming with other crack agents about the best way to nail felons.

It was the beginning of a deep friendship. Though only fourteen years her senior, Goody treated her like a daughter, advising her on career decisions and trying to set her up with the few men he felt were worthy of her attention. By the time she spent that first Christmas with him and his wife and two boys, the feeling of family had permeated their relationship. And when he was transferred to CDC-LED, he pulled enough strings to bring her along.

seven

Now Goody was out there on his own, a carload of killers probably bearing down on him at that very moment.

The farther Julia moved away from the last place the SATD had detected him, the more panicked she became. That spot was at least twenty miles behind her now. The two center lanes of the urban, six-lane highway had given way to a wide grassy median, and the speed limit had jumped to seventy.

Atlanta was gone, and so was her partner.

She continued her breathing exercises, but the tension wouldn't leave her. *Use it,* she thought. *Turn the stress into sharper focus. What happened? What went wrong?*

She chided herself for losing him. She never should have left the hotel, despite Goody's instructions. He hadn't been thinking clearly, all those guns, trying to protect Vero. And when she left the area, she should have remained closer; two blocks was too far.

Was she to blame for the SATD's malfunction? Once it was running, the program required nothing from the user but watchful eyes. Trouble with the host satellite was a slim possibility; geosynchronous satellites were famously reliable, which accounted for their proliferation.

In one of the SATD's more innovative constructs, the locator signal was routed through a commercial satellite. Commercial communication satellites tended to be more robust, making them less susceptible to adverse weather. More important, hiding the SATD's signal in a random, nongovernment satellite kept savvy criminals from blocking or scrambling it. Not even the operators of the host satellite were supposed to know the SATD was hitching a ride.

She thought now that they might have uncovered her covert intrusion, but the program was designed to maintain surveillance even while feeding false data to the operators who had stumbled onto it. To them, the SATD program would look like a minor system corruption. While they tried untangling the glitch, the covert user had ample time to switch host satellites. At that time, the "glitch" would vanish, without so much as a trace of the program's trespass.

In this case, the signal had blinked out without warning. When she had tried to shift host satellites, she could have been pounding on a dead keyboard for all the good it did.

Now that she thought about it, even the way it malfunctioned seemed odd. Most crashes resulted in the screen simply locking up; blinking cursors stopped blinking and keyboard commands yielded no computer activity at all, but the image always remained frozen on the screen. With this malfunction, first Goody's signal had blinked out, then the map had disappeared—

Almost as if someone had stolen it, one component at a time.

Julia cranked the wheel right and braked to a stop. She punched the gear lever into park and unsnapped her seat belt. Her hands flew to the laptop's keyboard. She used a special key code designed to override system failures to restart it, then waited for the operating system to load.

She tapped a staccato rhythm on the laptop's case as cold moisture seeped from her pores. The feeling that something hellish and huge had descended upon them threatened to cloud out all rational thought.

As if someone had stolen it . . .

Let me be wrong. Let me be wrong.

A few seconds later, the program came online. She instructed it to uplink to the same host satellite. The screen flashed the words MAKING CONNECTION . . .

Then CONNECTING TO: SATCOM6 455HR21911.89 v.62. *2

After a brief pause, as the laptop's hard drive whirled, the words on the screen changed to:

CATALOG B-TREE ERROR
RESOURCE FORK, BLOCK 672 (NODE 792, RECORD 4)
> ?

Julia moaned. The satellite was interpreting her current attempt to connect as unauthorized probing, so it was sending a false error message back to her to make her think the old program was nothing more than a system problem. This red herring would fool a good 99 percent of the world's satellite operators.

Julia knew better.

She bit her lip. The top secret program was to reside in the host satellite only as long as it received microbursts of passwords from the base computer every six seconds. That kept it from remaining in the satellite in the event the base computer failed before its user could instruct the program to withdraw. But her laptop—the program's base computer—*had* failed. And she had restarted it, which would have kept even a functioning system from feeding passwords to the program for more than a minute.

The old program should not have been running.

But it was.

And that meant only one thing: someone else was feeding it the correct passwords.

She snatched up the radio microphone and keyed the talk switch. "Goody! Goody! If you can hear me, listen." She enunciated her words carefully. "Turn . . . off . . . the . . . tracking . . . transmitter. Someone else is receiving the signal. Someone else is tracking you. Turn off the transmitter."

She tossed the microphone down. What else could she do? She could not defeat the program—not with the limited software utilities her hard drive contained, probably not with all the utilities in the world. Its programmers had anticipated that criminals would continue to increase their technical sophistication. They had made it nearly impossible to disable.

The best she could do for Goody now was to find him—fast.

eight

BLOOD FLOWED FROM HIM LIKE SAP FROM A BROKEN PINE, and dehydration parched his throat. His hands were sticking to the steering wheel. Donnelley focused on the road and tried not to think of his damaged body.

He was tilting forward and sideways now, keeping the wound away from the seat back. The hole in his flesh, piercing him with icy-hot ripples of pain, was just under his rib cage, between side and back. He looked at Vero. Dark skin. Black hair. Coarse features. Mexican or Brazilian, he guessed. The one thing he was sure about: the man was dog-sick.

"What's wrong with you?" he asked.

Vero's lips bent up on one side of his face. A new fissure opened in his bottom lip. "My employer fired me."

"Fired?"

"Instead of a pink slip, he gave me a virus. Not so strange.

Gangsters shoot each other. Makes sense biologists infect each other, no?"

"You're a biologist?"

"Virologist, really."

Donnelley thought about it, leaning more than he knew he should against the steering wheel. "So, what, like the flu?"

Vero laughed or coughed, he couldn't tell. "If only it was tame like that."

He glanced over. "Are you dying?"

"Oh yes, yes." He read Donnelley's expression. "It's not contagious."

"You sure? My throat's a little sore . . . Maybe it's just the dehydration."

"No, it's this. You got a cold, friend."

"But I thought you said—"

"What I have is no cold."

"But I caught a cold from you? You're not making any sense."

He waited for a response, but Vero just turned his head to stare out the glassless side window. After a minute, he started fiddling with his Windbreaker. Donnelley thought the zipper was stuck; then he heard the material rip. When he looked, Vero was removing something that had been sewn into the lining. He held it up, a black sliver of plastic the size of a postage stamp.

"This will explain," he said. "I made it for the CDC."

Donnelley squinted at it and held out his hand. When Vero hesitated, he said, "If that's what got us both killed, you gotta let me hold it, man."

Vero placed it in Donnelley's palm.

"Is this a camera memory chip?"

"Like it, but much higher density."

Donnelley closed his fingers over it. "You want this to get in the right hands, you gotta let me have it."

Their eyes locked.

"I'll take care of it."

Vero nodded.

Donnelley dropped it into the inside pocket of his jacket. "But if I find out the only thing on it are pictures of your family reunion," he said, "I'll come after you."

Vero smiled weakly and turned away.

Donnelley glanced at the police-band radio. It dangled from its bracket under the dash, torn open and gutted. *Looks like I feel,* he thought.

They'd been driving a long time when Donnelley saw the sign that marked the Georgia–Tennessee border. Given the tenacity of their assailants, he half expected another attack: a fiery ambush or even sudden death from a military-type strike—an Apache attack helicopter or a LAW rocket, maybe. He wouldn't put anything past them after the barrage they'd just let loose on him and Vero.

Time to pull over and let Julia catch up. If he didn't get to a hospital soon, his life would simply drain out of him. But the prospect of letting his guard down on an operating table without someone he trusted standing over him was more nauseating than the lack of blood. Besides, if he was going to die for something, he wanted to make sure it got into the hands of the good guys—whoever they were.

Where I-75 branched east, Donnelley went west, onto I-24 and into the heart of Chattanooga. Green hills rose around them, and a humid, musky aroma of honeysuckle filled the car. For the first time in over an hour, he smelled something other than his own blood. He glided into an exit lane and found himself on Belvoir Avenue. Turning east on busy Brainerd

Road, he spotted a good place to stop and cranked the wheel into a nearly deserted parking lot. He edged the war-torn sedan into an alley behind a brick building and killed the engine.

He stretched slowly, carefully, testing for aches and discovering which movements caused spears of pain from the wound. He found renewed strength, slightly, in having something to do. He shouldered the door open, the twisted metal popping and screeching. As he stood on shaky legs, he examined the rear of the building: lined with back doors, as he expected. He hoped the one he wanted was unlocked so they could slip in without being exposed to the main street. "Let's go."

"Go where?"

"A bar, my man. A dark, inconspicuous, everybody-minds-his-own-business bar. Last one in buys."

nine

THE CAR WAS TOO CLOSE TO THE BUILDING FOR DESPESORIO
Vero to open his own door, so he brushed away pellets of
glass and clambered out the driver's side, staying high to
avoid the crimson-drenched seat. Lots of blood, smelling like
raw meat.

He got out of the car in time to see Donnelley disappear
into the building. When Vero followed, he entered an office-
cum-storage room. Boxes marked PRETZELS, MARGARITA MIX,
and NAPKINS formed makeshift half-walls between steel
shelves, file cabinets, and a desk barely visible under a heap
of papers and magazines. Donnelley was apologizing to a
man in a filthy smock and pushing through another door
with a porthole window.

Vero caught the door swinging shut and saw another
door closing on his right. A dingy emblem on the door de-

picted the silhouette of a little boy peeing into a pot. The rest of the bar was equally drab and tasteless. Dim bulbs behind red-tasseled lamp shades barely illuminated each of a dozen maroon vinyl booths, which marched along one wall toward the murky front windows. Chipped Formica tables anchored the booths in place. Opposite the row of booths was a long, scarred wooden bar with uncomfortable-looking stools. Behind the bar, sitting on glass shelves in front of a cloudy mirror, were endless rows of bottles, each looking as forlorn as the folks for whom they waited.

He caught the strong odors of liquor and tobacco smoke, and the weaker scents of cleaning chemicals and vomit. In one of the booths, two heads bobbed with the movement of mug-clenching fists. A scrawny bartender with droopy eyelids picked his teeth with a swizzle stick and chatted quietly with a woman seated at the bar. Otherwise, the place was empty.

Vero walked into the bathroom. Donnelley was lifting his shirt away from the torn flesh in his side. He was cranked around, trying to assess the damage in the muck-spotted mirror. To Vero, he looked like an expressionist painting in which all the objects were the same color of too-vivid red: the shirt, the hands holding the shirt, the belt passing through pant loops. At the center of it all was the thing that corrupted its surroundings with its own gruesome color—a wound. The cut was crescent-shaped, its edges smooth. The flesh around it swelled before tucking into a finger-sized hole. While Vero watched, blood gushed out, flowed to the lip of the pants, and pooled for a moment before seeping in and dripping down.

"Oh," Donnelley groaned. "This is a bad one."

He pushed his index finger into the wound up to the first knuckle and growled through gritted teeth. When he pulled his finger out, it made a wet, popping noise. He fell to one knee, threw his head back, and sucked in air. Vero could hear the man's teeth grinding. Above the crimson mess, Donnelley's face was white as bleached bones.

He gripped the sink to pull himself up. Vero helped him. Donnelley turned on the water, doused his hand, then studied it. His thumb flicked at something on the tip of the finger he'd used to probe the wound. A long and deep cut. Blood welled up within its borders, then spilled out.

"That wasn't there a minute ago," Donnelley said.

Vero leaned closer. "Something's inside you? Something that slices like that?"

"Reckon so. Get me some TP."

Vero didn't understand but followed Donnelley's pointing finger to the tissue roll by the exposed toilet. He unraveled a wad. He leaned in to apply it to the wound.

"No," Donnelley said, stopping him. "Give it to me."

He stuck the wad in his mouth and bit down. He reached back with his left hand and jabbed the tips of his index finger and thumb into the hole, wiggling them to make room. He groaned, coughed, fell to his knees. His probing fingers wiggled farther in.

Vero held Donnelley's shoulders and stared in disbelief.

Donnelley yanked his hand back, holding something solid. He spit out the wad of tissue. His panting echoed against the walls of the small room. Perspiration coated his face in fat, runny droplets. Vero gently pressed another wad of tissue against the wound; in seconds, he was holding a blood-soaked clump. He tossed it into the trash and spun off another handful.

With groaning effort Donnelley stood, one arm propped against the sink, eyes closed, his head hanging down. Sweat dripped off the tip of his nose and strands of hair. The rhythm of his heaving chest gradually slowed. He raised his face and stared into the mirror. He looked down at the object in his palm.

Vero tried to identify it, but a pool of gore obscured its shape. "A piece of the car door?"

Donnelley shook his head. He stuck the object under the flow of water. Pink bubbles churned in the basin and vanished. He turned off the water, shoved a clump of tissue into the drain, and dropped the object into the sink. It made a metal *clink!*, then rattled thinly before sliding to a stop against the tissue.

It was black steel, the size of a dime. From its outside edge, three grooves spiraled slightly inward, forming three sharp teeth. A small hole pierced its center.

"What is that?" Vero asked.

"A fléchette," Donnelley said matter-of-factly, his voice raspy. He spoke through clenched teeth. "I've read about 'em. Soldiers used something like it for trench warfare."

"Those killers had *these* in their guns?" Vero was more angry than astonished.

"Probably—" Donnelley's breath hitched, his face contracted in pain.

The man's ability to behave in an almost normal fashion despite the gaping wound in his side was astonishing.

"Probably had a dozen or so packed into each shotgun shell. They'd tear a man to shreds. The car door slowed this one down before it hit me." He rolled his head in a circle, took a deep breath. "At the Academy," he said, "the first thing you learn about a penetrating injury is 'leave it alone.' Arrow, knife, bullet—don't try to take it out; leave it for the docs, who can clamp the artery that gets severed when it's removed, or take care of whatever complications arise." He shook his head. "I couldn't wait. That thing was tearing me up inside."

The two stared at the black disk in the sink as if it were a new species of poisonous insect.

"Tore you up bad."

"Tore me up *good*. Could have been worse, I guess. Let me have your jacket."

He put the disk in an outside pocket of Vero's jacket and slipped into it. It covered most of the bloodstain on his pants. He pushed his own bloody jacket into the wastepaper basket and tossed handfuls of tissue over it. The effort obviously pained him, but he held strong. He then reached up under his shirt and yanked something out. Donnelley examined a small box with a wire that abruptly ended. He reached under his shirt again and removed a steel disk with a short wire tail.

"The body mike broke," Donnelley said, seemingly to himself. "I thought I felt it ripping loose. Piece of garbage." He pushed it into a jacket pocket. To Vero he said, "Let's sit down and wait for my partner. I really need a drink."

JULIA MATHESON'S HEART POUNDED IN HER BREAST, A FIST wanting out. She had periodically listened for Goody's body mike and called for him on the radio. Her mobile phone lay in her lap, useless. It had rung several times, the word *Private* popping up on the caller ID screen. She had ignored the calls; Goody would have used the code they had devised. And she wanted to avoid Molland until Goody filled her in on his suspicions. The idea of LED involvement in the hit was ludicrous, but he had been clear about not involving anyone. She wasn't about to violate his confidence now.

She'd driven as far as Chattanooga without seeing another sign of him. She wanted to find solace in that, but it would not come. Just past the junction of I-75 and I-24, she'd turned around. Now she was heading back toward Atlanta, still looking and offering up silent prayers . . .

IN A CAR ON A QUIET STREET OFF BRAINERD ROAD, TWO MEN inspected their weapons: the driver with a NeoStead combat shotgun, the passenger with a Mini Uzi.

Mr. Uzi put the weapon in his lap and dropped down his visor. In the mirror, he examined his nose, swollen to twice its normal size and mottled in blue and red and even green—green! A fat gash like a little mouth right on the bridge. He touched it gently and flinched. "I can't wait to blow that dude away!"

The driver said nothing, just rubbed a silicone cloth over the shotgun's twin tubular magazines above the barrel.

The passenger watched him for a moment, then said, "I can't believe I lost my shotgun. I loved that thing." He watched a few more seconds. "We gotta go back and—"

"Don't even think about it, Launy," the driver said without looking.

"I meant after all this is—"

The driver turned. "Did you hear what I said? It's gone. We're not going back for it." He set the cloth on the seat and pivoted the magazines up at the rear. "Local PD probably got it now, anyway. Get another'n."

Launy slapped up his visor. "I was just saying . . ." He touched the side of his nose again and hissed. "What was that guy doing with a gun anyway? I thought he was CDC."

"He wasn't CDC. FBI."

"That would have been nice to know up front. How do you know?"

"I seen him before."

"Well, ain't that just dandy." Launy yanked a thirty-two-round magazine from the bottom of the Uzi's handgrip, tipped it to see the two topmost rounds, and shoved it back in. He was silent; then he held up the Uzi. "Now *this* is a fine weapon."

"No. I'm using the shotgun. Now shut up." The driver began dropping heavy shells into the magazine tubes until he'd loaded the NeoStead with twelve rounds.

They did their work in a green, late-model Chrysler, stolen from the outer edge of a mall lot where employees parked. They planned on being long gone before anyone discovered the theft, or the black Maxima—which they had hot-wired in Atlanta—stashed behind a tall clump of bushes.

A satellite phone on the seat chirped. Tethered to the phone was a CopyTele Triple DES cryptography device.

"'Bout time," Launy said.

"Shut up. Nobody wants to hear your whining." He punched five numbers into the keypad on the CopyTel, then answered the phone. He listened, said, "Yeah, got it," and disconnected.

He turned a strip of metal protruding from the ignition switch, and the car roared to life. He eyed his partner. "Now listen. We're getting nice change for this, and we don't have to sweat getting busted, not with these guys we're working for. It's a sweet gig. So be happy you got it, okay?" He paused. "You ready?"

Launy smiled like a dog showing its teeth. "Oh yeah."

The Chrysler pulled away from the curb and turned onto Brainerd.

ten

DONNELLEY LOOKED AT HIS WATCH. "SHE SHOULD HAVE been here by now."

"You haven't talked to anyone," Vero said. "How will your partner find us?"

Donnelley downed a shot of Jack Daniels and set the glass beside two empty ones on the table in front of him. He had poured one over the hole in his side. It had burned at first but felt better now. He wasn't worried about how the alcohol would affect his ability to outmaneuver his opponents; its dulling effect was less inhibiting than the pain, making him feel even more quick-witted than before the drinks. Besides, it would take a lot more than two shots to counteract the adrenaline coursing through his veins.

He nodded and canted to his right, squeezing a hand into his pants pocket. "My turn to share."

He held up what looked like a fat, black dime. A small slot in its side pointed at a *1* stamped into the black plastic case. Rotating the slot ninety degrees would leave it pointing at the numeral *0*. "I was going to attach this to your clothes sometime during our meeting. It would have allowed us to find you if you got cold feet and disappeared."

"I came to you."

"And look what happened. We could have been separated. They could have taken you. Never hurts to have one of these." He held it out to Vero. "Take it."

Vero thought for a moment, then shook his head. "No, it's not me that's important. Not anymore. You have the memory chip. You keep it."

Donnelley turned the transmitter over and peeled away a bit of paper. He retrieved the chip. After pressing the transmitter against it, he returned it to his pocket. The round paper he had pulled from the transmitter sat on the table. He tapped it with his fingernail. "The latest and greatest technology, tracking drug dealers and heads of state, and it all relies on two cents of adhesive."

Vero picked up a shot glass. Surprised to find it empty, he set it mouth-down on the table. "It has always fascinated me," he said, "that bombs get so much effort and attention, but hardly anyone thinks about the most important part, the delivery system. If it can't reach its target, what good is it?" He studied Donnelley's face. "This very issue held up my employer's plans for months."

"Plans for a bomb?"

"A virus."

"What plans, Vero? What does he want to do with this virus?"

"Kill people." He lowered his head, to Donnelley looking

very much like a shamed child. "Lots of people, women and children."

"Is he still . . . only planning?"

Vero's head moved: no.

"What is it? What's happening?" It dawned on Donnelley. "People," he said. "People make the perfect delivery system for viruses, right? It's you, isn't it?" He covered his mouth and nose. He thought of the time he'd spent with this man, in the car, here, and the ridiculousness of using his hand like a biofiltering mask. Hadn't he learned anything at the CDC? He let it drop back into his lap.

"I told you I'm not contagious," Vero said. He slid the upside-down shot glass in front of him from one hand to the other and back again. Quietly he said, "But I had a lot to do with all this. I worked on the project. I ran field tests, mostly in Africa."

"Africa? Is that where you worked?"

"The lab is far from there; that's the point. You shouldn't play with fire in your own backyard." He smiled thinly. "Plus, there's a lot of apathy about Africa. Westerners like to say that's not true, but it is. Deception is easier when people don't care."

"So why didn't you go to one of the CDC's offices in Africa? Or the European Center for Disease Control and Prevention in Sweden? It's much closer, and if time is a factor—"

"We only field-tested in Africa. I was here . . . to release it . . . the germ."

His head dropped farther, until it nearly touched the shot glass. His shoulders hitched, and Donnelley realized the man was fighting back tears.

Vero said, "*Que Deus me perdoe.*" He lifted a wet cocktail

napkin and wiped his face. He raised his gaze to Donnelley, as though seeking absolution.

"Wait a minute." Donnelley reached across the table and grabbed his shoulder. "Are you saying now, here? That's what you were doing here?"

Vero nodded, lowered his gaze once more.

"Where? What exactly is it?"

"I came down the coast," he said. "There were four of us, working each time zone. I got Boston, New York, DC. In each city, I picked up a package at a mail center. A canister. I'd go to a mall, sit on a bench with a coat covering it. Turn the valve."

"You exposed thousands of people to a deadly virus?"

He seemed to be intensely studying something on the bottom of the shot glass. "Rhinovirus, most of them. Most common of common colds. Spreads fast, though."

"You're not talking about a common cold."

"Remember what I said about delivery systems." He shot his gaze around, checking for eavesdroppers. He scratched the inside of his ear and looked at the blood on his finger-tip—some red and fresh, some brown and flaky. "When I got sick, I thought something had gone wrong. This wasn't sup-posed to happen. I called Karl. He—"

"Karl?"

"Karl Litt, my boss. A *monster*." He said it with convic-tion. "Karl, he sounded concerned, said, 'Oh no, Despesorio. Hurry, finish the job and come home.' But I know him too well. I heard it in his voice. There had been no mistake. But I should have kept my big mouth shut."

He punched himself in the cheek. Hard. Donnelley flinched but said nothing, could say nothing.

"I thought I could buy my way back, *threaten* my way home. I told him about my insurance policy."

"The memory chip."

"Instead of bargaining with me, he laughed. He said the list of targets had already gone out."

"Already gone out?"

"Made public. That way people would know it was planned, not just some act of God or biological accident. I told him I had more than that list. I had details about our field tests, the capabilities of our lab . . . He hung up on me. That's when I called the CDC. I thought . . . I thought . . ."

He shook his head, a slow, painful movement.

"Listen, you've got to—" Donnelley let the thought die. What Vero had come to reveal was *big*. He didn't want to blow it by saying the wrong thing, pushing the wrong button. Vero needed to be interrogated someplace safe, with one of the Bureau's interrogation teams—psychologists, mostly—and at least a few CDC scientists who would know the virologist's vernacular and the implications of his words.

He felt shaky, as though he'd been given a glimpse of the future, and it wasn't pretty. He shifted on the bench seat and saw the bartender watching him. When they'd first sat down, the man had come around the bar to take their drink order. Assessing them, he'd said, "Get you dudes something . . . beer, well drink, an ambulance?"

Donnelley said they had just walked away from a detox program. "Feelin' a li'l thin, ya know?" That seemed to satisfy him, but he'd been keeping an eye on them just the same.

Vero mumbled, and Donnelley leaned in. His words came in stuttering whispers, part confession, part rant. Donnelley listened, afraid to ask questions, afraid to disrupt what may have been the fevered speech of a sick man who didn't know he was talking. After a while—it could have been minutes or hours, Donnelley was so lost in the words—Vero grew silent.

His body jerked, as if startling awake from trance or sleep. Donnelley thought it had to do with his illness.

Vero leaned back. He used his hand to wipe tears from his eyes, pink spittle from his lips, snot and blood from his nose. His breathing was labored, deep, chest-moving breaths. Heavily bloodshot eyes locked on Donnelley's. He said, "I'm sorry. I—"

Donnelley stopped him. "We've got to get you someplace safe. You need medical attention, and you've got to tell your story." He touched the wad of napkins at his side. Again, it had become a sopping mess. Good thing the injury was in a part of the body that gave up its blood reluctantly; if it had been a head or chest wound, blood loss would have laid him out by now. He checked his watch and wondered if he was placing too much reliance on the SATD to lead Julia to them.

He surveyed the bar and slid out of the booth. "I'll be right back."

Vero grabbed his arm.

"I don't want to use my cell phone, in case someone's watching for it," Donnelley said. "Julia shouldn't use hers, either, but I can't contact her any other way. I'm going to call her from that phone over there."

Vero cranked his head to see the phone booth, how close it was to the door.

Donnelley leaned down to whisper. "Look, I know you've been through hell. You tell me you're dying and a lot of innocent people may die because the guy you're running from is neck and neck with Satan in the evil department, and I guess he is. You want to do what's right and tell someone about it. I appreciate that, okay? I'm going to get you to where you need to go; that's my job." He touched Vero's shoulder. "I don't disappear when things get hairy. You believe me?"

Vero stared into his eyes. Slowly he nodded.

"You can come with me if you want."

Vero smiled dully. "I trust you."

Donnelley concentrated on walking as steadily and normally as he could, ignoring a wave of nausea and spasms of pain. At least they weren't as bad as the lightning bolts he'd felt before. The phone was in an old-fashioned booth tucked into a dark corner by the front door. He slipped in and pulled the bifold door shut. In the ceiling, a fluorescent tube sputtered to half-life and continued to flicker after it should have given up; that and its brightness made his eyes ache. He backed the door open a few inches until the light went out.

He looked out at the mostly empty bar and the back of Vero's head. Not the *where* and *who* he'd prefer right now. His left arm had grown numb, so he let the handset hang from its metal braided cord while he punched in his long distance calling card number, the area code, and his home phone number.

After five rings, his wife's voice came on.

"Hello!"

His heart jumped at hearing her, then sank when he recognized their outgoing voice mail message.

"You've reached Jodi . . ."

His own voice: "Goody . . ."

Brice, trying to sound older than his ten years: "Brice!"

And the sweet voice of his six-year-old: "Barrett!"

All of them: "Leave a message, and we'll call you back," followed by uncontrollable laughter and *beeeeep*.

"Hey, guys. Just wanted to say hi. You must be out. Hope you're having fun. I'll see you soon." He raised the handset to the cradle, then brought it back. "I . . . I love you, Barrett. I love you, Brice. You be good now, okay? Honey . . . thank you for being so good to me. I love you. Bye."

He dropped the handset and held the disconnect button down for a few seconds, then dialed the calling card number and Julia's mobile phone. After two rings, he disconnected, then dialed again.

She picked up instantly.

"Goody!"

"Yeah, let's talk fast: unsecured line. I thought you'd be here by now. I'm hurt, kid. Real bad."

"Goody, listen to me." Her voice was higher-pitched and more panicked than he had ever heard it. "I don't have the signal. Someone else does. Do you hear? Turn off the tracking device, Goody! Do it now!"

"You don't—hold on." He fished the memory chip and transmitter out of his pocket. He used a fingernail to turn the slot in its side to the *0* position.

He closed his eyes to catch hold of his convulsing thoughts. If someone else was tracking them, this thing was bigger than he'd imagined. It boggled his mind to think of the equipment and covert intelligence necessary to intercept the SATD signal. It confirmed for him that someone inside CDC-LED, the FBI, or another federal agency was involved. And people like that didn't let their muscles relax once they had them pumped up; they'd be coming after Vero and him soon; they could be watching the bar even now. Still holding the memory chip, he scanned the confines of the dark booth. Laying the handset on top of the phone, he pushed up on the milky plastic panel that covered the fluorescent tube overhead. It rose about an inch. He pushed the chip and transmitter into the open space, but then the panel wouldn't lay flush.

He could hear Julia frantically calling his name. "Hold on," he said, loud enough to reach the handset. He felt around the perimeter of the telephone itself. Nothing. He leaned over and felt under the small wooden seat positioned in one corner. His hand slid over several clumps of old gum; then he found what he was looking for: a thin space between the seat and one of its supports. He transferred the chip to his other hand, then wedged it into the space, flat against the seat bottom.

Julia was ranting when he put the phone back up to his ear. He cut her off.

"Hey! Hey! It's your turn to listen to me, kid. I'm in the phone booth. In the phone booth."

"I understand that the line is not secure. Okay?"

He could tell she was absolutely panicked that he had not understood her before.

This time she spoke each word with painful deliberation: "Did . . . you . . . turn . . . *off?* . . . the . . . tracking . . . device?"

"It's off, it's off," he said. "How—"

"I don't know how, but you have to get away from there. Go now, Goody. Your location is compromised. Call me from somewhere else."

"I need to contact Casey, Julia. He's at Earl's place in Chattanooga. Understand?

"No, I . . ."

Come on, kid, Donnelley thought, *you have to remember.*

"Yes! I understand. But Chattanooga?" She swore. "I was just there. I'm about twenty miles south now. You got Vero?"

"I got him. And he's talking about some kind of bio-attack that may already be under way. I think there's a list somewhere of the cities they're hitting, something to do with a virus—"

"Tell me later, Goody. Just get outta there now."

"Look, if something happens to me and—"

"Nothing's going to happen if you get your butt out of there. Now go!"

"What's your ETA?"

"Give me fifteen minutes."

"You've got ten," he said and hung up.

He was turning from the phone when he saw them: two men in black knee-length coats. He couldn't think of all the reasons a person would wear such a thing in warm weather, but he knew of one—to conceal weapons. They had already passed the phone booth. He couldn't see their faces, but he would have bet his pension one of them had two shiners from a broken nose. They were heading directly for Vero in the second-to-last booth.

He pulled out his gun.

For Donnelley, the next seven seconds moved in excruciatingly slow motion.

Shouldering open the bifold door, he lunged through, pushing a scream out of his lungs.

The men spun. One raised a shotgun—something exotic, Donnelley thought. The other, the one on his right, had something smaller pulled up close to his torso: a submachine gun. Donnelley shot him. A red rose bloomed in the center of the man's chest, and he staggered back, dazed but not down. Donnelley pulled the trigger again, realizing his mistake even as he made it. He should have nailed each assassin with a double-tap before putting more holes in them. The shooter on the left was the one he had recognized, the Serpico for DEA. The guy brought his shotgun around, and Donnelley understood that the split-second decision to fire twice at the first one would cost him his life.

He was falling, one foot remaining in the phone booth. He had swung his pistol three-quarters of the distance to the other shooter when the shotgun boomed, hurling flames and dozens of razor-sharp disks directly at him. He caught a brief glimpse of the shooter's scowl, twisted into a perverted hybrid of man and demon.

When he was a kid, he had imagined that a sweet fragrance was the first evidence that heaven had opened its doors to receive you. But now the acidic odor of cordite from gunpowder stung his nostrils, and he thought, *Not sweet at all—it smells like death.*

He saw the sparkling of stars—disks catching the light—and behind them, the shotgun barrel's smoking black hole. Then the disks tore into him.

Not sweet at all.

Blackness.

eleven

THE BARTENDER'S NAME WAS JOHNNY. HE'D BEEN DOING this job for . . . he forgot how many years, maybe twelve. He liked the gig, because women liked bartenders. They especially dug a "mixologist" guy who'd perform for them, flipping bottles in the air and pouring a shot from way up high and catching it in a glass balanced on his foot, all the while wiggling his fanny to music Johnny thought had not survived the eighties. He wasn't one of *those* guys—though, truth be told, he broke a few bottles and spilled a paycheck's worth of booze on the floor seeing if he *could* be one of those guys when his uncle, who owned the joint, first hired him on.

Nah, he was the kind of bartender ladies liked *second* best. If they were nice to him, he gave them free drinks; the nicer they were, the more they could imbibe on the house. He hadn't wanted for a date since he'd started, though he had learned early on that you couldn't be too picky when your dates were more interested in Johnnie Walker than Johnny the Bartender. And it wasn't as if the work could ever be classified hard labor. In fact, Johnny couldn't remember a time when he'd broken a sweat on behalf of Babylon Bar, not even mopping the floor.

Until now. Drops rolled off his head and into his eyes, as if he were taking a shower. He wiped them away and peered around the edge of the bar, where he'd clambered when the shooting started. He'd decided long ago, if something like this ever went down, he wouldn't get stuck behind the bar like a fish in a barrel. He saw a Tarantino film where the bartender got it *just because*, and he'd been an easy target in that all-too-much-like-a-shooting-range space behind the bar. So that's why he was where he was, on the outside edge of the counter, farthest from the action without being seen and a screaming ten paces from the back office door, should the need arise to make a break.

He'd had his eyes on the two strangers pushing through the door, striding in like kingpins, when the guy who said he was from detox sprang out of the phone booth, gun blazing. As if he'd been waiting for them. Johnny had been on all fours and halfway to safety when he heard a big *boom!*—not the *crack* of the guy's pistol.

Coming around the bar, he'd had a straight view of the other detox dude in the booth—the one he'd heard called Desperado or something like that. Desperado had about jumped onto the table apparently, and when Johnny saw him, he was pushing off it and away from the shooters—still in the booth, but now where the other guy had been sitting. Desperado's mouth and eyes were as wide as any Johnny had seen, and he'd been trying to say something but couldn't get anything out except stammering sounds.

Johnny wiped the sweat out of his eyes, and peered around the edge of the bar.

One of the strangers was down. Looked as though he'd crashed against an empty table flipped facedown onto the floor. The guy from the phone booth was down too. Lots of glistening red—on him, around him, seeping out of him. The standing shooter was aiming a wicked-looking gun at him and seemed ready to pull the trigger again.

Johnny didn't want to see it and pulled his head back. When the expected roar didn't come, he looked again. The gunman had turned and was now facing Desperado, his big gun pointed at the man. Without turning his eyes away, he jabbed an index finger at Cheryl, who was—God bless her— still sitting on the stool where she'd planted her butt two hours before. Like pushing a button, the shooter's finger quieted her screaming, screaming Johnny hadn't realized she was doing until she stopped. He must have thought the sound was ringing in his ears from the gunshots. The shooter held his finger on her a few seconds longer, a warning not to start up again, Johnny thought. Then the shooter pointed at the two guys who'd been swigging watered-down Coors since opening time. They hadn't been screaming, just sort of gaping at the scene. The finger got their hands in the air as if they were being robbed. Maybe they were.

Then the man pointed at Johnny, right at him, peering around the bar, and Johnny thought maybe his bladder leaked a little. Just a little.

The shooter reached around to the small of his back and produced a chrome O. He threw it across the room at Desperado. It hit the table, slid off, bounced against the booth padding, and clattered to the floor. Johnny could see better now—two Os connected by a short chain: handcuffs.

The shooter nodded at Desperado. "Nice and easy," he said. "Put them on and—" A blaze of sunlight exploded behind the shooter, and Johnny realized the front door had burst open. A silhouette quavered between the radiance and the shooter, who was turning, yelling, "What the—?"

The door swung shut again, cutting off the blinding light. A tall, muscular man—Buddy Holly glasses with dark polarized lenses, light jacket, gloves, mussed-up hair—was two strides from the shooter. His fist came around and crashed into the shooter's head. From Johnny's vantage point, the head appeared to crumple under the blow like a melon. The body collapsed in a heap. The new killer's fist dripped with blood. Something stringy, clumpy, dangled from his knuckles. Johnny realized that what he thought was a glove was hard and black, with spikes, some sort of newfangled brass knuckles or—yes, now that he thought about it—a gauntlet. A knight's gauntlet, only black.

Cheryl was screaming again, whooping like a car alarm. Didn't seem to bother the newcomer, though. He reached into his jacket and withdrew a pistol with a long barrel. A red light shot out of it. Laser sighting—Johnny had seen it in a dozen movies. The man extended the gun toward Desperado. A red bead of light appeared on the man's forehead, followed immediately by a black hole and the sudden appearance of spattered brains and skull fragments on the wall behind him.

Johnny had no time to turn away. His bladder emptied. He dropped his head, gulping in breaths that seemed to lack the oxygen his lungs required. He heard sirens approaching. Someone must have heard the shots. Over time—he didn't know how long—his breathing relaxed. When he looked up again, the killer was gone. And so was the body of the guy he'd seen get shot in the head.

twelve

JULIA DASHED THROUGH THE AUTOMATIC SLIDING DOORS OF
Erlanger Hospital's emergency entrance, half expecting to see
Donnelley, Vero, and a group of hit men stretched out unconscious and bleeding on identical gurneys in the hall.
Instead, unfamiliar faces, miserably attached to a variety of
injured and ill bodies, turned toward her from rows of plastic
chairs. Keypad locks prevented her from getting to the treatment rooms. She stepped up to the nurses' station.

"I'm looking for a man—Goody . . . Goodwin
Donnelley. He would have come in within the past ten minutes or so. Injured, probably a gunshot wound, shotgun maybe
. . . a car crash . . . I don't know!"

The nurse, a stern-looking blonde who apparently saw no
use for cosmetics, stared at her impassively. "Are you family?"
she asked.

"No . . . I . . ." She showed the woman her law enforcement credentials.

After examining the ID for several moments, the nurse spoke slowly, as though dealing with a deranged person. "Ma'am," she said, "no one with injuries like that has come in, but I can—"

"He said *here!*" Julia interrupted. "He said to meet him at Erlanger!"

That was what he meant, wasn't it? Over a year ago, she had spent a pleasant afternoon with Goody and his family in his backyard. After charbroiled burgers and dogs, the boys had run off with friends, and she, Goody, and Jodi had sat around the picnic table, sipping Chianti and chatting. Somehow they'd gotten on the topic of TV medical dramas. Jodi had said that one in particular boasted the cutest doctors, to which Julia had replied that none of the current offerings could match Vince Edwards playing Dr. Ben Casey. She'd had the biggest crush on him, watching reruns as a kid. Despite Goody's and Jodi's lists of other candidates for TV's hunkiest docs, she hadn't budged. Ben Casey represented the perfect physician.

So when Goody had said that he needed to contact "Casey," she'd understood that to mean he needed a doctor. And when he'd said that Casey was at "Earl's place," certainly he'd meant Erlanger, Chattanooga's biggest hospital. At the time, she'd been positive that she had decoded his cryptogram. Could she have misunderstood?

Divulging his whereabouts with what seemed an easily deciphered code over an unsecured line told her his injuries were serious. He'd want the kind of immediate attention only emergency rooms offered. That such places were usually bright and busy was also an asset, though she doubted that killers who attempted assassinations in hotel restaurants and on crowded highways would think twice about blasting their way through an ER.

It dawned on her that he hadn't gone directly to the hospital; he had waited for her to find him. When she hadn't shown, he'd called to give her directions. He had wanted her with him enough to delay treatment and to risk exposure. He had wanted protection. Was he waiting outside for her, maybe passed out in a car? She started for the parking lot. A local cop in uniform passed her and keyed in the code that opened the doors into the treatment area. She followed him in, found a floor nurse, and asked about Goody.

"An ambulance is bringing in a gunshot victim now," the nurse explained. "They called it in a few minutes ago. Should be here in about two minutes."

"An ambulance?" She was having trouble thinking.

"Wait here," the nurse said sternly and darted away. Almost immediately she started talking again, but not to Julia.

"Dr. Parker. You got my page," she said to a man coming down the hall.

Everything about the man commanded attention. An unbuttoned white smock blew back under his arms, revealing immaculately tailored clothes: a gray dress shirt with subtle black and purple pinstripes and pleated slacks the color of ancient tombstones. Dishwater blond hair, trendily coiffed long on top and short on the sides, swept back from a broad forehead. Bushy eyebrows rode a strong crest above squinting gray eyes. His nose, straight but with a faint leftward bend at the tip, fit his face well. His stride was long, his gait confident.

The nurse reached him and turned to escort him toward a door next to one of the treatment rooms, apprising him of the situation as they walked. The pace of her speech had accelerated dramatically. "The trauma team's tied up in 1 with a boy who fell off his bike and suffered deep head lacerations and a concussion. Dr. Bridges is in 3 with a knife wound—"

"Somebody finally stabbed Dr. Bridges?" asked the man called Dr. Parker. His voice was deep but somehow soft, as if he'd considered each word and deemed it too important to rush or abuse. In such solemn surroundings, it took Julia a few seconds to realize that the physician was joking, despite the gravity in his tone and the scowl on his face.

The nurse giggled dutifully, then continued: "I *thought* you were still in the hospital. We have a GSW en route. Extensive chest trauma."

Gunshot wound! She's talking about Goody!

"The GSW is to the head, neck, chest, and abdomen," the nurse explained. "ETA any second. He's been boarded, intubated, and they got in two large-bore peripheral IVs—"

The two walked through a windowed door across from the nurses' station. A hydraulic closing mechanism hissed as it pulled the door shut behind them.

The wound sounded more severe than Goody had let on over the phone. And why an ambulance? He would have told her if the injury was that debilitating.

Julia looked through the door's window. The nurse was talking animatedly while the doctor slipped on green latex gloves. She stepped in. The doctor saw her and flashed a winning and obviously well-rehearsed smile.

The nurse made a beeline for her: "You can't come in here. You're—"

"I just talked to him," Julia said to the doctor, sidestepping the nurse. "He said he was hurt bad, but not—"

The nurse was insistent. "Dr. Parker, the patient's GCS is eight."

Julia turned to her. "What's that mean, GCS? Eight?"

Dr. Parker came up behind her and touched her arm. "It means he's verbally nonresponsive, close to comatose. Not a good sign, but we'll see when he comes in. I'm Dr. Parker, Allen Parker."

The nurse walked up with a glove stretched open and ready for him to insert his hand.

"Julia Matheson," Julia answered. She stuck her hand into her jacket pocket for her CDC-LED identification when a warbling siren reached her. It quickly rose in volume. Julia stepped into the hall.

Within seconds, an ambulance braked hard outside. Car doors slammed, and the automatic doors of the emergency entrance slid open on cue. Two uniformed EMTs, like a toboggan team at the top of a run, bounded noisily into Erlanger's emergency department pushing a gurney. One attendant held a clear plastic bag of fluid over the patient. The other pressed his hands against the patient's wounds, afraid, it seemed to Julia, of what might come out if he didn't. A steady stream of blood poured off the gurney, leaving a thick trail in its wake.

"Roll 'im in 2!" the nurse yelled, coming around Julia, pointing at the portal where open double doors revealed a bright, immaculate room waiting to be bloodied. Its tiled floor and walls, the grated floor drain, the smooth metal surfaces of the equipment—all betrayed the gorefest the room was designed to accommodate and contain.

Julia turned from it and rushed to meet the stretcher, anxious to let Goody know she was there for him. But the body on the gurney wasn't Goody—it couldn't be. It was drenched in red. Clothes and flesh hung in strips. She saw an arm that looked filleted. The part of the face she could see was . . . *gone.* She ran up to the gurney, in front of the attendant holding the bag. He crashed into her, and the whole production stopped.

"Hey!" the attendant yelled.

She leaned over the body, straining to see more of the face. An eye fluttered open, stared at her, closed again.

It was Goody.

She nearly screamed. Her hand clamped over her mouth. She felt her body go limp, as though someone had popped her spirit the way you pop a balloon.

The attendant pushed passed her. She stumbled backward, watched the gurney glide into Trauma Room 2. Then the door closed and she was standing in the corridor, numb and coated from waist to nose in Goody's blood.

thirteen

THE BODILY DAMAGE WAS AS DEVASTATING AS ANY ALLEN Parker had ever seen. Instantly, nothing else mattered: the room, the equipment, the trauma staff, his own physicality all fell away, sacrificed to the intense focus with which he attended to the patient's injuries. Everything around him paled as blood became more vivid, wounds more apparent, the needs of life more demanding. Information about the patient—called out by the staff or communicated as tones, bleeps, lights, and graphs by various machines—fell into the periphery of his awareness, absorbed without effort or recognition, but acted upon or mentally cataloged for later consideration. This was what it was all about: this one life, here and now.

His head darted to within inches of the gaping, bubbling wounds, then reared back to evaluate the injuries from different perspectives. He leaned over the body, then stood erect and slowly walked from head to belly and back again. As he went, he sealed holes in the body with squares of gauze, taping down three sides.

"Focus that light here. Four units RBCs, right? And get an operating room ready, fast."

He guessed that the carotid artery was intact, though only a surgical exploration could tell for sure. The internal and external jugular veins appeared ripped and oozing. He stepped around an intern who was busy injecting local anesthesia, skirting another who was tying off bleeding veins and arteries.

"He's 100 percent dead in the extremities," another nurse called out. "Fingers and toes are white."

"Bring that instrument tray over to me," Parker said.

The patient breathed spontaneously, but only barely. He hissed through shattered teeth, and air seeped out in gurgling bubbles through a dozen holes. Whatever had caused this damage was efficient and as ruthless as a starving shark.

"Where're the chest tubes? Come on, people!"

A section of ribs had turned into tiny fragments, which had shredded the right lung and disintegrated the liver.

"We need another surgeon. Find someone. Now!"

Blood pooled in open cavities. Pieces of flesh hung in strands.

"Get me suction. Clean here, here, and here. We're going to need more blood. Get the blood bank down here."

Parker didn't have to examine the abdomen to know the damage he would find there. A fetid stench suggested multiple perforations in the intestines. When he looked at the intestines protruding from the abdominal wall, he realized some would have to be removed altogether.

"Make it two surgeons . . . as many as we can get!"

Blood splashed and dripped and snaked toward the drain. Shock-induced endorphins probably—mercifully—prevented the man from feeling pain: a temporary reprieve at best, unless death snatched him from pain's grasp first.

Parker shook his head.

"If he codes, make it a DNR," he called out.

The *Do Not Resuscitate* order told the medical staff what they needed to know. Pulling out all stops to restore life upon cardiac arrest would most likely lead to an endless cycle of rescuing the poor soul from the brink of eternity, until he finally teetered over the edge forever. Restarting the heart could fool clinical death for only so long before the injuries caused biological death, in which all tissue dies: the end.

As a nurse blotted a section of the chest wound, Parker caught a glimpse of something too symmetrical to be organic. It appeared firmly embedded in the man's sternum.

"Whoa, whoa," he said. "What's this?"

Using forceps, he clamped the small, round object and tugged on it. He had to apply more force than he'd expected, but it finally popped loose. It was a black metal disk, razor sharp.

"Yow."

He dropped it into a stainless steel bowl. "Listen up, people," he announced. "It appears somebody has turned this man into a radial saw. Nobody sticks their hands in, got it? Use instruments—forceps and clamps. I want to see survey films of this whole area. Let's find out how many of these ugly buggers we're dealing with, and where they're hiding."

Nurses rushed to the table with masking tape and started marking off the edges of the wound.

The patient sputtered, and what came out sounded like a word. Parker turned to see the man's remaining eye focused on him. The gaze was piercing, intense. Jaw muscles bulged with effort, and the patient's mouth parted slightly. He was trying to talk.

Parker leaned his ear close. Hot, vile breath washed over him, then spatters of blood. Words followed. He bent lower, until his ear was nearly touching the man's mutilated lips. Parker's eyes narrowed, then grew wide. He tried to pull away, but the man's left hand had incredibly reached over Parker's head, holding him. The patient continued to speak in stuttering gasps.

After a long moment, Parker turned his face toward the patient's. "When?" he asked, a raspy whisper. He listened.

Blood bubbled out of the patient's mouth. His arm dropped off the table.

Parker looked around. The trauma team was busy. No one was looking; no one had heard.

"Who is this man?" he called above the cacophony. "Does anyone know?"

"A cop," someone said. "His partner is outside."

He gazed at the devastated face. He lowered his head again, turning his ear back toward the man. As he did, the electrocardiogram ceased its slow, rhythmic beeping to hum in endless, monotonous finality. The patient's heart had stopped.

"He's PEA!" somebody yelled out. *Pulseless Electrical Activity*, the condition that usually precedes asystole, or flatline. No one moved; everyone knew resuscitation was hopeless. They watched as Parker, still with his ear pressed to the man's mouth, gripped the patient's tattered shirt. He gave it a little shake, as if to rattle some words out of him. Then, slowly, Parker stood, staring at nothing, deep in thought.

"Doctor?" a nurse said. "Dr. Parker, are you all right?"

"Yes . . . of course." He rubbed his ear, smearing blood.

"Uh . . . mark the time." He looked at the wall clock. "Seventeen-oh-nine."

Nurses began stripping off gloves, shutting down machines, collecting gore-encrusted instruments. The various clamps, tubes, and lines still in the body would remain with the corpse until a forensic pathologist conducted an autopsy and declared the cause of death.

Parker tugged down his face mask and pushed through the doors to find Julia Matheson.

She was gone.

fourteen

TWO MINUTES EARLIER, SHE HAD WATCHED GOODY DIE. Gazing through the small windows in the trauma room doors, she had known there was nothing the doctors, nurses, and technicians could do to repair the injuries she'd seen. As soon as she had heard the cardiac monitor drop into a flat tone and someone call out, "PEA!" she felt a heavy weight drop in her stomach. Blood rushed to her head. The edges of her vision darkened. She felt herself sway, and she reached out, found something steady, and held herself up.

"Ma'am?" a voice asked.

She was gripping a young nurse's arm.

"Can I get you something?"

"Restroom?" Julia managed.

"Around the corner, down the hall, *on the right*."

The nurse raised her voice for the last three words—Julia was already around the corner, out of sight.

She barely reached the toilet when the contents of her stomach came up. She rose and leaned against the wall of the toilet stall, her cheek pressed to the cold steel, and wept. Her body hitched violently whenever she tried to stop, so for now, she let the tears flow. Images of Goody, of Jodi and the kids, kept swimming up from her memory, fueling her wracking sobs.

After a long time—ten minutes, maybe fifteen—the worst of it was over. Slowly, sadness gave way to anger; she felt it and seized on it. If emotions were drugs, sadness would be a depressant, anger a stimulant. She needed a heavy dose of drive to get through the next few hours, and eventually to find Goody's killers. If anger helped dull the pain of losing him and spurred her on, so be it.

She wiped her eyes and blew her nose. She hardly recognized herself in the mirror. She was pale, her hair disheveled, her eyes red. Somewhere along the way, her lip biting had drawn blood. A dark brown layer of it had formed on her lower lip. She splashed cold water on her face and tried to appear at least somewhat less homeless.

When she left the bathroom, her stride was strong, her shoulders square: she was on a mission to find whoever had slaughtered Goody, and why.

When she reached the ER, the trauma room doors were still closed. She pushed one open enough to peer in. The room looked like a battleground. Blood was everywhere, as were discarded gauze wrappers, bloody sponges, rubber gloves, strips of paper, and soiled towels. On a table in the center of the room, Goody's body lay under a stained white sheet, awaiting transport to a refrigerated cell, an autopsy

room, then the ground. She thought she should slip in, touch
his hand, but she couldn't do it.

I'm sorry, Goody. I'm sorry.

She wanted to continue talking to him like that, sending
words like a prayer to wherever he was, but she understood
the damage it would do to her composure, her resolve. She
moved her hand and let the door close.

She heard a noise and looked through a series of glass
doors to see the physician who had worked on Goody. Dr.
Parker, she remembered. She strode through the doors, not
noticing until she stood before him that he had stripped
down to his underwear. He was holding the gray pants she
had seen him wearing earlier, but they were stained with
blood. It had soaked through to his underwear and stomach.
The image of a battlefield returned; this man was one of the
combatants, away from the front, grateful to find that the
blood all over him wasn't his.

For a brief moment, surprise contorted his face. Then he
smiled, that same smile she'd caught before.

She spun around, saying, "Sorry . . . sorry . . ."

"Job hazard, I guess," he said calmly. "The blood, I mean,
not being caught with my pants down by a pretty woman.
That doesn't happen enough, I'm afraid."

She heard the snap of elastic and assumed that he had just
removed his underwear.

"Do you . . ." she started, getting over her initial shock
through the realization that he was flirting with her. His lack
of humility riled her, especially considering what had just happened, whose blood he was ridding himself of. "Do you
always take your clothes off in public?"

"Only after surgery. It's kind of a ritual we surgeons
have."

"I need to talk with you. The person you worked on, the one who died—"

"He was your partner, I know."

"He was my friend."

"I'm sorry."

"What can you tell me about his injuries?"

She heard the rustle of clothes.

"You can look now," he said.

She turned apprehensively, not convinced his invitation to look meant he was decent. To her relief, he had donned surgical pants.

"Actually," he said, "these scrub rooms are usually fairly private. I'd go up to the locker rooms, but they're on the sixth floor and, well, this is just more convenient." He opened a drawer, pulled out a folded smock, and handed it to her. "You'd better play doctor until you can change."

She looked down at her blood-soaked clothes. "Thank you."

"Are you a cop here in Chattanooga?"

"Federal. Out of Atlanta." She pulled out her identification and held it up to him.

He looked at it closely. "Centers for Disease Control," he said slowly.

His face paled, but she decided it was a trick of the light.

"I didn't know they had a law enforcement division."

"Part of Homeland Security. Mostly we're FBI special agents on permanent reassignment." She removed her business card from behind the ID card, jotted her mobile number on the back, and handed it to him.

"I see." He picked up a smock from a shelf, thinking hard about something. "So you investigate . . . what? Threats involving diseases, viruses?"

"Among other things. Doctor, what killed my partner?"

Parker shook his head. "Well, that's up to the medical examiner to decide, but an educated guess? Couple dozen razor-sharp disks, probably shot into his body from a large-bore firearm, like a shotgun."

"Disks?"

"Wait here." He walked through a glass door she had not seen before, which led directly into the trauma room. He picked up a small metal pan and returned.

Julia looked in and inhaled sharply.

"My thoughts exactly," said Parker. "Some of the disks were penetrating. That is, they entered his body and stayed there. This one"—he raised the pan, indicating the disk inside—"was lodged in his sternum. I suspect most of the disks probably went right through him and are embedded in whatever was behind him. By the looks of the injuries, they took a lot of his body with them when they exited."

"May I have this one?" she asked.

He squinted at her. "Is that okay?"

"We haven't established jurisdiction on this case yet, but we will. I might be able to get a jump on it if I can run this through our database, see if something like it has been used before in a crime."

"I see," he said thoughtfully. "Well, I don't see why not. The medical examiner will probably find plenty of others in the body, and the police undoubtedly already have all they need at the crime scene."

He took the pan to a sink and ran water into it. He said, "Was the man who was with your partner a cop as well?"

"No. Did they bring him in? I didn't—" She hadn't even thought of Vero. She had assumed, vaguely, in the back of her mind, that he also had been shot and killed, but she hadn't realized until that moment that she hadn't seen him come in.

If he had died at the scene, they would have kept him there for processing—photographs and such—and then taken him directly to the morgue.

Parker said, "One of the attendants who brought in Mr. Donnelley said the killer took the other man's body."

"Took it?"

"A witness said he shot him, flipped the corpse over his shoulder, and walked out the door."

A nurse opened the door behind Julia and leaned in. "Dr. Parker?"

"Yes?" he said without looking.

"There's a Detective Fisher on 3 for you."

"Thank you." He carefully drained the water from the pan. He opened and closed cabinets and drawers, selected a white and blue box the size of a pack of cards, and removed a pad of gauze from it. He used the gauze to pick up and dry the disk, then dropped the disk into the box.

"Apparently it was a pretty bizarre scene. Confusing." He handed the box to Julia. "Excuse me." He walked to a phone on the other side of the room. He raised the handset and said, "Dr. Parker . . . Yes." He looked at his watch. "I have an appointment off-site in forty-five minutes. How long will you be? . . . I see . . ."

While his back was turned, Julia slipped out. She couldn't see any reason Goody's admonition to avoid other law enforcement would be any less valid now that he had been killed. In fact, his death may have validated his concerns. She needed to know more about how he died, about who had killed him. The local cops would have plenty of details from the crime scene and any witnesses, but until she had a better grasp of what exactly was happening, she didn't want to see them. Or anyone else.

fifteen

KARL LITT'S SON, JOE, RAN DOWN THE GRASSY HILL, ARMS flapping like wings, legs moving faster than they could on flat terrain, his face brighter than the sun, laughing, squealing.

"Come on, son!" Litt called from the bottom of the hill. "She's gaining!"

Twenty feet behind the six-year-old boy, his mother scampered, reaching for her prey. She was obviously trying to prevent gravity from hurling her forward too fast, into her son.

Litt laughed. "You're almost there, Joe! Right here." He dropped to his knees, clapped his hands, and opened his arms wide to give the child a target. His son tacked left and ran for him. Joe appeared on the brink of a wipeout, but he stayed on his feet and picked up speed.

Instead, it was his mother who wiped out. Her feet pulled ahead, and when she tried to get her body lined up again, her arms and head and torso just kept going until she lost it, hitting the grass with her hands, then somersaulting once . . . twice . . . She twisted and began tumbling sideways, then backwards.

Litt's mouth fell open. He didn't know whether he should laugh or yell out to her. Then Joe slammed into him, and they both tumbled and rolled. They stopped, and Joe was under him, giggling uncontrollably. Litt raised his head, saw Rebecca lying still, and felt his heart skip a beat. She raised an arm and proffered a thumbs-up.

"Ha-ha!" he laughed to his son. "You did it. You beat the monster." He pushed himself up and pulled Joe with him. "See?" He pointed at the downed blonde beast.

Joe ran to his mother and nudged her with his sneaker. He turned back to Litt. "Let's fix her, Daddy!"

"Fix her?" Litt picked up his son and flipped him onto his shoulders.

"Wheeeeee!"

Litt looked down. His wife was staring at him with one eye, a tight-lipped smile on her lips. He winked at her, and she shimmered and disappeared.

Bam, bam, bam.

Litt looked up and around. His son was gone. His fingers touched his shoulder: just a bony old man's shoulder; no longer a perch for a little boy.

He was sitting on an unmade bed in a dark room, the only light coming from a black-and-white monitor on a dresser. It showed a man outside his bedroom. Gregor von Papen. While Litt watched, Gregor rapped again.

Bam, bam, bam.

Litt stood and shuffled to the door, kicking aside rumpled clothes, a magazine, a plastic cup. He leaned into the door, pressing his palms against it, head-height and shoulder-width apart, as though preparing to be patted down by police.

"What is it?" he called through the door.

"I have news," Gregor said.

Litt said nothing. Head hanging, he thought of the memory he had been lost in. Rebecca. Joe. Jessica. A tear that had just been sitting there fell from his eye. It made a faint flat sound when it hit the tile.

"Karl?"

"Yes?"

"I said I have news."

"What is it?"

Gregor hesitated, then said, "Atropos has succeeded."

Litt nodded. "Despesorio is dead?"

"Yes."

"He got the chip?"

Silence.

Litt snapped the dead bolt and yanked open the door. Gregor's face momentarily registered mild shock, and Litt knew he must look particularly awful. He'd done nothing to temper the pallor or scaliness of his skin. His eyes, usually shielded by sunglasses, must have been bloodshot and redrimmed. Since the accident, his irises had faded from cobalt to the faintest of blue, almost white. A quick glance would catch only pinprick pupils, which would seem alone in punctuating the eerie white orbs of his eyes, like periods without sentences. He blinked against the corridor's light.

Gregor took a step back.

"Tell me he retrieved the chip," Litt said.

"It wasn't on the body."

"Did he *take* the body?"

"Yes, he dissected it. It wasn't inside Vero, either. He

found the tracking device in Vero's leg. He wondered if that's what we wanted. I told him no."

Litt turned around. The dimness of the room soothed his eyes. He returned to the bed and sat, thinking. He asked, "Was he alone?"

"Some kind of fed was with him. He's dead too."

Litt nodded, then froze when Gregor said, "Atropos didn't do it."

Litt looked up. "Kendrick?" he whispered.

"I assume so. Atropos said it was a classic two-man hit team. Civilian clothes."

Litt smiled. "Atropos walked into *that*?" He shook his head in awe. "Worth every penny." He considered the scene a moment longer, then found his previous train of thought. "Did he check the fed?"

"He got out of there with seconds to spare. The cops were all over, apparently."

"So he didn't?"

Gregor shook his head.

"Well, he must. In all probability, Despesorio turned the chip over to the law enforcement officer."

"I'll let him know."

Litt picked up a pair of black sunglasses from a night-stand. Crumpled tissues fell to the floor. He stood and went back to the open door, slipping on the glasses as he did. He ran a palm from his forehead back over his nearly bald skull, flattening several long wisps of white hair.

"Tell him he must do it before Kendrick thinks of it. Kendrick no doubt believes we have already reclaimed the evidence Despesorio brought with him—if he knows about it at all. But it may occur to him to check the cop's body and personal effects. Atropos must beat him to it."

Gregor nodded and turned to leave.

"Gregor," Litt said, "remind him the chip was part of our agreement."

"Of course."

"I'll try to find out what Kendrick knows."

"You'll call him?"

"It's been a while. Time to catch up."

Litt scanned him up and down. They were the same age, but where Litt appeared at least eighty, Gregor could have passed for fifty, fifty-five tops. He was trim with a full head of salt-and-pepper hair, more pepper than salt. He always wore black SWAT boots laced up over his pant legs, a side-arm holstered to a tightly cinched utility belt, and camouflage clothes, a different style and pattern every time Litt saw him, it seemed.

"You look like a houseplant," he said.

Gregor glanced down at himself. "It's called Fall Forest."

"All the rage among heads of security, I presume?"

Gregor laughed. "I wouldn't know, but I am practically invisible in the woods."

"Good for you." Litt closed the door.

sixteen

His family had been dead almost thirty years. Joe had not seen his seventh birthday. Jessica had not experienced even one. His sweet Rebecca, his wife for twenty years—he had not been able to hold her as she died. He had not been able to say, *I'm sorry*. Kendrick Reynolds had not let him.

He wished, as he did every day, that they had had children earlier. If they had started growing their family when they were first married, maybe the kids would have been gone, away at college or on a road trip with friends, when Litt's work escaped the confines of his lab. Instead, they had waited. Litt had put his work first, as Kendrick had wanted. Up to that point, nearly his entire life had been in service to Kendrick. Since then, he had been in service to seeing Kendrick exposed, humiliated, dead.

Litt flipped a switch, and the room filled with red luminance, a color he found least irritating to his eyes. He sat at a small desk, swept away a pile of papers, and pulled a phone console close. He picked up the handset, punched in an encryption key and then a long string of numbers. He waited, listening to clicks and pops as the signal routed itself through a dozen different networks in as many countries. Finally he heard ringing on the other end. It was a dedicated line and completely untraceable.

When Kendrick Reynolds answered, Litt said, "I skunked you again."

"Good evening, Karl," Kendrick said, his voice slow and slight. The man was in his nineties. It was a wonder he could even talk, let alone scheme the way he did.

"Your man defected and got as far as the CDC's doorstep. You're getting lax."

"But I got to him before you did. That's all that matters."

"Okay, I concede your victory . . . this time." Kendrick paused, then said, "You were always competitive. A poor loser and a poor winner. I thought you would outgrow it, but you never did."

"And the only person you've ever cared about is yourself. Once, I thought I'd misjudged you, but I hadn't."

Litt closed his eyes. He did not want to exchange petty insults. Why were they compelled to tread these waters time and again?

"You mean I made you believe there was more to me? Pray tell, when?"

Litt pressed his lips tight. "When . . ." He pulled in a deep breath and let it come out slowly. He imagined his anger leaving with it. He realized his fingers were aching from squeezing the handset and forced them to relax. "When you gave me your blessing to marry Rebecca. But now I know you were only tolerating me, appeasing me, to keep me compliant."

"You've been reading too much Freud."

"You never cared about her. Or Jessica. Or Joe. It must have infuriated you that we named him after my father and not you. I realize now that you had hoped for a way to get my family out of the picture. And you finally found one."

"Karl, you're wrong. You know I always loved—"

"Just curious," Litt interrupted, bringing the conversation back in line, "how did Despesorio—my defector—come to your attention? Do you have a keyword tap on the CDC phones?"

The old man coughed, his mouth obviously turned away from the phone. Ever so polite. Then he said, "And at USAMRIID, the World Health Organization, all six of the world's biosafety level-four labs . . . everywhere someone with knowledge of you or your operation might show up. It was only a matter of time, Karl."

"It's been thirty years."

"The world is getting smaller. Technology is getting better. You can't hide forever."

"We'll see."

Silence.

"Karl, we can work something out."

Litt pressed the handset tighter to his face. "You mean before I expose you, before I shatter whatever legacy you think you've built?"

"I mean before you do something you'll regret."

"The only thing I regret is ever trusting you."

"I know you're close to something, Karl. Word is, you've stopped taking orders for bioterrorism products. It's not because you've won the lottery, so I figure you've got your crew working on something else, something big enough to forgo cash flow. That tells me you're confident in whatever it is, and you're close to rolling it out. One of your scientists defected. I'm guessing he had an attack of conscience. That—and the very nature of the work you do—tells me that what you have in mind is very nasty."

He sighed into the phone, a raspy gasp that turned Litt's stomach.

"Listen to me. Maybe you're right, maybe I care only about myself, maybe I've always been that way. But that's not you, Karl. I've seen your capacity to love. Has your heart really hardened so much?"

"Yes." A cold, solid syllable.

"I'm trying to tell you: You don't have to do what you're planning. We can work something out."

"I've worked it out, and you're too late."

"What?" Kendrick said. "What have you done?"

"You'll find out soon enough."

"If that's true, why did you hire killers?"

Litt laughed. "You know as well as I do, for every exposed secret, ten new ones need protecting. Now, more than ever, I need my privacy."

"Since you've played your hand?"

"You can say I waited for a royal flush."

"Did you get everything back?"

He's fishing, Litt thought. "I'm short one biologist."

"Another one?"

"No, the same one. He was a good man."

"Apparently too good for you."

"Good-bye, Kendrick."

"Karl."

Litt hung up. Kendrick was difficult to read. For him, the

day's events could be over . . . or he was still investigating, seeing what was there to find . . . or he had the chip. Litt didn't put much stock in this last possibility. He believed Kendrick would have hinted that the game was over, that after all the battles he'd lost, he'd won the war. More likely, he would continue to poke around, maybe find Despesorio's trail or something he'd left behind. Litt hoped Atropos was as good as his reputation.

"Soon it won't matter," he said out loud. "Old man, you're about to find out just how rock-hard my heart has become."

KENDRICK DISCONNECTED AND SAT IN HIS WHEELCHAIR, staring at the phone. One hand picked at the wool blanket covering his legs. His other hand went to his mouth. He snipped off a sliver of fingernail between his teeth and examined the result. God was gazing at him, and he shifted his eyes to gaze back. Nestled in a felt-lined cup holder in the arm of his chair, a God-head pipe cast a disapproving look on Kendrick's agitation.

"I know," he whispered at the face, "but it's him, not me. What choice do I have?"

Kendrick had first beheld the ceiling of the Sistine Chapel in 1958, when he attended the funeral mass of Pius XII as Eisenhower's secretary of state. The potency of Michelangelo's brush had stunned him: the luster of Ezekiel's garments, evil Haman's dramatic crucifixion, the rising saints and tortured sinners of *The Last Judgment*; all of it rendered among intricate columns and arches and pedestals that the artist had painted on the ceiling's smooth plane. But nothing took his breath away like the visage of God as He was creating Adam. Its combination of strong features and tender expression portrayed the perfect balance of power and compassion, superiority and love.

Back in the States, he found himself pondering that sweeping beard of Michelangelo's God, the granite nose and forehead, the purposeful eyes. In God's face, Kendrick discovered the potential of man, the symbol of the way he wanted to live out the rest of his life. He secured the finest raw meerschaum Eskischir had to offer   this was three years before the Turkish government banned the export of meerschaum block—and sent it to the most renowned Viennese carver. What he received back was a three-inch-tall, three-dimensional carving in white meerschaum clay. It matched the Sistine head of God right down to the bulging vein in His temple, the arch of concentration in His brow, the way His beard rose up the jawline only to the earlobe. It was a masterpiece of a masterpiece.

It was also a pipe, with an amber stem curving up from the back of the head and a bowl whittled into the crown. Over the years, the meerschaum had absorbed nicotine from countless bowls of tobacco, coloring and highlighting the creases of God's face in a cinnamon glow. It was aging much more gracefully than Kendrick's own craggy countenance.

He was convinced the face on the pipe changed ever so subtly, even if only in his mind's eye, to help guide him. When he was having doubts, God gave him a look of strength, of encouragement; when he was righteously angry, God scowled at the offender with him. Now God was saying, *Take care of this, Kendrick. It's why I gave you so much strength, so many resources.*

After a long moment he gestured, and a man in Air Force blues stepped over.

"Sir?"

"He was trying to find out if we had something on him. And he claims to have set something in motion. Send in another team. We need to locate whatever it is he's missing."

The captain walked away, his heels clicking on the hardwood floor and echoing slightly in the big, antebellum ballroom that Kendrick had converted into his command center. Leaving his home had come to require more energy than he could afford to expend. But he could not retire or die until he had tied up the one loose end that could wipe out everything he had worked for, his country, his name. He had to find Litt and eliminate him forever.

He considered calling the captain back to remind him that the last team had been sloppy, hardly the surgeon Karl had found. More like surgeons with chain saws. But he decided the method wasn't his business; he cared only about the outcome. Granted, last time the outcome stank, but he wasn't in the field. He had learned a long time ago to let the experts do their thing. Give them an objective and get out of their way.

Would innocent civilians die? Maybe. He hoped not, but he hoped even more for a way to stop Karl.

He avoided making eye contact with God.

seventeen

FOR A MAN OF LETTERS, JEFF HUNTER FOUND HIMSELF
often thinking about numbers. On his mind at the moment:
six. That was the average number of work-related questions or
suggestions he fielded during his morning journey from the
doors of the *New York Times* building to his desk on the third
floor. More than the hellos or the great-story-yesterdays. No,
what he could count on hearing was something like, "That
drug dealer didn't really tell you that, did he?" or "I heard
from a source that you got that detail wrong," or—the winner by a mile—"I've got a great story for you, Jeff!" Six times
on average. Once, the day after his Pulitzer nomination,
twenty-eight people suddenly had brilliant story ideas Jeff
just had to pursue. Twenty-eight. Only a dozen had congrat-
ulated him.

Today the lobby security guard scored number one:

"Hey, Mr. Hunter, that story you did on college hazings? I was wondering, my nephew—"

"Can I get back to you about that, Tom? Kinda in a hurry."

He didn't slow down. To the elevators, push the button. Janet from HR evened things out: "Hi, Jeff. Are those new glasses?" Then she blew it: "If you have a minute, I thought of something you should write about. You know EQ—emotional intelligence quotient? I just heard of this test—"

As if he needed ideas.

He arrived at his cubicle, having fielded five opportunities for distraction. Not bad. But then he checked his e-mail—not part of the morning's count, but with a scoring system all its own. Forty-four new messages, even with a kick-butt spam blocker and his own kill filters that automatically deleted e-mails containing such obnoxious words as "idea," "lawyer," and George Carlin's "Seven Words You Can Never Say on Television." He tended to get a lot of messages with at least one of those nasty seven. At least he used to, prior to creating the kill filters.

One wife. Three kids. Two mortgages. A salary just over six figures.

Numbers. *Maybe I should have been an accountant.*

Except he loved being an investigative reporter. Corruption, greed, abuse of power—what could be better than uncovering these deeds and exposing the perpetrators? In Hunter's book, nothing.

He started sorting through the e-mails. Delete. Delete. Delete.

He came to one with the subject line, "The story of the century"—a slight twist on the usual "Story of the year!" He opened it and was surprised to find it blank. Some story. Then

he noticed the attachment, something called "First_Strike.xls."
A spreadsheet. Or, more likely, a virus.

"I don't think so," he said out loud and hit the delete key.
He'd gone through a dozen more e-mails when he thought
about the spreadsheet again. What if it really was a big story?
The blank message was a deviation from the norm; most
people didn't seem to know how to stop once they started
typing a message to him.

He opened his trash folder, then double-clicked on "The
story of the century." He checked the return address. It was
an anonymous e-mail resender he recognized. He received at
least a few nasty-grams a week with return addresses that
were untraceable, thanks to Web sites that believed in a person's right to anonymity. In his experience, anonymity over
the Internet meant trouble. Then again, Deep Throat went
nameless for thirty years. Most whistleblowers preferred it
that way. He eyed the icon that represented the attached file.
If it was a virus, the company's computer guys could take care
of it. And his computer backed itself up every evening, so he
wouldn't lose much, in a worst-case scenario. He selected the
file and opened it.

His monitor displayed a list of names, addresses, and, on
most records, what appeared to be social security numbers.
He scrolled down. The list went on and on. He hit the button that jumped him to the last entry. Exactly ten thousand.

Scrolling back up, he recognized some names—politicians, celebrities, business leaders. Of course, these could be
average joes who only shared the names of famous people.
There was also a large number of names he didn't recognize.
What did any of these people have in common? Why were
they on this list? Why was he sent the list, and who sent it?
The social security numbers bothered him. The list could

have come from one of the stolen data files that made the news every week—hacked credit card companies, hospitals, schools. Hardly the story of the century.

There was only one way to piece this puzzle together. He chose a name at random, opened an Internet phone directory, slipped on his telephone headset, and let his computer dial the number.

THE CAR, SLEEK, BLACK, AND LOW, ROARED THROUGH THE STREETS of Paris at dizzying speeds. It plunged into a traffic tunnel, slalomed between pillars, and zipped past slower cars.

"This is where Princess Di crashed," Bobby Waddle said. His eyes darted like Geiger counter needles as he assessed approaching dangers and opportunities to skirt them. He risked a quick swipe at his nose and wiped what came away on his jeans. He sniffed hard to avoid another such distraction.

Next to him, Cole Martin scrunched his nose. "Who?"

"She was going to be queen of England. Mom liked her."

Bobby's car left the ground as it came out of the tunnel onto Pont de l'Alma. Biting pavement again, the rear tires spun with unfocused power and caused the back end to skitter into the side of a taxicab. Sparks flew, and the speedometer instantly dropped ten miles per hour. He was doing only eighty-five now.

He glanced at the rearview mirror and didn't like what he saw: another sleek sports car, this one red, gaining quickly. He pushed a button and released a thick stream of oil onto the roadway. His rival spun out of control and crashed into a bus.

"No fair!" Cole yelled.

"The oil was an upgrade I picked up on the last lap,"

Bobby said, laughing. He coughed and reminded himself not to laugh.

Cole threw down his controller. On the lower half of the television's split screen, his car was on fire. Words flashed over it—RESPAWN: HIT BUTTON A.

"Come on. It's no fun by myself," Bobby said. His eyes never left the screen. His fingers moved over the controller with robotic efficiency.

"You always win!" Cole complained.

Bobby set the controller in his lap and turned to his friend. He coughed. His chest felt tight, and it hurt. "I've been playing longer than you. You want me to let you win?"

"No. I just . . . I don't know. I don't like this game anymore."

"Wanna play Halo?"

Cole shook his head.

"Quake?"

"No."

"What do you want to do?"

"How about Nerf-gun tag?"

That sounded good. They'd been on the Xbox for about an hour, as long as his mom allowed him per day.

"It," he said.

"You're always it."

"All right, you be it." He turned off the TV and dropped the wireless controllers into a drawer. As they were heading out the back door, the phone rang.

Bobby's mother yelled down the stairs: "Bobby, could you get that, honey?"

"Aw, Mom!" But his words weren't as loud as he thought they should be. His lungs just couldn't push them out. He decided it was easier to answer the phone than to argue.

"Hello?" He watched Cole pick a Nerf gun out of the toy box on the deck and check it for sponge bullets.

"May I speak to Robert Waddle, please?" A man's voice.

"Who is this?"

"Jeff Hunter, from the *New York Times*."

"We already get a newspaper."

"I'm not calling about a subscription. Is Robert Waddle there?"

Cole was waving at him to come. He waved back.

"That's me, but nobody calls me Robert. Just Bobby."

"You live in Castle Creek, right? New York?"

"It's next to Binghamton."

There was a pause. "Is your dad also named Robert?"

"His name was Philip. He's dead." He was getting annoyed.

"I'm sorry. Did he die recently?"

"When I was a baby."

"When you were what? I'm sorry."

"A baby. I have a cold."

"How old are you now?"

"Ten. I'm not supposed to talk to strangers."

Cole had jumped off the deck and was making his way toward the woods at the back of the property. Bobby wanted to play around the house, but Cole thought because Bobby wasn't there, he got to choose the rules. Dang it.

"That's right, you shouldn't. But let me just ask one thing. Has anything unusual happened to you lately?"

"Like what?"

"Oh, I don't know. An accident, or has anybody—"

"Bobby, who is it?" His mom whisked into the kitchen and held out her hand for the phone.

"Some guy . . ." He placed the handset into her palm, glad to be done with it, and bolted toward the door.

"Whoa, whoa, whoa," his mother said. She raised a finger to tell him to hold on. "Who is this, please?" She listened for three seconds, then hung up. "I don't have time for salesmen. Did you sweep the garage like I asked?"

"Yes, ma'am."

"You're so good. Come here." She touched his forehead. "Still warm. How do you feel?"

"Stuffy. Tight right here." He patted his chest.

"Worse than this morning?"

"A little."

"That means a lot. Don't stay out too long, and stay out of the brook."

"Aw, Mom."

"Do you want to not go out at all?"

He shook his head.

"Okay, have fun." She slapped his bottom, and he ran out the door. Cole was nowhere in sight.

A KID. WHAT WAS IT ALICE SAID IN WONDERLAND? CURIOUSER and curiouser. Jeff Hunter typed a note on the line that contained Robert Waddle's name. He scrolled down a ways and selected another.

"THE LOBSTER CAKES AND DOM PERIGNON SOUND LOVELY," Gretchen Gaither told the woman sitting beside her on the couch. Her smile faltered slightly. "But they're out of our price range."

The woman touched Gretchen's hand. "For your fortieth anniversary? Why not splurge?"

She thought about it. It would be nice. Just this once. She

knew Jim would go along with it . . . and then quietly work a few weeks of double shifts to pay for it. She couldn't do that to him.

"I'm afraid not," she said. "What else do you have?"

The woman looked disappointed—or disgusted. She leaned over to a large volume of menus and photographs on the coffee table, flipped a few pages, then a few pages more. "Bruschetta and Torciano Fragolino? Fourteen dollars a bottle."

Gretchen nodded. Jim would have hated this meeting with the caterer. It would have reminded him that things hadn't turned out the way they had dreamed. Still, he had always provided for their needs and had found a way to put their two children through college. It had been a little easier when she worked as a substitute teacher. But two years ago, her arthritis had grown too painful to ignore or sufficiently medicate. And an already tight budget became even tighter. She'd told him that their anniversary needed no special commemoration, other than their own remembrances of the happy times they'd shared. But he had insisted: "Ask the kids to come; invite some friends. Let's have a little party—catered, because the guest of honor shouldn't do the work."

"How many people?" the woman asked.

"About thirty, with the kids and their families."

The caterer looked around the small living room. "Have you thought about renting a banquet room? They can be had for a very reasonable price."

"Our backyard has hosted many a birthday party," Gretchen said, smiling at the memories. "I think it'll do for this."

The phone rang, and she excused herself.

She found the cordless handset on the dining room table. "Hello?"

"Gretchen Gaither?"

"Yes?"

"Jeff Hunter, with the *New York Times.* Do you have a few moments?"

AFTER SPEAKING TO THE GAITHER WOMAN, HUNTER DISCON-nected with a mouse click. Retired schoolteacher. No recent problems with financial institutions or anyone else that she could think of. Seemed like a sweet lady. He could tell his call had spooked her. He hoped she didn't follow up with a call to the news desk or, worse, to the police. He wasn't ready to answer questions, and he wasn't ready to let the list go.

ANDREW WALLENSKI LOOKED AT THE WALL OF THE BOYS' REST-room and shook his head. Kids these days. To know such words in middle school was bad enough, but to actually spray paint them on a public wall! No respect. Not for property. Not for the people who had to clean up their messes. If they were his kids, they'd show respect, that was for sure.

He opened the can of white latex paint and poured it into a pan. He'd tried scrubbing graffiti off the walls before. The wall paint had come off with the spray paint, and he'd had to re-cover the entire wall anyway. Waste of time. Waste of paint. Fool kids. He draped a drop cloth over the tops of the urinals and had run the roller up three feet of wall, dulling but not obscuring a big letter *S,* when the mobile phone in his back pocket jangled.

A DOZEN CALLS LATER, HUNTER HAD NOTHING. HE'D SPOKEN TO a mother in Denver whose infant son was on the list; a sixteen-year-old girl in Dallas who was late for her waitressing job and didn't want to talk; a father in Chicago who wanted to know why a stranger was asking about his seven-year-old daughter; and two women and three men, all of whom had no clue why they'd be on a list sent to a news reporter. Of course he'd encountered wrong, unlisted, and disconnected numbers; busy signals; unanswered calls; and answering machines. But none of those counted. No journalist worth his press pass let that stuff deter him from a story. Problem was, he wasn't sure he had a story. Just a list of names.

He had called a *Times* entertainment reporter in LA to ask about the celebrities on the list, but she had nothing to report. Biggest news was that the workaholic director Lew Darabont, also on Hunter's list, had failed to show up for a script read-through—the first time in his career. A studio publicist announced that Darabont was suffering from exhaustion and would take a few days off.

Hunter then reached a senator at his Washington office. No news there, except that he was furious over a narrowly defeated tort reform bill he had helped draft. He ranted for three minutes, then apologized, saying he hadn't gotten much sleep the night before. "Fighting a cold," he'd explained. "It's got me down, and I think it wants to be the flu."

That was another thing Hunter had discovered. There seemed to be a high percentage of people with colds. Hunter didn't know when cold season was and wondered if it was at different times of year in different parts of the country. He made a note to check it out.

He'd talked about or to five kids and twelve adults, nine males and eight females, six well-known people, and twelve nobodies. Scattered around the country. No rhyme, no reason. No story.

A cub reporter appeared at his desk. The kid was helping him research a story on transit cops making a sport of beating up vagrants in the subway tunnels. He was excited about interviews he had conducted and wanted Hunter to listen to the MP3 files. Hunter took a last look at the mysterious list of names. He closed the document. Just another WAS story—wait and see. He had eighteen others like it.

eighteen

JULIA MATHESON CHECKED INTO A DOWNTOWN MOTEL under her married sister's name and paid cash. It was the kind of place that didn't ask for identification or a major credit card, and couldn't care less who you were or what you did in the room, as long as you didn't destroy the property and you paid in advance. She requested a room on the back side of the building, out of sight of people cruising the boulevard.

The room had brown indoor-outdoor carpeting, a chipped Formica table bolted to the wall next to the bed, a threadbare bedspread, and a hand-printed sign on the back of the door that read NO COOKING IN ROOM. The smell of fried hamburgers tinged the air.

Julia dropped her purse and laptop case on the bed, along with a big bag from Wal-Mart containing a change of clothes, a gym bag, and other items. She went to the window and opened it, then fell onto the bed beside the bags. Most of the acoustic spray had come off the ceiling, probably a little here and a little there for the past thirty years. There was a big brown-rimmed water stain in one corner. She tried identifying the other splotches: ketchup, coffee, a smashed insect. She sighed and closed her eyes.

What was she doing here? She should have been back in her duplex in Atlanta, cleaning up the dishes, helping her mother to the tub. She needed to call her. It wasn't that her mother's MS rendered her completely helpless, but more that she'd be worried. Julia rarely came home late, and when she did, she always called first. She didn't know what she'd say. Not anything that would make anyone tapping the phone decide to stake out the house and wait for her or anything that would give away her location.

Listen to her: tapping the phone!

But that was her reality right now. Someone with loads of intelligence and highly sophisticated technical capabilities had attacked them and killed Goody and Vero. They had intercepted the SATD signal, which this morning she would have said was impossible. And Goody had recognized one of the assailants, an undercover cop. What did that mean? Was a government agency involved in the hit? A rogue director? Or was the guy freelancing?

Now that Vero was dead, was it over? She didn't know, but she remembered something Goody had said during the investigation of a serial killer: "There's no end to evil."

She wondered if Jodi Donnelley knew that her husband was dead. Probably Edward Molland, the LED's director of domestic operations, had told her. Julia wanted to be there, to hold her, to comfort the boys. At the same time, she wished there was no reason to comfort Donnelley's family.

She opened her eyes, turning her mind away from what she wished. It all hurt too much. She needed to keep her head straight, her thoughts on the problem.

She sat up and scooted back to lean against the wall, the nearly disintegrated foam pillow propped behind her lower back. She pulled her knees up and hugged her legs. Her heart felt wedged in her throat.

Okay . . . Goody called a little after six. Despesorio Vero showed up at CDC. What kind of name is that? What was that accent? Mexican? Did he travel to the States, or did he live here? Why did he want to see Mark Sweeney? National Center for Infectious Diseases . . . National Center for Infectious Diseases.

Pressure behind her eyes. She wanted to cry . . . and she didn't want to.

What are the five stages of grief? Or are there six? Denial . . . anger . . . depression . . . No, bargaining, then depression . . .

Ahhhh! Goody went into the Excelsior. The SATD was working. His wire was working. Some white noise, maybe the hotel's AC. He ordered orange juice; then Vero came in, asked if he was Sweeney.

Her top teeth found a ridge on her bottom lip, the scab from having bitten into it earlier. She bit down, feeling the pain, letting it move her away from her grief. She tasted blood.

He said Vero didn't look well. Then . . .

She remembered the gunfire, how loud it was through the earpiece. Goody had yelled. People were screaming in the background.

She closed her eyes, pinching out a tear. She bit harder on her lip, swallowed against the lump in her throat, fought the flood at her eyes.

IF JULIA HAD DISTRACTED HERSELF BY STEPPING OUTSIDE AND looking north, she would have seen in the distance the shape of Missionary Ridge. It was discernible at that time of evening by the lights radiating from the large homes perched on it. If it had been pointed out to her, she could have seen, near the very peak of the mountain, a light glowing in the study of the recipient of Goody's last mortal words.

Dr. Allen Parker sat at his desk, a fire roaring in a nearby hearth, Mozart's *Requiem* streaming through ceiling-mounted speakers. He was torn between two piles of books and papers. One pile contained everything he needed to finish an article he was writing for the *Journal of the American Medical Association* on the benefits of partial liquid ventilation for patients with severe respiratory failure. It was already three days overdue.

The other pile interested him more. He pulled a book off the top of the stack—*Field Virology.*

"Okay, Mr. Donnelley," he said out loud. "You got me. Now let's see if you knew what you were talking about."

He turned to the table of contents, ran his finger down the chapter titles, then turned to chapter 39. A single word in large type at the top of the page read FILOVIRIDAE. As he began to read, words and phrases seared into his mind—*hemorrhagic fever, outbreak, abrupt onset of illness, death, no known vaccine.* A headache brewed behind his eyes, but he continued reading. *Epidemic. Biosafety level 4. Human pathogen. Mortality.*

Occasionally he'd look up from an article or book to Google a phrase on the iMac on his desk. One online search would lead to another, and twenty minutes would pass before he'd return to the hard copy he'd been reading.

More than a few times he'd light a cigarette and promptly forget about it. He'd find a butt attached to a delicate cylinder of ashes in the ashtray and have to light another one. In his study, he puffed away as if it were the best thing he could do. Erlanger had become smoke-free, forcing him to smoke outside with the other diehards. It made him feel ostracized and dirty. More times than not, when people saw him in the hall heading for the door with cig and lighter in hand, they'd say, "Doctors smoke?" like *Cops commit crimes?* He'd answer, "This one does."

He liked to think he didn't care what people thought, but he did. At thirty-six he was already one of the leading thoracic surgeons in the country, thanks to a nearly flawless record in the operating room. That, and a procedure he had invented that happened to save a senator's life. He had been featured in *Time* magazine as a "Top Ten Doc"; other articles followed in news, medical, and financial publications. Even his house got coverage in *Architectural Digest* and *Southern Living*. Before long, movie and television producers began offering ungodly sums for his opinion of their shows' medical veracity. He was one of the few practicing surgeons with a Hollywood agent, a tidbit he carefully dropped into as many conversations as possible.

Parker pushed back his chair and stood. The tambour clock on the mantel told him it was a little after nine; he'd been in research mode for over two hours. The rest of the house was dark, except for the light over the stove, which spilled into the hall and glowed faintly outside his study doors. It reminded him that he had thrown a Hungry Man turkey dinner in the microwave and forgotten about it. He snatched the nearly empty pack of Camels off the desk, shook one out, and lit it with habitual fluidity. He held the smoke in his lungs for a reassuring moment, then sent it billowing over his head. Then he sat down again, pulled the iMac monitor closer, and tapped into a medical database.

It was going to be a long night.

nineteen

FINALLY, SOME GOOD NEWS. LITT HAD JUST HEARD FROM one of his "control subjects"—people on his First Wave list whom he had paid to keep him informed. A school janitor in Chicago had called to let him know that a *New York Times* reporter had contacted him. The reporter wanted to know why the janitor's name was on a list he had received.

Litt knew it was too early for the reporter to develop definitive conclusions about the list. But either the reporter would make follow-up calls and realize everybody on the list was getting sick, seriously sick, or he would become aware of news reports around the country of people getting sick and eventually make the connection. It wouldn't be long before one of the reporters who received the list realized that someone knew who would get sick *before* they'd gotten sick.

And that's when Litt would make his entrance onto the world stage.

All he could do now was wait. But he was anxious, and for years his only source of relaxation had been lab work. So he left his room and headed for his laboratory. He would find something to do.

Litt walked stiffly, feeling the lack of fluid in his joints, feeling bone rub against bone. It didn't help that his skin itched all over as well—more than usual. Talking to Kendrick had taken its toll. It had dredged up painful memories, which took away from his ability to handle the here and now.

Kendrick Reynolds. He wished he'd never met the man, even if it meant dying on the docks with his father. He took that back. He had not met Rebecca then, and that was an experience that made everything else bearable. She was morphine in an otherwise painful existence.

He smiled, felt his bottom lip crack. Doubtful you'd find that line in a love song. But it was true. And it was true that she was gone, leaving only the pain.

His father had expected better for him. Then the Reich had fallen, and so had his father. *Que será,* he thought bitterly.

A fluorescent tube overhead sputtered and hummed. He shuffled a little farther to a bench and sat. Today, he was tired. A good day to stay in bed. If only he had that luxury. He closed his eyes.

And remembered.

1945

TEN-YEAR-OLD KARL LITT YEARNED FOR SLEEP. HIS MUSCLES and tendons throbbed with fatigue; his eyes were burning embers pressed into his head. Still, he willed his body to stand tall. He resisted the temptation to gaze at the peacefully sparkling stars and tendrils of fog wafting over the harbor's black water. Doing so would surely lull him to sleep. He could not afford that.

He fixed his gaze on the *Unterseeboot* moored at the battered wharf. Scars from vicious battles creased and pocked her metal skin. Unimaginable clashes had beaten and blasted away huge chunks of gray paint. She appeared ready for scuttling, not for sailing the most crucial mission of the war.

The U-boat rose on a swell from a deep ocean current. Shadows shifted on her hull, and her entire length seemed to flex into bands of impenetrable flesh, unbeatable muscle. In fact, she was only one in ten U-boats to make it this far. She had cast hundreds of Allied ships to the sea floor. On this voyage, however, she was fangless; the captain had jettisoned the torpedoes to accommodate more precious cargo: gold, scientific equipment, Aryan blood.

Cartoonish insignias had replaced U-boat identification numbers when the war started, an attempt to mystify the Führer's *U-bootwaffe*. The one on this submarine—a grinning devil—glared with vivid white eyes from its position on the partially crushed conning tower. Karl glared back, daring the seafaring imp to blink first.

The shadow of a workman splashed against the conning tower, obscuring the devil face. Karl watched the man shuffle up the gangplank, hugging what appeared to be an extraordinarily heavy crate. Red-faced, he waddled to the open deck hatch, set it down with a thud, and slid it into the arms of another, who would stow it in the belly of the metal beast.

Karl watched the man lumber away from the hatch, chapped hands kneading his lower back. When the man reached the gangplank, Karl shifted his vision to the conning tower again. He had stopped tracking the workmen's pendulum-like movements from wharf to U-boat and back again; the glare of the naked bulbs near the crates shot daggers into his eyes.

He surveyed the dock. The few fathers who had arrived here stood away from one another, watching the workmen with dazed expressions. Karl had the great privilege of witnessing this historic event to its end. It was a privilege commensurate with the daunting responsibility he bore for their survival—for the survival of the Reich. Like the creaking war vessel before him, his adolescent shoulders did not appear up to the task. But only the sons and daughters of the Reich's top scientists could possibly carry on the battle now; they had been trained, they were ready.

Absently, he ran a hand over his filthy jacket.

Standing at rigid attention next to him, the boy's father tugged on the front of his own jacket for what must have been the hundredth time. He was trying to flatten wrinkles that were stiffened by too much sweat and blood and grime ever to lay smooth again. With blown-out knees, unraveled stitching, and rumpled hat, the uniform was at odds with the man's proud posture. Only the Ritterkreuz—the cherished Knight's Cross of the Iron Cross that hung around his neck—gleamed in the lamplight.

Josef Litt was a man of exquisite refinement. If not for the triumph of knowing his life's work would continue through his son, he would find the humility of his current situation unbearable. He wore the uniform and title of an *SS-Oberstgruppenführer*, a lofty military rank reflective of his authority, but certainly not of his duties. Although he had killed, he was no soldier. In the lab he had shown how men in white coats could turn men of muscle into pathetic drones. His experiments had earned him the attention of the Supreme Commander. Before long, he was head of a top secret research laboratory, with an SS regiment—and title— at his disposal.

Karl was proud of his intimate knowledge of his father, an otherwise guarded man. He turned to appraise the familiar, crisp profile of the man who was now entrusting the Aryan dream to him.

Approaching footfalls drew his attention to the wharf. One SS soldier had broken away from the other four. Three diamonds on his left collar marked him as an officer. His gray uniform looked disheveled and grubby, but it was a model of German aristocracy compared to Karl's clothes.

The soldier moved to within a handsbreadth of Josef Litt. He angled his head away from the boy and bent closer and whispered in his father's ear.

Josef nodded tersely, without hesitation.

The soldier glanced back at the workmen. Finished, they were talking quietly and waiting for their pay so they could go home and at long last fill their families' bellies. He pulled a Schmeisser submachine gun from a strap over his shoulder. He positioned the weapon so only the boy and his father could see him yank back its bolt, chambering the first round. He flicked his eyes toward Karl. The look surprised the boy; the man's face reflected doubt, even sorrow. Then the soldier turned away, leaving Karl to wonder. With the gun hidden behind him, the soldier marched toward the workers.

Karl felt his father's hand on the back of his head. The elder Litt's voice was cold as an executioner's blade.

"Sei fleißig, mein Sohn." Learn well, my son.

THE HARD LESSONS HAD STARTED SIX DAYS BEFORE, WHEN HIS father had awakened him after midnight. "It's time, Karl," he had said breathlessly.

"I'm ready, Father."

In the anemic light of the foyer, there was a teary farewell with Karl's mother. Hair in curlers, she wore a thin beige nightgown that smelled vaguely of sweat. She alternately embraced him crushingly, kissed his face, and babbled about how much she loved him. He stood stoically unresponsive; her antics shamed him. She had known for more than half a year this day would come. Karl broke free of her arms and strode out the door without looking back.

Several trips along the rubble-strewn streets of Berlin filled the car with three other children—two boys, one of whom wept incessantly, and a cheery little girl who informed them that she was five. Travel was slow as they moved against a pounding tide of refugees heading into Berlin.

Two hours later, they lost their car to three German army officers determined to escape the wrath of both the Allied war machine and an increasingly unstable Führer. What followed was a blur of trudging through fields and swamps and dense forests.

The thought of missing the U-boat made his father nearly insane with panic. They caught an hour's sleep here, a couple more there. They rummaged through heaps of trash and the clothes of decaying corpses, looking for scraps of food. Josef feared all pedestrians, and vehicles even more so. He instructed the others to hit the ground and stay flat at his signal.

Once, Josef told the children to wait, and he loped off toward a farmhouse. Karl thought he looked like a wounded beast, bounding toward shelter under the glare of a hateful moon. He returned thirty minutes later with two loaves of bread and a small bag of carrots and potatoes. The bread was splattered with a dark, coppery-smelling liquid, impossible to identify in the night. The group ate it without question.

Sometime after that, a fat man in tatters sprang out from behind a stone wall. He grabbed at the children, demanding food. Josef rushed to him and knocked him into the mud. In an instant, he was sitting on the man's fat belly. A huge knife appeared. Josef pressed the blade against the man's bulging neck. Karl saw muscles strain in his father's jaw and forearms and caught a flash of gritted teeth: the wounded beast cornered.

"Don't try me," his father said. "You won't survive to tell the tale."

They did not move for a long moment; then his father pushed off the man and started walking again. Always walking.

The downed man gasped for breath. Blood flowed from what looked to Karl like a small, smiling mouth etched into his neck. But the man pulled himself up, held a dirty handkerchief to his wound, and stumbled off in the other direction.

They staggered into Rostock on the Baltic Sea late the next afternoon. After three years of Royal Air Force bombings, the town was a crumbling mess. Tiny billows of dust danced like ghosts in the empty streets. Shutters clung to darkened windows. If the Brits had failed to completely destroy the place, they had succeeded in beating the spirit out of its people.

They rounded a ravaged brick building and faced the harbor—but no U-boat. The opaque water was smooth and undisturbed. The scorched pilings of shattered docks jutted from the water like rotten teeth. Only the nearest dock had barely survived, the huge sliding doors of its warehouse intact and drawn tight.

Karl turned to his father, who did not look devastated as Karl had expected, only worried. Josef held his hand up to Karl—Don't panic, it said—and walked on, his hand still raised, forgotten.

As they drew closer, one of the warehouse doors screeched open, and SS soldiers stepped out. The SS commander explained that the U-boat was waiting thirty miles offshore. Josef's mood lifted; he laughed. "Call it in," he said.

Karl lumbered into the gutted warehouse. A ragtag bunch of children—most of them nowhere near puberty—sprawled in boredom and fatigue over mountains of crates. He discovered later that they numbered thirty-five, including himself. Among them were a half dozen men, unshaven, unbathed, and looking utterly miserable. The scientists and chaperones his father had told him about. Water from an early-afternoon rain shower dripped off exposed rafters, producing a light melody on the crates and concrete floor.

He located a boy about his size, sitting on a short stack of pallets, and hobbled over to him. Karl had lost a shoe in a treacherous ravine several days before and now wore only a bulky rag on that foot.

"What's your name?" Karl demanded.

"Gregor." His voice was weak, as though he had no energy for the task. His face was scratched and dirty. Karl knew his was the same.

"Your shoes—give them to me."

Gregor looked him up and down. "No."

Karl moved in quickly. One hand clenched Gregor's neck, the other caught the arm that had come up in defense. He touched his lips to the boy's ear. "Don't try me," he whispered harshly. "You won't survive to tell the tale."

He took a step back and smiled wickedly at Gregor's

stunned expression. Then Gregor lowered his head and untied the shoes.

SIH HOURS LATER, HE WATCHED AS THE SS OFFICER WITH THE submachine gun hidden behind him used subtle hand signals to organize his soldiers into a crescent around the dockworkers. The military men eyed the officer for a signal, as an orchestra would watch its conductor. Just as one of the workers tossed a cigarette aside and turned his head in suspicion, the officer nodded. He swung the gun around and started firing.

When the other soldiers joined in, the sound was like the sky ripping open from one end to the other.

Within seconds it was over. Smoke billowed like souls into the night, disappearing as it caught the wind and escaped the light. After a moment, the boy felt his father's hand pressure him to walk forward toward the U-boat. At the gangplank, they turned to each other. All the things he could say and do ran through the boy's head, but finally he simply held out his hand to give his father a handshake. Instead of grabbing Karl's hand in return, his father thrust his arm forward, head-high, and said quietly, "Heil Hitler!"

Karl straightened and returned the gesture. Their eyes locked, and the boy whispered, "Heil . . . Father." He hungrily scanned his father's strong features. The man smiled softly and lowered his arm. Josef snapped his head at the warship, and Karl boarded.

From the bridge atop the conning tower, he watched the wharf shrink with distance. He had turned and was about to climb into the sub when a single sharp crack of pistol fire startled him. When he jumped back to the rail, he saw all the men who'd stayed behind: his father, the soldiers, and the scientist-chaperones. They were huddled on the dock, faces turned down, looking at a body. One of them leaned over and picked something up. He held it to his head, a shot rang out, and he fell. Another man stepped forward, picked up the gun, and repeated the process.

Karl watched his father stoop down, stand up, and stick the barrel of the gun into his mouth. His arm appeared to be shaking, but at that distance, Karl couldn't be sure. He was facing the harbor, seemingly watching the U-boat.

Does he see me? Karl wondered.

For a moment, Karl forgot who he was supposed to be. Gone from his mind were the grueling lessons he had endured since age three: what it meant to be part of the Master Race, to be Josef Litt's son, to be a scientist with special knowledge of nature's way . . . None of it mattered now. Only his father's acknowledgment.

His father yanked the gun out of his mouth and stared across the increasing expanse of water toward the U-boat. His shoulders seemed to fall slightly.

He does! He sees me!

He was about to raise his arm and call out when the U-boat, which had been making a wide bank out of the harbor, suddenly passed a shoulder of land, and the dock vanished. Five seconds later, the last shot rang out.

Karl stood on the bridge a long time, sea spray slapping his face, stinging his eyes. Finally he lowered himself into the boat.

WHEN THE CAPTAIN TOLD HIM THEY WERE BOUND FOR BAHIA Blanca, Karl had imagined emerging into a bright Argentinian sun. But when they disembarked forty-five days later, it was into another moonless night. Soldiers in green uniforms ushered them toward a waiting bus. They filed past a tall man with a young, earnest face.

"Wait!" the man said in German. He had an unsure smile on his face. He turned to look back at the U-boat, at the crew unloading boxes of unused supplies under the supervision of armed soldiers. To the children he said, "Where are the adults? Where are the scientists?" His German was heavily accented.

Karl stepped forward. "We are the scientists."

The man's smile broadened, then disappeared.

"Are you Herr Reynolds?" Karl asked.

"I am."

The boy withdrew an envelope from inside his shirt and held it out to the man. "My father asked me to give you this."

Reynolds tore open the envelope and read the letter inside, glancing often at the small faces before him. He lowered the letter and closed his eyes. When he opened them, he had reached some sort of decision.

"Very well, then," he said. His voice was strained. "Welcome, all of you!" He sighed and gestured toward the bus. "Please . . ."

The bus took them to an airfield; a plane took them to America.

Kendrick Reynolds eventually found families for the other children. Karl he adopted—though Karl refused his name. And while the boy's dockside claim that he and his peers were scientists had been an exaggeration, most of them were extraordinarily brilliant children with a foundation of scientific knowledge rivaling postgraduate students. From this foundation, Reynolds developed a program that made him powerful and wealthy. And Karl grew to love the man.

Until the betrayal.

twenty

THE FIRE OCCASIONALLY FLICKERED AND FLARED AS IT found a remnant of virgin wood to consume. But mostly it smoldered resentfully as it faded away. Still, the stone hearth held its heat and sent it into the den. Allen Parker came back to the world and realized he was hot. He pushed back from his desk, dead tired. He'd learned more about the topic of Donnelley's deathbed remarks than he'd ever wanted to know. Acid churned in his stomach.

He shut down his computer, saved the Mozart CD from yet another play-through, and meandered out of the den, switching off lamps as he went.

He stepped into the kitchen to turn off the light over the stove and remembered again the turkey dinner he'd left in the microwave. He pulled it out, peeled back the cellophane, and held up two pieces of meat with his thumb and index finger.

He lowered them into his mouth and switched off the light with his other hand. In the master bedroom, he turned on the bedside lamp, stripped off his clothes, and pushed them into a chute. He heard them fall softly into a basket in the basement laundry room, where Maria, his part-time housekeeper, would wash and press them.

He walked naked into the bathroom and up to a panel set into the tile near the doorless shower stall. It was more of a shower *room*, really; some families lived in smaller spaces. He pushed a button that would bring the water temperature and pressure of the showerheads to a preconfigured setting. He checked himself out in the wall-sized mirror opposite the shower, pulling his belly in a little. He didn't look too bad, considering.

A bit of the exhaustion washed away under the steaming shower jets, replaced by a healthy, relaxed tiredness. He cranked his neck around, letting the stream massage his muscles. The heat, the pulsating pressure, the tropical sound of the water splashing against the tiles and reverberating between the walls—it all made holding on to the day's tension impossible. He was just rinsing the shampoo from his hair when the phone rang. He darted out of the shower, snatched a towel off a rung, ran into the bedroom, and grabbed the receiver on the fourth ring.

"Dr. Parker," he announced.

"You're out of breath, sir. You all right?" It was a man with a heavy Southern accent.

"Who is this?" He patted his face with the towel.

"Name's Detective Fisher. I'm investigatin' the murder of Goodwin Donnelley—the man you worked on in the ER today—and the other man who was killed with him."

The clock beside the bed glowed 11:18.

"Isn't it a little late to be calling, Detective Fisher? I'll be happy to talk with you in the morning, but I—"

"That's not why I'm callin'. I mean, not really. We've got ourselves a situation here, and we have reason to believe your life is in danger."

"My life?"

"Two of the nurses who assisted you with Donnelley died tonight. They were murdered."

"Murdered?" He sat heavily on the bed.

"As well as one of the EMTs who brought 'im in, I'm afraid. Tell ya the truth, Doctor, it wasn't until we got the call on him that we made the connection. We checked with the hospital, and they confirmed that the two women and the EMT assisted Donnelley after the shooting."

"What are you saying, Detective?" He wanted to hear it outright.

"What I am tryin' to tell you, Dr. Parker, is that some-one—or multiple someones—is killin' off everyone who came in contact with this Donnelley guy before he died."

"Why?"

"Maybe you can help me with that one. I understand Donnelley spoke to you?"

"No."

"Well, sir, that's different from what one of your nurses, Gail Wagner, told me not ten minutes ago. If you—"

"Four nurses assisted me," Allen said, changing the sub-ject. "What about the other two?"

"Like I said, I talked with Ms. Wagner by phone just a few minutes ago. We're sendin' a car over to her apartment right now. We can't reach the other nurse or the other EMT. And nobody seems to know where that special agent woman went."

"Julia Matheson?"

"Yeah, that's her. Even her own office in Atlanta's scratchin' their heads over her whereabouts. I hope that's not a bad sign. We've also picked up the bartender where they gunned down Donnelley and Vero, but I suspect nobody wants him. I think whoever's behind these killings is concerned about some kind of deathbed confession, somethin' Donnelley wouldn't have told just anyone unless he thought he was dyin'." Fisher waited for him to comment. "What's your take on that, Doctor?"

Allen said nothing.

"Dr. Parker, these murders all went down within the last two hours. Someone is moving mighty fast here, *mighty* fast. Now, sir, I'm sending over—"

A shadow flickered in the hallway outside his door, where the moonlight spilled in from the living room windows. For an instant, the dappled light was totally obscured—*not* the result of a passing bird or breeze-blown branch. Allen's stomach clenched tight, and his heart seemed to stop before kicking into high gear. The security system was not on. By habit, he set it right before climbing into bed. That way, he didn't have to disarm it to answer the door or wander outside. Some nights, he didn't use it at all.

"Okay?" Fisher was saying. "Dr. Parker?"

"I'm sorry?" His head was swimming. He couldn't move. From his position he could see down the entire hall that bisected the home's front half from its back. All he saw was blackness, spattered as usual with diffused moonlight. He couldn't tell Fisher he thought someone was already in the house. That might encourage them to abandon all caution and hurry to kill him. He figured his best chance for survival lay in not being caught off guard.

"I said I'm sendin' a cruiser over to your house right now,

for your own protection. Lock your doors and windows, and stay inside till it gets there. Don't open the door unless you see it outside, okay?"

"Uh, yeah, okay."

Could the intruder be listening in on an extension?

There was a moment of silence on the phone. Fisher obviously expected Allen to ask more questions, express more concern, protest this disruption of his life.

"Thank you, Doctor," Fisher finally said and hung up.

twenty-one

ALLEN DROPPED THE CORDLESS PHONE ONTO THE BED. Keeping his attention on the doorway, he reached under the bed and pulled out an aluminum baseball bat. In college, a series of dorm room break-ins had taught him the emotional comfort of accessible weaponry.

He backed into the bathroom and punched the button that turned off the shower. As the last droplets fell to the tile floor, he heard a thin creak come from somewhere down the hall. His mind flashed through an inventory of the house: What in it creaked? Which hinges needed oil? Which floorboards were loose? None came to mind. He was still holding the towel in his left hand. He let it drop; what was pride next to survival?

He tiptoed to the bedroom doorway, bat held high in both hands. He stepped into the hall and stopped, listening intently while letting his vision adjust to the dark. The light from the bedroom spilled into the hall only a few feet before surrendering to shadows.

Murdered, the cop had said. But he hadn't said how. Shot? Stabbed? Bludgeoned? Torn apart?

Stop it! Doesn't matter. Dead—that's all that counts. Don't want to be dead. Don't want to be dead.

Slowly he began to distinguish subtle shades of gray: the darker area of the linen closet door; the place where the hall opened up to the big foyer and living room; the place farther along the black, black hall where the weak glow from the embers in the fireplace barely marked the opening to the den.

He lifted his foot and inched it forward with the slowness of a cat's yawn. He set it down carefully, then waited, listened. He repeated the process with the other foot. His breathing seemed extraordinarily loud. He tried to take slower, shallower breaths but managed only a few before his lungs cried out for more oxygen to fuel the surge of adrenaline in his bloodstream. He had to will his leg to start another step.

He jumped as a flash of movement down the hall caught his eye. Gone now. Black moving in black. Someone could stand in the darkest parts of the hall, he realized, without being seen. And to that person, he would be perfectly silhouetted in the lighted rectangle of the bedroom doorway. The image of a hideous dark figure running toward him filled his imagination for a split moment. This was too much. He backed into the bedroom and shut the door.

Murdered.

He felt the breeze on his bare back. He turned to see the sheers that covered the glass opposite the bed billowing away from an open sliding door. He'd been in the room to change clothes and then to shower, and neither time had he opened that door. His mind raced.

The door was open. He hadn't opened it.

He could see the whole room fairly well, except for behind and under the bed and in the bathroom and walk-in closet. He weighed his options: bolt for the front door and hide outside? or into the bathroom, and hope no one was lurking there? or shut and lock the sliding door, search the bedroom, and guard it until the cops arrived?

He didn't like any of them but opted to stay in the bedroom. Trying to leave no flank exposed, he shuffled sideways toward the sliding door. He held the bat high in his right fist, keeping his left hand open and up in a posture of defense. As he moved closer to the door, the far side of the bed came into view. No one there.

He shuffled past the open bathroom and closet doors, the blackness within each seeming to shift ominously, teasingly. He strained his eyes, expecting one of the shadows to peel itself free and flash toward him. The tips of his left fingers were now touching the fluttering sheers. To shut the door, he had to reach out and grab the handle. If someone was waiting on the deck outside, he wouldn't know it until they were face-to-face.

He stretched through the sheers for the handle. For one suspended instant he peered out into the blackness of the deck, imagining the sparkle of a blade slicing through the air to impale him.

Then he got hold of the handle.

At that moment, when he was at the apex of his stretch and was just reversing direction to pull the door shut, he first felt, then heard footsteps on the carpet directly behind him. Without looking, barely thinking, he swung down with the bat and felt it connect with something—*someone!* In the edge of his vision, he saw a man, big, with something raised over his head. He used his grip on the door handle to propel himself forward. He felt wind on his back. Something made contact, searing pain just below his shoulder blade. He swung his leg around and through the opening. In two steps he was at, then over the railing . . . falling through darkness.

The grassy earth below caught him with unkind arms. He crumpled, slamming his head painfully against it. He sprang up and ran for the woods where his backyard ended. He heard a *thunk!* and a divot of grass exploded near him, flying into the air and back down.

He was being shot at!

Fifty feet to the woods.

An irregular dot of bloodred light hovered like a firefly on the grass in front of him. Allen realized that the assailant was using a laser sight to target him. It spasmed back and forth, then vanished as it found his back. He jerked to the right. Immediately he heard the *thunk!* again. Another divot erupted from the yard.

Twenty feet.

He crashed into the heavy foliage . . . tumbling over the first thick branches . . . rolling onto heavy loam, twigs, more branches, stones . . . smashing into a thick oak. A dozen small wounds opened on his naked body. He rose facing his yard and saw a shape, black against the gray silhouette of the house, leaping as he had over the railing. The laser shot off into the sky, visible only when it pierced some mist. Before the figure landed, Allen was running again, blindly crashing through the deep woods. The ground fell away sharply. His bare feet slammed down on bruising round rocks and cutting sharp ones. Skeletal fingers of tree branches clawed at his face, his arms, his legs.

He plunged madly down the hill, trying to recall the

topography, the placement of the area's roads and houses below. He wondered wildly if he'd find refuge or if a bullet would find him first. He heard the crunch of twigs behind him and pushed harder, rebounding off trees, tumbling and leaping forward, tumbling again. Holly bushes raked their thorns across his skin. His chest slammed into an unyielding branch, knocking him off his feet. He landed hard . . . was up again . . . pounding down the hill . . . slipping on ferns . . . flinching as limbs lashed his face, back, legs . . . fighting the urge to stop, to rest, to think.

The night had robbed the leaves and wildflowers of their brilliant daytime colors, leaving them with only shades of gray. He plowed through them, scrambling into prickly brambles, falling into blankets of ankle-high plants.

The moonlight was more hindrance than help. It cast a maze of shadows before him, deceiving him time and again, causing him to flinch away from thickets of razor branches that weren't there, only to send him crashing into ones that were. Far worse, he imagined its apathetic glare illuminating his pale skin like a beacon for his pursuer.

Trying to avoid catching a bullet in his brain, he added to his chaotic scramble a series of erratic zigs and abrupt zags. He knew this method of escape was noisy and didn't care: speed was his advantage now, not stealth.

He leaped over a thick clump of tangled vines, roots, and shrubs. His foot came down hard on earth that gave away. His leg sank into the ground, broke through something with a sharp *crack*, and stopped when the surface was up to his waist. His head flew forward. He raised his hands before his face before it hit a large, flat rock.

The wind knocked out of him, he gasped for breath as a plume of dust mushroomed up from the hole. The soil around his sunken legs began to collapse into the hole, wedging him more firmly in the earth. His foot must have crashed through a dried and rotten root system, the broken ends of which were now digging painfully into his foot, ankle, and shin.

As his breath came back, he waved away the dust and found himself staring at a name etched in stone: Ed Johnson. A notorious name in these parts, belonging to a man hung in 1906 for rape. Allen was in the old Negro cemetery, which dated back to the Civil War. He had fallen into Ed's grave, and what he had thought was a dried root system was more likely a rib cage. The ancient bones gouged at his ankle, ripped at his calf. He leaned onto his side and wiggled his leg. Something chalky ground under his heel. He turned onto his stomach, reached for the top of the headstone, and tugged. The earth around him shifted, and he pulled free.

He scampered away from the hole on all fours, then rolled onto his back, breathing hard. Trees converged high above, forming a leafy canopy through which moonlight seeped like rain. Those tall leaves danced on a breeze that Allen couldn't feel. Beyond them, faint wisps of clouds drifted by, flush with lunar radiance. Between the canopy and loamy ground, a fine mist hovered, stirring faintly.

He remembered that the cemetery occupied a patch of land where the slope leveled before dropping off again. It was a disrupted place. Time had seen the surface either collapse in on rotted caskets or swell into great mounds, pushed by unknown forces from below. The result was land as wavy as windblown seas. The wood itself contributed to the sense of fracture. It had moved in to reclaim its estate, sending dense bushes in to obscure toppled headstones, pencil-thin pines to impale graves like vampire stakes, gnarled roots to reach up through the ground like hands of the dead pleading for release from this distressed place.

Resting now, Allen began to feel every bruise, every cut, every abrasion on his body. His muscles hurt, and his lungs burned. Acid churned in his stomach. He couldn't stay there; he had to find help. He listened for the snap of a twig, the scuff of a shoe. He rose to a sitting position and started to tuck his legs under him. If he stood slowly and walked carefully, he might be able to quietly weave his way down the mountain . . .

He stopped.

The hazy, red beam of a laser panned the night air on a plane three feet above his head and stopped on the trunk of a tree six feet away, a burning red dot as vicious as a demon's eye.

twenty-two

JULIA WOKE, STILL SITTING ON THE BED, HER BACK AGAINST the wall. She moved her head, feeling her neck tendons stretch and pop. She wiped drool off her chin. Most likely she had been snoring as well. Drooling and snoring—the only time she did either was when she was exhausted. This time it wasn't physical but mental and emotional exhaustion she had succumbed to.

She looked at the clock. It was late, but she needed to check on her mother. If she was having a bad day, she may not have moved from her bed, which meant no food, no drink, no meds. She kept a bedpan handy, but she hated to use it, and having it sit there dirty was to Mae Matheson akin to messing on the carpet.

Julia rolled off the bed, fished an anonymous calling card out of the Wal-Mart bag, and left the room. She found a phone booth at a gas station a mile from the motel; calling home, she would be more vulnerable to a trace than if she were to call nearly any other number. Mae answered on the fifth ring, sounding groggy.

"Hi. Are you okay?"

"Julia? I didn't hear from you. Where are you?"

"Mom . . ." Her voice cracked. Tears marshaled in her eyes. *Not now. Mom first.*

"Have you been up? How are you feeling?"

"Oh yes, I'm fine. I made a sandwich and watched *American Idol.* I'm telling you, if that Jesse wins, I'll be so angry. He can't carry a tune in a suitcase . . ."

Julia listened, smiling sadly. She could tell her mother was truly feeling okay—not good, but okay—and not just saying it, which she sometimes did even on the worst of days. She didn't want Julia changing her life to accommodate her illness—at least not more than she already had. But Julia suspected her denials had more to do with kidding herself that she wasn't as ill as she was.

"Mom, I gotta go. I won't be home tonight—something came up."

"Oh, I see."

No, you don't, but what you're thinking is better than the truth.

"Do you want me to call Homecare?"

"Don't be silly. I'm fine."

"I'll call tomorrow, then. You know the number if you need help?"

"I do, but I won't." Being stubborn now.

"I love you, Mom."

"Love you, honey."

She cradled the receiver and held on to it. She wished

things were different. But who didn't? She sniffed, ran the back of her hand over her eyes, got in the car.

Before she arrived back at the motel, again her mind started grinding through the day's events, transcribing conversations, forming questions, following leads. She felt overwhelmed by the number of fragments of information to sift through. Her experience had taught her that while all the clues available might not lead to a solution, they always led to another clue. Eventually the solution presented itself. The next clue was somewhere among the known facts; she simply had to find it. She was overlooking something.

Goody said Vero was talking about a virus . . .

Looking, thinking, trying to understand . . .

twenty-three

THE GLOWING RED DOT OF THE LASER LINGERED ON THE tree an instant, then slid off and continued its sweep over the cemetery.

Allen hunched down on folded legs beside a massive bush, majestically draped in silky leaves and bejeweled in fat berries. Slowly he turned to look in the direction of the laser's origin. The bush blocked his view of the assailant's passage—and concealed *him* from his pursuer.

He heard the soft crunching of footfalls moving leftward as he looked up the hill. The assailant was coming down at an angle that allowed a controlled descent, not on the steep course Allen had barreled down. Most likely he was tacking, trying to stay as true to Allen's course as possible. Then he came into view on the left side of the bush, sixty feet away. A dark figure that seemed too angular and moved too fluidly to be human. No matter where he walked, he remained a shadow, black upon black. Only the bright red point of the pistol's laser sight at the tip of his right arm broke the inky monotone of the night.

The figure turned and strode toward him, rising and falling with the crests and depressions of the insane landscape. Mist swirled in his wake, spiking upward, then settling like flames.

Allen nearly bolted for the edge of the cemetery, where the hill continued its descent back to civilization. For a quarter of a second his muscles contracted, ready to spring. Instead, he inched under the bush, sliding his legs along the ground to avoid jiggling the leaves. He bent himself into a crescent and pushed his torso under the perimeter of the plant, using his hand to gently push the leaves over his hip and shoulder.

The assailant stopped ten feet from him, miraculously still in deep shadow. His body faced the shrub under which Allen shivered, but his head was rotating back and forth, scanning. Allen held his breath, hoping his body didn't scream for oxygen too soon, as it had in the hall outside his bedroom. The fierce shadow figure stood there, emitting a sound Allen couldn't place—

Chick-chu, chick-chu, chick-chu . . .

—and scanning, listening . . . *twenty seconds . . . thirty . . .* Allen's chest hitched as his lungs started to protest.

. . . forty . . .

The man spun ninety degrees and strode toward the edge of the cemetery.

Gasping air as quietly as possible, it came to Allen that it was frustration, not discovery, that had motivated his pursuer's aggressive approach toward the shrub. The man had realized that his prey could be anywhere in the woods, or even out of them by now.

Allen lifted a branch out of his way and parted his knees slightly so he was looking through them at the assailant. A black shadow against the darkness of the nocturnal woods. It was as though he had brought the shadows with him, had cloaked himself in a darkness that no light could penetrate. Yet the figure's physique was obvious. Muscular arms, legs, chest. Tall. Powerful.

From the way the man's head was moving, Allen guessed that he was scanning the woods below the cemetery. Then the figure turned around.

Allen heard a soft metallic *click,* and the laser flicked out. The figure marched toward him again, taking wide strides that quickly closed the distance between them. He stomped right past Allen, hit the uphill edge of the cemetery, and began the ascent toward the house without slowing. Thirty seconds later, the woods consumed the sound of his passage.

Fear kept Allen from moving for a long time. Finally he slid out from under the bush and stood. He looked uphill and saw nothing but black trees, bushes, leaves, and vines advancing toward his house, disappearing into the night. He stared at individual shadows, trying to find one that was man-shaped, hoping he wouldn't. Shades shifted subtly, by wind, not man. When his unblinking eyes began to tear, he lowered his head, cupping his face in both hands.

His body ached with a hundred cuts and bruises. His heart hurt from riding so high in his throat. The strong stench of his own perspiration was nauseating. His mind threatened to fold into itself.

Then he was over it.

He lifted his head toward the leaf-obstructed sky, inhaled

deeply, and resolved to fight, to win, to live. He ran his palm over his side, brushing off dirt and leaves and little twigs that had embedded themselves into his skin. He ran his fingers through his hair, dislodging debris. The act of standing and squaring his shoulders made him feel less like a kicked dog. He made his way to the other side of the cemetery, then stepped down the slope to begin the trek off this mountain. He picked up speed as he descended, crashing through branches and bushes.

By the time he was halfway down, a plan had begun to form. When he saw the first glimmer of electric lights through the trees, he knew what he was going to do.

twenty-four

"EVIDENCE!"

Julia said it out loud to the empty motel room.

If someone wanted to warn the CDC about an impending bio-attack, wouldn't he bring some kind of evidence to prove he wasn't a nut?

She thought back to her last conversation with Goody. He'd reminded her that their communication was not secure. He'd said he was injured. She'd warned him of the compromised SATD signal. He'd said he'd turned off the tracking device. Wait. First he had said he was in a phone booth. But why would he have said that? She'd thought he was reiterating the unsecured status of the line, but it wasn't like Goody to state the obvious. And it had come at an odd time, after she informed him of the SATD problem. He'd told her to hold on, had left her hanging for half a minute, then came back with that cryptic message about the phone booth.

That was it! It was *cryptic*.

I'm in a phone booth.

No. *I'm in* the phone booth. Okay. *That* phone booth.

Then he had said it again. Emphasizing the sentence's importance? Yes, but something else . . . something . . .

He had not repeated the first sentence verbatim. No *I'm* the second time . . .

I'm in the phone booth. In the phone booth.

He'd meant "*It*—the evidence—is in the phone booth, the one you will know about if I don't make it back to retrieve the evidence myself."

That had to be what Goody wanted to say. She knew how his mind worked. Everything fit. Some kind of evidence was in that phone booth, and she was going to get it—as Goody had intended her to—right now. She dashed out of the room, slamming the door behind her.

ATROPOS FUMED. HE STOOD IN A THICK COPSE OUTSIDE PARKER'S house and watched two cops pound on the door. The cruiser had been pulling into the drive as he came around the house after coming back up the hill, where he'd lost his quarry. He had ducked into the trees just as the headlamps swung past his position. After a long moment, they tried the knob. One cop, a woman, stepped off the tiled stoop and shined a beam around the grounds. It panned over Atropos's hiding place. He didn't budge. The other officer joined her. They surveyed the home's huge facade, whispering. Another flashlight snapped on. The two moved away from Atropos's position and rounded the far corner, sweeping their lights across windows, bushes, the yard.

Parker had reacted much more quickly than he'd expected. The man's survival instinct was calibrated high. Atropos liked that, the challenge of it.

He looked down at the pistol in his left hand and unscrewed the silencer from the gun's barrel. The sound-suppressing coils inside had absorbed too many shots already to remain effective. He dropped it on the ground, pulled another one from his jacket pocket, and attached it. Then he tucked the massive gun into a custom nylon holster under his left arm, where he hoped it would stay. Perhaps now that Parker had escaped, he still had a chance to use the gauntlet on him.

He flexed his gauntleted fist. *Chick-chu, chick-chu.*

He looked at his watch, then back up at the house. Parker was long gone, at least for now. But a guy like that, living in a place like this by himself—he loved his stuff. He'd be back, probably later tonight. Atropos would be waiting.

For now, he had another target to pursue. No current location, but he had some ideas, some places to check.

Moving out into the yard, he turned to make sure the police officers hadn't reconsidered their plan to circum-navigate Parker's residence. A faint glow of flashlights played against the trees on the far side of the house, growing fainter, moving away. He walked along the hedge, following the drive back to the street, where he'd stowed his rental between other cars a few blocks away.

twenty-five

"HELLO?"

"*This is the BellSouth automated operator. Will you accept a collect call from—*"

"It's Allen! Pick up!"

"*Press 1 to accept. Press 2 to deny.*"

"Hello?"

"*Press 1 to accept. Press 2—connecting now.*"

"Stephen! It's Allen . . . Hello? Stephen?"

"I'm here. Just a little surprised."

"It's that kind of night. I need you to—"

"Where are you? Why'd you call collect?"

"I'm in town, but I don't have any money."

"That's a first."

"Listen—"

"Allen. Is this about Mom and Dad? Dad? Is he okay, man?"

"Dad's fine. Mom's fine. Everybody in the whole world is fine except me. Just shut up a second and listen, will you?"

"That's the Allen I know. Go ahead."

"I need you to come get me. Right away."

"*You* need me? Never thought I'd hear that. Are you hurt? You sound—"

"Whoa! You're moving your mouth again . . . Sorry. Look, physically, I've suffered a few lacerations, bruises, but I'm not seriously injured . . . yet."

"Yet?"

"I'll explain later. You need to come get me right now. This very minute. Pick me up at the Texaco at the corner of McCallie and Dodds. You have a running car, don't you?"

"Yes, Allen. I have managed to purchase a car and actually keep it running."

"What kind?"

"What?"

"What kind of car!"

"A Vega. Seventy-four. Hope it's good enough for you."

"What color?"

"Maroon . . . and orange and gray. The passenger-side door is blue. The hood's kinda reddish, pinkish—"

"Corner of McCallie and Dodds."

"Gotcha."

"And, Stephen?"

"Yeah?"

"Bring some extra clothes. You know, shirt, slacks, shoes. Some underpants."

"This I gotta see."

STEPHEN PARKER CRADLED THE PHONE SLOWLY. SPONTANEITY was out of character for his brother. So what was this? Had he been robbed? Carjacked, more likely these days. But why not call the cops? Or one of his friends? Stephen hadn't been one of them for years.

He probably had been with someone he shouldn't have— the wife of a colleague maybe—and had to keep her involvement quiet. Or the husband had done the damage, and now all Allen wanted was for the situation to go away.

He sat on the edge of his rumpled bed and pulled on an equally rumpled flannel shirt.

He stood and walked into the two-room cabin's main living area, dropped his hulking weight into a nappy old chair, and grabbed his well-worn cowboy boots. Physically, Stephen was more bear than man: His bones were big and broad, arranged to a height of six foot five—all of it wrapped in thick bands of muscle. His body was nearly covered with a dark pelt of thick, curly hair; it exploded from his face and hung like an animal that had latched on and died. His face, as much as it showed, was bearish too, with thick features and kind, heavily lidded eyes.

He moved into the area of his home that served as a kitchen, duly designated by the floor's pocked and stained linoleum; no covering at all protected the rest of the cabin's plywood floors from the feet that trod on it, or in turn protected the feet from it. From the cupboard under the sink he withdrew a paper grocery sack. In the bedroom again, he packed the bag with clothes and rolled the top closed.

He snatched a ring of keys from a nail by the front entrance and went out, pulling the door shut but not locking it. He bounded over the crumbling wood step that he kept meaning to repair.

Heading to his car, parked in the narrow space between the small church he led and his cabin, his thoughts returned to his brother. They hadn't even spoken in eight, nine months. They had nothing in common except their parents.

Allen thought Stephen had betrayed the family name by rejecting a career in medicine. Following the path forged by their father and grandfather was not only a privilege; it was expected.

Oh well, Stephen thought for the thousandth time. He'd tried being philosophical with his family, then pragmatic and pleading; in the end, it always came down to disappointed resignation: *Oh well.*

He reached the car door and stopped, throwing his big, hairy head back to look toward the sky. "Lord," he said out loud, "whatever's happening with Allen, let me do right by him. And more important, let me do right by You. I thank You, Lord, for giving me this chance."

He folded his body into the small seat of the Vega. He used it mostly to pick up supplies in town and visit parishioners; otherwise, he didn't stray too far from the church. The starter chattered and whined before finally turning over and spurring the engine into action. A cloud of black smoke erupted from the tailpipe and engulfed the vehicle. Stephen punched the accelerator to escape the fumes, spewing sand and pebbles back at the smoky beast as it disappeared into the woods along the thin dirt drive.

twenty-six

THE BAR'S WINDOWS WERE DARK, ITS DOOR SHUT, BLOCKED by yellow crime-scene tape. A police cruiser was parked directly in front of the entrance. Of course the place was guarded; the daylight massacre of a federal agent and his charge made it a red-ball case.

As Julia drove past, she saw a single patrolman behind the wheel. The dome light was on, and he was reading a paperback. *Smart,* she thought. *Destroy your night vision and make it easy for perps to see you before you see them.*

She drove a few more blocks, turned left, and parked on a dark residential street behind an abused pickup. She popped the trunk lid and got out. From a metal bin in the trunk, she selected an assortment of rusty tools and a tire iron.

Traffic on Brainerd Road was light; she darted across unnoticed. She made her way to the trash-strewn alley that ran behind the businesses and turned toward the bar. The grungy backs of buildings towered above her on the right; an alternating cycle of tall pine and chain-link fencing lined her left. Tree limbs leaned over the boards, and leafy shrubs pushed through the fence. Purple Dumpsters hulked like sleeping bison at regular intervals. Where it wasn't pitch dark, it was deep gray. She trotted toward the bar.

On the way over, she'd used a pay phone to call the Chattanooga homicide desk. She'd given them the name of another female federal agent. A Detective Fisher was lead on the case. The on-call detective had offered to patch her through to him, but she'd said her involvement was too preliminary to bug him. She'd needed only a few facts: primarily, location and a basic chronology of the crime: *Yeah, I know our people are all over it, but I'm just typing up a summary for my boss, and you know how it is, trying to get a straight answer from a team of twenty hotshots.*

Two aspects of the crime were immediately intriguing. First, after Goody shot one of the assailants, the other was killed by a third assailant. The prevailing wisdom was that he had been a third member of the hit team who'd decided not to split the fee, though he could have been a separate hit man altogether, not associated with the first team, or some guy who'd stumbled onto the hit and acted to protect himself.

Then why'd he take out Despesorio Vero, as witnesses said he did?

That was the nature of crime investigations: anything goes, no matter how implausible, until other theories build more supportive tissue.

The other interesting element was a set of handcuffs found near Vero's body. According to the bartender, one of the first assailants had tossed them to Vero. You've got your target covered by a shotgun, and you tell him to cuff himself. You're not trying to kill him; you're trying to take him alive. Why?

She'd considered asking for access but quickly rejected the idea. If anyone in law enforcement saw her retrieve evidence, they could confiscate it. Plus, if the people behind Donnelley's murder had moles in law enforcement, could she trust any cop? No, she wanted to examine any evidence she found herself before turning it over to the investigative team—and only after she trusted the integrity of those involved.

She had reached the parking lot that flanked the side of the bar. The moon illuminated a single car, closer to her than the bar. It appeared empty. She ran all out, staying as close to the fence as the litter and bushes allowed.

The bar's back door and jamb were metal. A heavy-metal plate, welded to the door, covered the latch and dead bolt. Even the hinges were not exposed. The nearest window was barred. She tried the tire iron on the door. It didn't budge.

She shook her head. No way she was getting through it. She pulled out her CDC-LED badge and identification and marched out of the alley and along the side of the bar toward the cruiser. She stepped off the curb and went around the back of the car. She rapped on the driver's glass and leaned down.

The cruiser was empty. The dash-mounted lamp burned brightly; a Dean Koontz novel lay tented on the bench seat. But no cop. She stood and looked over the roof at the bar. She noticed its open front door. Just then, the windows flashed with light, and the peal of three rapid gunshots ripped into the night.

She ducked and withdrew her pistol. In the field, she kept a round chambered, saving the extra second it would take to pull the slide in an emergency. Still, she double-checked by pulling back on the slide a half inch. The brass casing of a .45-caliber bullet sparkled as it caught the street-lamp's glow. She lowered the gun to her side and pulled back on the hammer with her thumb.

She'd detected no impacts to the cruiser, so unless the shooter was an atrociously bad aim, the shots were not meant for her. She rushed to the door and slammed her back against the brick between the door and the huge front window. She threw her head around to look in the door and pulled it back in one quick motion. At the rear of the customer area the office door was half-open. Weak light spilled out into the bar. Silhouettes of halogen lamps on tripods, left by the crime-scene techs. Had she noticed movement? She couldn't be sure. She looked again. Saw nothing.

Arms locked straight before her, pistol at chin level, she swung around and stepped through the door. She panned her pistol to the right, toward the phone booth. Nothing. Back toward the rear of the bar. She smelled perspiration, her own, and the faint odor of blood and the much sharper tang of cordite. Now she saw the smoke, drifting lazily in the scant light from the office. She took another step. So dark.

She stopped at the edge of the bar counter, leaned over. The darkness was complete: she could be looking right at someone hiding down there and not know it. She didn't have a flashlight. She didn't want to turn on the bar lights—even if she did know where the switch was located.

Julia felt exposed. She put her gun and the palm of her other hand on the bar top, hoisted herself up, and dropped behind the counter. She felt shelves of glasses, cleaning supplies, bags of something, pretzels or nuts probably, then the thing she expected: a small refrigerator. She cracked the door open.

White light burst from it, revealing an area behind the bar free of bad guys. She crouch-walked to the end of the bar and went around it.

She heard the metallic *chink* of door locks, then hinges creaking, fast and high-pitched. Someone had swung open the back door, the one she had tried to jimmy. She stood and ran toward the office, then stopped and crouched again. A body lay sprawled on the floor. The cop from the cruiser. He was spread-eagle, facing up, eyes open. The chest of his blue uniform glistened in a way it shouldn't have. He still clenched his gun in one hand; a flashlight had rolled several inches from the other. The dim office light caught the edges of the flashlight's shattered lens and bulb.

She squinted at the office door's porthole window over the top of her pistol. She scanned past the booths, then back to the office door. Bathroom doors ahead, on the left. She pivoted around to assess the area behind her, then back again. Only then did she move up to the body. Keeping her vision on the hovering white dot of her gun's front sight and the office door beyond, she reached down to feel his carotid artery. No pulse.

She stepped over him and moved quietly to the office door. A small, green-shaded lamp sat on a cluttered desk, casting the room's only light. The back door stood open.

Outside, a car door slammed. She ran through the combination office-storage room, weaving around stacked boxes and unused equipment. When she entered the alley, she spun left into the parking lot. A sedan was squealing out onto Brainerd, tires smoking, engine revved to critical mass. Julia raised her gun and fired three rapid shots. The back window shattered and rained out onto the trunk and black-top like the jeweled train of a wedding gown. She started to squeeze off another round when the car disappeared beyond a building.

She dashed back through the back door, into the customer area, over the corpse, and directly to the phone booth. She holstered her weapon, stepped in, and shut the doors. The light flickered on. Not knowing what she was looking for, if it was breakable, she moved carefully. She stepped on the tiny seat and pushed her palms against the plastic light cover, raising it up. She contorted her hand up into the space between the panel and the area above it, slowly feeling around its circumference. The panel gave up its hold and fell past her to the floor. Ceiling and lighting fixture exposed, she found nothing. Next she checked the phone itself: the coin-return slot, the outside edges where it mounted to the booth. She used a pocketknife to pry the instruction card out of its metal frame. Nothing stashed behind, no messages written on it.

She was thinking about looking on the booth's roof when she slipped her hand beneath the seat and felt wads of rock-hard gum and firm, angular ridges that could be anything. Her heart stepped up its pace. She fell to her knees, pushed her head against the wooden side panel, and looked under. Too dark. She felt along the edges, the brackets holding the seat. Then something moved. She dug at it, and it slid out from a bracket. A small square of plastic.

A memory chip!

The tracking device was on it. *Goody, you sly fox,* she thought. He had turned the transmitter off but kept it with the chip so that anyone looking for it—Julia, anyway—would know immediately that he had placed it there.

With a tight grip on the chip, she opened the bifold doors, extinguishing the light. She made her way back to the rear door and stepped into the alley. She was halfway across the parking lot when she heard the first police sirens. The cop who'd been killed probably noticed a light or something inside, called for backup, then rushed to keep his appointment with death. She hurried into the alley on the other side, letting the shadows envelop her. When she reached the end of the block, she heard a chorus of sirens reach a crescendo, then drop off as tires screeched to a halt. She looked back to see red and blue lights splashing against the fence at the back of the parking lot—and something else.

A shadow. It had moved quickly into the gloom against the fence a half block back. Concealing her fear, she stepped casually around the corner of the last building on the block. She slipped the chip into the wide back pocket of her pants. She removed her pistol and moved to look back down the alley.

Shadows, just shadows.

She stood, continuing to stare into the blackness. Nothing moved. The lights at the far end wavered like a psychedelic dream. Slowly she backed away from the building's edge, turned quickly, and ran across the side street to the next dark alley.

It was when she was almost at the end of that block that she heard a shoe scraping the asphalt directly behind her.

twenty-seven

THE CHEVY VEGA HITCHED AND SPUTTERED AS IT CAME OFF I-153 and onto Shallowford Road. The houses here roosted close to the street, not large, but well built and warm.

The car slowed as Stephen Parker tried to force the gearshift into second. The gears grinded in protest, then quieted as the lever slid into place. He popped the clutch, sending a plume of oily smoke out behind him, and the car lurched forward. He let up on the accelerator when he sensed he was traveling the posted speed; the speedometer needle had not budged from its peg at zero since Stephen could remember.

He had crossed Missionary Ridge and was watching for Dodds Avenue, which would be coming up in another two blocks or—

A ghostly figure bolted up in the headlights.

Stephen slammed on the brakes, bracing himself against

the wheel. The car shimmied to a stop. With startled eyes, Stephen glared out at the apparition in the street.

It was Allen. Seeming as startled as Stephen, he tottered faintly in the whitewashed glare, clenching a filthy beige blanket around him. He came around the passenger side, yanked the door open, and climbed in.

"You can close your mouth now," he said.

"What is this?" Stephen yelled, his voice trembling at the lower end of the chromatic scale. "I almost turned you into road pizza, man! I thought you said the Texaco!"

Allen was unmoved. "I couldn't risk staying there. Probably the first place they'd look. Let's get this thing moving."

"They?"

"Just go."

"Where?"

"Back to your place." Allen looked at him. "That okay?"

"Fine by me." Stephen shoved the stick shift into first, made a U-turn, and gunned it toward the highway. "Who's *they*? What did you do, Allen? How serious is this, man?"

Cranked around in the seat, Allen watched the pavement pay out behind them. He turned, scanning out the side windows, then glanced again through the back-hatch glass.

"I have no idea who they are, except that one of them floats around like a shadow and has one big, honking gun. As far as I know, I didn't do anything. And it's as serious as life and death gets. Okay?"

"But you . . . I just . . . *Man!*"

They drove a few miles in silence, and Allen started to relax. He lifted his face upward, resting the top of his head on the seat back, and just *breathed*. After a few minutes, he lowered his head, looked around as if for the first time, and said, "Nice car."

"Cute blanket."

"Yeah. It was a seat cover in some old Buick. Did you bring the clothes?"

"'Course," Stephen affirmed, nodding toward the back.

Allen pulled the paper bag into his lap and fished out the underwear. He pulled them on; they floated around his middle like bloomers.

Stephen glanced at Allen. What he saw made him look twice. "You look like you just escaped the Chinese Torture of a Thousand Cuts."

"Feels like it."

"Care to share?"

"No."

"Come on, Allen. Here you are naked as a baby seal, cut to shreds, on the run from . . . who knows? Tell me something."

"I need to think it through first, all right? Everything happened so fast, I really don't know what's going on. I'll try to—to be up-front with you. Really."

"Uh-huh."

A few more miles in silence. When Stephen had coaxed the Vega up to speed on I-153, Allen said softly, "Thanks for coming to get me." He never took his eyes off the patch of road illuminated by the headlamps.

twenty-eight

THERE IT WAS AGAIN.

A shoe scuffing the ground. Just a few feet behind her.

Julia lunged forward, tucking her upper body down and throwing her feet over in a somersault that lowered her profile, propelled her away from the attacker, and enabled her to draw her gun in one quick motion. She'd practiced it many times, but this was its first practical application. As her right foot touched ground again, she spun on it, raising her pistol, ready to fire from a squatting position.

No one there.

Just shadows—again.

A Dumpster, fifteen feet away. Trash and weeds cluttered the ground around it. Everything was bathed in the absence of light. Nothing moved except the occasional leaf or corner of some crumpled paper in an unfelt breeze.

But she'd heard it, the scrape. She'd even *felt* the presence of someone. No one could have hidden so quickly, vanished so completely. She was acting spooked. *Acting?* She *was* spooked. Her nerves were frazzled. Of course they were, but enough to make her see predators in the shadows, hear phantom footsteps? She didn't think so.

She rose and, holding the pistol close to her leg, traversed the rest of the block. Again she rounded the last building's corner, as casually as her excited muscles would allow, then plastered herself against the brick. She waited, listening, gun at the ready. One minute. Not a sound. Two. Nothing. She peered around the corner. In the distance, two blocks away but seeming farther, the police lights performed their silent ballet. Otherwise nothing moved, nothing appeared out of place, though darkness shrouded most of the back street.

Julia holstered her gun, turned, and walked away from the alley toward Brainerd and her car on the other side. An ambulance flew by in the direction of the bar, lights and siren blaring. She crossed Brainerd. At least a dozen cruisers were in front of the bar and around it into the parking lot. If a federal agent's murder couldn't light a fire under their investigative behinds, the death of one of their own would make them positively combust.

She stepped up to her car and unlocked the door, moving quickly. Before anything could rush out of the shadows at her, she was in the car and gunning the engine. She cranked the wheel sharply to get around a pickup parked in front of her, then punched the gas. She turned left, intending to travel on Brainerd, away from the activity at the bar, and wind through the city to her motel.

She had driven six blocks and had signaled to turn when

a hand reached around from the backseat and gripped her throat. She jerked with surprise, and the car careened sharply as it turned the corner. She hit the curb. Two wheels rode on the sidewalk. She corrected the vehicle.

Still the hand held firm—tight but not choking. Julia thought one of the tires was losing air, but that's not what was making the sound.

It was her assailant, his lips near her ear: "Shhhhhh . . . Shhhhhh . . ."

She grabbed his forearm. It wasn't flesh; it was hard as steel but . . . not steel, warmer, textured in a way steel wasn't. A hard plastic maybe, and huge. It was some kind of . . . gauntlet. He applied more pressure, and she let go.

"What—?"

"Shhhhhhh . . ."

At McBrian, she ignored the stoplight and made a wide arc to the left, into the westbound lane.

Finally he spoke in whispered tones. His voice was gentle, pleasant.

"Keep both hands on the wheel," he said.

She nodded.

"Pull over."

"No."

He squeezed harder.

"Make a right up here and stop." The consonants were sharper, the gentleness gone.

"I said no," she repeated, driving past the road he wanted.

The grip contracted. She now found breathing difficult. Her pulse began to throb in her temple. Fragments of her assailant's features floated in the rearview mirror: eyes that flashed green whenever they passed under a streetlamp, messy jet hair, glasses.

"I won't hurt you," he whispered. "I've been sent to deliver a message."

"I don't believe you." Her voice was raspy.

"If I wanted to kill you, I would have."

Julia thought about that. It wasn't true: she had not given him the chance. She'd hopped into the car and taken off too fast. Since then, the car had been in motion. Killing her while she drove risked an accident—attention and injury to himself. But why hadn't he waited to reveal himself until she stopped again? Killing her at a stop sign or light would most likely prevent an injury accident, but not necessarily an accident altogether. In death her foot might jam down on the gas pedal in what coroners called a cadaveric spasm. He couldn't wait until she reached her destination and turned off the car. What if she was meeting the police? The last reason she could think of for his not waiting to kill her until she stopped on her own was that the farther she drove, the more distance she put between him and his own transportation. Then he'd have to either drive her car back, with or without her body, or find another way back. Did killers consider such things? She guessed they did.

"So?" he said. "Pull over."

Instead, she punched the accelerator. The car roared ahead, past other vehicles, through stoplights.

The hand clenched tighter.

twenty-nine

ALLEN HAD SLIPPED INTO STEPHEN'S OVERSIZED CLOTHES by the time they pulled into the space between the church and his cabin.

"This is it?" Allen asked incredulously.

"Home sweet home," Stephen confirmed and climbed out.

The cabin was behind the rear wall of the church. The parking lot lay on the north side of the church, in front of the cabin, giving the appearance that a visitor could go either to the church or to Stephen's cabin, as though the cabin were historically significant. Dense pine forest surrounded the property. The dirt road leading to it ended at the clearing, where the gravel parking lot started. The lot had been rutted dirt until last year, when the tiny church finally had enough funds in the coffers to grade the area and pour the gravel.

Stephen led the way. At the porch steps, he avoided the middle one, pointing at it for Allen's benefit. When they were both inside, he said, "Want anything?"

"A shower."

"Bathroom's over there. Want something to drink, eat?"

"Water's fine." He hitched his head toward the bathroom. "Mind?"

"Mi casa, su casa." Stephen was weary, but his broad smile conveyed the sense of hospitality he genuinely felt.

"Muchas gracias." Allen sauntered into the bathroom, looking like a child in his father's clothes. "Towel?"

"Cupboard on the right."

Allen closed the door slowly, looking beat in every sense of the word.

Stephen went into the kitchen area. He filled two plastic cups with ice and water and placed them on the coffee table in front of the couch. "Water's here when you want it!" he yelled at the bathroom door before plopping onto the couch. He looked at the wall clock. After one. He always rose by five—an internal clock sort of thing—so he wasn't going to be worth much tomorrow.

He stared at the bathroom door. Allen was in deep trouble this time, no doubt about it. He wondered if he could or even should help him out with whatever it was. Sometimes the best thing you could do was let people sort out their own problems. He supposed it depended on how nasty the trouble could get.

A square of light from an approaching car splashed through the front window and panned across the wall of books. It was a pattern he knew well: as the car made the last turn in the drive before entering the parking lot, the light would sweep across the books, usually stopping between

Matthew Henry's *New Testament Commentary* and *Clear and Present Danger.* Then it would shoot up to the ceiling as the car entered the parking lot, sliding to about center-room before creeping toward the door as the car approached the porch.

This time, however, the light vanished after hitting *Dracula*. Stephen sat upright on the couch. The car had stopped before entering the parking lot. That, mixed with the hour and the night's odd events, set off all kinds of alarms in his head. He rose and walked carefully to the window. The car was moving slowly in shadows, headlamps off, closing the thirty-foot gap to the clearing. When its bumper settled over the edge of the parking lot's gravel, it stopped.

And there it sat, in the gray haze of the night. The occupants would know someone was home. They'd see the Vega parked between the buildings, lights in the cabin. Was this the bogeyman Allen was running from?

"Allen?" he said softly. No answer. He repeated it, louder. He could hear the shower running through the bathroom door. It stopped. "Allen?"

"What?"

"Come here!"

The headlamps flicked on. The car started rolling again. Into the clearing. Moonlight peeled back the shadows like a CEO whipping off the covering of the company's newest model.

A Corvette—new enough to have headlamps that didn't retract into the front end.

It rolled slowly into the parking lot, then angled toward the cabin. The brake lights came on, making the trees behind it glow red. It stopped. He could see the ovals of faces inside, swiveling as the occupants surveyed the area. Then the car continued its slow progress toward the cabin.

Stephen pulled his face away from the window and leaned his head against the wall. Could be cops, bad guys, or simply people who'd gotten lost on their way back from the Drestin Dinner Theater. More than a few folks had stopped by for directions over the years.

The Vette stopped out front. He heard car doors open and slam. He moved to the door. Should he open it or ignore the knocks that would start in about five seconds? If the strangers needed help, he'd want to help them. If they meant harm, wouldn't they find a way in anyway?

He opened the door, flipping on the bright porch light as he did. Two men looked up at him, startled. Stephen grinned at them. One of the men stood at an angle in front of the car. He had short red hair and a zillion freckles. Something in the man's eyes caused Stephen to pause. He looked at the other man, older than Freckles, maybe forty. He sported a bushy mustache and black, black eyes.

Stephen heard the bathroom door open behind him.

"Did you say—?" Allen started.

Stephen looked over his shoulder at his brother. In the bathroom door, a towel around his waist, Allen was hunching over to gaze past Stephen. His mouth dropped, and his eyes grew wide.

"Stephen! No!" he yelled. "Shut the door! Don't—"

Stephen turned back to the men. Freckles was swinging a shotgun from around his side. He raised it, leveling it at Allen. One eye closed as he took aim.

The gun roared.

thirty

THE CAR BARRELED DOWN BRAINERD ROAD, SWERVING slightly through pools of halogen streetlights and traffic signals—green, yellow, red.

Julia gasped for breath, one weak hand touching the gauntlet. The attacker's fist closed, pinching her trachea like a straw. Fat dots of purple and red began to crowd her vision. In a mad effort to get free, she yanked the wheel sharply right, smashing into the door of a parked car. Sparks and headlamp glass pelted the windshield; metal screamed, because Julia could not. The assailant in the backseat merely swayed . . . and loosened his grip. She gulped in huge breaths, her lungs on fire, her throat raw.

They were traveling now at more than sixty miles per hour along one of Chattanooga's busiest streets, a feat impossible to duplicate in daytime traffic. Now, at a quarter after one, Julia took advantage of the absence of commuters.

"Slow down," the assailant hissed, punctuating his words with light squeezes. Each one sent a bolt of pain up her neck and into the back of her right eye. Panic stirred within her, ready to free her mind of all restraints. He squeezed again, this time holding the pressure.

"I mean it," he said. "If you draw attention to us, I'll break your neck without a second thought."

She eased up on the accelerator; he eased up on her neck. The speed dropped to fifty, then forty-five.

"Good girl."

The car sailed through a red light, eliciting a loud honk from a car Julia didn't see.

"I understand," her captor whispered. "We've got something like a Mexican standoff here, don't we?"

The speedometer needle hovered around forty.

"You must be trying to guess my next move," he said. "Let me help you: right now, I'm considering my choices. I can kill you now and take my chances in a crash. Of course, I'd try to grab the wheel and steer to safety. That might work. Or I can wait until you have to stop—for traffic, an empty fuel tank, whatever. It has to happen sooner or later."

He let her ponder those options.

"Or you can pull over, I'll give you the message I was asked to convey, and be on my way."

Julia continued driving. A bead of perspiration broke off her brow and slid into her eye, stinging it. She tried to blink it out. Coppery blood on her tongue: she had reopened the cut in her lip. She didn't believe for a moment that he had a "message" to deliver—at least not one that involved leaving her alive. He wanted to instill doubt, to give her a flicker of hope. Hope would keep her from acting drastically and could possibly get her to pull off onto a darkened side street, where murder was much more comfortable.

"You know?" he said, his voice growing deep with menace. It sounded to Julia that he said the next sentence through clenched teeth. "I like the one where I kill you and take my chances."

Abruptly, he dropped his head lower. A police cruiser was approaching from the opposite direction a half block away.

"Don't—*don't* flash your brights," he said, every word as firm as the grip he had on her neck. "Don't make a face or twitch a finger. If you signal them in any way, I'll keep you alive long enough to choke on their blood."

She'd never believed anybody more.

The cruiser drew closer. Streetlamps illuminated the faces inside. Two patrolmen. Probably frustrated by orders to carry on as usual, while a cop-killing investigation was unfolding farther away. The officer in the passenger seat said something sharp. The driver agreed with a frown. They could be talking about their wives, for all Julia knew.

They were no more than twenty feet apart when Julia cranked the wheel into the police cruiser's lane.

THE FRECKLE-FACED ASSAILANT HAD TRIED TO TAKE A STEP toward him while firing the shotgun. As he was closing his eye to aim, his foot came down on the rotted step that Stephen had meant to repair. It splintered under his weight, sucking his foot into its maw. The gun boomed, taking out a head-sized chunk of the cabin's siding directly above the door, showering Stephen with splinters and dust.

Stephen stormed out the door, raising his elbow in the

jaw-splitting fashion he hadn't postured since his days as a college linebacker. As Freckles was arching forward and down from his crash through the step, Stephen's elbow caught him squarely in the forehead. The impact sent him reeling back in the other direction. Stephen grabbed the shotgun by its barrel; it slipped easily from Freckles's unconscious hands.

He spun the gun around, raising it toward the other assailant, who was bringing a pistol around from behind his back.

"Freeze!" Stephen screamed.

The man didn't even pause. His pistol just kept coming, two seconds from fatal effectiveness. Stephen grasped the man's intention to go down fighting.

"Ahhhhh . . ." Stephen bellowed, the sound rising like a furnace under extreme pressure. He hurled the shotgun at the man, who raised an arm to parry the blow. By the time he swatted it away, Stephen was within striking distance. He planted a massive fist into the man's head, striking the temple. The man crumpled under the impact.

Stephen stood over him, startled by his own abilities. He bent and picked up the pistol and shotgun. Freckles had landed flat on his back on the car's hood, one leg stretching into the hole in the steps. His sport coat had flopped open, revealing an underarm holster. Stephen took that pistol as well. He saw the outline of a billfold in the coat's inner pocket and tugged it out. It flopped open, revealing a badge. Hamilton County Sheriff's Department. He slipped it into his back pocket. He took a few paces toward the woods and threw each weapon into the darkness. He checked the other man for ID and didn't find any. Then he strode into the cabin, calling for Allen. He found the bathroom door shut and locked. He shouldered it open. Allen's bare feet were slipping out a small window over the old-fashioned tub.

"Allen!" Stephen leaned over the tub to look out. Allen was scampering away on all fours, gripping clothes in one hand, a pair of shoes in the other. "Allen!"

He stopped and cranked his head around.

"Come around front, man," Stephen said.

He walked through the house and stood on the porch. Neither assailant showed signs of revival. He stepped off the porch and leaned into the Vette's open window. He came out with keys and a device that was larger than a cell phone and had a foot-long cylinder jutting from it. Stephen recognized it from *Blue Planet*, one of his favorite shows: it was a satellite phone, good almost anywhere in the world, not reliant on local networks or relay towers. The phone was tethered to a box that looked like a modem with a keypad. He had no idea what it was—he must have missed that episode. He turned around to see Allen coming out of the breezeway where he'd parked the Vega.

"Oh, wow," Allen said. "Oh, wow. You did this? Wow!"

It was the first smile he'd seen crease his brother's face that night. He pointed at Freckles. "That one's a cop."

"What?"

"Had a deputy sheriff's badge."

Silence.

"I don't think he was here as a cop, though," Stephen said. "He tried to shoot me without saying a word, and this is no cop car."

Allen swore.

"Get in the car. I'll be right there." Stephen took a step toward the woods and hurled the keys deep into them.

"What was that?"

"The car keys."

"What? Why?" Allen asked. "We should take their car. It's a lot nicer than yours. Look at it."

Stephen thought about it. "Too late now."

"What are those?" Allen asked, pointing.

"A satellite phone and some other gadget."

"Well, don't throw those away. Maybe we can use them."

"How?"

"I don't know, but we need to find some advantages here, right? You never know. What would it hurt?"

"Whoever these guys were communicating with can probably track the signal," Stephen said.

"Then turn it off. We'll turn it on to use it now and then when we're moving, so they can't pinpoint us."

Stephen was doubtful.

"Come on, man. We need *something*."

"All right, here." He handed the equipment to Allen. "Now get in the car."

He jumped over the porch steps and clomped into the cabin. A minute later, he came out carrying a paper sack. He switched off the cabin's overhead light and shut the door.

When he climbed into the Vega's driver's seat, Allen asked, "Where are their guns?"

"I chucked them."

Allen threw up his hands in exasperation.

"What would *you* do with guns?" Stephen asked and cranked the ignition. After some coughing and sputtering, the engine backfired once and settled into a fitful rhythm. He moved the stick shift into first gear and eased the Vega out from between the two buildings.

Allen threw his hand in front of Stephen's face, pointing. "Look!" he said.

The mustachioed cop was leaning into the car, pulling at something behind the seats.

"What's he doing?" Allen asked.

"Can't be good." He popped the clutch and pointed the lurching Vega at the road.

The man ducked out from within the car and stood, a weapon in his hands. It looked like the kind of thing Arnold Schwarzenegger favored, like it could blast holes in mountains. The man scowled at Stephen and Allen.

"Go! Go! Go!" Allen screamed.

The car fishtailed, moved closer to the drive.

"He's cocking it or whatever—!"

They came off the gravel, onto the dirt road, sliding between the first trees.

Metallic thunder filled the air. Trees exploded around them. Gas pedal jammed, Stephen glanced at Allen and saw only impossibly huge eyes.

Clouds covered the moon, drawing darkness over the road. For a moment Stephen had the wild idea that it was symbolic, God's way of portending their deaths. The car jolted sideways as a barrage caught the rear panel behind Stephen's seat. A jagged hole opened up on both sides of the car. Then Stephen swerved around the first bend, knowing they were invisible to the assailant now. All the same, he drove like the devil was on their heels.

After several miles, they crossed an ancient wood bridge over Chickamauga Creek.

"Where's the road?" Allen asked, as though he thought the assailants had taken it. "The paved road?"

"I'm not going to take any paved roads if I can help it. We're going deeper into the woods until we can figure out what to do next."

Allen began putting on Stephen's extra clothes for the second time that night.

Stephen looked over, shook his head.

"I wasn't about to tear through the woods naked again," Allen said.

"No, looked like you were crawling to me."

Allen said nothing.

"Look, Allen—"

The car went across a particularly deep rut. Their heads banged the roof.

"Look, whatever our differences are, we're in this together now. Whatever *this* is. You gotta let me know what's going on."

Allen nodded. "Get us someplace safe, and I'll tell you what I know, which isn't much."

thirty-one

JULIA SAW AN INSTANT OF SHEER HORROR ON THE POLICE officers' faces before their cars collided. The headlight beams merged, growing intense between the two cars before bursting; hoods crumpled; windshields spiderwebbed, then shattered. The collision was deafening, two mountains crashing together.

Julia vaulted forward. Her seat belt locked, catching her so rigidly she felt a rib crack. Her air bag erupted like a kernel of giant popcorn, smashing her back. The assailant's arm tore from her neck. She sensed his body crumpling against the seat back before starting to flip over it, hip and leg first. A moment later, her seat belt *kachinked* open, her door popped wide, and she tumbled out. Trying to stand, she stumbled, stood, weaved.

Metal clanged to the ground somewhere, glass tinkled, radiators hissed, liquid dripped, one of the police officers screamed in pain or rage or both. She turned to the cruiser. The cop in the passenger's seat was pushing down an exploded air bag.

His door swung open, and he stepped out, clutching the window frame for support. He had the crusty face of a life-long beat cop, overweight, near retirement. He looked utterly stunned. A ruptured cigarette was smashed against his cheek, strands of tobacco flaking away as he moved. He spotted her, and his face hardened.

She held up her palm. "Federal agent!" she yelled, her voice hoarse but clear. "FBI!" She could explain the difference later. She staggered toward the policeman, pointing at the twisted metal of her car. "There's an armed man in my car. He tried to kill—"

"Are you *insane?*" he snapped.

"I've got an armed gunman situation here!" She couldn't believe she was having to do this. She stepped closer, instinctively picking the cop's name off the patch on his shirt. "Officer Gilbert, my name is Julia Math—"

"Hold it right there!" He put a hand on his gun but left it in its holster. "Show me some tin, lady, or you can spread-eagle on the ground right now!" He slapped the cigarette off his face.

She glanced over at the wreckage of her car, saw no sign of the killer. She removed her identification wallet from her front pants pocket, then held it up. The cop—Gilbert—signaled her to step closer. A red crease split open across his forehead as a bullet grazed him, and he fell back. Julia turned toward her car. Through jetting steam and wafting smoke, made nearly opaque by one still-blazing headlamp, she saw the killer behind the glassless windshield frame of her car. He was leaning on the center of the dashboard, his right arm draped over it as if he were chatting it up at a neighborhood tavern. One side of his face glistened with blood. In his left hand he held a bulky semiautomatic pistol, surely a .45. Already big, the addition of a long sound suppresser made it look more like a small machine gun. He turned it toward her. A point of red light flashed in her eyes.

She dropped straight down, hearing the *thunk!* of the shot, followed by the tinny sound of the spent cartridge clattering against the crumpled hood. Before she realized it, her pistol was in her hand.

Officer Gilbert leaped to his feet, the red graze on his brow glowing like war paint. He had drawn his pistol and come up shooting. From her hunkered position, Julia could not see the killer, but the cop obviously thought he had a target. He rattled off six rounds as fast as he could pull the trigger. He was clicking through the paces of reloading before the sound of the last shot faded away.

She scanned the street. No civilians. Good. The closest businesses were a closed bookstore and an all-night Laundromat that appeared empty. She sprang up, the bead of her pistol's front sight hovering over the spot she'd last seen the killer. Gone.

The other cop, the driver, clambered out, falling on his hands. He yanked out his legs and stood with a dizzy swagger. He was pale, but Julia suspected that was his usual complexion: tall, skinny, midtwenties, a shock of orange hair burning the top of his head. Blood pulsed from his mouth. It was a fighter's injury: he'd lost a central incisor, rupturing a small artery in the upper gums. Dazed, he bent into the cruiser and emerged with a shotgun. He pumped the slide, chambering a shell. He spat out a mouthful of blood and yelled, "Whatcha got?"

"Gunman! In the car. I think he nicked me."

Neither man showed a trace of panic or fear, just determination and a healthy measure of ire.

Dang, they breed 'em tough up here, Julia thought. Crouching, she darted behind the cruiser.

The killer popped up from behind the dash, fired, and disappeared. She felt the slug zing past her head.

Both cops let loose with a volley of thunderous shots, evaporating huge chunks of metal and dash and seat upholstery.

Why is he staying in the car? she wondered. *Something's wrong.*

As if in answer, the assailant sprang up from behind the trunk, his laser-sighted weapon already leveled at them. Before they recognized his presence, he fired and vanished. The bullet shattered the window of the open driver's door and tore a hole in the chest of the orange-haired cop. He cried out and flew backward, knocking Julia to the ground and pinning her feet.

"Stinky! Stinky!" Officer Gilbert called. At least that's what she thought he said; it could have been "Stanky" or "Spanky." The officer's name patch was no help: the bullet had ripped right through it.

Gently, quickly, she pulled her legs out from under him. He gritted his teeth, grimaced, rolled his eyes toward her. He looked so young. She got her legs under her and crouched down, ready to leap, run, or roll. With one hand she applied pressure to the wound; the other gripped her pistol.

Gilbert was already screaming into a microphone, stretching its coiled cord out the door as far as possible.

"Officer down! I need backup! Now! Now! Now!" He gave the cross streets. A female voice squawked in reply.

He dropped the microphone, bobbed his head up and

down, high enough to see the wrecked car through his own broken windshield. "How is he?" he asked, not turning to look.

"Alive. Looks bad."

Stinky was holding on to consciousness by a thread.

Gilbert jumped, seeing something. He rose, thrust his arms over the roof, and fired three rounds.

And waited.

Nothing.

Sirens swelled in the distance, approaching fast.

A flicker caught Julia's attention, and she looked down. A red spot of light hovered on Gilbert's ankle.

"Move!" she yelled and leaped toward him, too late.

His ankle exploded as if from an internal detonation. Before the next event happened, she knew it would. The cop yelled and fell to the street. A red spot appeared in the center of his forehead, seeming to have already been there, waiting for him. The back of his head ruptured with the assailant's exiting bullet. The killer had calculated that maneuver with obscene perfection.

"Noooooo!" Moving low, close to the rear tire, she hooked her gun under the car and rapid-fired along the ground in the general direction of the assailant.

On the opposite side of the cruiser, a police unit roared onto Brainerd from a side street and squealed to a stop, headlamps illuminating her Taurus. The assailant fired at it from behind the trunk. Brainerd filled with a kaleidoscope of lights as a half dozen cruisers converged on the two wrecked cars, three from behind her car, bathing the assailant in white light. He spun on them, shooting huge holes into their windshields. Doors flew open, cops beat it for cover behind their cruisers.

The assailant bolted away from the car, running for an

alley between the bookstore and Laundromat. As he did, he shot at Julia. The red point of his laser zigzagged around her as bullets plunked half-dollar-sized holes in the cruiser's sheet metal and shattered the asphalt in front of her. The tire behind her ruptured. Holding her ground, she fired back. As his foot touched the curb, one of her bullets struck his shoulder, spinning him around. He glared at her, his eyes wild.

She froze. Only a second . . . less. But in that time, he leveled his gun at her. She didn't see but felt the laser center on her forehead.

A thousand banshees screamed—it took her a moment to recognize the sound of many guns firing at once.

The assailant, still glaring at her, spasmed as round after round tore into his body. Blood and gore sprayed out behind him. Store windows erupted. White powder burst from brick facades, so fine and abundant the buildings appeared to be smoldering.

He would not fall. He jerked his head to look at the police, at the muzzle flashes and smoke that marked his demise. He swiveled his gun toward them and returned fire. He seemed to be absorbing the firepower and hurling it back.

Julia rolled behind the cruiser, trying to press her body into the street. From this prone position under the rear bumper, she took aim at the crazed assailant. She'd heard of doped-up druggies, so numbed to pain, so high on artificial stimulants that it took a virtual army to bring them down. But this was something . . . different.

Later, every cop there would admit to their colleagues, their wives, or themselves, feeling the same sense of astounded terror, like waking to the realization that everything you thought about the universe was wrong. Despite the killer's uncanny ability to withstand horrendous injuries, nothing startled them so much as the unflinching concentration he displayed when he changed ammo clips. In the midst of an unceasing barrage of gunfire, he swung another magazine up to his gun just as he fired his last round and the slide locked open. The spent clip dropped away. He jammed in the new one with the ease and thoughtless habit of checking the time. Shattered and shooting, he had somehow kept track of his every shot, knowing the precise moment to change clips. The process delayed his shooting no more than a second.

The moment the new magazine was seated into the handle of the gun, his free hand dropped down to his belt, where another magazine was clipped. His hand stayed there, ready.

Then his chest erupted in a mist, and he toppled.

The quaking of guns ceased. Silence rushed in to fill the void like water into a new footprint; its presence felt heavy. All eyes watched the body sprawled across the curb. A sheet of blood fanned out on the sidewalk from the chest and shoulders; rivulets of it began snaking from under other parts—head, arms, legs—and flowed into the gutter.

Somebody coughed, breaking the spell; another cursed loudly. Then the air filled with the sound of guns being reloaded, magazines refilled, spent shells being kicked on the ground and swept off car surfaces.

Julia watched as three patrolmen cautiously approached the body, shotguns poised to continue the onslaught should the body so much as twitch. They were spaced well apart to avoid being slaughtered as a group.

A noise erupted from the killer. A melody. Lights appeared on what Julia had thought was another magazine clipped to his belt. It was the man's cell phone, and it was ringing.

The three cops instantly locked into combat firing stances.

The musical ring tone was a song Julia knew: Pink Floyd's "Comfortably Numb." After about ten seconds, it stopped.

One of the cops glanced over his shoulder, checking his comrades for guidance they didn't have; another inched forward, kicked away the assailant's pistol, and stretched his hand to the assailant's neck. An eternity later, he gestured that he'd found no pulse. While the other two covered him, the first hefted the body on its side to cuff the hands behind the back. Julia had seen corpses cuffed before, but never with so much gravity. The cop ran a hand along the body's perimeter, pulling a heavy knife from an ankle sheath and the cell phone from the belt. He tossed them aside.

Julia closed her eyes and lowered her face to the pavement, feeling tiny pebbles bite into her cheek. She was grateful for their solidarity, for how *real* they felt. She stayed like that as EMTs assessed Stinky—he was alive with surprisingly strong vitals—and until a cop came over and pressed his fingers to her throat.

"I'm okay," she said and cupped her face in her hands.

thirty-two

GREGOR WOKE FROM A DREAM IN WHICH HE WAS FIELD-stripping a rifle, alone in a vast arctic landscape. The rifle made sense: he'd broken down and cleaned and reassembled a fair share of them. He wasn't so sure where the winter conditions came from. His foster parents had lived in Wyoming, which certainly got cold and snowy, but nothing like in his dream. Maybe it had something to do with his thirty-year stretch in a tropical climate. No snow. Ever.

His room was dark, except for a soft, unfamiliar light. At the very moment that he saw the light was coming from one of the two cell phones on his nightstand, it rang. Its previous ring must have been what pulled him from his imaginary midnight wandering.

"Yes?" It came out as a croak. He repeated the word.

He recognized the voice on the other end, and his mind

cleared immediately. The voice recited a code phrase. Gregor thought for a moment, then returned the proper reply. He listened. "But aren't you there now? . . . Chattanooga, Tennessee . . . Of course, I can resend the files, but—hold on, let me get a pen."

He threw back his blankets, swung his legs off the bed, and turned on the bedside lamp. Something wasn't right. The great warrior Ts'ao Kung said the essence of battlefield success was "to mystify, mislead, and surprise the enemy."

The enemy! Gregor thought. *Not your allies, not your commanders!*

Code phrase or not, the call worried him. But the man was not someone you questioned or angered. He possessed the phone number, the code phrase, the voice. Gregor didn't know what else to do. He stood and stumbled toward his desk for a pen.

He wished he were back field-stripping a rifle in subzero temperatures.

thirty-three

JULIA WASN'T ABOUT TO HANG AROUND. SHE'D BEEN TRY-
ing to avoid cops all day, and now she was surrounded by
them. It wouldn't be long before they found their composure
and wanted to know more about her involvement. She'd be
brought in to police headquarters and questioned until the
FBI or CDC showed up to relieve them of the burden that
was Julia Matheson. No doubt there were people in several
agencies who had questions for her.

At the moment, each member of the local PD was busy
describing the action from his or her own perspective. There
was the kind of laughter that comes after extreme stress, and
cops saying, "No, no, no, this is the way it went down," and
cops who were in a blue funk about the casualties, and cops
who wanted to fight because they didn't understand how
someone could laugh at a time like this. There were few, it

seemed to Julia, who had set all that post-traumatic stuff aside and were going about the business of securing the crime scene and interviewing witnesses. Those who were doing their jobs moved slowly, distractedly, and focused primarily on where the assailant's body fell.

She went to inspect her car. She found what had kept him in the car long after he should have bolted: in the accident, his right arm had apparently become wedged between the crumpled hood and dash. He'd only escaped by slipping his arm out of a wicked-looking gauntlet, leaving it behind. A string of blood dripped from it as if it were a severed arm.

She told a patrolman that she needed to pry open her car door and borrowed his crowbar; she had left her own crowbar with the other tools stashed in the alleyway behind the bar. She levered the hood metal back enough to wiggle the gauntlet loose, then dropped it into a deep canvas book bag, along with a few papers scattered about the interior. Then, acting as if she were doing exactly what she was supposed to be doing, she marched around the corner and kept on going until she reached another major street and hailed a cab.

She was in her room and slumping on the bed before the extent of her injuries became apparent: She hurt everywhere. Her side throbbed where the rib had fractured; her hips ached from thrusting against the seat belt; her throat still felt as fragile as blown glass; various spots of pain flared on her face and arms where fragments of erupting asphalt had bitten into her.

She pulled the memory chip from her pants pocket, turned it around in her fingers. So small. In centuries past, when people fought over a small item, it was usually a jewel or a key to a locked treasure, maybe a deed to some estate or a religious relic. Now, as often as not, it was information. And a *lot* of information could fit on a tiny square chip like the one she held. Didn't look like much. Worth ten bucks in a computer or camera store. But throw some information on it, and it became invaluable. She thought of the cost so far. Goody. Vero. The cop Gilbert. Even the assassins—the two killers who'd died in the bar and the one tonight. Not that their lives were worth anything, but they did contribute to the tally. And those were only the deaths she knew about. What had happened before Vero tried to get this chip into the right hands?

I hope you're worth it, she thought.

She scooted back on the bed, grabbed her laptop, and turned it on. She leaned over and rummaged through the computer case until she found an adapter card, which she pushed into the computer's expansion port. When she pushed the chip into that, the screen immediately flashed a pattern of multicolored static and froze.

Julia winced.

She restarted the computer four times: twice she started it with the chip already slotted, and twice she waited until the operating system had booted. Each time, it crashed the computer.

Groaning, feeling every bruised muscle, she rolled off the bed, grabbed her purse, and left the room. At the pay phone outside the motel office, she used a calling card to dial a long-distance number.

"Wha—?" She heard a male voice say on the other end of the line.

"Bonsai?"

"Who's this?"

"Julia. Don't say my last name."

"Like I would. What time—?"

"Late. I need your help."

"Call back in the morning, Julia. No, I'll call you. I'm really beat, you know, with the new kid and all."

"Goody's dead." There was so much silence, Julia said, "Bonsai?"

"Goody?" He was stunned. "When?" No sleep left in his voice.

"Today. Yesterday, now. There's some weird stuff going down. I need your help, and no one can know. Can you help?"

"Sure, yeah, whatever."

"Can you get to a secure phone?"

"This one's good. I sweep it every day."

Of course he does.

"I have a memory chip. It's—" She read a shallow impression in the chip's plastic case. "An SDx30. I'm pretty sure it's at the heart of what got Goody killed. But I'm afraid it got damaged."

"What's it doing?"

"Whenever it tries to mount, the computer locks up."

"It's a full-volume encryption. Everything it needs to know it's a computer file—the hibernation files, swap files, the resource fork, all of it—is locked up. It's a pretty recent development in data security. Your computer doesn't know what to do with it, so it just dies."

She felt a wave of relief. "Can you do anything with it?"

"Probably. I'll need to send you an app that'll tell your computer not to attempt mounting it. Then you can send it to me."

"Bonsai, could you go somewhere else to receive it?"

"Are you talking about the tap the feds have on my T1?"

"You know about that?"

"What kind of hacker would I be if I didn't? I got a second T1 nobody knows about."

"I should have known."

"You got Wi-Fi?"

"With a trace-interlock."

"Nice." A trace-interlock was like an antenna for wireless Internet connectivity. It pulled in Wi-Fi signals within a mile radius and ran a quick decryption on any firewalls it encountered, granting the user access without passwords. It was built into the SATD software.

He gave her a Web address where they would meet online to swap files. He also issued her four pass phrases, which she would need to communicate with him online, one pass phrase at a time.

"I need to get back to my room and reboot," she said.

"My site has a VOIP function," he said. "You know VOIP? Voice Over Internet Protocol?"

"I know it."

"We can talk that way. It's secure."

Walking back to the room, she thought about Bonsai. He'd been a seventeen-year-old high school geek in Denver when he'd hacked into the Strategic Air Defense computers at NORAD's facility inside Cheyenne Mountain. He had done it only to see if he could, but Air Force brass, NSA goons, and the FBI came down hard on him. Before he'd fallen victim to a merciless judicial system, however, Donnelley had fought for his rehabilitation, pointing out the value of the kid's incredible computer savvy to national law enforcement. Prosecutors had reluctantly agreed, and Bonsai became a freelance computer hacker for the U.S. government.

The skinny kid with flaming acne and long oily hair had proved to possess one of the sharpest security minds in cyberspace, going on to make a six-figure income showing corporations the chinks in their firewalls—a computer system's version of a vault door. Now twenty-one, he had a wife and a newborn boy—Baby Bonz, Goody had called him, though his name was Christopher. Bonsai credited Goody for his freedom. Julia knew he had always wanted to repay the favor. News of his death must have cut deep.

Repositioned on the bed, Bonsai's Web site on the screen, Julia waited for him to send her the application she needed. She started the transfer of the encrypted memory chip data. A bar graph appeared, indicating that the transfer would take a long time, maybe hours. Bonsai's T1 line was fast, but Julia's Wi-Fi was slow; transfers always moved at the slowest speed in the conduit.

"Julia?" His voice came over the laptop's speakers.

"Hmm."

"Go to bed. I'm going too. I'll get on it as soon as I get the whole thing."

"Thanks, Bonsai."

She watched the bar graph. Progress was marked by a blue bar moving from left to right. She stared at it for five minutes, and it barely moved.

It might have locked up, she thought. *I should call Bonsai, see what he thinks . . .*

But then she was asleep.

thirty-four

ETERNAL NIGHT.

The morgue was as black for the shadowy figure gliding through its halls as it was for the bodies tucked coldly into the endless rows of metal cabinets. If human eyes had caught a glimpse of the fleeting shadow, they would look again and see nothing. It moved quickly along the edge of the corridor. Silent. Aware.

No amount of Clorox could eliminate the smell of death from the air. The figure inhaled the odor, discerned the metallic blood scent from the pungency of flesh.

A door opened, seemingly of its own accord. The shadow slipped through.

A fine beam of light erupted from the shadow, glinted off the lipped edges of an aluminum table. It flashed up to the far wall, which was sectioned into three-foot squares, each with its own stainless steel handle and dangling tag, a copy of the one tied to the big toe of the corpse inside.

A hand formed out of the shadow. Clad in black leather, it snatched the tags, turning them toward the light: Willows, R. . . . Jeffreys, M. . . . John Doe.

The hand stopped as the shadow contemplated the non-name: *John Doe.*

It lowered to the handle. A metal latch clicked, airtight seals ruptured, steel rollers slid on metal. A white sheet billowed up, drifted down.

The drawer slammed shut. The shadow hand continued past the names. Then stopped again.

Another John Doe.

Another click. Another *tissshhh* of escaping air. More rollers. The flutter of a sheet as the beam fixed on a face, pale and frozen as statuary.

The beam clicked off. The shadow, blacker than the dark air around it, engulfed the body. When it retreated, the body was gone.

A SOUND STARTLED JULIA OUT OF SLEEP. SHE WAS SITTING ON the bed, leaning askew against the wall where a headboard would be in a nicer motel. Sunlight filtered through the tattered curtains, brightening the room almost reluctantly.

Julia looked around for whatever had awakened her. Bolts of pain shot up from her stiff neck. She became aware again of aches in her throat and side and other injuries, but realized they were less severe than they had been the night before.

She started to rise, and her leg bumped the computer, which had toppled off her lap and onto the bed sometime during the night. She tilted it up to look at the screen and tapped the track pad to bring it out of its own automatic slumber. The screen lit up. It showed Bonsai's Web site and the words TRANSFER COMPLETE.

The computer must have chimed to signify that Bonsai had received the file. That was fast. She looked at her watch and realized it hadn't been so fast. It was 9:28 a.m. She'd slept for seven hours. She wondered how long it would take for him to figure out the encryption.

She picked up her cell phone from the bedside table and turned it on. It rang immediately.

Yes!

"Bonsai?"

"Where in the name of Clint Eastwood have you been!"

She instantly recognized the gruff voice of Edward Molland, her boss. Each word rang as sharp as a rifle shot.

"I have been dialing this number since yesterday afternoon."

She thought of slamming the phone down, just dropping it and leaving the motel.

"The phone was off, sir."

"Well, why haven't you called? Why didn't you check in with the Bureau's Chattanooga office? Man alive! The fiasco down here. The death of a federal agent, Julia—*Donnelley!* And whatever that was you were involved in last night—the bloodbath they called me about. Sounds like you were smack in the middle of it, then just disappeared. They wanted to put an APB out on you, get a warrant for your arrest—*your arrest,* Julia! I convinced them to wait. Now you have to convince *me.*"

"Arrest me? On what grounds?"

"You name it. You know how this works. At the least,

you're a person of interest. They want to talk to you, and they'll find a way to haul you in, if you don't haul yourself in first."

"I'm trying to work a few things out first."

"Work what out? Julia, you are a federal agent. You are part of a spin-off agency of the FBI, if you need to be reminded. We have procedures, protocol. You've broken at least a dozen regulations that I know about. This is not like you, not like you at all."

He didn't say anything for a long time, and she didn't know how to respond. She wanted to cry or scream or . . . something. She could picture Molland, tapping manicured nails on the surface of his immaculate desk, hair just right, suit tailored just so, looking more like a politician than a chief law enforcement officer. Oddly, she wondered if someone was sitting on the black leather sofa in his office. If so, would their expression convey professional concern for her behavior or conspiratorial delight at having found her? She pushed the thought away. If there was a mole in the agency, the chances of it being Molland were slim. Goody had always trusted him. That was why he'd agreed to leave the Bureau for CDC when Molland had asked.

He cleared his throat. "What's the take on that guy you and the locals zapped last night?"

"I have no idea, sir. Hired gun. Very professional."

"You know he's gone?"

The blood in the base of her neck chilled, then cascaded down her spine.

"What do you mean?"

"Someone broke into the morgue this morning. Stole the body."

The room grew darker, as if the sun had slipped behind a cloud.

"Why?"

"That's the question. Coroner went in this morning, and the corpse was gone. Like he got up and strolled out."

"He had to have been shot two dozen times."

"That's what I heard."

Long pause. Molland spoke again, his voice much softer, even compassionate.

"Look . . . Julia. I'm sorry about Goody. I can't tell you how much. I know you two were close. I understand that you panicked, freaked out. But it's time to get back on track. Let's catch his killers, huh? What time can you be here? One? Two?"

"I need more time," she blurted. "I mean, I haven't slept, and I need to get organized." What she really needed was to sort through her notes and memory, then make a definitive decision either to go to the Bureau with her suspicions or to go somewhere else, like directly to the attorney general. She also wanted to give Bonsai time to decrypt the information on the chip.

"Okay. I understand. How about three?"

"Tomorrow morning would be better."

"Tomorrow?" He didn't say anything for a while, then: "Okay, look. You've been through the wringer. Take the day off. Be here first thing in the morning, right? My office."

"Thanks, Ed. See you tomorrow."

"Julia?"

"Yeah?"

"First thing in the morning. I mean it."

She disconnected and set the phone back on the bedside table. She had taken two steps toward the bathroom when it rang again. She picked it up and looked at the caller ID. *Private number.* Bonsai or Molland again. She pushed the talk button.

"This is Julia."

"We need to talk."

"Who is this?"

"Dr. Parker. Remember? We need to talk," he repeated.

"Parker?" She'd forgotten about leaving her number with him. "What do you mean, we need to talk?"

"Somebody tried to kill me last night. Twice."

"What? Who? No, wait—" Her head was spinning now. She expected Rod Serling to step through the door, calmly introducing the *Twilight Zone* episode her life had become. *Meet Julia Matheson. Lonely federal agent. Her job requires her to think in terms of black and white, in logic and fact. But she's about to discover a place where logic and fact have no meaning. A place called . . . the Twilight Zone.*

She said, "Are you where I can call you back in three minutes?"

"A pay phone."

"Give me the number." She memorized it. "Okay, three minutes."

Julia hung up, dug into her purse for coins, and walked in her stocking feet to the pay phone outside the hotel's management office. She dialed the number and dropped in the coins. When Parker answered, she said, "All right, who tried to kill you?"

"Three different people. One of them had a badge."

"A federal agent?"

"A local cop, a sheriff's deputy, I think. Another was a big guy, had a gun with a laser—"

"A gauntlet?"

After a moment, he said, "I didn't see anything like that. But he was fast and moved better than you'd think for a man that size."

"Glasses?"

"Yeah . . . thick black frames. You know this guy?"

"He attacked me last night too. He died in a shootout with the cops."

Parker made a noise that might have been a gasp or murmured profanity. She watched through the office's front window as an old man came out from a back room, absently rubbing his chest under a stained T-shirt. He spotted Julia and waved.

Parker said, "So? Can we meet?"

"Me, as a cop?"

"No, not really. Maybe . . . Not officially. I don't know."

She laughed. "I think I know what you mean."

"Just you. No other agents, no cops, no surveillance."

"Just me."

"Okay. Meet us at the Appalachian Café on Market Street in Knoxville at—"

"Whoa, whoa. Knoxville?"

"There or nowhere."

"You're afraid of being in Chattanooga?"

"You're not?"

"I'm shaking in my socks. Who's 'we'?"

"My brother. He was with me last night. Noon?"

"Noon it is. Appalachian Café." She hung up.

A dozen thoughts tripped over themselves for her attention: the stolen body, the meeting with Parker, his attempted murder, Molland expecting her tomorrow morning . . . She squeezed her eyes shut and willed them all away. *Not now, not now.* Mentally, she constructed an agenda: shower *(yes, long and hot . . . okay, not so long; Knoxville is a two-hour drive)*, enter the new data into her case journal *(skip that, no time)*, check out of the motel *(can't stay anyplace too long)*, hop a cab to a car rental company to replace her agency car, shoot up to Knoxville.

She went back to her room, stripped off her clothes, and laid them out on the bed. She added *Call Mom* to her list. Then she stepped into the steaming jets of the shower and let the pounding water wash away her concerns, if only for a short while.

SHE FOUND A DIFFERENT PHONE BOOTH TO CALL HOME. HER mother sounded tired, but she claimed to be mobile. She insisted she didn't need help. The next call Julia made was to Homecare, the home health agency. The company had a check-in service; a nurse would swing by the duplex every four hours to make sure everything was as it should be. That ought to drive her mom crazy.

thirty-five

GREGOR KNOCKED ON THE OBSERVATION WINDOW UNTIL Karl Litt turned from a biosafety cabinet. His arms were pushed into gloved ports that allowed access to the cabinet's sensitive contents. Gregor motioned, and Litt nodded, pulled his arms out, and spoke to a young man standing beside him. A moment later, the laboratory door opened and Litt stepped through.

"A lead on Parker and the Matheson woman," Gregor said as Litt stripped off surgical gloves and smock and dropped them into a bin.

"Can we count on it?"

"Coffee?"

The compound's break room always featured a half pot of vile black sludge. Litt loved the stuff.

Litt nodded and stepped up to a metal door and absently

passed his face before a square panel of black glass set in the wall. Behind the glass, an infrared camera scanned his physiognomy, creating a pattern of the invisible heat generated by the blood vessels under the skin. The scanner compared this thermal image with ones filed in its hard drive. Finding a match, it disengaged the door's lock.

When Gregor had first heard of a foolproof identification system that recognized individuals' unique thermal facial patterns—distinguishing even between identical twins—despite aging, cosmetic surgery, and the total absence of light, he had lobbied Litt to get the compound's security doors retrofitted for it. Years earlier, they had agreed to spend the bulk of the organization's financial resources on research and security, and because Litt had recently landed a lucrative contract to supply a Middle Eastern dictator with biochemicals, he had consented to Gregor's request.

They stepped into another corridor, this one much dimmer than the one that serviced the labs. Only one in three fluorescent tubes worked, and many of those sputtered on the brink of death. A dank odor filled the air. In some sections, the "corridors" were nothing more than large, corrugated-metal tubes, dripping water from the rivets and buckling and splitting like overstuffed sausages where earth pushed through. The military base had been abandoned over forty years before and wasn't in the best condition when new. Now it threatened to disintegrate back into the surrounding land, though Gregor knew Litt had done his best to keep it operational.

Falling in step beside the other man, Gregor continued. "The transaction-monitoring people have an affinity agreement with an organization that intercepts telephone transmissions. So, say your subject's away from his usual Internet service provider and uses a credit card number to temporarily tap into a new provider—something that happens frequently, I take it, if the subject suspects his lines are bugged. The transaction-monitoring guys pick up the credit card sale, which includes the new IP address he's using, and that, in turn, is associated with a phone or data line. The phone guys step in and, *bam*, instant bug."

"Parker accessed the Internet?" Litt asked.

"No, he called the female federal agent, Matheson. He's not stupid, he watches TV, so he goes to a pay phone—and uses his *credit card* to make the call." Gregor grinned.

"Ahh," Litt said, appreciating the irony.

"So the phone bug kicks in—it's all automatic. Now we not only know which phone booth the guy is using—we got his conversation too."

"We got it?"

"MP3. I had it in my BlackBerry two minutes after he hung up. I forwarded it to Atropos."

"What'd he say?"

"No response yet."

They reached the break room, saw a biologist with a magazine and a mug seated at the only table, and stepped back into the corridor.

"Our accountant called this morning," Litt said quietly.

"Atropos doesn't come cheap."

"He mentioned another offshore transfer. Twenty thousand."

Gregor nodded. "That was to the service that gave us the lead on Parker."

"Doesn't matter. Soon enough, we'll be able to buy Anderson's entire firm." He scanned the dilapidated corridor. "*And* get this place fixed up."

The biologist exited the break room, greeted Litt and Gregor, and headed toward the labs. The two men went in. Gregor poured them each a cup of coffee, and they sat at the table. Gregor stared into the liquid's shiny black surface.

"Something else?" Litt asked.

Gregor shrugged, sipped from the cup. "It's just . . ."

"What?"

"So close to fulfilling the dream, Karl. I'm just thinking—" He looked into the black orbs of Litt's glasses, saw himself reflected in each lens. "Look, I don't have a problem with killing kids, as a means to an end."

"You don't believe it's necessary?"

He shrugged. "Strategically, I think it's a mistake."

"Our experts disagree. The plan was maximum impact. The public has to *feel* it, Gregor. It has to hurt."

"I just think there will be a backlash where children are involved."

"We want a backlash—against Kendrick, against his deceit, against his government's complicity."

"But is the list about getting attention or . . ." He tried to find the word.

Litt beat him to it. "Vengeance?"

"Your family . . . Who wouldn't want revenge? I'm just wondering if putting so many children on the list . . . I know it will wrench people out of their complacency, but might they not want your head instead of listening to the reasons you are striking back at them?"

"At first, maybe. Then they will say, 'Who has brought this on us? Who has awakened this monster?' And they will find Kendrick and their own government. They will bring down their own house from their grief and anger."

"I hope you're right."

Litt pushed back from the table, his chair screeching against the tile. He stood. "Either way, Gregor," he said, "it's too late now." He picked up his cup and left.

Gregor didn't move for a long time. He had studied war. He understood the power of demoralizing an enemy's citizens, of crushing their spirit and their will to fight. But he also knew that the tactic could backfire and result in a more determined enemy. Perhaps that wouldn't be so bad, he thought. He was sure Karl would respond in kind. Ten thousand this time. How many the next? One million was not out of the question. Karl didn't care. He had stopped caring decades ago.

Take my family, he imagined Karl thinking, *and I will slaughter your children.*

thirty-six

THE APPALACHIAN CAFÉ OCCUPIED A RUSTIC BRICK BUILD-
ing on a cheery block of downtown Knoxville, complete with
wide sidewalks and a line of alternating old-fashioned streetlamps and mature trees. Modeled after the favored eateries of
Europe, the café boasted a large front patio where wood-
framed umbrellas shaded white metal tables. Now lunchtime
on an outside kind of day, every table buzzed with business
types. Microbrewed beer disappeared by the vat, along with
whole crops of the latest trend in spinach salads. The image
made Julia yearn for the day before yesterday, when she and
Donnelley might have lunched in such a place and razzed
each other over some investigative faux pas.

As she came up to the wrought-iron rail that separated
the patio from the sidewalk, she scanned the diners for
Parker. Everyone appeared to be laughing or smiling, which

made her conscious of her own pouting mouth. Then she saw him, sitting across the table from a huge man who'd blocked him from view seconds earlier. They didn't look like brothers. He spotted her and nodded in greeting. She liked that: no conspicuous waves or shouts. Whether that meant he knew how to keep a low profile, she'd find out soon enough.

She had to enter the restaurant to get to the patio. The place exuded a smell like roasted almonds that made her mouth water despite her upset stomach. Only then did she realize that she'd last eaten more than twenty-four hours ago. Perhaps it was hunger and not only grief causing her stomach pains.

The hostess escorted her to Parker's table. Both men stood. They were positioned across from each other, leaving two chairs between them at the round table: one facing the street, the other facing the restaurant. She'd have preferred a seat where she could watch both of them at once. She settled for the one facing the street, putting Parker on her left, his brother on her right. She slipped the new gym bag off her shoulder and set it on the ground.

"I'm glad you came," Parker said, sitting again, scooting his chair close to the table.

She smiled politely and noted that he was wearing brand-new clothes, complete with factory-fold creases. Her new blouse had hanger marks on the shoulders, which her blazer hid. She took in the other man, his brother. He had to be one of the biggest people she'd ever seen. The hairiest too. But he possessed kind eyes and a ready smile. Where Allen was undeniably charming, perhaps a little too slick, this man was utterly and instantly likable. She hoped she wasn't simply needing a kind face and imagining it where it wasn't.

"We couldn't think of anything else to do," Allen said. "We

had our reservations. I'd just as soon trust the waiter as a cop right now."

"I know how you feel," she said.

He gave her an inquisitive look, but she turned away.

"You're Dr. Parker's brother?"

"Stephen." They shook hands. In his, hers was small and pathetic looking.

"And call me Allen, please."

"You don't look like brothers."

"I got the looks," Allen said. "He got the . . . hair."

Stephen winked at her.

"Are you a physician?"

"He almost was," Allen said, a little harshly, Julia thought. "He dropped out two months short of graduation. He—"

"Allen, let's not go there." Stephen turned to Julia, his face softening. "I'm a pastor, and I have no idea what I'm doing here."

"Weren't you with Allen last night when he got attacked?"

"Yeah. I still don't know what I'm doing here."

She got it. What normal person would guess he'd be attacked by assassins and have to run for his life? "Me too. Allen, you too?"

"I know that everything was fine until your partner wound up on my operating table."

He was glaring at her, seeming to expect an answer to a question he hadn't asked.

"What are you saying?" she said.

He shifted in his chair. "I don't like being chased from my home. I don't like being shot at. I don't like my life being disrupted."

"You're acting like I had something to do with that."

"Didn't you?"

"No. I don't like it either. I've got a mother at home with multiple sclerosis, and I can't get to her, can't help her. The man you watched die on your table was my partner, yes, but he was also my best friend. He recognized one of the men who killed him. He thought he was a federal agent. So until I find out what's going on, I can't go back to my own agency, and I can't call in the troops. I'm out in the cold, and you're making it colder."

The confrontational expression remained hard on his face; then it softened and he said, "You hungry?"

"Famished, I think."

Allen gestured to the waiter, and all three ordered.

Julia unrolled flatware out of a cloth napkin, shook it out, and dropped it into her lap. As she did, she asked, "What kind of food do you like, Allen?"

He paused to look at her. "Steak, mostly. Seafood. Italian. Anything prepared well."

"I'm partial to Cajun. Blackened catfish, jambalaya, mmm. Where were you born—around here?"

"Chattanooga. Our father's a GP there, as was his father."

"Family business."

"Yes," he said, his eyes on Stephen.

Cool's the word, she thought. Allen didn't fidget. He looked her straight in the eyes. In her experience, the cooler the customer, the easier it was for him to lie. That was her reason for asking unimportant questions—she wanted to witness his behavioral baseline when he wasn't lying. Later, if his behavior changed, she would have cause for suspicion.

"So," she said, "what happened yesterday?"

He shook his head, then nodded, glanced at his brother, opened his mouth, shut it again. Clearly he wasn't sure where to start.

"Let me tell you my end," she offered. She told them about the call to pick up Vero, the hit attempt and escape that separated her from Goody, the loss of the SATD signal, Goody's call, the hospital. She explained how she went to the bar to examine the crime scene, but excluded mention of the memory chip. She didn't want to reveal her entire hand until she knew these men better, knew what part they would play in this situation's resolution, if any. She described her encounter with the assassin and the end he met.

Allen said, "You said the cops killed him. You think he's the same one who attacked me at home?"

She nodded. "Big guy, glasses, laser-sighted handgun."

Allen began his story with Goody's presentation in the ER. He described the wounds and the razor disk he found lodged in Goody's sternum.

As hard as she tried to stay objective and removed, Allen's words sliced her heart, just as those disks had sliced Goody. She was certain the memory always would. To get her mind off the details of his death, she said, "The only common denominator between us is Goody. So you think the attack against you has to do with him?"

"Absolutely. Just before I was attacked, a police lieutenant called. He said several other people who'd been with Donnelley between when he was shot and when he died in the trauma room were attacked and killed."

Julia's face expressed the shock she felt. "The killer must have been looking for something. Or else trying to keep people quiet about what they think Goody might have said. Did he say anything to you?"

"Oh yeah. For one, he said filoviruses are man-made."

"Man-made? You mean . . . like in a lab?"

Allen nodded. "And we're talking some nasty stuff.

Marburg. Ebola. Severe hemorrhagic fever. Internal organs start to decay as though you're already dead, but you aren't. Your blood loses its ability to clot; then your endothelial cells, which form the lining of the blood vessels, fail to function, so blood leaks through. Soon it oozes from every orifice—the obvious ones and even from your eyes, pores, and under your fingernails. Then you die."

Julia wasn't hungry anymore.

"Most people think of the outbreaks in Africa," Allen continued. "But Ebola has struck in the Philippines, Italy, England. The strain known as Reston takes its name from the town in Virginia where it was first discovered. In 1996, a case of Ebola was reported in Texas. Marburg was first recognized in Marburg and Frankfurt, Germany, and Belgrade, Yugoslavia."

"But *man-made*? What does that mean?"

"Just that, I guess. Somebody *created* it. It was genetically engineered. Whenever a terrible new virus is discovered, everyone just assumes it was some kind of natural mutation or that it's been lying around dormant for tens of thousands of years until something—man's encroachment into its territory, presumably—reactivated it or exposed humans to something that was always there."

"Of course we'd think that," Stephen interjected. "After all, who'd want to *make* something that terrible?"

"But maybe somebody has," said Allen.

"Is that even possible?" Julia asked.

"With what's going on in genetics these days, anything's possible," Allen said. "When Marburg first surfaced, doctors thought they were dealing with a strain of Rhabdoviridae—rabies. Maybe somebody genetically altered a rhabdovirus, I don't know, but on closer inspection they realized what they had on their hands was an entirely new family of virus. Filoviruses . . . Ebola is completely unlike any other known human pathogen. Its physical appearance is long and thin, like a snake—appropriate, considering its stealthy and deadly disposition. And it secretes an unusually high concentration of glycoprotein that shields it from the immune system. That means there are no vaccines and no cures."

"If you get it, you die?"

"Not necessarily. Some victims survive. No one knows why."

"But that's changing," said Stephen. "Allen looked into it last night. Ebola is getting worse, more virulent, as if someone is *improving* its effectiveness."

Julia stared at Stephen, then turned to Allen for confirmation.

"It's true," he said. "The first Marburg outbreak had a 28 percent mortality rate. Ten years later, the Ebola-Zaire's mortality was up to 75 percent. In 2001, it hit 90 percent. It's now one of the most lethal viruses ever known."

"As if that weren't enough," added Stephen, "transmission of the disease is getting more volatile. Earlier strains showed no signs of spreading through the air. Direct transmission was by contact with blood and other secretions containing high titers of virus. Then, about ten years ago, the Army reported that healthy monkeys caged across the room from monkeys with Ebola got infected. The Ebola had become airborne. Was this a natural evolution of the virus?" His bushy eyebrows shot up. "Or the fruition of someone's efforts to make the disease more deadly?"

Julia shook her head. "But why? I mean, it doesn't make sense."

"It makes perfect sense," said Allen. "Think about it. A

disease with no known cure. No way to vaccinate against it. The person who controls such a thing could hold the world hostage. Symptoms of Ebola exhibit quickly, often just a few hours after infection. And it kills quickly, usually within a couple weeks. The short incubation means a tight quarantine can keep it from spreading out of control. But if someone were to systematically infect pockets of the population, he could wipe out whole societies without losing much control over its spread."

The table fell silent for a full minute. Julia stared down at her half-eaten sandwich, watching the tuna salad ooze from the croissant. She couldn't grasp the full implications of Allen's words; her mind would not project itself past the popular horror stories of Ebola's effects on the human body. But she did know that if people had created this disease, they would kill to keep it secret.

In fact, she thought, *such people would be highly proficient at killing.*

thirty-seven

HE WAS ALMOST THERE. TEN MINUTES, ACCORDING TO THE rental car's GPS. Seven minutes, the way he was driving. He anticipated finding three targets. He'd try to take one alive, use him or her to retrieve his employer's property. He had never failed an assignment, and he didn't want to start now. Truth was, however, he didn't care too much about the property . . . or his employer. He *did* care about the targets.

He cared a *lot* about *them*.

Tension in his face. In the muscles of his forearms and hands. Bad for battle.

He focused on the sound of the radio coming through the car's cheap speakers: a country melody . . . heavy metal . . . some loudmouth ranting about a local politician's drive to . . . classical music—Vivaldi, the driver decided. The Red Priest. And what had that politician been up to? He wanted to raise the cost of parking meters—yeah, that was it. The radio jumped to the next station on the dial. A commercial for "champagne homes on a beer budget . . ."

He felt calmer.

Champagne homes on a beer budget. Who thought up these things?

His foot edged down on the accelerator, and he shot through a light just as it turned red.

GPS said eight minutes. He said five.

thirty-eight

"THERE'S ONE MORE THING THAT LENDS CREDIBILITY TO what your partner told me," Allen said, poking at the fries on his plate. "No one has been able to find where Ebola resides when it is not in monkeys or humans. It disappears for years at a time, but no reservoir has been found, despite testing thousands of animals and insects." He gave her a sideways glance, as if to say, *Are you following?*

"You're suggesting it can't be found in nature because it's not there."

"Pretty *and* smart," he said with a wink at Stephen. "The reservoir is actually a test tube in some mad scientist's lab. He keeps it there until it's time for another field test. Then back into nature it goes so he can watch what happens."

"Wait a minute," Julia said. "Isn't it possible that a virus can mutate itself in the ways you've described, for no other reason than its own survival?"

"Certainly."

"And scientists still might find a nonhuman reservoir in nature and figure out natural reasons for those other odd things about Ebola, right?"

"It's possible."

"I mean, you *are* viewing the evidence through the lens of suspicion."

"And in the context of a murderous cover-up," he agreed.

"Why wouldn't somebody have blown the top off this years ago?"

"Julia, I can only guess." Allen snatched a fry off her plate, bit it in two, and flicked the remainder at Stephen. "Maybe these guys are good at hiding. If they have been introducing Ebola into the population every time they needed to test it, they've been smart about it; probably giving it to monkeys first, or even infecting humans *through* monkeys, to throw investigators off the trail. In Africa they found the perfect red herring: poor countries where shoddy communication, transportation, and medical expertise combine with rough terrain and a staggering number of possible insect and animal vectors to hinder ecological investigations and throw a cloud of mystique over the whole puzzle. It *is* the Dark Continent."

"You're forgetting the more probable reason," said Stephen. "Look at the situation we're in. We may or may not know something, yet somebody is going all out to silence us. How do we know that other people, people before us, haven't *tried* to blow the top off, only to be stopped? By all indications, we're messing with powerful people."

They sat quietly for a while, looking at their partially eaten lunches, at each other, but not really at anything. The shadow under their umbrella seemed to have darkened.

"Okay," Julia said, pushing away her plate. "Let's say someone *is* making Ebola. Unless they're doing something more, I can't see—"

"They are," Allen said. "I think they are. The way your partner put it was—and I'm not trying to embellish or interpret—'bio . . . attack . . . filovirus . . .' I asked when. He said, 'Already happening.'"

Julia said, "'Under way'? That's what he said."

"We've got to do something," Stephen said, leaning in.

"I agree," she said. "But what?"

Allen said, "The sooner this breaks open, the sooner the heat's off us."

"Any ideas?"

"The media. Newspapers, television. It'll make headlines for a year."

"Allen, it's not going to happen," Stephen said with a dismissive wave of his hand. His frustrated tone told Julia the two had already covered this ground. "There's not a news organization in the country that'll touch this story without proof."

"Look!" Allen leaned on his elbows over the table, bringing his face to within a foot of Stephen's.

The wooden pole of the umbrella perfectly separated their firm profiles. The image reminded Julia of a billboard she'd seen outside Atlantic City for what promoters billed "the fight of the century." The Parkers made credible stand-ins for the boxers: handsome Allen would be the media darling—witty, enchanting, nimble of tongue and foot. But hulking Stephen would be the hands-down favorite, a monolith of unyielding muscle. She suspected that their discord ran deeper than the disagreement at hand.

"I know people, media heavyweights, who could help," Allen continued.

"You could be joined at the hip to Katie Couric—it's not gonna matter."

"You have a better idea?"

Stephen turned to Julia. "You're FBI?"

"Sort of. Like a division of it."

"Can we go there?"

Allen jumped in. "I told you, I'm not going to—"

Julia held up her hand to stop him. "Yesterday morning, I would have said there wasn't anyone in my agency or the Bureau I wouldn't trust. Now I don't know. What I do know is someone highjacked a satellite signal that's supposedly impossible to highjack. At least one, maybe two, hit squads are in play; they're not being discreet and they're not afraid of killing federal agents. At least two of them were probably cops, so whoever hired them has connections within the law-enforcement community. All of this may have something to do with a man-made virus, which means either terrorism or the military. It's hard for me to imagine that the government isn't involved in this at some level. The muscles that are flexing are way too big to be private."

"The media, then," Allen said, leaning back, vindicated.

"I don't think so," she said. "I agree with Stephen. Unless you have hard evidence to support your claims, no reputable news agency will come near this. Your connections might get you lunch and a pat on the back, but that's all."

She raised her hand again to halt Allen's objection. "I'm not saying this isn't a huge story, but to newspeople, your saying that it is doesn't mean squat."

It was clear to her that Allen was not accustomed to being contradicted. The flesh on his face seemed to harden. His tight lips pushed out a bit, sliding back and forth slowly, as though he were working on a jawbreaker. His eyes bore into hers, unflinching. He'd obviously perfected this countenance of wrath to a degree that caused nurses, med students, and even colleagues to acquiesce rather than endure the gaze.

She leaned into it. "Contacting the media now will do nothing but tell our pursuers how much we know and where we are."

"The killings," he said. "The condition of Donnelley's body, his words . . ."

"Just words," Julia said, firm. "And nobody heard what he said but you, right?"

"You don't believe me?"

She hesitated a beat. "I do, because Goody told me some of the same things. And I'm not the media. You'd have to convince some pretty jaded people whose livelihood depends on checking and double-checking the facts. Even if they were to give you the benefit of the doubt, they'd keep the story under wraps until they investigated, until they were *sure*. That would give the people after us time to do what they probably do best: silence nosy journalists and their informants."

Allen blinked slowly. He was listening.

"Going to the press would put the spotlight on us, not them. Of course, you could sell the story to one of those grocery-store gossip rags. It'd be right next to a feature about the three-headed pig-boy who ate his neighbor."

His facial muscles relaxed. A slight twitch at the corner of his mouth formed into a shallow smile. This seemed to signal a kind of forgiveness of her insubordination. He glanced around, as if realizing for the first time where they were. He nodded. "So where does that leave us?"

Julia looked at Stephen, his big, hairy face open to her,

anxious for an answer. She moved her attention back to Allen. He was more cynical than his brother, more cocksure, even now, when he was scared and unsure.

"Where that leaves us is alone."

thirty-nine

"So what do you suggest?" Allen asked.

She returned his gaze for a time, then turned her head to stare vacantly at the sidewalk beyond the patio's perimeter. Feet clad in various forms of shoes strode across her field of vision, but her mind registered none of them. Their situation was like a hole, into which she tried to fit a myriad of solutions. As idea after idea flashed into her mind, she'd size it up, hold it next to the hole, discard it for the next one. After a minute she looked up.

"Evidence. Whatever we eventually do—go to the media, go to the cops—we need to bring evidence. I have something from Vero, a memory chip. It may be all we need, but it's encoded. I may have fixed that, but until we know for sure, we should turn over a few rocks, see what we find."

"*We're* going to investigate?" Allen's voice was high with disbelief.

"Have to," said Julia, distracted by the plan forming inside. "I can pull some info off of various data banks, find out what the Bureau knows, maybe the status of the investigation in Chattanooga. That may lead us to more clues, more avenues of discovery. We don't know yet what we're looking for exactly, but that's how all investigations start. Before you know it, the pieces fall together, and you have enough to make a case."

"Where do we start?" Stephen asked, ready.

"I'm thinking . . ."

"Well, no matter how you cut it, we're on the run," Allen said. "I've never been on the lam before, but I imagine it can get expensive—food, transportation, hotels."

"And no credit cards," Julia said. She'd obtained her new car this morning from a rent-a-lemon place that accepted an extra fifty bucks and photocopies of her driver's license and LED creds in lieu of a major credit card. Now she was almost out of cash, and she hadn't considered where she would get more without leaving a paper trail.

"How about this?" He nodded at a business across the street. "That's a branch of a bank my dad uses. We called him this morning. He arranged a cash withdrawal in Stephen's name. I don't have my ID. We get the money, go somewhere, decide what to do."

"You've thought this through," she said, impressed.

"Leave it to Allen to nail the money angle," Stephen quipped.

"Speaking of which . . ." Allen's eyes made a sweep of the dishes.

Stephen pulled out his wallet and dropped two bills on the table, a big grin pushing away the hair around his mouth.

"Allen sans cash," he said. "I never thought I'd see the day. Be right back."

He stood, stepping back from under the umbrella to avoid pushing it up by his towering height. He stepped over the patio's railing into the blazing sun. He squinted in one direction, then the other, waited for a car to pass, and jogged across the street. Julia marveled at the gracefulness of his movements.

"I need to make a call," she said. She tossed her napkin onto her plate and stood, pulling the gym bag up by its strap. "I saw a phone inside."

"I'll go with you."

"Suit yourself."

She tugged open the big French door that serviced the restaurant and stepped in. Over her shoulder, she said, "I'm only calling my mother. You don't have to—"

Then she saw him: crossing the street, as though he'd been watching them from a nearby storefront, and he'd seen Stephen go into the bank. Everything faded away. She saw only him, moving as if in slow motion, letting a car pass, darting behind it. Straight for the bank.

"What? *What?*" Allen's words sounded muffled, far away.

Jet-black hair, sticking up in spots. Thick-framed glasses. Tall and muscular.

"Julia, you're pale as a ghost."

She pushed past him, back onto the patio.

"Allen . . ." She pointed.

The man was standing in front of the bank's front window, peering in.

"What? I . . ." Allen started, then: "That looks like . . . I thought you said he was dead. You said he got blown away. That can't be him."

"It *is* him. That's the guy I saw the cops kill last night."

Her hand went to her pistol. It rested on the handgrip as she watched the assassin pause for a woman exiting the bank. He slipped into the space behind her, and the glass door closed. He was inside.

forty

"IT WASN'T HIM." ALLEN WAS LEANING CLOSE TO HER, HIS hand on her shoulder. Already they were drawing stares.

"You know it was." *But how?* She had not seen a bruise or cut or bullet wound.

He echoed her thoughts: "How can that be?"

"I don't know. I just . . . *don't know.*" Her mind poked at possibilities, but none of them made any sense. "We have to get Stephen out of there." She pulled out her mobile phone, flipped it open, and dialed 411.

"I thought we didn't want to use cell phones."

"They already know where we are." She recited the name of the bank. Ten seconds later, a computer voice informed her it was making the connection at no additional charge.

Allen said, "He might follow Stephen into the bathroom. Or the way these guys are, just go after him right in the lobby."

"I know, Allen. Shut up a second."

The receptionist inside the bank answered. Julia made her voice low and gravelly. "There's a bomb inside the building. In two minutes, you're *soup*." She flipped the phone shut. Two minutes would not give the bank manager time to consider his options.

"Soup?" Allen asked.

"Nice image, huh? If you were that receptionist, think you'd be giving the manager an earful about evacuating the building?"

"I'd probably just leave."

She looked at him. If he was joking, he showed no sign of it.

"Let's hope she's cut from a different bolt."

She hoisted the gym bag to her side, pulling the strap over her head to cross her body like a bandolier. She didn't want to lose it if things got crazy. They walked around the tables in front of them and stepped over the railing. She hoped Stephen would pile out with the crowd and beeline it for them. She'd lead them around the corner to her car, staving off the killer with her pistol, if necessary.

The bank doors swung open, and a nicely dressed woman shot out at the head of a massive knot of people. They pushed and shoved and exploded from the narrow doorway, spilling into the street. Cars braked and stopped. Somehow, the word had spread to the three-story building's upper floors; Julia could see bodies moving quickly out of the front-facing offices.

"Yell at him when he comes out," she said. "Tell him to run, just run. Anywhere."

She stepped off the curb. She was considering going into the bank. A movement in a second-floor window caught her eye.

It was Stephen.

He was looking through the closed window at the insanity on the sidewalk below; then he raised his head, searching for Allen and Julia. She waved her arms. He spotted her and shrugged.

Come on! she motioned.

He nodded and pushed up on the frame. It wouldn't budge. He leaned over and made a hammering gesture. Someone had nailed the windows shut, probably upon retrofitting the building with central air. He tried again. She could see his face contort. With a crack she could hear from across the street, the window frame splintered, and the glass panel rose six inches . . . Another heave and it opened to a foot . . . then another two—enough for him to climb through.

She ran to the street's center line, sensing Allen behind her. Cars had stopped in both directions as bank customers and office workers milled about on the far side of the street. Heat radiated from the blacktop. Beads of perspiration sprang out on her forehead, her upper lip.

"Get out now!" she yelled.

The crowd, noticing the big man somehow stuck in the doomed building, joined in. Shouts rang out: "Come on, man!" "Get out!" "Jump!"

But the second floor was too high above the concrete pavement.

"He's in the bank, Stephen!" Allen called. "The killer!"

Stephen's face changed from confusion to concern. He began assessing his options. He eyed the arching fabric canopy jutting out from an expensive perfume shop next door.

"Hang from the ledge! Hang and fall! Now, Stephen, now!"

He nodded and immediately swung his leg through the

opening. The crowd roared its approval. Crouching on the ledge, facing the window, he assessed the distance down, scanned the edge for handholds. His right hand clutched an envelope. He began to lower himself from the ledge when a shadow flashed in the room behind him. Wood and glass exploded over him. A fist shot out, grabbing hold of the hair on top of his head. Stephen jerked his head around, tethered to the fist. He wrenched his head back hard and lunged away from the window as far as his arms would stretch. A black arm and fist came out of the window, missing his face by inches.

Julia pulled in her breath. The fist bore hard spikes in the black knuckles—the killer was wearing the gauntlet she had retrieved from her mangled dashboard. Her hand dropped down to the gym bag hanging at her side. Through its nylon walls, she felt it, solid as a fossilized arm.

Another gauntlet!

This assailant was not merely similar to the one she'd seen killed; he was precisely the same.

She drew her pistol and watched as Stephen kicked off of the building, flying backward.

forty-one

THE GAUNTLET HAD NOT MISSED STEPHEN'S FACE. HE FELT it nick his brow. Warm liquid stung his eye. The black fist retreated, pistoning back for another strike. If the assailant leaned out, the fist would reach his head.

Stephen released his grasp on the window frame, focused all his strength into his legs, and pushed out, cranking his body sideways as he did. The arm crashed through the remaining glass, reaching for him. Pellets of glass hit his face, flew past him. The attacker's head and shoulders leaned out of the window. He had chiseled features, a twisted mouth, blazing green eyes behind nerdy glasses.

Stephen hit the canopy with a great *whup!* His left shoulder caught a rib of the iron frame; the awning buckled, following the downward momentum of his body. Pain flashed up his side into his jaw. Maroon canvas enveloped him, closing out the sky above. He slammed to a stop. He thought he'd hit the pavement, then realized he was cradled in a hammock of fabric, rocking slowly. He scrambled to break free, probing for the ground with his foot. He found it, not far away, and spilled out onto it. His shoulder radiated lightning bolts of pain, and his arm felt numb to the elbow. He realized he was still holding the envelope of cash. He shoved it into his back pocket.

In the street to his left, Julia crouched in a target-shooting stance, holding her pistol in both hands and pointing it, lock-armed, at the window above. Stephen turned to look, saw nothing.

"This way!" Julia yelled, pointing in a direction that would cause him to cross in front of the bank. Her eyes never left the shattered window.

He hesitated, puzzled. She had approached the café from the opposite direction. Then it came to him: the crowd he'd only half noticed from the window had grown exponentially in the brief time it took him to make it down to the street. Gawking people stood at least ten deep in a wide semicircle, of which the bank was the epicenter. But no one dared to approach the area in front of the bank or the sidewalk for thirty yards on either side; Julia had chosen the path of least resistance.

Allen darted past her, toward the end of the block. That was enough to prompt Stephen to run as well. Julia moved sideways fast, keeping the gun poised at the window. She joined Stephen on the sidewalk on the opposite side of the bank from the canopied store.

The crowd made a sharp sound as if they were catching their breath all at the same time, apparently seeing something that was out of Stephen's view.

Another window above him erupted.

As the first fragments of debris struck his head, Stephen grabbed Julia's arm, pitching her forward, away from the destruction.

Then it came: big and heavy, smashing into the pavement behind him.

He swung around. A body was crumpled low, covered in glass and wood chips. For a moment, he was certain the assailant had hurled somebody through the window, hoping to crush Stephen. Then the shoulders moved, shaking off the debris. A face turned up to him. It was his attacker. He rose, shedding glass. Blood trickled from cuts in his forehead and cheek.

Stephen assessed the situation, realized that running was pointless. The man would overtake them all with predatory ease.

Stephen took a step back and opened his arms, a gesture of peace. "What is this, man?" he asked.

The assailant grinned, humorless and cold. But it was his eyes that convinced Stephen: he was here to kill. Nothing was going to stop him.

Nothing but me, Stephen thought.

He brought his left leg forward and shifted his hips back over his right leg—a *hu kool chase* stance. He was ready to kick or defend.

"Stephen!" It was Julia. "I got him. Get out of the way!"

The killer moved in, thrusting his armored fist forward, cat-quick.

Stephen parried the blow with an upward sweep of his left forearm. The impact was like slamming into a car bumper, but he succeeded in knocking the fist off course. Even before their arms made contact, Stephen's right arm sailed forward, the heel of his palm aiming for the spot between the nose and upper lip. A well-placed blow would cause incapacitating pain.

He never made contact.

As if time skipped a few beats, the killer was gripping Stephen's wrist, stopping the locomotion power of his hand two inches before its target.

The assailant glared at Stephen, inches from his face. Stephen saw nothing in his opponent's countenance but animal fury. Then the killer twisted his lips into what might pass as a smile in certain demonic circles and nodded. The gesture said, *Touché*.

"We don't have to do this," Stephen said through clenched teeth. He knew they did, but deep inside, he remembered the last time he had battled; his conscience didn't want to be here.

The assailant pulled down fiercely on Stephen's arm, bringing his knee up at the same time, calculated to shatter the radius and ulna.

Anticipating the motion, Stephen swiveled his hips. The blow struck him hard on the thigh. Turning his defensive movement into an offensive one, Stephen swung his leg between them, then around his opponent's side. He yanked his leg back. It collided with the killer's leg, on which all his weight rested. His mind jumped ahead, working through the motions he'd make as his opponent hit the ground.

Which he never did.

Normally, a man will protect himself in a fall by swinging his arms toward the ground, but the killer never released Stephen's right wrist. Instead, he used it to hold himself up and pivot around with the force of Stephen's kick. Before Stephen realized what was happening, the killer's back was to him, and he felt himself pulled by his arm over the killer's head. He collided with the sidewalk. He sensed movement over him and rolled. The gauntlet smashed into the pavement where his face had been, kicking up rock chips and a quick plume of concrete dust.

If he'd kept rolling away, as his mind screamed at him to do, he knew his opponent would jump ahead, pin him, and kill him. Instead, he rolled back, grabbing hold of the killer's arm with both hands. Before the killer had a chance to kick, Stephen hoisted his lower body into the air and planted a stunning blow with the tip of his boot into the top of the man's head. Anchored by Stephen's grip on his arm, the killer staggered . . .

Then dropped his knee onto Stephen's forehead.

forty-two

LIGHT SWAM BACK INTO HIS MIND, FORMING ITSELF INTO images: the building on his left, blue sky, white clouds, a flash of leg, and the killer standing over him, poised to bring his spiked fist into Stephen's head.

Stephen swung his arm straight up, aiming for the clouds high above. He struck the killer between the legs.

The gauntleted warrior tumbled away.

Stephen rolled and pushed himself up. He kicked out, catching the man in the side. As the killer staggered back, Stephen lowered his torso and kicked his booted heel into his opponent's sternum.

The killer flew backward into the bank's display window, crashing through and disappearing behind a waterfall of shattering glass. A huge pane sliced down like a guillotine. An instant later, Stephen caught the full force of a roundhouse kick to the side of his head as the killer leaped over the glass-toothed sill. Stephen's head snapped back painfully. He wanted to fall, to let the black cloud hovering at the edge of his consciousness engulf him and just . . . fall. Instead, he jerked his head upright and raged the black cloud away—just in time to see a saber-sized sheet of glass arcing on a horizontal plane toward his neck, blurring with speed.

He ducked.

The glass, clasped in the killer's hands, disappeared in a screaming, dissolving collision with the brick that flanked the bank's windows.

Stephen drove his head into the killer's stomach and felt the pain of a fist gripping the hair on the back of his head. Rather than pull back, he pushed forward, knocking his opponent off balance. They both went down. As the killer hit concrete, Stephen somersaulted over him, using the momentum to tear his head away from the fist.

He felt like he'd been cracked on the back of the head with a lead pipe. He blocked out the pain; it was something he was getting used to.

He rolled away, tumbling out of the killer's reach. On his feet, down for mere seconds.

The killer too—standing ten feet away, bent at the knees, arms out like an attacking wrestler. He rocked slightly on the balls of his feet, ready. The man was tall, only slightly shorter than he was, maybe six foot four. At roughly 260 muscular pounds, the man's proportions were similar to a body builder's; he possessed none of the lankiness common among tall men. Through the unzipped opening of the black Windbreaker, a dark green pullover clung to bulging pectorals. Quick eyes watched Stephen's every move.

Stephen sucked in a deep breath, then another. Sweat stung

his eye. He tasted blood: a lot of it. A chill trickled down his spine as he realized the killer was breathing in the unhurried rhythm of a body at rest, barely perceptible in the shallow rise and fall of his massive chest. No perspiration at all. Just blood. Cuts and gashes and scrapes freckled the killer's face and one visible hand . . . a hand that still clutched a clump of brown, bloody hair and what looked like—a piece of *scalp*.

The attacker raised his fist to examine his prize. He focused on Stephen and smiled.

"That's *gotta* hurt," he said in a strong voice, no trace of humor. He casually pushed the hair into the breast pocket of the Windbreaker, seeming to dare Stephen to retrieve what had been taken from him.

"Stephen!"

It was Allen, behind him some distance. Panicked, by the sound of his voice.

The killer glared.

"Run, Stephen!"

"Stephen, I can get him." Julia's voice, closer. Cool as a whole patch of cucumbers. "Move out of the way."

He glanced back quickly. Julia was on the sidewalk right behind him, thirty feet—

"Watch—!" she screamed, and he dropped straight down, knowing what was coming. The gauntlet passed over him, so close he felt it stir the hair remaining on top of his head. He rolled into the killer's legs, but the killer leaped away so fast it was as though he had never been there. Stephen swept his massive leg around, appearing to target his opponent's ankles, but intending only to buy enough time to jump up.

When he did, he found the killer several steps away, nearly under the uncrushed part of the canopy that had cushioned Stephen's fall.

The man moved to strike a blow to Stephen's chest, but pulled away at the last moment.

Stephen kicked out, realizing too late that his assailant had feigned the punch to draw him in.

The killer caught hold of his leg, pinning it between the crook of his left arm and one of the poles that held the canopy frame. Stephen tugged, but he might as well have had his foot encased in the foundation of a building. He bounced on one foot, trying to keep his balance. He swung around to twist free, but the killer moved with him, countering his movements.

Pain fades in the heat of battle as the mind locks in on survival. But even a brief reprieve in the action can send it rushing back, as it did now for Stephen. His head felt cleaved, his shoulder savagely wrenched.

His opponent flashed that evil smile again, superior, unflinching.

As if in slow motion, the killer's arm, spiked and rock solid, pivoted back, then surged forward. Stephen tried to bring his arm around to block the blow but missed. He twisted sideways and felt the crushing impact on his ribs. The air burst from his lungs. He hitched for air that wouldn't come. Then he saw the killer bring his arm back for another strike. His enemy had been targeting his head all along; Stephen knew this one would find its mark, a blow he wouldn't, couldn't survive.

Then a gunshot rang out, sharp and close. Sparks sprang like fireworks from the pole in front of the killer's face.

Stephen was free, falling, crashing to the ground.

Another shot.

Vaguely he sensed someone running toward him, past him, stopping at his feet: Julia, gun in hand, taking aim. Someone else, Allen, rushed to him, tugging at his arm.

"Stephen! Come on, man! Let's go!"

Allen straddled him, lifting him. Stephen felt all the pain in the world shatter his body. He growled more than screamed. Allen raised his palm, drenched in blood, and grimaced.

"Can you move?"

The question prompted him to try. Catching a rush of adrenaline, he rose, then staggered. Allen moved to his left side, slipping under his arm, and maneuvered him away from the canopy. Stephen gasped for air, found he could breathe again. Fire radiated from numbness on his left side, pulsing fingers of it reaching toward his heart, his head, making his legs weak.

But with each step, each breath, he felt stronger. He pushed away from Allen to stand on his own. He was shaky, still in pain, but otherwise okay—he thought.

It'd take more than that to keep this old fighter down.

He sensed chaos all along the block, people screaming and scattering at the sight of guns, others watching the action from behind cars. Somewhere in the distance sirens wailed. He turned. Julia was occupying the spot where the killer had pinned him to the canopy pole. Gym bag slung over one shoulder, she clutched her gun at the end of two stiff arms, aiming. He looked past her in time to see the killer peer around the corner of a recessed entryway two storefronts away. She'd managed to drive him away, but not far. Julia fired, and a brick erupted near the killer's head.

"Go!" she yelled. "Go!"

A huge black gun sprang out from the entryway, turned toward them, spat smoke. Julia dodged to the left. Allen pulled at Stephen. Both spun and moved down the sidewalk, close to the buildings. The best Stephen could muster was a loping gallop. Allen moved in to help again, supporting and steering him.

At the corner, Stephen paused long enough to see Julia moving backward toward them, pistol poised. Then he and Allen were around the corner, into a different world where crowds didn't gather to witness bloody battles. Halfway down the block, in the circular drive of the Marriott-Knoxville's entrance, guests pulled luggage from their cars' trunks. Taxis and private vehicles lined both sides of the street.

A shot rang out, and Julia rounded the corner, crashing into them.

"Move it! He's coming!"

They bolted toward the hotel entrance; then Julia yelled, "Wait! Wait! Not there. It's too obvious."

She scanned the narrow stores that occupied this half of the block. All the shops carried expensive jewelry, clothes, and objets d'art. Their facades were all display windows and glass doors, which led no doubt into tastefully sparse show-rooms; none looked like a particularly shrewd place to hide. Certainly they had back rooms, but not necessarily rear exits.

"The hotel!" Stephen rasped. "It's the only way!"

"No, here!" Allen said, pointing at the curb.

"What?" Stephen asked.

"Yes!" Julia said. "Under the cars! Now!"

She dove into the space between two parked cars, pushed the gym bag under the front one, and disappeared after it. Allen shoved Stephen toward the car behind hers and shim-mied under the vehicle behind that. Stephen hunkered down and slid into the narrow space. Something bit into his back, and he pushed closer to the asphalt, scraping his body along. He craned his neck to be sure his legs weren't exposed.

Through the slim opening between the high curb and the car frame, he witnessed the killer's head pop around the corner. Gone again. A second later, he swung into view, a silenced pistol extending from one arm. Failing to spot his quarry, he lowered the gun and stepped to the first display window. He moved to the next window, spinning around between the first and second to check the area across the street and down toward the hotel. He moved with fathomless agility, like water erupting from a fountain. He flowed past Allen, past Stephen.

A boy of about thirteen on a skateboard approached at top speed, the wheels of his ride *clack-clack-clacking* on the pavement seams. The killer's arm shot out. He grabbed the boy by the shirt and lifted him off the skateboard, which sailed on without him.

"Where are they, boy?" the killer hissed into the teen's face. "A woman. Two men. Where?"

"I . . . I . . . don't know what you're talking—"

He tossed the boy aside like dirty laundry. The kid tumbled on the cement, coming to a stop facedown. When he lifted his head, he was staring right at Julia.

forty-three

THE BOY'S EYES WERE HUGE. HIS MOUTH QUIVERED, AND she was sure he would scream out.

She raised a finger to her lips.

The boy rotated his head a bit, saw Stephen under the car behind her. He swiveled around to look over his shoulder. The killer was glaring into a store window thirty feet away. He turned again to Julia, frightened eyes staring into frightened eyes. With a slight smile, he hopped up and bolted away from the killer, toward his wayward skateboard.

More man in that boy than I thought.

As the killer made his way toward the entrance of the Marriott-Knoxville, Julia tried to anticipate his moves. Would he assume they took refuge in the hotel? Would the lobby area occupy his time long enough for them to escape? Or would he simply threaten the valets for information, as he had the boy? Perhaps this time with his pistol—picking off one to motivate the others.

Yes, she suspected that was his style.

Even if no one had seen them dive under the cars, the valets would surely convince him that the three hadn't entered the hotel. He'd keep tracking them outside, eventually thinking to look under the parked cars.

So what to do?

A pebble bore into her elbow. She tried to push it away and knocked her head painfully on the car's undercarriage. Something warm and wet touched her scalp—blood or oil. No matter . . .

He was almost at the hotel entrance. Could she bear to see him sacrifice a life in his search for them? No way. A threatening move was all it would take to push her into offensive action.

Images of last night's firefight brought a dark cloud of pessimism to her thoughts. Acid roiled through her stomach, and her mind ached at the need to know how this man had survived, how he had *come back*. Even in the heat of battle, the perplexity of it pushed at her thoughts. Had last night really happened at all? Had she been hypnotized? Drugged? Was she going crazy?

Not now, Julia! she scolded herself. *Focus.* Focus on this killer—whoever, whatever he was.

He had turned from the window and was scanning the row of cars parked along the street, paying particular attention to the taxicabs closest to the hotel entrance. He stepped to the next store's window.

She fished something out of a side pocket of the gym bag, then twisted around to look back at Stephen. The big man was absolutely *packed* under the vehicle. Bits of gravel clung to his beard, and a smudge of grease marred his forehead. His face expressed miserable distress. He spread his hands and opened his eyes wide, as if to say, *What are we going to do?*

She signaled him to stay put. Behind him, Allen was making emphatic hand movements at her, shaping his hand into the form of a pistol and jabbing it toward the killer: *Shoot him!* She gave Allen the stay-put signal as well. She crawled on her belly until her head was even with the front bumper. The car in front of her was a taxi. The killer had just stepped to the next store window when she made her move: she crawled out from under the car, staying low; then she turned onto her back and pushed herself under the taxi. A few moments later, her head popped out from under the vehicle on the street side. As she expected on this hot day and with the engine turned off, the cabbie's window was down.

"Hey," she whispered sharply. When there was no reaction evident in the elbow that protruded from the window, she tapped on the door. The elbow disappeared, and the car rocked a bit as the cabbie looked around.

"Down here!"

The door opened just a crack, and a startled face looked down at her.

"What the—?" he began, but she stopped him by displaying her badge and photo ID.

"Shhhhh," she whispered. "I'm a federal agent." She flipped her credentials case closed and raised the other hand, which held a wad of cash. "Take this, close your door quietly, and I'll tell you what I need you to do."

He hesitated briefly, then did as she had instructed.

While he was counting the bills, she whispered, "Don't look my way. Just do what you were doing before I got here." She lowered her head to see that the killer had reached the hotel and was scanning the area. She tucked her head under the car before a passing vehicle took it off. She whispered louder.

"Okay, listen. Give me fifteen seconds to get out from under here, then burn rubber outta here. Make a U-ie and haul down the street as fast as you can. Don't stop for anything—lights, traffic, anything. Got it?"

The whispered voice floated down from the cabbie's window. "Lady, you only gave me forty-seven bucks."

"It's all I have. If you get in trouble with the cops, with your boss, the Bureau will straighten it out. All you have to do is push it for about five miles, and you're forty-seven dollars richer. Deal?"

"Yeah, yeah. Fifteen seconds."

She backed away from the edge of the cab. Then she saw the killer and froze. He had a valet by the hair, bending him back and gripping his neck with a gauntleted hand. She knew too well what that felt like. She was reaching for her pistol when the cab's engine roared like a waking beast. She moved away fast, banging her head on the muffler. She'd just rolled onto her belly and slipped back under the other car when the cab screeched in reverse, slamming into hers. Grime rained down on her. She wondered frantically if the cabbie had misunderstood or was trying to annoy her, then realized that he had to pull away from the cab in front of him to get out. The rear tires started spinning on the blacktop, generating an unbelievable amount of smoke and sound.

The cab shot out into traffic, cutting a semicircle across three lanes, and sped away in the other direction. Horns blared and wheels locked in a chorus of wailing tires. Several cars smashed into each other.

And the killer did precisely as she had anticipated.

He dropped the valet and galloped into the street after the cab. His feet flashed by Julia's hiding place. She turned to watch his progress, but he was instantly out of sight, lost among the traffic. She heard cars a block away sounding their horns and locking their brakes. The cabbie was doing quite a job for forty-seven bucks.

She was out from under the car in seconds, chunks of greasy dirt falling from her hair and clothes.

"Allen! Stephen! Move it!"

She draped the gym bag's strap over her shoulder and stood on her tiptoes. The killer was two blocks away, only a half block from the cab. He stopped. Julia's breath wedged in her throat—she knew what he was doing. The back window of the cab shattered, shot out by the killer's silenced weapon. The cab veered and bounded onto the sidewalk.

I got him killed!

But it kept moving, coming off the sidewalk and swerving around a parked car. It made a sharp turn and disappeared. It took the killer a full ten seconds to reach the same spot and disappear himself.

Sirens warbled around the corner where the bank stood, then stopped. Witnesses would soon inform the police of the direction they had fled.

Allen and Stephen reached her side, congratulating her for a brilliant move.

"It's not over yet," she said. "Stephen, you going to make it?"

He touched his side and grimaced. "Yeah. Nothing a tight Ace bandage and some ibuprofen won't ease."

"Good enough." She ran to the first taxi in line.

forty-four

AFTER THEY'D CLIMBED IN, THEY WAITED FOR THE DRIVER, who was standing outside his open door, looking in the direction of his apparently berserk colleague. "Driver, we're in a hurry!" Julia called.

He slid in behind the wheel, hooked an arm over the seat back, and glared at them. "I ain't going to do what Frankie just done," he said.

"We don't want you to," Allen said. He held his hand open to Stephen, who pulled the envelope out of his back pocket, groaning when he twisted, and placed it in Allen's hand. Allen pulled out a hundred-dollar bill and held it up. "Will this get us to Maryville?"

Julia was squeezed between Stephen and the door. Through the back window, she'd caught a glimpse of the killer darting between cars, moving quickly toward them.

"Let's go!"

"I can get you there," the driver said slowly, seeming to talk to the money, "for this here tip *plus* the fare there and back."

"Sounds good."

The hundred dollars disappeared into the driver's shirt pocket. He settled himself in behind the wheel and started the meter.

The killer was a block away. His arms pumped like an Olympic sprinter's—an Olympic sprinter with a really big gun.

"Go!" Julia pulled her pistol from its holster under her arm but kept it hidden beneath her jacket.

"Look, lady—"

"Another hundred," Allen said, digging in the bag, "if you do what the lady says. Now!"

The driver slammed the shifter into drive and punched the accelerator.

The killer stopped to aim. Leveling the pistol at the taxi, he jerked toward the sound of squealing tires behind him. He leaped to avoid being struck by a car, came down on its hood, and flipped off, disappearing from Julia's view. When he reappeared, he jumped on top of the car's hood. From that vantage point, he raised his gun again.

Julia caught the glint of the laser's ruby sparkle. Then the cab veered around the corner at Locust Street and roared toward the highway a block away. She holstered her weapon.

Allen tossed the hundred into the front seat, where it disappeared into the driver's shirt pocket. He turned to Julia. "Since when are killers resurrected?" he whispered. It sounded like an accusation.

Stephen groaned and said, "What are you talking about?"

"She said that guy back there was the one she saw shot to death last night!"

"Obviously someone else."

"It was the same person," Julia said.

"Same clothes maybe," suggested Stephen. "Same team of assassins, even. That would make sense if they were recruited under the same criteria: big, bold, tough as nails."

"No. It was him." She touched a sore spot on her neck where his fingers had dug in. "I don't know how to explain it."

A flash of memory caught her off guard: a seventh-grade science assignment to collect as many spiders as possible over a single weekend. Cobweb spiders, wolf spiders, jumping spiders, sac spiders, daddy longlegs. But the crowning jewel of any collection was a black widow. She'd known the prize would be hers. After exhausting the dark recesses of her house, she moved outside, overturning countless boards and stones. Finally she flipped over a chunk of concrete, and there it was: glossy black, the size of a large marble— skittering right toward her bare knee as she knelt in the dirt. She barely jumped away in time and trapped it under a mayonnaise jar. Watching it try to escape, she sensed its dark hostility toward her. The trick would be to kill it without harming its body. She spent hours pushing alcohol-drenched cotton balls under the glass rim. The thing crawled over them, almost mocking. Finally she shot a stream of insecticide at it. It slowly rolled over and pulled in its legs like a fist. Cautiously she removed the jar, then the cotton balls.

It sprang to life. Moving for her, *touching* her hand before she could pull away. Stunned, crying out, she slammed a rock down on it, again and again.

For weeks afterward she'd awaken in the deep hours,

drenched in sweat, swatting away dream spiders that dug into her skin with their fangs.

Something about that spider stayed with her—its intense desire to get her, even defying death for one last chance.

This man, this killer, reminded her of that indomitable black widow.

But he was infinitely more frightening.

"All I know," she said, "is that I saw that man, that one at the bank, blown to bits last night. A cop checked his pulse."

"Could he have been wearing a flak vest?" Stephen offered.

She scowled. "There was so much *blood*."

The brothers stared at her, Allen with doubt in his eyes, Stephen with compassion.

She turned away, caught her reflection in the glass. "I don't know," she said quietly. "Maybe I'm going crazy."

A dark silence filled the cab. At another time the taxi's strong stench of pine cleanser might have offended her; now she was thankful it masked the odor of blood from Stephen's shirt. After pulling onto I-129 south and finding a comfortable speed, the driver snatched the mike off the in-dash CB radio.

Julia leaned forward to touch his shoulder before he keyed it. "What are you doing?" she asked.

"Need to call the fare in. Company regulations."

"Hold on a sec." She turned to Allen, shook her head. He nodded and scooted to the edge of the seat.

"A third hundred," he said, "if your records and your memory say you took us to Oak Ridge."

As the driver appeared to study the road ahead, his hand hooked itself over the seat, palm up. Allen slapped the bill into it. The money joined the other hundreds in the driver's shirt pocket.

"Four-fifteen," he said into the mike.

"Go ahead, four-fifteen," a woman's voice squawked.

"Got a fare to Oak Ridge. Let you know when I'm back."

"Ten-four, four-fifteen. Hey, Manny, you know anything about the excitement in the vicinity of Church and Market?"

"Negative, Nora. What's up?"

"Sounds like a bank robbery."

Manny's shoulders stiffened. Allen glanced nervously at Julia.

"Frank's been screaming at me through the box for ten minutes. Says someone shot up his steed."

"Wow," he intoned stoically to Nora, then clipped the mike to the radio. "Those hot C-notes you been feeding me, Jack?" He kept his eyes on the road.

"No," Allen said. "The bank wasn't robbed. If it was, our deal is off and you can come clean about where you really took us. Okay?"

He didn't answer immediately. "That's Oak Ridge, right?"

Allen sighed. "Right."

"Funny how that town looks more and more like Maryville every day."

forty-five

THEY MADE THE HALF-HOUR DRIVE INTO MARYVILLE IN RELA-
tive silence. The driver queried them for knowledge of the
events back on Church Street, but they claimed ignorance.
When they responded to his attempts at small talk in mono-
syllables, he flipped on his radio to a country station and
didn't speak again.

A few times, Stephen groaned quietly. He simply smiled
reassuringly when Allen or Julia turned to him.

Allen's head ached with disturbing thoughts. What had
he gotten himself into? In the space of one day, he'd been
driven from his home, nearly murdered several times, and
thrown into a fugitive run with the brother he hadn't seen in
two years and a streetwise federal agent.

He glanced at their profiles. They were deep in their
own thoughts. As he watched, Stephen closed his eyes slowly,

exhausted and hurting. As much as Allen begrudged his brother's choices, he admired what he'd just done. The fact that Stephen had held his own with an obvious warrior boggled his mind.

And Julia. He shook his head in wonder. Even while the killer was battling Stephen, her decisive action was stunning. Running *toward* the guy as he was about to crush Stephen's head, firing off round after round, driving and holding him back so they could make their escape—all while the killer was shooting back! Some of it was a product of her training, sure, but either you were born with courage or you weren't; no amount of instruction could instill raw bravery. Reliving those harrowing moments heightened his sense that something special had occurred.

He'd heard about men in combat who found themselves surrounded and outnumbered. Later they'd claim that everything had come together in that moment: with bullets and shrapnel whistling past their heads, they instantly remembered minute details of every evasive maneuver they had ever learned in training or in the field; they could accurately predict every inch of terrain they had never seen; their marksmanship became flawless, their feet sure. Only after escaping certain death did they realize that they had done things they could never, ever repeat or explain. But they had *survived.*

What Julia and Stephen had done back there was something like that.

His eyes traced the contours of her face, turned in profile. The strong forehead, straight nose, full lips. She was gorgeous—not in a fashion-model way, but with the kind of delicate beauty that shocks school-age boys into realizing there are things about girls worth noticing. Still, Allen found himself appreciating her for qualities the mirror could not reflect:

the quickness of thought and fearlessness that had saved them from the killer. He couldn't remember the last time he'd felt desire for a woman because of her strength of character, intelligence, compassion, or other uncaressable trait. The realization that he felt that way now made his stomach tumble, a thrill he had not experienced in years. He was vaguely aware that his attraction for her benefited him in a more valuable way as well: it took his mind off the predicament they were in.

Thirty minutes after leaving Knoxville, the taxi rolled into Maryville. Julia stared out at the passing buildings. She seemed to seek out each street sign as they passed it, nodding as though committing the name to memory—familiarizing herself with a locale from which they may have to escape. Very professional. He smiled, but the necessity of her precautions made him unable to hold it.

She noticed his attention and smiled, sweet but absent, then returned to her reconnaissance.

Allen looked out his own window. As he watched the sun-drenched town unfold in all its disarming beauty, he felt a pang of envy for those who lived peaceful lives here, or visited with nothing more pressing on their minds than finding the nearest gas station or restaurant or bathroom. Maryville, nestled in the shadows of the Great Smoky Mountains and liberally studded with century-old buildings and trees in full bloom, made him ache for his own hometown, the near-perfect life he'd carved there for himself. His face flushed with anger at the faceless people who'd taken it from him.

Julia's voice distracted him.

"Pull in here."

Allen followed her finger to a Motel 6 sign just ahead. The driver whipped into the parking lot without slowing and jerked to a stop in front of the office at one end of the

L-shaped structure. Bright blue and orange doors alternated like opposing sentinels before the rooms at ground level and behind the wrought-iron railing of a second-story balcony.

Julia and Stephen clambered out as Allen paid double the fare. He climbed out on the driver's side and watched Julia over the roof as she pulled a newspaper from a machine, folded it, and slipped it into an open side pocket of the gym bag.

"Take care, buddy," the driver said, and Allen believed he meant it. Their melancholy silence had conveyed the true depth of their plight more than he'd realized.

"Just remember our deal."

"Oak Ridge."

Allen slapped the roof in acknowledgment, and the taxi pulled away.

forty-six

IN THE SHADE OF THE BALCONY, STEPHEN STOOD SOLID AS a totem pole, stone-faced and still a bit dazed by his injuries, which had to be cleaned and dressed.

Allen wanted a few hours of shut-eye for himself. He reached for the office door, but Julia stopped him.

"Not here," she said. Through the glass door, they could see that the office was unoccupied. Behind the brochure-crowded counter, a shadow moved on the open door to a back room. Julia hitched her head to the side, urging the men to follow her. They moved quickly into a breezeway at the elbow of the building where an ice machine and a soda dispenser hummed quietly.

"We're not going to take any more chances," she said. "The people after us are too determined and too resourceful. There's another motel about a mile back the way we came."

"Think the cabbie will rat us out?" Allen asked.

She smiled. *Rat us out.* "The killer saw us take off in the taxi." She combed her fingers through her hair, a quick, unconscious motion. "He was trying to shoot at us and dodge traffic at the same time, but I'm sure he took note of the taxi number or license plate. The guy's too proficient not to. The cabbie may or may not stick to his story about dropping us off in . . . Oak Ridge, you said?"

Allen nodded. "Yeah, it's a small town about the same distance from Knoxville as Maryville, but in the opposite direction. I figured the cabbie's odometer would support the story."

"Let's not count on it working. Sooner or later, our enemies will figure they've been duped. You figure that killer could pressure the truth out of the cabbie?"

"Without breaking a sweat," Stephen said. If the strong resonance of his words was any indication, he was feeling better.

"How are you doing?" Julia asked.

"Flesh wound."

"So what was that kung fu stuff back there?" Allen asked.

"Tang soo do, actually," Stephen said. "Like tae kwon do, but its emphasis is on respecting the humanity of your opponent. The object is to use only the moves and the force necessary to stop an attack, escalating the severity of your blows only as the threat becomes greater."

"How much greater could that warrior's threat have been?"

"Shoulda brought a rocket launcher."

"You should have brought some brains," Julia snapped. "That was a stupid move, taking him on."

Stephen looked hurt. Allen realized that Julia's bold actions had impressed his brother as well.

Stephen said, "I knew if we just ran, he'd overtake us,

shoot us or something. I thought the only chance we had was for me to confront him. Turned out that was like a gazelle picking a fight with a tiger."

"I thought you did well," said Allen. "And you're right; we'd probably all be dead if you hadn't fought him."

"And that's how we'll all end up if we don't get moving." Julia shifted the gym bag to her right shoulder. "Let's take a back street to the motel."

The thought of a cool, dark motel room made Allen drowsy. He'd risen early yesterday after a restless night, only to put in a typically hectic day, followed by a decidedly untypical night of escaping from gun-toting killers. Three hours of fitful sleep in the cramped front seat of Stephen's Vega just didn't cut it. He heard himself say, "Four hours of undisturbed slumber sounds like nirvana to me."

"No sleep, Allen. We don't have time. I have some calls to make, and you have some errands to run."

Her words knocked him back a step. Who was she to determine their agenda? Returning her direct gaze, he sensed that the way he responded would shape an important dynamic to their relationship. He'd always been a leader himself, yielding authority to no one, especially a woman. She might have more experience in covert matters, but did her knowledge of the criminal mind and her prowess with weapons give her a right to assume control of their destinies? As he opened his mouth to protest, the ice machine loudly dumped a tray of ice into its holding bin.

Allen jumped and snapped his head toward the machine, feeling Stephen tense up beside him. Julia didn't flinch, merely continued to watch him. It seemed that surviving in the shadowy underworld of dark villains had made her unflappable. He had to admit, regardless of her gender and age, she was the most qualified to see them through this insane battle.

"What?" she asked.

"I think I feel a second wind coming on."

She spun and strode out the far end of the breezeway, heading for the street that ran parallel to Broadway Avenue.

He was glad she hadn't smiled. Stephen stepped past him, briefly patting him on the back with a mitt-sized hand.

"I will not give sleep to my eyes, or slumber to my eyelids," he said and walked on.

"Come again?" Allen moved to catch up with him.

"Psalm 132. David was determined to build God's temple. Julia is determined to triumph over these people after us." Stephen was walking in great strides now, either feeling no pain or simply ignoring it. The right side of his shirt clung to his skin. The blood on it had spread like a perspiration stain under his arm, spanning down to his hip.

"We have been moved already beyond endurance and need rest," Allen recited. At Stephen's inquisitive look, he said, "John Maynard Keynes, first Baron of Tilton."

"'Be strong, show yourself a man.' First Kings."

Allen laughed. "'A dying man needs to die, as a sleepy man needs to sleep, and there comes a time when it is wrong, as well as useless, to resist.' Steward Alsop."

"Oh-ho!" Stephen roared, ready to counter.

They walked on like that, lobbing the wisdom of others at each other. Julia marched silently ten feet ahead, leading them toward the motel. While the bright sun warmed their skin, a gentle breeze sweeping off the mountains kept them from perspiring. Traversing this quiet back street so soon after arriving eased their sense of being pursued. This place, where an occasional dog barked from its backyard home and children drew hopscotch grids with colored chalk in driveways, was galaxies away from the pit that spawned germ-creating madmen and their bloody minions. Tension evaporated in the heat like morning dew. For a few minutes, they even felt safe.

The slowing movements of Julia's head revealed that her darting scrutiny of their surroundings had turned to careful observance. They deviated from their course once to patronize a drugstore she spotted across Broadway. Stephen purchased medical supplies and an XXL T-shirt emblazoned with the message HUGGABLE, which he probably should have slipped into at the store, but he decided to wait until they were ensconced in the motel. All three picked up toiletries.

Ten minutes later, Julia brought the group to a halt.

"Okay, there's the motel." A portion of its sign was visible over the roof of a house. "Allen, we'll say we're married. Stephen, hang out here for about fifteen minutes; then come. Our room will be the one with the washcloth sticking over the top of the door. We'll try to get one around back."

In the glow of the first brotherly camaraderie he had experienced in years, Allen had almost forgotten their fugitive status. "Why should he wait here?" he asked.

"Two shall live where three would die." She grinned and walked away.

"Shakespeare?"

"Julia Matheson," she called over her shoulder.

Allen threw Stephen an exasperated look and hustled after her.

forty-seven

ALL THE ROOMS AT THE MOTEL FACED BUSY BROADWAY Avenue, so Julia insisted on keeping the curtains closed. Even with the lamps on, the room, decorated in brown hues, appeared murky. It was the sort of room for illicit rendezvous, drunken binges, suicide. Allen was sure it had seen its share of each; the stark ugliness of it alone could drive someone to self-destruction. As Julia fiddled with the zipper of her gym bag, he plopped onto the bed and pulled a pillow over his face.

"Did Goody say anything else?" she asked.

He lifted the pillow up to look at her.

"You said he mentioned Ebola, that it was man-made, coming here . . . Anything else?"

He thought. "He said something-*pora*. I didn't catch all of it. I thought maybe *purpura*, a rash of purple spots caused by internal bleeding. It fits. He mentioned some names. Karl Litt."

"Lit? L-i-t?"

"I guess. I Googled *Karl L-i-t* and *L-i-t-t*. Nothing. He said to tell Jodi and Brice and Brett—"

"Barrett."

"Barrett. He said to tell them he loved them."

"His wife and sons," Julia said, dropping down on the bed, the laptop forgotten in her hands.

"And you."

"Huh?"

"After 'Barrett,' he said 'Julia.'"

"He did?"

"'Tell them I love them. Jodi, Brice, Barrett, Julia.'"

Stephen's hearty thumps resounded through the door. Allen rose with a groan to admit him.

"Check the peephole," Julia said, turning away, wiping her eyes as if she were scratching an itch on her eyebrow.

"I am, I am," Allen said, though he wouldn't have without her warning.

Even through the peephole's fish-eye lens, there was no mistaking the hulking figure outside the door. Allen pulled it open. With the sun at his back, Stephen looked truly haggard. His hair and beard stood out in all directions; a tuft of fur protruded from a place just above his belly where his shirt had lost a button; blood, road dirt, and concrete dust scuffed his clothes; the lines on his face were deeper than they'd been the night before. Clutching the crumpled bag from the drugstore, he was a poster child for the homeless and destitute. He sauntered in, lowered himself into an armchair nearly as tattered as he. He stretched out his long legs and planted his feet on the bed.

"I'm feeling my age," he moaned.

Allen took the bag from him and said, "Take off your shirt."

"I'm all right." He raised his arm in protest and stopped short, skewing his face in pain.

"Yeah, right. Take it off." Allen began lining the supplies up along the bottom edge of the bed. "Needle and thread. Did you get needle and thread?"

"It's in there." He tossed the shirt into a wastebasket by Julia. She moved it into the bathroom.

"Get me some hot water while you're in there," Allen called. He found the small travel packet of thread and needles at the bottom of the bag and opened it. He knelt beside Stephen and started examining the worst of his wounds. "So where'd you learn that 'dang you too' stuff?"

"Tang soo do. One of my parishioners runs a *dojang*. He thought it would help with my coordination and keep me in shape."

"It worked," Julia said, setting down an ice bucket of steaming water and two washcloths next to Allen.

"I attend his class twice a week and perform *katas* every day." He glanced under his arm at Allen, seeming to assess his interest.

"*Katas?*"

"Formal exercises against imaginary opponents. They teach you how to control your breathing rhythm and eye focus; they develop balance, gracefulness, strength . . . stuff like that."

"What level are you?"

"Second dan black—ahhhhh!"

"Sorry," Allen said, dabbing at a particularly dark clump of blood. "Black belt? That's how you took down those guys at your cabin?"

He glanced at Julia, heading into the bathroom. She looked back and winked. If she realized he was trying to distract Stephen from the repairs he was making to his flesh, then Stephen probably realized it too; he was allowing himself to be distracted.

Stephen frowned. "The first one caught me off guard, the assailant, I mean. I just gave him an elbow in the face, pretty sloppy. My *sa bom nim* would have a fit."

"And the other?"

"I was getting into form with him. I gave him a hammer-fist strike to the temple." He laughed. "I'd never seen it for real. Incredible."

Allen threaded a needle, prodded a spot on Stephen's side, and poised the needle over it.

"You still into meditation?"

"Keeps me sane."

Julia stepped from the bathroom as she brushed her teeth. Allen could tell she didn't want to miss the conversation.

He flashed a big smile at her. "He used to disappear inside himself so deeply, he wouldn't hear us yelling at him."

"I heard you."

"We used to say he was heavily meditated."

Julia laughed, a nice sound.

Allen said, "You know, being a toothbrush is the worst job in the world."

Stephen blurted, "Tell that to the toilet paper!"

Julia laughed again, spraying tiny droplets of toothpaste.

"Hey," Allen said, "you stole my joke," and Julia laughed harder.

After a few moments, she spoke around the toothbrush. "I thought meditation was something Buddhists and New Agers did."

"Depends on where your mind's at. I meditate on the ways of Jesus."

"But he got into it before all that Jesus stuff," Allen said, unable to keep a measure of disdain out of his voice.

"All right," Stephen said. Soothing, placating.

"This is going to hurt," Allen said.

"Just do it."

Allen looped the thread through a dozen times, cinching each stitch to close the wound. He remembered a joke about a new doc trying to suture a man with palsy. He turned to tell it, but Julia had disappeared back into the bathroom. A few minutes later she came out, but he wasn't in the mood anymore. Instead, he asked Stephen, "Having a black belt, what do you think of the Warrior?"

Warrior. With all the labels that described him—enemy, pursuer, assailant, killer, assassin—the three of them seemed to have settled on warrior. The title was disturbingly appropriate.

"One bad dude."

"I mean in skill, fighting skill."

"Allen, were you watching? He had me, would have killed me if Julia hadn't chased him off. He is faster, smarter, stronger than any man I've sparred with. He moved like he knew everything I was going to do and responded to it as though he'd had weeks to think it over."

"But we got away."

Stephen said nothing.

"You seemed . . ." Julia paused, thinking about her words. "*Hesitant* to engage him."

When Stephen didn't respond, Allen said, "He's a pacifist."

Stephen shook his head. "C. S. Lewis said that unless you can show him that a Nazified Europe would be better than the war that stopped it, he could not be a pacifist. That's how I feel."

"I've never seen a pacifist fight like that," Julia said.

Allen said, "I'm surprised you fought at all, after what happened."

"What happened?" Julia looked between brothers, getting nothing back.

Allen said, "He—"

"I just swore off . . . being like that. That's all."

Allen bit his tongue. He leaned back on his haunches, inspecting his work and the work yet to do.

Despite the brief tension, a peace settled over them then—the tranquility that comes from being at ease with the people around you. The shared experience of fighting for survival had connected them in a way Allen didn't understand. He felt it, nonetheless, and apparently the others did too.

Julia was slouched in a chair, seeming to assess both brothers. A smile quivered against her lips like an incomplete thought.

Memory has a tendency to seize upon moments that seem to an outsider mundane and unremarkable. The occasion is special only to participants, and even they often don't recognize it as memorable. This moment would prove to be like that. They would remember the stillness in the midst of chaos, their casual postures in the shadowy room, the sense of camaraderie.

The calm before the storm.

forty-eight

THE GAUNTLET CAME DOWN HARD ON THE TABLETOP. IT SAT there, empty and cold and very frightening.

"It's the Warrior's arm," Stephen said, quietly awed.

Julia nodded.

Allen hopped off the bed for a closer look. Sure enough, the black, spike-knuckled gauntlet he'd seen shatter through the bank window lay motionless on the dresser. Somehow it seemed more sinister now. Before, he had not seen it in its entirety, bulging with artificial muscles, curled into a taloned claw. He reached for it, hesitated, then gripped its forearm. It was warm, like flesh, but firm as bone. He lifted it, surprised by its lightness.

"It can't weigh more than a *pound*," he said, stunned. He tilted it. The fingers closed into a fist—

Chick.

He jumped back a step, letting the gauntlet slip from his grasp. Both Julia and Stephen jumped as well, thinking the thing had snapped at Allen or done something equally startling.

"That's the sound I heard last night in the cemetery," Allen said, staring at the gauntlet, now palm-up on the carpet. "While the Warrior was searching for me: *chick-chu, chick-chu,* rhythmic like that."

"Clenching and unclenching his fist," Julia said.

Allen nodded, watching the gauntlet as if he expected it to scurry toward him.

Stephen picked it up. He pushed his hand into it, reaching straight out. The gauntlet instantly took on the appearance of black skin, buckling a bit the way skin would when Stephen turned his palm up, bulging in the forearm when he squeezed his fist. "Incredible. Where'd this one come from, Wal-Mart?"

"It was left in my car by the Warrior, the one who got blown away last night," Julia said, holding out her hand.

Stephen slipped it off—reluctantly, Allen thought—and presented it to her.

Julia returned it to the gym bag. "Just another mystery, I guess. I don't know how much good it'll do us, but it is evidence . . . of some kind." She tossed a folded newspaper at Allen. "Find us something to drive. Private party. Not too expensive. Something we can sleep in, if necessary."

"We can sleep in anything."

"Comfortably, I mean. A van or station wagon."

"I guess I can handle that." He snapped the paper open.

Julia said, "Whatever you find, make a big deal about looking it over; then tell the seller you prefer paying in cash. I doubt he'll object. Have him drive you to that FirstBank we passed on the way in. While Stephen keeps him occupied, go ask the teller to break a hundred, and make sure you get one of those little cash envelopes. Before you leave, put the whole purchase price in the envelope. Then hand it to the seller."

"Why the big production?" Allen asked.

"The alternative is to whip out a few grand in hundred-dollar bills. Just a bit suspicious. The cabbie thought there was a bank robbery in Knoxville. The media coverage might mention us, might not. In any case, we need to deflect suspicion as much as possible."

Allen smirked at her. "You ever get tired of thinking?"

"Not when my life depends on it."

Stephen picked up the drugstore bag and headed for the bathroom. At the door, he turned back toward Julia. "Seems like you're gaining momentum. Feeling better?"

Her face was grim. "I'm just tired of holding the dirty end of the stick."

ATROPOS SAT BEHIND THE WHEEL OF HIS RENTED BUICK AND watched the Yellow Cab garage across the street. Sunlight poured into the canyon of buildings and blazed against the surface of the windshield, making it impenetrable to inquiring eyes. Good thing, too, for the stony scowl of the face inside was the seed of nightmares. If moods were animals, his would be an enraged tiger, hateful and destructive. The events of the night before had left him irreparably damaged. A black void swirled through his being, and only the blood of those responsible could possibly fill it. His soul's need for their deaths was more acute than his body's need for oxygen.

He thought of the targets. Julia Matheson. Stephen Parker. Allen Parker. They had been full of fear and terror.

They knew they could not win but had fought and run out of instinct. In the end, instinct would fail. Where strength and skill were lacking, only hope had a chance to prevail, and he had given them no reason to hope. The ones who lasted longest were the ones who held to their belief that they would live—until their stopped hearts told them they didn't.

But there was something about them . . .

He felt a pang of anxiety, just a fleeting flash of doubt. Trusting his own instincts, he pursued it. The big one, Stephen, had strength and a few good moves; he'd give him that. The woman was brave and feisty. That meant she couldn't be counted on to behave the way most of his targets did when they knew he was after them. She wouldn't cower. He had not seen the doctor in action, except to run. But he *was* a physician. Probably intelligent. If he wasn't merely a savant in the medical field, if he possessed the ability to focus his intellect on things outside his field of expertise— an ability few seemed to have, in Atropos's experience—then the three of them together might make a challenging opponent. He'd have to pick them off one at a time. He'd have to stay sharp.

This headache wasn't helping. He'd downed half a bottle of Tylenol in the past two hours; it hadn't taken the edge off at all. He pulled off his glasses, pinched the bridge of his nose. He ran his fingers back through his hair, slipped the glasses back on.

A cab was pulling into the garage, *his* cab. The prey's accomplice had returned before the end of his shift, as Atropos knew he would. His wallet undoubtedly fattened, the man would have seen no reason to sweat through another three hours of drudgery. Predictable. Equally predictable was the lie he'd tell about the destination of his last fare and, ultimately, his telling of the truth as the bridge of his nose slowly collapsed.

Chick-chu. Chick-chu.

Atropos waited for the man to emerge and head for his personal car. When he did, Atropos hopped from the Buick and darted across the street, a disarming smile creasing his lips and a black-fisted hand concealed in his jacket pocket.

forty-nine

ALONE IN THE SHADOWS AFTER ALLEN AND STEPHEN LEFT
to buy a conversion van, Julia felt her adrenaline ebb. Malaise
pressed on her like a warm blanket. She flung open the curtains, hoping the sunlight would dispel the room's gloomi-
ness, and the traces of her own. A quick scan of the parking
lot and the street beyond, then she stepped clear of the window. Previously, she'd wanted the curtains shut because of
Allen and Steven's naïveté concerning covert operations. Her
experience in babysitting government witnesses had taught
her that most people will habitually step up to open windows
at least a few times, even when they know better. Using the
computer at the table and moving along the edges of the
room, she would be invisible to the traffic on Maryville's
main thoroughfare in front of the motel. An enemy directly
outside the window would see her, but that would mean their
enemies had found them anyway.

Which was a possibility she couldn't dismiss. The Warrior's appearance in Knoxville confirmed her suspicions that the people after them were powerful and resourceful. And Allen's comment about the "resurrected" killer had jarred her. She'd decided during the cab ride not to ponder the metaphysical implications of a killer who appeared to have come back from the dead to hunt them. That an assassin with obvious black-op experience had targeted them was enough; contemplating anything deeper threatened to unravel the moorings her mind had on reality. Besides, asking unanswerable questions only fostered frustration and drained brainpower from more productive endeavors. Whatever the explanation, he was after them. Her job was to keep them alive.

She pushed her hair back with both hands, feeling the grit and grease from the undercarriages she'd crawled beneath. She walked slowly into the bathroom and pressed her palms against the countertop, leaning over the sink. One of the two fluorescent tubes above her flickered madly, transforming her reflected face into something from a carnival fun house. The brown of her eyes, eyebrows, and hair, the maroon of a small cut on her cheekbone she didn't remember getting, appeared black against the white of her skin.

She splashed cold water on her face, then did it again. She poured it over the back of her neck, ran streams of it into her hair. *Yes.* Her skin thirsted for the water's briskness, its energizing purity. She threw her arms back to let her jacket fall to the floor, followed by her cream blouse. Water cooled her chest, streaked over her belly. The next thing, she was naked under the icy jets of the shower. The cold robbed her breath but ignited her mind. In minutes, she felt new, ready.

Then she added heat to the stream and lathered soap over her body and shampoo into her hair. She leaned against the tiles and watched the suds spiral down the drain until the water was clear. A sharp toss of her head snapped the water from her hair, and she stepped out. In the mirror, her skin glowed a healthy pink.

Okay, she thought. *Time to get to work.*

SHE SAT CROSS-LEGGED ON THE BED, THE COMPUTER IN HER lap. She called up the Web site Bonsai had given her. It was blank except for a single rectangle in the middle of the screen that read CLICK ME. She did and was prompted to enter a pass phrase. The third one she entered caused the words in the box to change to PLEASE WAIT. She worked a towel over her moist hair. She hoped that Bonsai had been able to decipher the chip and that it contained enough evidence to end this thing.

He worked out of a home office in Morrison, Colorado, a quaint tourist town in the Rocky Mountain foothills west of Denver. She pictured him there now, playing his computer keyboard with the vigor of a virtuoso pianist. In fact, he bore a fair resemblance to a young Beethoven: wild hair, fiery eyes, stern mouth. She assumed the acne had cleared up by now. When he typed, fingers blurring over the keys, his head bobbed spastically to a tune only he could hear.

A minute later she wondered what she was waiting for, if a glitch would keep her waiting forever. Not like Bonsai, but nothing was sure with computers or the Internet, regardless of the skills of the person trying to tame it.

Then a voice came through the speakers. "Julia?"

"Bonsai! Did you crack Vero's code?"

"Nope."

Her stomach lurched nauseously.

"Nothing to crack," he continued.

"What?"

"It's not encrypted. It's a new type of digital media, very cutting-edge. High-resolution, lightning-fast rendering, incredibly dense code. It requires an unholy amount of computing power to drive it. What compact disks are to eight-tracks, this thing is to anything on the market today."

"So, what? I need special hardware?"

"Not anymore. I linked with some buddies at MIT's computer lab. After some trial and error, they were able to supply me with a program that converted this code to one that a top-of-the-line Pentium can handle."

"So what's on it? What kind of files?"

"Mostly video. You lose quite a bit of resolution in the conversion process, so it's grainier than the original, and the image stutters a little, but you can see it okay. What kind of brain you running?"

"The Bureau's best. Custom configured to power some pretty incredible satellite communications software."

"The clock-speed has to be *fast*, Julia. Nothing you can pick up at Sears. I mean—"

"Prototype Athlon two-gig processor, two gigs of RAM, a gig dedicated to video rendering, and a half-tera hard drive."

"Yow! Okay, then. I'm ready to send when you are."

"I need another favor first."

"What do you have in mind?"

"Hack into the Knoxville Police Department and the Tennessee State Criminal Investigation Division for any pending investigations of clone-phone dealers in the 423 area code. Make sure it's not a sting operation, just an investigation.

I also need the name of one of the dealer's customers. Cross-reference it with recent busts; I don't want the dealer talking to the guy. Doable?"

"Consider it done. VOIP me in thirty minutes."

fifty

ATROPOS CONSIDERED THE POSSIBILITY THAT HIS PREY HAD changed hotels, but dismissed it. They probably thought the Oak Ridge ruse was evasive enough. If they *had* gone somewhere else, the chances of finding them without his employer's help was slim. This place was the best lead he had.

He turned right onto Houston Street, which intersected Broadway Avenue at the Motel 6 where the cabbie said he'd dropped them off. His eyes darted over the L-shaped structure, taking in the ground-level breezeway and housekeeping cart parked in front of an open door on the second-floor walkway. Continuing past, he noted the alley that separated the motel from residential backyards. The small, opaque windows of bathrooms dotted this side of the building: each a point of egress. He'd watch for one of them to come out for ice or snacks or to use a pay phone. But if he had to hit the room, he'd have to move hard and fast: no return fire, no retreat.

He made a U-turn at the next intersection, pulling to the curb when he came abreast of the motel. The office was visible through the glass of a station wagon parked in front of the room closest to him. He could barely make out what appeared to be vending machines in the shadowy breezeway. A bright square of sunlight glowed like a movie screen where the breezeway opened up on the other side of the motel. He stared for a long time, looking for the silhouette of a head to break out from the sharp lines of the machines. Satisfied that the three had not posted a sentry there, he shifted his gaze to the cars in the parking lot. One of his prey could have broken into a car to keep watch. That it appeared they had not taken such precautions confirmed his suspicion that he was dealing with amateurs, despite the woman's position as a federal agent. She was accustomed to hunting, not hiding.

Approaching the office from the front seemed safe, but first he would inspect the surrounding area: Where were the nearest police cruisers? The likely avenues of escape? Places where his quarry could hide should they evade his attack, and where he could hole up if something went wrong?

He reached for the gearshift lever on the steering column, and a glimmer against the matte of his gauntlet caught his eye. Instantly he knew the cause and reached for a handkerchief in the leather pouch around his waist. In his anxiousness to get to Maryville after interrogating the cabbie, he'd neglected routine maintenance. He wiped at the glimmer first, then rubbed vigorously over and between each spike and each finger. He tossed the cloth into the passenger seat, where it landed soiled-side up: thick red smears against the sun-brightened white.

He rolled away from the curb with one last look at the motel. As he turned onto Broadway, he began scrutinizing every person, vehicle, building, and passageway he saw.

BONSAI CAME ONLINE AS SOON AS JULIA SELECTED THE CLICK me button.

"So, anything for me?" she asked.

"Do hackers like computers?" He explained the information he'd found in the Knox County Sheriff's Department database.

She wrote two names and a phone number on a notepad. "You're brilliant. I'll get back to you when I'm ready to receive the data from the memory chip." She shifted on the bed and tucked a bare foot under her bottom. She caught a whiff of something unpleasant in her dirty clothes and ignored it. It would have to be good enough to have clean hair, dry now and brushed loosely back from her face. She pulled the room's phone off the nightstand and dialed the number Bonsai had supplied.

"Sky Signs," a male voice announced.

"I need some phones."

"We do skywriting, lady. Weddings, birthdays, something to cheer—let Sky Signs write it in the stratosphere."

"Cute."

"Thanks for calling."

"Whoa, I still need some phones."

"I told you, we don't do phones."

She glanced at the notepad. "That's not what Aaron Horvitz told me."

A pause.

Bingo.

"Who?" the man asked flatly.

"Thought Aaron mentioned he was a good customer of yours . . . Colin, right? Maybe I heard wrong."

"Gimme your name and number."

She did, and the line went dead. She shot out the door and across the parking lot to the pay phone she'd visited before checking in with Bonsai. It was one of those booth-less phones, encased in a blue egg-shaped shell. She tucked her head close to the phone, hiding from passersby on the street behind her. Mr. Colin Dorsett was undoubtedly try-ing to reach Aaron Horvitz to vouch for her. Sad thing, though: according to Bonsai, police had taken Horvitz into custody two nights ago for discharging a firearm into the foot of a rival drug dealer during a bar fight. She was bet-ting that Horvitz had more pressing concerns than appris-ing his supplier of stolen and reprogrammed cellular phones of his new residence in the county clink. The pay phone began ringing.

"Yeah?" she answered.

"Aaron ain't answering."

"So?"

"So I don't do business with strangers."

"Look," she said, sharp. "Aaron said his name was good as gold with you. He's not going to be too happy to find out it ain't."

Dead air, then: "Whaddya want?"

"Four flip phones with fully juiced batteries, a car power cord, a USB adapter."

He spit out a colorful word. "You starting a telethon?"

"Something like that. While you're at it, I need a few others things. I'll make it worth your while." She told him what she wanted.

The man reluctantly agreed and quoted an extravagant price. He was trying to allay his concern with cash.

"Fine," Julia said. "Bring them to the Hungry Farmer on Henley Street at five." Their taxi had passed the restaurant on their way out of Knoxville. She knew through Bonsai that the cops were onto Dorsett's clone-phone business. She couldn't risk their seeing her at his counterfeit storefront.

"Hey, I don't make house calls, lady. I don't care who you know."

"Tell me business is booming after *60 Minutes* ran that piece on clone-phone crackdowns. No way, buddy. Make a swing by the Farmer for me, or I'll spend my money somewhere else."

It's what eventually got them all: greed.

"All right, five o'clock, but I ain't coming in. I'll be driving a red convertible Camaro. Come out when you see me, cash in hand."

"See you then," she said, sweet as candy.

fifty-one

ALLEN JUST DIDN'T GET IT, AND STEPHEN SHOULDN'T HAVE been surprised. He shook his big head and steered the van onto Broadway Avenue. After the Vega, it was a pleasure to drive such a smooth-running machine; that he actually *fit* in it was icing on the cake.

"It's not like I assaulted the guy," Allen said, continuing their argument.

"You said his van was a piece of—"

"That's called negotiation."

"You were antagonizing the man!" A light turned red, allowing him to turn the full force of his gaze on his brother.

"Oh, bull," Allen countered snidely, which was really no counter at all. "He didn't take offense."

"He almost decked you."

"I would have let him if it lowered the price."

"How can you spend so much money and be so cheap at the same time?"

"How green do you want it?"

Stephen glared at him a moment, then realized he was talking about the traffic light and accelerated through the intersection.

"Besides, he could have told us to take a hike if he didn't like my attitude," Allen said.

"Some people don't have the luxury you do to turn their backs on cash. Not that you ever have." It was a wonder they had come from the same family. The next light turned yellow, and he slowed for it. He seemed to have caught the red side of Broadway's traffic-light cycle. Fortunately, they were only a few blocks from the motel.

Abruptly, Allen fell to the floor between the two front captain's chairs. "Turn your head to the left!" he yelled, motioning wildly in that direction. His terrified expression compelled Stephen to obey.

"What?" he asked.

"Don't look, but the motel . . ."

He flicked his vision at the Motel 6, catty-corner on the right. The massive figure of the Warrior filled the open office doorway. He had his head cranked around, looking into the parking lot, toward where Stephen waited for the light to turn green. Stephen turned his head away. He felt the skin on his arms rise rapidly into goose bumps. There were maybe fifty yards between them. The Warrior could look right at him if the thought crossed his mind.

A horn behind him blared.

"Oh—" Green light. He glanced over. The Warrior was talking to someone in the office. Stephen made a panicked decision to turn away from the motel, instead of driving past it. He checked for cars in the left-turn lane, signaled, and edged into the intersection. A pickup was approaching from the other direction, and he braked for it, realizing too late that he could have darted across ahead of it. If a siren erupted from the van and flashing lights sprang up on its roof, he would not have felt more exposed. Another car pulled out from a liquor store, filling the gap between the truck and a knot of cars racing forward from the intersection a block away.

"Come on, come on," he said under his breath.

"Just go!" From his position on the floor, Allen was blind to the traffic.

Stephen hunkered low in the seat and looked over. The Warrior had come out of the office. He was standing in the sunlight, squinting at the cars in the parking lot.

The car behind him honked again. Stephen jumped. The Warrior turned to look. He put his hand against his brow to block the sun. The horn blared again, longer. Now the Warrior was striding forward, across the motel parking lot, directly toward Stephen.

Why is this guy honking? Can't he see the traffic?

He realized the rear of the long van was blocking the lane that went straight through the intersection. Deciding to turn had been a mistake.

He calculated he could cut through the traffic behind a car and pray the oncoming drivers were attentive enough to slam on their brakes hard enough and fast enough to avoid colliding with him. He saw an opening and knew there wasn't room. He was going for it anyway.

Dear Lord, don't let anyone be hurt.

He moved his foot off the brake and glanced quickly at the Warrior, thinking he may have to duck away from a gunshot. He was gone. Stephen jammed the brake pedal. Then he spotted him, staring into a parked Toyota. The Warrior moved around it to examine the interior of the next parked car. He seemed to have discounted the commotion in the street as being none of his concern.

Stephen closed his eyes, let out a long breath.

"What? What's happening?"

"Nothing. We're outta here." The light had turned yellow, stopping the surge of oncoming cars. Stephen roared across and into a residential neighborhood.

Allen grunted as he began pulling himself up.

"Stay down, Allen!" Stephen said, urgent, wide-eyed. There was something about his brother sprawled on the floor of the van that lifted his spirits. He turned his head to hide his smile.

THE ROAR OF A BIG ENGINE AND THE SQUEAL OF TIRES BECKoned her to the window. Pistol in hand, she pressed against the wall, flicked her head around the sill, and pulled it back again. A dark blue conversion van, idling directly in front of the room, not parked. Had to be the guys. But why the Jeff Gordon theatrics? A car door slammed. Allen ran around the front of the van. She holstered her weapon and swung the door open.

"Let's go!" he said, still outside. "The Warrior! He's at the Motel 6."

"That was fast. He'll know we didn't check in."

"Then he'll start checking around." He was grabbing the few items he and Stephen owned, tossing them into the drugstore bag.

"He may not be alone," she said, disconnecting computer cables with one hand, pushing components into the gym bag with the other. Allen stepped into the bathroom, used his forearm to sweep whatever was on the counter into the bag, and followed Julia out of the room.

Stephen pulled away before she had the side door shut, and that was fine by her. He bounded over a curb onto Broadway, jostling her headfirst into one of the plush rear seats. For a while she watched out the tinted rear windows for a vehicle pulling up fast or following at a consistent distance. Nothing.

"You saw only the Warrior?" she asked.

"Isn't he enough?" Allen had a smudge on his cheek, but his hair was perfect. It came to her that she'd never seen it any other way, even after crawling out from under the car.

"I need some navigation," Stephen said.

"Knoxville."

"You gotta be kidding. The airport?"

"Hungry Farmer Restaurant. I've arranged to pick up some new phones, ones that can't be traced back to us."

"And then?"

"And then we find out who wants us dead so badly."

Neither man had seen her withdraw her pistol, and both jumped when she jerked the slide back and let it return with a resounding *ka-chink!*

fifty-two

THE VAN WAS PERFECT. BESIDES TINTING ITS WINDOWS, someone had put curtains over the side and back windows. Curtains also separated the front seats from the rear of the van, but were now pushed to the sides. A foot-wide board could be placed on supports so that it spanned the width of the van directly in front of the rear captain's chairs, or stowed under the seats. A mattress on a plywood board took up the last four feet of the interior. Julia could have done without the stench of cigar smoke, but by the time they reached the parking lot of the Hungry Farmer, she had the table cluttered with computer gear and had forgotten all about the repugnant odor.

"Drop me off, and park across the street," she told Stephen. She took a table by a window looking out on the parking lot and ordered coffee.

Halfway through her second cup, a red Camaro pulled in, its beige canvas top up. She was out of the restaurant before the car came to a complete stop. An obese man behind the wheel eyed her suspiciously. She squatted by the window and tossed a wad of cash onto his bulbous stomach. He counted it and handed her a plastic grocery bag. She looked inside and nodded, and the car pulled out faster than it had pulled in. Thirty seconds later, Stephen picked her up in the van.

"I wish everything went that smoothly," she said, slamming the van's sliding door. She moved into the captain's chair behind the driver's seat and laid a phone down on the table beside the computer. She dumped the rest of the bag's contents into the chair next to her: three more cell phones and another bag of items from Radio Shack.

"Where to?" Stephen asked.

"Take us to an east-west interstate."

"Which direction?"

"Doesn't matter. Find a rest area or truck stop."

He thought about it. "We're not too far from I-40."

"What's east?"

"Next big city, Charlotte."

"What's west?"

"Nashville."

"I-40, James."

Stephen got the van moving.

Allen turned around in his seat. "What's with the phones?"

"Each one has been reprogrammed with a cell phone number that someone retrieved by monitoring the calls in a congested area, like rush-hour traffic."

Allen nodded. "The people looking for us don't know to

monitor the airwaves for these particular numbers. We can use them without the bad guys tracing the signals back to us."

"Except that I want them to find these two." She held up a phone in each hand.

"I don't get it."

"You will. But first, here . . ." She handed him a mini-cassette recorder still in a Radio Shack box, two AA batteries, and a cassette tape. She began pulling a second recorder out of its box. When both recorders were ready, she said, "Pretend it's a phone. Hit the record button when I hit mine, and chat with me."

"What do I say?"

"Follow my lead."

fifty-three

"PLAY IT AGAIN."

Kendrick Reynolds sat in his wheelchair next to a computer workstation, a pair of noise-eliminating headphones clamped over his ears.

The technician used a trackball to manipulate controls on the monitor. Voices came over the headphones.

". . . killed Goody." A female voice.

"Who?" Male.

"My partner, Goodwin Donnelley. The guy who died on your operating table yesterday."

"Right. Who killed him?"

"I don't know, but Despesorio Vero died too." She sounded exasperated. *"He was the guy who was trying to get into the Center for Disease Control. They were in some bar in Chattanooga. Goody went to your ER. Vero's body disappeared."*

Behind Kendrick, Captain Landon held a single headphone cup to his right ear. He said, "The key-phrase trigger was *Karl Litt*. When the monitors recognized the phrase, the recorder kicked in."

Kendrick moved a cup off one ear. "But we can't hear it in context?"

"Key-phrasing entire geographical areas means monitoring every conversation, millions of them. It's not like monitoring a handful of lines or even every line in an office building. We can't use record-and-erase technology on geokeys. Our systems are already taxed—"

"Just say no, Mike." Kendrick looked up at him. He was sure what the captain saw when he looked back was a tired old man. He hated that.

"No, sir. No context on the key phrase *Karl Litt*."

He hated that too: not knowing how much these people knew, how much Vero had told them. He had to find them, interrogate them, and confiscate whatever evidence Vero had passed on to them. There were two issues now: finding Karl and keeping a lid on projects that were never meant for public scrutiny. He hoped catching up with these three would solve both problems.

The technician at the controls spoke up. "They're still talking."

"What? How long have they kept this connection open?"

"Twenty-three minutes. I'm streaming it live now. Should I bring the audio current?"

"Go ahead."

"*. . . but that's impossible. If Despesorio Vero did have information, he would have told Goody.*"

"*Donnelley?*"

"*Yes.*"

"What about this Karl Litt guy?"

"I don't know . . ."

Kendrick closed his eyes slowly. He pulled the headphones off and laid them on the workstation. "They're moving?" he asked with a quiet sigh.

"Yes," said the technician. "They're both on I-40. The woman's heading west out of Knoxville, toward Nashville. The man's heading east, between Thorngrove and Danridge."

Kendrick shook his head. It wasn't them. As a federal agent, Matheson would know about key-phrasing. But she wouldn't know how much more advanced military technology was over what the Justice Department had access to. She would be accustomed to systems that missed more key phrases than they caught. That's why she repeated the names—Karl Litt, Despesorio Vero, Goodwin Donnelley. Decoys only worked if people went after them.

"Send one team each to intercept them," he ordered. He could not risk being wrong. "Tell them to tread lightly; I don't think it's them. And, ruling out anything along I-40, try to get a handle on where they're really heading."

"THAT WAS FUN," ALLEN SAID FLATLY.

They had recorded their conversation, duct-taped the recorders to the phones, had one phone call the other, and sent them in different directions—one under the tarp of a ski boat attached to a Suburban and one in the open bed of a pickup truck. Julia had no doubt their pursuers would key in on the signal. Their ability to intercept the SATD and find them in Knoxville told her they had the technology and were actively seeking them. She only hoped it would take them a long time to track down the cell phones. On the recordings, she hadn't mentioned any possible key phrases for fifteen minutes. That would give them time to distance themselves from the phones. The mini-cassette tapes were thirty minutes long. After that, the dead air would cause the phones to disconnect. If their pursuers had yet to find the phones, they would not be able to pinpoint the signals—because there would be no signals—and would have to search everywhere along I-40.

Except, she thought with dismay, *if they used an infinity transmitter to call the cell phones and force the lines to stay open until they found them.*

She'd forgotten about that. If it wasn't one thing, it was twenty.

"So you think they're off our tail now?" Allen wanted to know.

"For a while . . . I hope."

"Now what?"

"We find out what Vero gave his life to bring to us."

She told them about the memory chip, where she'd found it, and how she had to contact a friend to help her access the data.

"You have this chip, but you can't read it, and you don't have the data your friend converted? So what's your plan?" Allen looked as though he'd been hit with a bat.

"I'm going to get the data, Allen, all right?" She wanted to smack him. In his smug expression she saw someone used to predictability, someone who didn't just prefer order over chaos but required it. She saw . . . She saw someone who was frightened and wanted everything to go back to normal. She realized they were all on edge. His frustration came from the same well as hers.

"Look, I don't have all the answers. I don't have *any* answers, really. All I know is we have to keep moving, keep looking for reasons why this is happening and how we can put an end to it. We just don't know enough at this point."

She plugged her laptop into a cigarette lighter receptacle, then connected the other cell phone she'd purchased to the laptop. Allen watched her.

"While we're moving," she explained, "I can't use the device that connects me to Wi-Fi, and I don't want to stay in one place long enough to get the file transfer. So I got a third clone-phone. Bonsai gave me a direct number to his server. It'll be slow, but it's secure and we can do it while we're heading back to Atlanta."

"That's what I don't understand," Stephen said from the driver's seat. They were traveling south on I-75, which would take them through Chattanooga and on to Atlanta. "Why there?"

"Atlanta? It's where all this started, for Goody and me anyway. And it's my home turf; I may be able to tap some resources I couldn't somewhere else."

"Like what?" Allen asked.

"I don't know, Allen. Maybe it's just a comfort factor."

Consulting a notepad, she punched a number into the cell phone. A moment later, the laptop indicated that it was connected to a server. She called up Bonsai's Web site and started the transfer of Vero's data.

"This is going to take a while."

"What's a while?" Allen asked.

Julia shrugged. "I'll know in a minute." She waited for the program to receive enough data to extrapolate an estimated completion time. "I'm hoping we can view it before reaching Atlanta."

"That's about three, three and a half hours," Stephen informed her.

Three digits appeared on the screen. She stared at them numbly, then reported, "Six hours and twenty-three minutes."

When you start marking time by the number of attempts on your life you've survived, six hours seems an eternity.

She cleared her throat.

On the way to meet the clone-phoner, they'd stopped by a grocery store for a supply of food and drinks. Now Allen reached into a small Styrofoam ice bucket in the foot well and pulled out a Pepsi. He handed it to Julia.

She nodded her thanks and took a swig.

They rode in silence. Stephen clutched the wheel in both hands and checked the side mirrors with obsessive frequency. Allen rolled an unopened Dr Pepper between his palms and stared out the windshield. Julia leaned back, hiked a shoeless foot up onto the chair, and thought about the events since Goody's phone call yesterday morning. She carefully considered every word she could remember, every move she'd made or seen, searching for a question that needed answering, a clue that needed exploring. They were there, waiting for discovery. They always were.

fifty-four

JORGE PRIETO WATCHED HIS BLOOD DROP A DOZEN FEET and disappear into the rich, dark soil below. He had long stopped trying to snort back the constant flow that poured from his nostrils, or blot it with the thin cotton sleeves of his khaki coveralls. Cradled in the fork of two limbs in a thirty-meter copaiba tree, he painfully sucked in air through clenched teeth, trying to relieve his burning lungs without making a sound. It had taken all his energy to break away from his captors and make it this far.

Not far enough! Gotta move! Move . . .

But his aching body urged him to wait, just a few more minutes of rest.

Brought in blindfolded five weeks ago, he had no idea how much farther to the compound's perimeter. A kilometer? Twenty? No matter, he had to make it, had to.

Before he could suppress the urge, he coughed, hawking up something from deep inside. Stifling a groan, he listened for pursuers. He heard nothing but the ghostly howl of wind flitting through the treetops. He planted his sweaty face on a forearm and waited for the feeling that his organs were shifting freely within his body to pass.

What had they done to him? *What?*

When the pain had come, cramping his stomach, raising the temperature of his skin, he'd cursed *Karai-pyhare,* the evil troll whose invisible caress left victims shaken and sick. A silly superstition, he knew, but childhood beliefs die hard. His adult mind recognized the symptoms of influenza. Then the headaches, dizziness, nausea, and perspiration spiraled higher, like a brewing storm, and he realized something far more serious had hold of him. *Dysentery,* he thought when blood showed up in the toilet, *maybe jungle fever—malaria.*

He thought of how his captors had seemed obsessively concerned over his condition, attaching a million confusing machines to him and running all sorts of tests. He'd asked about chloramphenicol for dysentery or chloroquine for jungle fever—medicines you learned about growing up poor on the Tropic of Capricorn. They had shaken their heads dismissively.

That's when I knew you'd done something to me, you devils, you monstruos*! I saw it in your faces and knew I had to get away . . . had to warn others . . .*

Most everyone, it seemed —his fellow "prisoners," the guards, himself—had cold symptoms to greater or lesser degrees. The ones who had complained of cramps or bloody noses disappeared within a few days. If he was going to make a move, it had to be quick.

The crack of a twig startled him. His face made a sticky suction sound when he raised it to glare into the dense subtropical forest. Pitch-black shadows made darker by irregular spots of bright sunlight—nothing more. Even the contraptions hidden in the trees—the tiny cameras and monstrous machines that defied imagination—were invisible to him now. He turned to face the ground, and a ribbon of blood spiraled down like an eel escaping into the deep.

In his mind's eye, he saw Juanita floating up to him as if through water: her cashew-colored skin, mahogany eyes, soft lips . . .

No! He must not let his thoughts scurry away, but they were becoming so slippery, so rebellious.

Concentrate! Escape! You don't belong here. You are not a prisoner.

And that was true. He had done nothing wrong, nothing to deserve imprisonment. Jorge Prieto had always accepted personal responsibility, had always tried to do the right thing. When he slipped, he worked hard to make amends. Had he fled when Juanita said she was with child? No. Casper Merez had even pushed a half million guaranis into his hand—a month's wages!—and told him, "Go, Jorge. Such a burden is not for a seventeen-year-old boy. Go find the man inside first." But the man was already there, and he had married the girl instead. Now, twelve years later, he and Juanita had not just one but four *niños*, three girls, darkly pretty like their mother, and a boy, strong and forthright like his father.

And did his family starve when their mouths became too many for their backwater town of Piribebuy to feed? No, he had moved them to Itaipu, where construction on the world's largest hydroelectric plant paid him for as many hours as his back could bear.

Always food on the table, shelter from the elements. The minimum a man provides his family.

Maybe he should have worried more about the many people who vanished from Itaipu. Some said it was the demon *Kurupi*, who came in the night to feast on human flesh. Others thought those gone had tired of the bone-breaking work and fled back to their poorer but happier villages. He had not known what to think, had not really thought about it at all. Feed his family, be a man—only these things mattered.

Now Jorge Prieto knew better. The truth had come to him instantly in the form of two men leaping from a slow-moving van, clubbing him, shackling him, dragging him into their metal lair.

Kurupi, yes—but with the faces of men.

He pushed into a sitting position, his legs dangling through the fork, his back hard against the massive tree trunk.

As much as he wanted to provide again for his family, he wanted more to tell them that he had not simply *left* them. What had his disappearance done to their hearts? It was a twisting knife in his own chest to ponder the question.

So he had watched for a chance to escape. This morning, it had come.

Movement in his peripheral vision.

A guard emerged from the darkness, stepping silently over the muscular roots of a mahogany tree. The man, clad in shades of green, carried an assault rifle, panning its barrel as his eyes scanned the forest before him. He did not look up. When he was directly underneath, Jorge Prieto leaped through the fork, aiming his legs on each side of the soldier's head. They crashed down together, the other man cushioning Prieto's fall. Still, Prieto rolled away in agony, every organ blazing with its own unique pain. He vomited, crimson streaked with oily black swirls. Dark mist moved through his brain, stripping away rational thought. But he knew he had to get away, as an animal knows when to hide, when to run, when to strike.

He pulled the weapon out from under the collapsed soldier and staggered away. Unsure of what made him look back, he did—in time to see the soldier on his knees, pulling a pistol from a holster at his hip. Prieto swung the automatic rifle around and squeezed the trigger.

THE SOUND SHATTERED THE CALM JUNGLE. BIRDS OF ALL SIZES and colors burst through the leafy canopy, adding their own panicked squawking to the rustling of the countless plants they disturbed. Soldiers instantly hunched lower, pivoting in the direction of the machine-gun fire. Gregor von Papen, nearly invisible among the mottled greens and tans of the forest in his camo, considered drawing his sidearm, decided not to, and marched into the barrage's dying echo.

Gregor thought of this as his *descabellar*, the final kill offered a retiring matador. He wasn't retiring, of course; he would die commanding security forces. But Litt had proclaimed an end to his need for test subjects.

"We've arrived," he'd said. "Target practice is over. Let's get on with the war." He wanted all the prisoners gone immediately. "Managing them will put a strain on our resources during this critical time," he'd said.

So this morning, while loading the prisoners into a truck for transportation into the jungle, where the others were buried, Gregor had arranged an opportunity for one of them to "escape."

Humid air carried an almost inhuman scream to him,

wavering insanely until it formed into words: *"Morir, Huicho! Bajar infierno! Bajar infierno!"* Back to hell! Back to hell!

Near. More important, the reproach came after the gunfire, meaning their prey had armed himself. The few guards left in the compound started to converge on the sound. Gregor whispered quickly into his headset, and they backed off. He didn't want to lose any more men.

Besides, these men respected a leader who exhibited the kind of bravery he demanded. Respect bred loyalty, so he always watched for ways to improve it.

Walking forward alone, he pulled his BlackBerry out of its holster and examined it. It monitored and controlled all of the compound's outside security systems. At the touch of an icon on the screen, he could turn electric fences on and off, lock and unlock gates, arm and disarm surface weapons, and access the lighting system. Gregor had read in a security publication that small transmitters could be added to cameras to relay their images to handheld devices like his. He hoped to convince Litt of his need for the upgrade.

He cut through the forest's shadows like a cat on the prowl. The BlackBerry confirmed that the compound's Deadeye system was inactive. Only recently developed by Lawrence Livermore National Laboratory, the device monitored an area for gunfire. When its infrared sensors detected a gunshot, its computer would calculate the projectile's point of origin and instruct its own weaponry to return fire. Regardless of how well the assailant hid himself, two seconds after pulling the trigger, he'd be dead.

Designed to protect high-ranking officials in motorcades and at public appearances, and to combat sniper activity, the Deadeye was a perfect addition to the compound's perimeter security. Suspicious of the compound's guards, covert activities, and the steady disappearance of people from surrounding towns, some local rebels had taken to ambushing vehicles coming into the compound and shooting at guards from the cover of the jungle. Such assaults had stopped after the Deadeye system mowed down three of the guerrillas.

Private organizations were not supposed to possess military-grade weapons. However, Gregor had discovered long ago that nothing was out of his reach as long as Litt's band of merry scientists kept producing the germs dictators and terrorists desired. With its constant exchange of illegal merchandise, barter was the currency of choice on the black market. The Deadeyes had been a gift from the U.S. government to Israel to combat sniper activity on Route 1, between Tel Aviv and Jerusalem. Several wound up in the possession of Hamas sympathizers, who preferred biological agents over anti-sniper weapons.

Gregor used his thumb to punch the button that activated the Deadeyes. The icon changed from "safe" green to "unsafe" red. Up ahead, he heard labored breathing and the crashing of a body breaking through heavy foliage.

He stepped behind a tree and yelled, "Jorge Prieto!"

The crashing sounds stopped.

"Jorge! There is no need for this! We want only to help you!" He spoke in the man's native tongue.

"Go away! *Huicho!*"

He nodded to himself. To the Guarani Indians, *Huicho* was an ugly little demon, a chummy companion of Death. He had long, dirty hair, skin the pallor of a corpse, and a fetid odor. The creature caused repugnance and terror. Gregor wondered if Prieto had ever laid eyes on Litt. He bent around the tree and caught a flash of khaki.

Prieto was staggering at the edge of a pillar of sunlight at the far side of a small clearing, looking for his pursuers. He was hugging himself with one arm; the hand of the other arm gripped a Beretta AR-70 assault rifle. Blood covered his face from the nose down, giving him the appearance of wearing a harlequin's half mask. His eyes were wide and blinking continuously, whether from the sun or perspiration or troubled vision Gregor didn't know.

He felt a pang of pity for the man. What must it be like to feel your insides turning to jelly? To have no clue why? He doubted Prieto would appreciate his own sacrifice. Could such a simple man grasp the grandeur of being the last experimental host of a virus that billions would come to fear? Or of being one of the first to experience a new generation of manipulable "designer" viruses? Ignorance is not always bliss, for here was a man who knew nothing but pain and fear, and none of the reasons that would make him proud to endure them.

Better to end it quickly.

Gregor stepped out from behind the tree and into the clearing.

Prieto jumped at the movement. He squinted at Gregor, obviously unsure if he had spotted a man or a bush. Then he focused on Gregor's face, which Gregor had not bothered to cover with camo. The Indian hunched lower and leveled the machine gun. Its barrel wavered wildly.

Gregor waited. When Prieto started backing slowly into the shadows, Gregor made a show of reaching for his holstered pistol. Startled by this, Prieto bared his teeth and fired. Dirt exploded fifteen feet in front of Gregor, who didn't so much as flinch. The high-pitched whine of an electric motor sounded to Gregor's right as the Deadeye rotated its weaponry. Prieto heard it, too, and shifted his gaze just as the Deadeye

let loose with a five-second burst from its M134 minigun—
five hundred rounds of 7.62mm ammunition spread over a
six-foot radius. The effect was similar to an explosive charge:
Jorge Prieto ceased to be.

The Deadeye's Gatling-style barrels continued to whirl,
filling the comparative silence with a metallic death rattle.

Gregor could make out the circular pattern cut through
the jungle as if a rocket had passed, taking Prieto with it. Small
trees fell to the ground, severed in two. Leaves floated down,
having been torn from their branches and hurled skyward. The
air was hazy as the slate-colored smoke of gunpowder drifted
up from the Deadeye's hiding place in the trees, and the green-
hued mist of vaporized foliage floated down.

Booted feet stomped behind him. He punched the Black-
Berry's Deadeye icon again and watched it turn green. The
last thing he needed was for some excited guard to shoot off a
round and awaken the hideous Deadeye to their presence. He
strode forward, searching the ground. He stopped when he
spotted a pair of legs . . . just legs. The rest of Jorge Prieto
fanned out from the knees in a glistening, lumpy mass. A
guard entered the clearing, then stopped, wide eyes taking it
all in. Two medical technicians arrived. They, too, stopped
short, eyeing Gregor as if he'd perpetrated the destruction
with his bare hands. He bent down to scoop up the dented
and perforated AR-70. A piece of its polyurethane stock fell
away. He saw that a fist still clenched the grip, and remembered that *Guaraní* meant "warrior." The man had died as his
ancestors had lived—fighting. He tossed the rifle to the guard,
who shied back before catching it with fumbling hands.

"Clean this up," Gregor ordered and marched away.

fifty-five

ALLEN BOLTED UP, A NIGHTMARE CLINGING TO HIM LIKE A bedsheet. He gulped for air even as the fear faded into his subconscious. For an instant he thought the warm moisture drenching his hair, streaking his chest, was blood; then he realized it was perspiration, lots of it.

The sound of another breath caused him to freeze.

He jerked around and recognized the van's interior. Stephen was reposed in the driver's chair, which was collapsed into a sort of narrow bed. Faint light coming in through the windshield caught the tips of his whiskers and hair, giving his head a fuzzy, surreal quality. But his soft, bass snore was real enough, and Allen found some comfort in that. He became aware of a rhythmic patter echoing through the van. It took him a moment to identify it as light rain falling on the roof. He shifted his gaze and made out Julia's head between the passenger door and seat. He thought he could hear her shallow breathing. In all, he found the sounds soothing.

The army blanket that had covered the mattress when he crawled back to it was now bunched up in a corner. He shifted to slide the makeshift curtain away from one of the square back windows and smelled the stale odor of uric ammonia. The former owner had mentioned having small children, and Allen envisioned stains the ragged shape of countries on the bare, pinstriped mattress beneath him. It gave him a token appreciation for the dark.

Stephen had parked at the far end of a shopping center's parking lot. A twenty-four-hour grocery store in the middle of the strip dwarfed the peddlers of videos, liquor, stationery, coffee, electronic components, and other assorted luxuries of modern life. Allen spied a pickup truck and a dilapidated VW bug a few slots and one row over. Because the cars were too far from the grocery to belong to shoppers, he assumed their owners were store employees. A regular pattern of lampposts poured pools of rain-hazed light onto the vast asphalt. One such lamppost rose out of sight just to the right of the van's rear window but returned no light. He scanned the pavement below for broken glass, saw none. He doubted Stephen would have thought to shatter the bulb, but Julia would not have hesitated.

He eased down on the mattress and gazed through the window at the clouds. Beyond, stars twinkled as raindrops passed over them. He wondered how long until the sun came up and the others woke. Then he drifted off again. When his eyes fluttered open, it was daylight, and the van was moving. Stephen and Julia talked quietly in the front seats. To orient himself, he turned back to the rear window. The sun stung his eyes.

"Good morning." It was Julia, looking much more refreshed than he felt. She had spun her chair around and was ducking under the table that held her computer equipment. She positioned herself in the bucket behind Stephen.

"Is it?"

"We're alive," Stephen called back. "I'd say that makes it a good morning."

"I suppose." Allen groaned and swung his legs off the mattress. He tugged at his shirt to align the buttons with the center of his chest and asked, "Where we going?"

"McDonald's," Stephen chimed. "Hungry?"

"I don't know yet, but I sure could use a mug of java." His mouth tasted like something had died in it, probably smelled like it too. Julia was massaging her neck, and he remembered the awkward position she had slept in. He felt a little guilty that he'd hogged the only bed, but only a little. He lined up the toe seam of a sock and pulled it up. He looked up to find her smiling at him.

"What?"

"Nothing," she said, shaking her head slightly.

That smile. She really could break hearts without any trouble.

"It's just that I've never seen your hair mussed up before."

His hands flew to his head as if she'd said his hair was on fire, and he began combing it with his fingers. Her smile broadened, and as much as he could have bathed in her charms all day, he was irked to realize that he was the cause of her amusement. He noticed the laptop lid was closed. When he'd decided to check out the mattress, it had been open and still receiving the decrypted data from Julia's friend.

"Did you get the data?"

She grinned and nodded. "It took even longer than the

program had calculated. It was still downloading when we parked and fell asleep. When I checked this morning, it said FILE TRANSFER COMPLETE. I almost opened the directory, but I figured you two would want to be part of it." She was almost giddy.

"Doesn't matter to me who checks it out." Allen shrugged. "As long as it's something we can turn over to someone else and get back to our lives."

The van stopped, and Stephen killed the engine. Through the windshield, a pair of men in paint-stained coveralls pushed through a glass door marked with golden arches.

Stephen turned to face them. "So, what say we stoke up on some greasy fast food and do some good today?"

The three collected their toiletries, invaded the restaurant's washrooms, ordered breakfasts, and met back at the van, bags of food in hand. The men climbed into the front seats while Julia took her position facing the laptop. Immediately she began clicking away, taking bites out of a biscuit whenever the computer paused to perform a command. The aroma of Egg McMuffins, hash browns, and coffee quickly usurped the odor of old cigars as the van's dominant smell.

"Okay," she said after a few minutes.

Allen tossed her a quick glance, then turned his full attention to her when he noticed that she was sawing her top incisors over her bottom lip. He wondered if she'd have much of a lip left when this thing was over.

"Ready to see what's on that memory chip Vero left?"

Allen thought she was trying to sound optimistic. Truth was, they were all hoping for something that probably didn't exist: an easy answer to their dilemma—*any* answer to their dilemma.

Stephen choked on his coffee. It spewed from his mouth

and into the forest of his beard as he snatched at a pile of napkins and slammed them over his mouth. He turned his watery eyes toward her.

"I'll take that as a yes," she said, popping the cables from the back of the laptop and positioning it on the chair behind Allen so all of them could see. She collapsed the van's pseudotable as though she'd been doing it a long time, put it on the floor at her feet, then turned back to the laptop. The fifteen-inch screen was black except for a palette of five colorful buttons hovering in the lower right corner.

Allen recognized the symbols on the buttons from audio-cassette players: a triangle with the acute angle facing right for PLAY, a triangle pointing left for REWIND, two vertical lines for PAUSE, and a square for STOP. The fifth symbol he didn't recognize; it looked like the circle and crosshairs of a rifle scope.

Julia moved a cursor over the palette of buttons.

Something struck the van.

Thunk!

Her pistol appeared in her hand so quickly, Allen wondered if it had always been there. As for himself, he might not have even noticed the sound, had Julia not moved so urgently. Before he realized it, his head was between his knees. He steeled himself for the windshield's inevitable shattering under the impact of the next round. His mind filled with things he wanted to yell out: *Start the van! Step on it! Let's go!*

But he heard Stephen's words first: "Whoa! Whoa! Whoa!" He was leaning almost out of the chair to stop Julia's movement toward the sliding door. "The door lock, Julia!" he said. "I just locked the doors." He reached his hand back and toggled the switch twice: *Thunk! Thunk!*

She stared at him in disbelief, whether at Stephen's actions or her own, Allen couldn't tell.

"It *is* loud," Stephen said apologetically, with a sideways tilt of his head.

She settled back in her chair, calmly slipping the weapon under her blazer. "It's okay," she said, closing her eyes. "Bit jumpy."

I'm just glad she's on our side, Allen thought.

Her lips stretched into a fat grin; then her eyes snapped open. "Told you I was raring to go." She reached out to the computer and clicked PLAY.

fifty-six

THE BLACK MAN EMERGED FROM A DOORWAY SET IN A whitewashed wall. With a perfectly round head and pencil-thin body, he resembled an upside-down exclamation point. He wore blue jeans, which were mostly white and hung loosely on his narrow hips, and a threadbare flannel shirt, buttoned tight at the neck. Dangling from the tips of three fingers was a beat-up metal lunch box, the kind kids toted to school in the sixties. Whatever had decorated it—images of the Brady Bunch, Speed Racer, or King Kong—had long since faded and chipped away. After appraising the sky, he started up the unpaved street, his heavy boots kicking up little plumes of dust. He glanced over his shoulder and stopped. A big smile broke like a crescent moon on a starless night. He raised his unencumbered hand and yelled, *"Moyo Wanji!"*

"What's that? What'd he say?" Allen didn't take his eyes off the screen.

Julia shook her head. Stephen said, "Shhh." All three had rotated their captain's chairs to face the laptop. By now, each was leaning forward—even Allen, whose nonchalant posture had succumbed to intense curiosity around the time the man on the screen had assessed the sky for rain. If the McDonald's restaurant suddenly exploded, it was doubtful the three people in the blue conversion van would have noticed—except maybe to turn up the volume on the computer they encircled.

From the left side of the monitor, another man came into view, dressed in equally depreciated clothes, carrying a stained paper sack. He said something unintelligible and clapped the first man on his back. As the two continued on, the camera jerked and followed, wobbling with the camera operator's hurried gait.

A column of numbers lay to the right of the video image. The first appeared to be a date, European style with the day first—5 April of last year. Below that, presumably, the time the video was shot—06:08:21 when the action started and now just changing to 06:11:00.

Julia thought the next number, 00:01:49:15, was a tape counter in National Television System Commission protocol: hours, minutes, seconds, then frames, which were ticking off at a pace of thirty per second. This was no amateur shoot; whoever had filmed, edited, and compiled this demonstration was professional.

As the camera followed the two men through the grungy streets of a small village, Stephen stretched across to tap at the number below the counter.

"See that?" he asked.

"Some kind of countdown," Julia observed. "Seven hours and four minutes—to something." She suppressed the urge to look at her watch, almost forgetting that the events playing out on her computer screen were now thirteen months old. Still, that backward-moving timer gave her the chills.

The men on the screen walked into a square where an old military-type truck idled loudly, belching clouds of oily exhaust from a rattling tailpipe. The truck was a sick shade of greenish-yellow, except for spots of pea green on the cab doors where insignias had been stripped away. Other men, all black, converged on the truck from different directions. In turn, each man climbed aboard, disappearing within the truck's canvas-covered bed. When the "star" of the video—that's the way Julia had come to think of the round-headed man—disappeared into the shadows, the image flickered once and went black.

Julia realized she'd been holding her breath. She let it out and pulled in another.

A new scene appeared with a jolt of the camera—a close-up of a pudgy man with an enormous gut and a yellow hard hat. He was barking out orders in a tongue so foreign it made Julia's head hurt. From behind came the sound of motors, raised voices, and the staccato rhythm of construction. After a moment, the camera swung to an area where a small group of men were slamming axes into trees. The camera zoomed in on the one in the center—Julia's star.

"The countdown," Stephen whispered.

It read -00:13:58. Julia's stomach tightened. A car horn from the laptop's tiny speakers drew her back to the video. The horn blasted for about five seconds. In that time, the star looked up, dropped his ax, and started meandering toward the camera, head hung as his left hand massaged his right bicep. The camera pulled back and hobbled away, taking a position some forty feet from the army-style truck. Again men converged on it, each with the day's physical agony showing on their bodies: filthy clothes, hair hued tan with sawdust and forested with spiky wood chips, grimacing faces, joints so stiff Julia could almost hear them creak. Shadows pooled at their feet, betraying a midday sun.

Each leaned into the back of the truck and emerged with a sack or box. They moved to the shade at the edge of a dense forest and sat. They pulled unwrapped clumps of a doughy substance from their containers, then worked vigorously to transfer it to their stomachs. The star ate quietly, perfectly centered in the camera's eye. The camera jiggled occasionally but otherwise remained stationary.

"Anyone got a fix on the location?" Julia asked without turning away from the screen.

"Haven't seen enough of the landscape," answered Allen. "I'd guess the language is an African dialect—a form of Swahili, maybe."

"So, Africa?"

"Just a guess. The town was pretty impoverished, and that foliage appears equatorial. Africa, South America, Southeast Asia. Our best clue—"

Julia stopped him with a raised hand, palm out.

The countdown had reached -00:00:55, and heads began turning skyward, apparently hearing something not yet detectable to the camera's microphone. Their eyes scanned aimlessly, then focused on something up and to the left of the screen. Over their apparent words of curiosity came the escalating drone of an airplane motor, like the hum of an approaching giant. Someone pointed, and one by one the men stood.

At this point the camera swung away from them, catching a white flash of sunlight before finding blue skies over the leafy tips of trees. A black dot grew quickly into a single-engine plane, coming in low over the forest. In an instant it swooped down, blurring hugely in the monitor. As the camera followed, it spewed a fine mist from its undercarriage.

"Crop duster," Allen remarked, stating the obvious out of sheer befuddlement.

The plane banked right, leaped over the trees, and disappeared.

Angry words poured from the speakers as the camera panned to the men speaking them: *"Wadika!" "Unakwenda wapi!" "Salop!"*

"That was French!" Stephen said. "I heard *salop*. That's French for . . . Well, it's not a nice word."

"Nimekasirika!" "Espece de pauvre con!"

"French again. *Con* means idiot."

As the mist blanketed them, the workers closed their eyes to it, coughed, and shook their fists at the spot where the plane had disappeared. Brushing off a flourlike dust, they spoke in sharp tones to one another and spat at the ground.

"Wait a sec," Julia said, moving a finger to the keyboard and causing the image to freeze. "The countdown's at plus twenty-two seconds now." She moved the cursor on the screen to the REWIND button and tapped her finger. In reverse, the workers appeared to powder themselves with dust that magically floated off their bodies and sailed into the air. Julia froze the image again. "Negative five seconds." She started clicking a button. "Four . . . three . . . two . . ."

"The mist from the plane is just coming into view at the top of the screen," Allen pointed out. Despite Bonsai's predictions about the converted file's poor quality, the resolution was perfect.

"One."

The mist was just hitting the tops of their heads.

"Zero."

The star's head was only a vague shadow behind the layer of dropping mist.

"That's it," Julia said. "The countdown was to this point."

"When whatever was in that mist hit their lungs," Allen said.

Dead silence filled the van like smoke as the three gazed at the image on the screen. After a few moments, Julia clicked a button to reactivate the video in real time. They had already seen this part: the men hurling insults at the sky, dusting themselves off, checking their food for residue . . .

"So what African countries speak French?" Julia asked, turning to Stephen and shifting in the big chair to tuck a leg under herself. She kept flicking her eyes toward the screen, waiting for something new. Despite being with two civilians, mentally she had donned her investigator's hat and was getting into the rhythm of corporate deductive reasoning.

"Zaire," Allen said. He whipped a crumpled pack of Camels out of his breast pocket and shook one out. After tossing it into his lips, he said, "It's obvious, isn't it? Ebola? Zaire?" He replaced the pack and removed a bright red Bic lighter from the same pocket; instead of lighting up, he rolled it between his fingers and raised his eyebrows at her. "The two are practically synonymous."

"It adds up," Stephen agreed.

Julia nodded and turned back to the screen. She wasn't really sure why it mattered at this point, but Donnelley had taught her that every fact, no matter how seemingly insignificant, played a part—sometimes a crucial part—in unraveling the mystery at hand.

"Okay, Zaire," she said quietly and watched as the camera panned slowly over the faces of the complaining men, lingering a moment on each one as if to record their identities.

"I don't like where this is heading," Allen said.

She brushed her bangs away from her forehead. Without turning away from the screen, she said, "If we really are dealing with Ebola, I think we just witnessed the intentional infection of these people."

"What bothers me more is that Ebola spreads through body fluids, blood usually." Allen shifted, agitated.

Julia paused the display as the camera was pulling back to frame the entire group again.

Allen's unlit cigarette wagged like an accusatory finger when he spoke. "As far as we know, no one has ever been infected by an airborne strain. Monkeys, yes; never a human. Big difference. If the vector to transmit the disease was in that dust, it's a strain more dangerous than any we've ever seen. And it's gone unreported."

"Maybe nobody knows," Stephen whispered.

"Look at the date," Allen said, indicating the screen. "Whoever's controlling it has had over a year to perfect the delivery system. A crop duster when this video was made—what now, a breeze?"

Julia stared at him a long time, lost in thought. At last she punched the button that continued the video.

fifty-seven

THE VIDEO FLICKED TO A NEW SCENE.

The doorway set in a whitewashed wall again—the skinny black man's home. The date and time set the moment at the fifth morning after the crop duster's visit to the man's work site. The man's friend approached the door, knocked. A woman answered, worry as plain on her face as the bright red housedress on her body. She shook her head and closed the door.

Blackness.

The scream pierced through the speaker even before the shadows swam into recognizable objects on the screen. The man—Julia's star—bellowed in agony from a battered cot in a small, dark room. Naked to the waist, he was curled in a fetal position, clutching at his stomach, rubbing his chest. Perspiration sluiced in thick streams from every inch of exposed flesh. With savage effort, the man hooked his head over the cot's edge and vomited into the black hole of a rusty pail.

"Lord, have mercy," Stephen whispered.

Positioned somewhere above the cot, the camera perfectly framed the convulsing figure. The woman who had answered the door glided into view and began wiping the man's head and neck with a drenched cloth, comforting him with soft cooing.

With a bolt of quick static, the day passed. The man still lay in a knot, wet, miserable, accepting water from a rag pressed to his fever-blistered lips; only the time on the display had changed. Another flash of static and the man was blistered and bleeding, flailing on the bed, splashing ribbons of blood across the walls and curtains. His mouth stretched in a silent scream. His eyes, solid red, searched blindly for help.

Julia's palm covered her mouth.

A man in a blood-drenched smock, a stethoscope slung around his neck, tried to hold down the dying man. A woman in a white-and-blue dress—a nurse, Julia thought—covered her mouth much the way Julia did and backed away from the bed and out of frame. A geyser of blackish blood erupted. The doctor staggered back, arms raised against the horror before him.

The body convulsed, then was still.

Soft chanting now; the mournful throb of a single drum. A corpse, wrapped from head to toe in white linen, lay like a ghost on a chest-high bier. Weeping softly, the woman who'd comforted Julia's star, his wife perhaps, dipped a flambeau into the kindling under the body. Within seconds, flames had completely engulfed the corpse.

"The medical staff didn't report the cause of death," Allen said, shaking his head. "Health officials never would have released the body."

The camera panned over the faces of the mourners, many of them recognizable from the work site scene when the crop duster had vomited its obscene cargo over them. As smoke darkened the sky, the scene faded to black.

The next act opened at the work site, familiar men laboring under a scorching sun.

"Not again," Julia lamented. The date display had jumped ahead two months.

But the crop duster did not return. In fact, nothing dramatic occurred in the two minutes the camera lingered there, zooming in on individual faces in calm order. Each went about his duties, seeming to have forgotten the death of his friend. The scene played out like an epilogue, as if to say, *Life goes on.* If Kafka or Tolstoy had directed the video, this was the way he would have ended it.

Another slow fade. All that was missing, Julia thought, was the word *Finis* in scripted letters.

After several flashes of static, another video sequence started—this one far different in quality. The image, grainy from low light levels, filled the monitor. Gone was the column of numbers that had recorded the time, date, and other bits of cryptic information. Where the first video had all the markings of a professional recording, made for evidence or analysis, this one more closely resembled a home movie. As covert as the preceding footage obviously was, this current stock seemed more so: most of the time something like a flap of cloth blocked a portion of the lens; the angle was from about knee-high, as if the operator had held the camera like a briefcase—or *in* a briefcase, thought Julia—and nothing was framed quite right. Most disturbing, visually and viscerally, was the image's constant vibration.

"Why is it doing that, that shaking?" Stephen asked.

"Bad tape in the camera, maybe?" offered Allen.

"Fear," Julia said. "Over the past decade, the Bureau has taken to wiring informants and undercover agents not only for sound but also for visuals with miniature cameras. We see that shaking a lot. The guy's scared stiff."

Under a slate sky, the camera panned over a collection of rusty Quonset huts. They rose like the humps of a sea monster from a field cleared of all foliage except for wisps of dry prairie grass. Here and there, the camera caught men with guns standing or strolling, paying no particular attention to the camera operator. In the distance was a tall chain-link fence, double coils of gleaming concertina wire balancing on top. Beyond that a dense jungle grew. Directly in front of the hangars was a long patch of ground, level and clear of foliage.

"That's a landing strip," Allen said.

"So it's an air base?" Julia asked.

"Except for the armed men, it looks abandoned."

Stephen stroked his beard in thought. "Don't drug cartels operate out of abandoned airstrips?"

"Yeah, and look how green and lush that jungle looks," Allen said. "More Amazonian or Asian than African."

Julia said, "I don't think this is about drugs."

The scene changed, and the camera was moving through a dim corridor. It approached a door, then went through it into a brightly lit, refurbished corridor. Windows were set in the walls on each side, lighted from within. The camera approached a window. Reflected in it was a ghostly image that quickly sharpened.

Julia froze the frame. Caught in the glass, a man held a briefcase under his arm.

"Look," Julia said, pointing to a black circle in the side of the briefcase, facing the glass. "Wanna bet that's an opening for the camera lens?"

The man recording his own reflection appeared to be Hispanic, with tight curly hair and heavy features.

"He matches the description of Vero from the bartender at the place where he and Goody were killed," she said. She studied the face a moment, then restarted the playback.

The reflection faded off the glass as the camera focused on what lay beyond—a room lined with beds. On every one lay a man or woman, some tossing in anguish, others still. Machines monitored their vital signs. IVs snaked into most of the arms.

"Some sort of sick ward," Stephen said.

Turning from the window, the image blurred. When it refocused, a man was walking toward it. At first Julia thought he wore a mask of a skull. His eyes were big black holes, his skin bone-white and gaunt. As he approached, she saw it was no mask. Sunglasses covered his eyes, but the rest of the visible head was disturbing: wispy, white hair clung in patches to the scalp, and the face was more than gaunt. It was as though someone had stretched cheesecloth over a skull. A lipless mouth stretched into a wide grin, showing canted and missing teeth.

Julia's heart leaped, and the camera flicked off.

fifty-eight

WHEN THE SCREEN HAD BEEN BLACK FOR A GOOD FIFTEEN seconds, Allen exhaled loudly and said, "I didn't see anything that proves Ebola is man-made, or that these guys did it. At best, it showed that there's an airborne strain of Ebola."

"And that someone's intentionally infecting people," Stephen said.

"There were two video clips," Julia said, thinking. "One appeared to be of a man in Africa being infected with Ebola. I'm making lots of assumptions, I know. The second was not action-oriented and was in a different setting. There's nothing that obviously connects the two, but they must be related somehow."

"Somehow," Allen repeated. He leaned back in the passenger's seat, fishing a crumpled pack of cigarettes out of his breast pocket. He examined the package, saw it was empty, and tossed it over his shoulder onto the dash.

Julia's eyebrows furled together. If Vero had intended to expose the true, malicious origin of Ebola, why wasn't the evidence on the memory chip? What had he set out to prove?

She had been staring at the computer, without really seeing it, when two white-lettered words appeared on the dark screen:

ERSTE ANGRIFF

"Who's that?" Stephen asked.

Allen said, "I don't think it's a who. *Erste* is German for 'first.'" He scrunched up his face. "I'm not sure about *angriff*. Something like 'battle' or 'fight.'"

"First battle," Stephen whispered.

They waited for more . . .

Then it dawned on her. The self-starting video sequences had fooled her into regarding Vero's memory chip as a DVD, which would naturally unravel linearly to the end. But it wasn't. It was a computer data chip with files that had to be opened. The video clips were nothing more than digital multimedia files, like word processing documents and spreadsheets. Whatever this was, it wasn't self-opening.

Julia moved the cursor over the words, and the little arrow turned into a pointing hand. "It's hypertext," she said. "It's linked to some other file."

She clicked on the words. Instantly a list of names began scrolling past, lightning fast. She tapped a key, and the list froze.

"Anthony Petucci," she said, pointing. "The actor?"

Stephen bent near to read aloud. "Howard Melton. Isn't he a senator? Janet Plenum, governor of Oregon."

"Lew Darabont," Allen said. "I love his movies."

Julia said, "Hasn't he directed something like four or five of the top ten films of all time?"

She moved the cursor over one of the names. Again it turned into a pointing hand. "They're linked too." She tapped the cursor button.

New words filled the screen:

RICHARD KENNEDY

SSN: 987-65-4320 B. 04/21/55

OCCUPATION: CEO, NANOTECH SOFTWARE, INC.

HOME ADDRESS:

1910 WHITEHORN DRIVE

SAN FRANCISCO, CA 94120

<HIDDEN FIELDS FOLLOW—DO NOT MERGE>

APPENDECTOMY, 11/02/92

MOUNT SINAI HOSPITAL, LOS ANGELES

CONTROL CODE: 469878884-L

"He's one of the richest men in America," Allen said.

"Appendectomy?" Stephen said. "What kind of database is this?"

"A big one," Julia said, bringing the screen back to the list of names. She scrolled down a few screens. Tapped on a name, closed it . . . then another . . . and another . . .

"There's an odd assortment of the famous and the average," she said after a while. "Politicians, celebrities, business leaders, an auto mechanic, housewives—look at this . . ."

HUNTER, BABY BOY

SSN: N/A B. 09/15/06

OCCUPATION: N/A

HOME ADDRESS:

4250 MICHIGAN AVENUE, APT. 312

CHICAGO, IL 60611

<HIDDEN FIELDS FOLLOW—DO NOT MERGE>

PKU, 09/17/06

MEMORIAL HOSPITAL, CHICAGO

Control Code: 842074654-M

Stephen shook his head. "A baby. Didn't even have a name when this information was collected."

"PKU," Allen said. "That's a blood test all newborns get."

"Why is he here," Julia whispered, "on a list with the rich and famous, on a chip people are dying over?"

She went back to the names, let it scroll to the end. It took several minutes. She wasn't sure why, but watching those names zip past, knowing they were somehow linked to Donnelley's death, Vero's death, the gruesome murder of that man on the video, made her feel sick.

Stephen must have been uneasy too. He shifted nervously. "How many?" he asked.

"I don't know. Five thousand? Ten?"

"What's it matter?" Allen said, patting his breast pocket, finding nothing. "We don't know the significance of these names. Could be a Christmas card list, for all we know." He opened the glove box and began rooting around. "What are we going to do, phone up Richard Kennedy and everyone else who's on it? 'Excuse me, sir, do you happen to know the guy who's planning to invade the U.S. with the Ebola virus?'"

Julia suspected that apprehension was a strange guest in Allen Parker's psyche; showing anger was easier than facing a new emotion. She waited for something else to materialize on the screen. When it didn't, she leaned over the laptop and started typing. She was digging for more information the way Allen was hunting for a cigarette. Both came up cold.

She slid back into her chair, seeming to be swallowed by it.

"What now?" Stephen asked.

She took a minute to answer. The chip wasn't what she had hoped it would be. It contained no quick solution, no proof of who was doing what to whom and why; it didn't even contain evidence they could use—not without knowing what it was evidence of. Like most evidentiary material, it was maddeningly ambiguous, needing to be united with other puzzle pieces before its value became clear. She wanted to kick the computer right off the chair but didn't have the energy. Finally she took a deep breath and raised her eyebrows to him. "We've been here too long. Let's get moving."

"Anywhere in particular?"

She skewed her mouth, considering. "No," she said and laughed a little. "Nowhere at all."

fifty-nine

ABOUT TEN MINUTES INTO THEIR JOURNEY TO NOWHERE IN particular, Allen said, "The planes."

"What planes?" Stephen asked. "You mean the crop duster?"

"That's what got me thinking, that and the airstrip on that base." He had been riding with his feet up on the dash like a teenager. He brought them down and turned to Julia. "Would you agree the people trying to kill us are professionals?"

"Professional hit men? Yeah, seems that way to me."

"Then they're probably not from Atlanta. Certainly not Chattanooga. Not enough work for them."

She saw where he was heading. "They flew in for the job."

He nodded. "And I'll bet they didn't take commercial flights. They've got special weapons. Need to move quickly, on their own schedule. They don't want too much scrutiny."

"So a chartered or private plane?" Julia said.

"That's what I'm thinking."

"And landing at the airport leaves a record, a lead."

"Not necessarily. Airports aren't required to log every landing. Most do since 9/11. Sometimes there's a record only if the plane paid for fuel or overnight parking."

"There'll be records," she said. "Goody's killers didn't make their return flight, and the Warrior stayed awhile. Parking fees are a gimme."

"Can you access airport records?"

"Hey, I'm a federal agent—I can do anything." She smiled and reached down to maneuver the makeshift table off the floor. Allen moved to help, but she had it in place between the front and rear chairs before he could decide which part of the board to grab. She transferred the laptop to it.

"Seriously, this thing is loaded with programs that can worm their way into most computer systems. They're designed for on-site searches of computers used for criminal activities. You wouldn't believe the gimmicks perps use to prevent their data from making it to a tech lab. Magnetized doorways that wipe out hard drives as police carry them through; reserve batteries that blitz the data with a power surge, triggered by mercury switches to detect movement or zero-current switches that detect when the computer is unplugged. One child pornographer booby-trapped his computer with homemade C-4. It was rigged to detonate if the computer was lifted off of a pressure-sensitive pad. We spotted it before it hurt anyone, but it would have vaporized the evidence, along with the house and a half dozen cops. Anyway, it's best to seize the data right at the scene. I have programs that slice through the toughest computer security systems like they weren't even there. Where do I start?" Her fingers were poised over the keyboard.

"Try General Aviation, Chattanooga Metropolitan Airport."

She scooted closer to the computer, eyes flicking from keyboard to screen and back.

"See what they show for landings, parking, fuel sales, maintenance."

A few minutes passed. Then she swiveled the monitor around for Allen to see.

He leaned in. "Those are the flight progress strips."

"Going back two weeks," Julia said, smug. "But this is where I hit a brick wall. I have no idea what to look for."

"Let me see." He pulled it closer, squinting at the entries.

"How do you know all this?" she asked.

"I've always loved private aviation. I took some private pilot lessons but never finished. Got too busy. Sometimes I still park by the airport to eat my lunch, watch the planes come and go. Here, look at this." He read it aloud: "Fourteen-eighteen. Cessna Citation CJ2. N471B."

"Yeah?"

"How many four-million-dollar private jets fly into Chattanooga?"

"The timing's right. Just before the killings at the bar."

"You think that's the plane that brought in the two-man hit team?"

"It's the Warrior's. The first two assailants pursued Goody and Vero from Atlanta. The second set of assailants, the ones who came for you at your house, you said one of them had a cop's badge. A local cop. Maybe by then they were getting desperate, hiring whoever was available."

Allen said, "The FAA maintains a plane registry right on the Internet. We can find out who owns that Citation without jumping through techno-hoops." Something on the screen caught his eye. "Hold on. Oh-five-fifty-one, Cessna Citation . . ."

"This morning? He left?"

"Yesterday morning. Another landed. N-number: N476B."

"Two Citations? Sixteen hours apart." Julia was thinking out loud. "Could the same people own both?"

"Same type of plane with almost sequential tail numbers? Very likely." Allen read again from the screen: "Oh-eight-twenty, Cessna Citation."

"*Another* one?"

"The first one, N471B, took off yesterday morning, two and a half hours after the second arrived."

"What are we supposed to do now?" Stephen asked from behind the wheel.

She gave herself a moment to think. "I suppose we find out who registered the Cessnas. Probably a dummy corporation, owned by another dummy corporation. But if we burrow deep enough, maybe cross-reference the names we dig up with other clues we find along the way, we'll uncover something solid."

Allen didn't look happy.

"Welcome to detective work," she said. "Ninety percent of criminal investigations is following paper trails, digging through computer files, reading receipts and depositions and ledgers until your eyes are ready to fall out. Forget *CSI*; it's more like wait a minute." She spun the laptop around, away from Allen.

"Hey."

She began typing, staring at the screen.

"What?"

"The hard drive. Can't you hear it? It's working too hard. Someone's hacked into my computer."

sixty

"YOU'RE IN THE AIRPORT'S COMPUTER," ALLEN SAID. "MAYBE they're trying to hack you back."

"That's not they way it works. If they detect the breech, they just cut you off. Someone's going through my files."

"So cut them off."

"I'm trying. They've got some kind of protection against that. I've never seen anything like it."

An observer catching her flexing bands of jaw muscles, the determined flash of gritted teeth, would have guessed that she was battling for her life. And they'd have been right: Survival on the run was like a knife fight. The outcome was rarely determined by the planting of one deadly blow, but by the number and depth of slash after slash after slash—until the one most slashed bled to death. She could not afford the injury of giving away access to her computer, whether the intruder's motive was to find out its contents or destroy its data.

"Disconnect the phone," Allen said.

"If I can stop him, maybe I can find out who it is." She keyed in more commands. "It's not working." She reached for the phone line. The screen went black, and a line of white text appeared at the top:

> *Ms. Matheson?*

Allen, unable to see the monitor from the front seat, asked, "What is it?"

She told him, then typed:

> *Who is this?*

The answer:

> *A friend.*

"What's going on?" Allen stood to lean over the top, bumping the table and nearly dumping everything to the floor.

Julia caught the computer and phone, stabilizing them on the table once more. "Allen! Sit. I'll tell you. He says he's a friend."

"A friend? *Your* friend? What's his name, Bonsai?"

"Shhhhh! This isn't Bonsai. Just be quiet and listen."

Speaking the words, she typed:

> *I don't need any more friends.*

> *That's not what I've heard.*

She read the response aloud, already typing her reply:

> *How do you know me?*

> *I've been waiting for you. I knew you would eventually think to check the airport records. I'm surprised it took you so long.*

Allen whispered, "Is he still going through your hard drive?"

"No, he's just talking." She wrote:

> *Why did you hack me?*

> *Just trying to make a connection.*

"That's not true," she said. "He was digging. I think he realized I was onto him and decided to take another approach, instead of just getting cut off."

> *Ms. Matheson. Your enemy is my enemy. Does that not make us friends?*

> *No. Who is my enemy?*

> *Atropos.*

"I've heard that name," she said, but she typed:

> *I don't know who that is.*

> *The man who tried to kill you, Dr. Parker, and Mr. Parker.*

"The Warrior," Allen said.

The words continued:

> *Of all the people who kill for a living, he is the worst.*

Julia closed her eyes. It was coming back, who Atropos was. She typed:

> *Atropos is a myth.*

> *A myth that almost killed you.*

> *Whoever he is, he's only a hired gun. Are you his employer?*

> *Atropos is purely freelance.*

> *Did you hire him?*

> *No. You know who did.*

"What's he mean, we know?" Allen said after she read the line.

"I don't know."

The answer came over the screen:

> *Litt.*

"Karl Litt," she said, her mind racing. "Goody said his name. We used it in our fake conversation, the one we recorded. They *were* listening. That may have been the one key phrase they caught. He must think we know more about him than we do." She typed:

> *Are you Karl Litt?*

> *Litt hires killers. He does not engage in conversation. He does not have the resources to find you the way I did.*

"I don't know," she said. "He seemed to find us in Knoxville without any problem. Either this guy doesn't know Litt's capabilities, or he just wants us to think he's more powerful than Litt."

> *How do I know you don't want us dead as well?*

> *Ms. Matheson, I've traced you to your computer, which means I know the cell phone number you're using. I could have simply remained silent and sent people to your location.*

"Except that I realized he had hacked me. I wouldn't have continued using this phone."

"But what if he hadn't rooted through your hard drive?" Stephen said. "Couldn't he have found the number you were calling from without your ever knowing?"

She nodded. "He might have thought he could get away with both—getting a traceable number for us *and* finding out what's on my hard drive. But we caught him, so now he's trying to say what a stand-up guy he is."

> *So, friend, what is your name?*

> *It doesn't matter, just that we can help each other.*

"I don't trust people who won't say who they are," she said. "All right, then . . ." She moved her fingers over the keyboard and punched in a series of commands. She stopped and leaned back. "Let's see how you like that."

"What did you do?" Allen asked hesitantly.

"I sent a worm back to him," she answered with a smile. "Right now it's rooting its way into the other computer. And it's sending data back to us."

"Like what?"

She shrugged. "Letters, address book data, financial information—the kinds of things people keep in their computers. The first thing it looks for are program registration records. They usually contain the name and address of the computer owner."

A box floated on the screen, showing the quantity of data her worm had pulled in from the other computer. The number grew larger as she watched. She typed:

> *How can we help each other?*

Nothing. Ten seconds. Twenty. Then the number in the floating box stopped changing.

"He cut me off." Her fingers moved over the keyboard.

> *You there?*

Nothing.

"He's gone."

"You shouldn't have hacked him," Stephen said.

"Why not?"

"He said he could help us."

"And what makes you believe him?"

"What he said, that he could have just sent people after us."

"We don't know he didn't."

She rebooted the laptop with plans to run a spyware-detection program when it was up again. She didn't want something lurking in her computer she didn't know about.

"Who's Atropos?" Allen asked.

She shook her head. "A fantasy. Supposedly he's the world's best assassin. He can hit anyone, anywhere. Never fails. Always gets away."

"He didn't get *us*," Stephen said, defiant.

"Yet," she said. "Most assassinations don't happen the way they do in the movies. They're rarely clean, quiet kills.

Sometimes it takes four or five attempts to hit the target, over days or weeks. Of course, getting them on the first attempt is best; later they're on guard, probably got some beefed-up security. It gets tougher. Then again, the assassin learns more about his target with each attempt. Patterns and weaknesses. So as long as he doesn't give up until the job is done, he's considered successful."

"Why did you say he's a myth?"

"Maybe *legend* is a better word. The stories about him get wilder every time you hear them. He's killed dictators protected by armies. He's been credited with killing someone in Asia and then, within an hour, killing someone else in America. The story goes, he comes from a long line of assassins. In the eleventh century, an 'Atropos' helped Frederick Barbarossa seize control of the Holy Roman Empire. Six hundred years later, Elizabeth Petrovna of Russia was found dead in her bedchamber; despite the official explanation of a sudden illness, some historians claim she was assassinated by a man named Atropos. During World War II, Atropos claimed Allied spies, politicos, and important industrialists as his victims. Just some spot examples I remember. Besides the name, each succeeding assassin shared one trait: he killed with a spiked gauntlet."

"Oh, man," Stephen said. "You're creeping me out."

"I think that's the idea. He's the boogeyman for historians and CIA types."

She disconnected the phone from the laptop and turned it around in her hand while she talked.

"I guess he's kind of a cult celebrity," she continued. "Look on the Internet. There are fan clubs dedicated to this guy. Some say he was reared from infancy on the skills of his family's tradecraft. At six years old he learned how to pick locks. At eight he learned that severing the spinal cord at the base of the neck prevents targets from getting off one last shot after you've killed them. It's this lifelong training that makes him so good. And some people think his very lineage adds to his prowess, that each generation yields a better assassin than the generation before him—not because of the training, but because it's in his blood."

"Knock it off," Allen said, flashing an unsure smile.

"You asked," she said.

"Maybe there's something to it," Stephen said. "After all, Julia, you saw him come back from the dead."

Her mouth went dry. She *had* see him slaughtered, only to appear the next day, ready for a fight. That was creepy enough, but did it lend credibility to stories about him? To her, it did.

The tinted window next to her hinged at the top. She levered open the bottom to its maximum opening of about four inches. She was about to drop the phone through when it rang.

She looked at Allen, who scowled.

"Private number," she said and answered.

"Touché, Ms. Matheson."

The voice made her think of her great-aunt's letters. The writing was thin and shaky, as though written on a paint mixer.

"I thought you'd like that," she said.

"You're a very capable woman. As I said, I believe we can help each other."

"Without knowing who you are, I don't want your help, and you certainly won't get mine."

Silence.

"At this point," he said, "I must tell you that we are dealing in matters of national security. I must be assured that anything I tell you will be kept in the strictest confidence. This goes for you and Allen and Stephen Parker. I am recording this conversation."

"You're kidding, right?"

"I've very serious. Divulging what we say to *anyone* —the media, your mother—will result in your arrest and imprisonment. Is that clear?"

Her stomach tightened. Did he say *mother* simply to stress the comprehensiveness of the prohibition, or was he *saying* something? Did he know about her mother, her being alone, her illness? Was he threatening her?

"We've got killers after us, and you're telling me you'll throw me in jail for talking?"

"I can't say more without your indicating that you understand the confidential nature of our conversation and the consequences for violating this confidence."

She suspected he was more interested in establishing his credibility with her than binding her to a gag order.

"I understand and agree."

"And what is your whole name?"

She told him.

"Now, please, let me speak to Dr. Parker and his brother."

She hesitated. Was he trying to establish that they were together? Was there any reason to keep it secret? She couldn't think of any. She handed the phone to Allen.

He listened, then said, "Allen Douglas Parker." Listened. "I agree." He handed the phone to Stephen, who went through the process, then held the phone over his shoulder for Julia to take.

"Okay, now—"

"My name is Kendrick Reynolds."

"Kendrick Reynolds?"

Allen's eyes got big. He mouthed the name.

"Do you know who I am?"

"Of course. Former secretary of state. Former director of the CIA. Advisor to—what?—eight presidents?"

"Ten," he corrected.

"Billionaire," Allen added.

"I assume," the man claiming to be Kendrick Reynolds said, "you can confirm my identity through the computer files you stole."

"You said you can help us."

"I *can* protect you."

"The way you protected Goodwin Donnelley and Despesorio Vero?"

"My point exactly. They were on their own, away from my protection. Their fate does not have to be yours."

"And how do we help you?"

"I believe you have something Despesorio Vero was bringing me."

"To you? He showed up at the CDC. I heard tapes of his calls. He never mentioned you."

"I am the only person who can stop Karl Litt."

"From doing what?"

"Honestly, I do not know." He sounded even more tired than previously. "But considering Karl's . . . expertise, I have some ideas."

"Such as?"

"A biological attack on the United States."

"And who is Karl Litt to you?"

"A bad investment."

"You're in business with him?"

"He worked for the government at one time. Now he doesn't."

Allen touched her shoulder. He whispered, "Could they be tracing the call?"

She nodded. "Give me a number where I can reach you."

"Ms. Matheson, you can end this now. Thousands of lives—"

"A number or we never speak again."

She waited. After a long moment, he recited a number and a security code. She closed the flip phone and dropped it out the window.

sixty-one

KENDRICK REYNOLDS CRADLED THE HANDSET AND LOOKED at his assistant. Captain Landon watched him carefully, unsure of Kendrick's mood.

"Interesting," was all Kendrick would say. He pulled a breath through the mouthpiece of his God-head pipe, found it had gone out, and plucked it from his mouth.

Maybe it was for the best that Julia and the Parkers knew precisely who they were dealing with. He didn't know about Stephen Parker, but reports on Allen Parker pegged him as some sort of medical Einstein, and just now Julia had made her intelligence abundantly clear. These were the kind of people who didn't believe in "the man behind the curtain"; they wanted names and faces and résumés.

Now they have mine, he thought.

That both frightened and exhilarated him. If laying himself bare before people who had the evidence not only to destroy his future but to dismantle his past resulted in finding Litt and burying that very evidence against himself—well, this could turn out to be his most brilliant play yet. What a way to end his career. Absently, he ran a finger over the face of God.

Of course, Matheson and the Parkers themselves were loose ends that would need tying up. But for now, he needed only to get his hands on whatever it was Vero had left and Litt was trying to get back. Something, definitely. The woman had all but admitted to having it.

His eyes refocused on the captain. "Anything?" he asked.

Captain Landon checked his monitor. He pushed a button and spoke into a mouthpiece clamped to his head.

Kendrick wheeled himself back, spun his chair, and positioned it near a recliner. He reached out and got hold of a wooden cane. He rocked his body out of the chair, leaning heavily on the cane. Aiming for the room's exit, he took two halting steps. His third was more sure.

"Sir?" the captain called behind him.

Kendrick didn't look back or stop his gait; he was shuffling but moving along at a good clip.

"The cell phone has stopped moving. Our team will intercept it in twenty minutes."

Kendrick waved his free hand. "Ah! She got rid of it. We can only hope she calls."

Seventy seconds later, he made it to the door and stepped through.

"DO YOU TRUST HIM?" STEPHEN ASKED. HE WAS STILL STEERing the van through the streets of Atlanta. Being a moving target gave them a small measure of comfort.

"Not as far as I can throw this van," Allen said.

"I don't know," Julia said.

"Look," Allen snapped, "he wants the evidence kept secret and claims Vero was bringing it to him. That means he's involved."

"He's offering to help," Stephen reminded him.

"What else would he say? 'I want to kill you for the evidence and because you know too much. Let's meet'?"

"He may be our best chance of getting out of this mess intact."

Stephen wasn't completely convinced of his own words, Julia could tell, but he wanted to examine all the possibilities.

"Our best chance of getting killed, more likely," Allen said. "For all we know, Kendrick Reynolds is behind this whole thing. It makes sense: he's got the money and the power to do everything we've witnessed. Finding us. Sending cops to kill us—Julia, you said it had the government's fingerprints all over it; this guy's as *government* as they get. Hiring 'the world's best assassin.' Come on!"

She let Allen's voice fade into the throaty drone of the engine. Deep in concentration, she stared out at the city, at its eclectic people and architecture, at its silent clash of old and new, beautiful and ugly. She was vaguely aware of sunlight slicing through the van at a different angle each time Stephen rounded a corner; of the rising temperature, turning the air muggy and soporific; of an increasing sense of being nothing more than a bit player in a tragedy already written and rolling along toward an unknown climax. All of it could have too easily congealed into an atmosphere of hopelessness.

For that reason, Julia accepted this new wrinkle, this stranger bearing gifts or traps, as a challenge. If Kendrick Reynolds turned out to be what he claimed, a friend, then she'd lose nothing by waiting a little longer, learning a little more. If he was another face of the monster that pursued them, she was hell-bent on knowing that before their next encounter. His offer of assistance could be an oasis or a mirage. She wasn't going to stop looking for water until she knew for sure.

At last she said, "He may be able to help us, but he wants us to help him too. He's asked us to turn over the data from the memory chip. He's in a much better position to know what any of it means. Maybe sharing it with him will give him the ammunition to fight our foes for us. Then again, what if his seeing the evidence means he no longer needs us or wants to help us? We'll have lost a bargaining chip. I think we need to know more before we make that decision."

"So, what?" Stephen asked. "Investigate more?"

"That's my two cents," she said. She picked up another cell phone and began readying it for use.

Allen tapped the top end of a pack of Camels against the dash. He glanced back at her. "Now what?"

She powered up the laptop. "Atropos is still looking for us. The airport records show his plane is still in Chattanooga, right?"

He nodded.

"Then let's go to Chattanooga."

sixty-two

SILENTLY, ALLEN SLIPPED OUT THE DOOR BETWEEN TWO hangars and began making his way toward the tarmac. Thick shadows had already filled the man-made canyon he traversed, but the orange glow of dusk still blazed at its far end like fading embers. The fingers of his left hand skipped lightly along the corrugated metal side of the hangar he had exited; his left arm cradled a package hidden beneath his beige Windbreaker.

He crossed the narrow alley and stopped with his back pressed against the other building, two feet from the corner. He scratched savagely at his beard, flipped his salt-and-pepper ponytail off his shoulder. Three quick breaths, then he edged to the corner and peered around.

Beyond the hangars stretched three rows of parked airplanes. Most were compact, two- and four-man rides, tied down to keep them from flipping in a stiff wind. Here and there private jets gleamed above their propellered brethren. And past them all, well away from the rest, sat the one he had come for —a white Cessna Citation CJ2, tail number N476B.

He was about to swing out into the open when he glanced in the other direction—toward the majority of buildings, the terminal, and the control tower—and saw a white pickup truck speeding along the taxiway toward him, amber strobes flashing atop its cab. He stepped back into the shadows.

This is not a good idea, Allen thought as the truck flashed past the alley.

Trouble was, it was their only idea that didn't involve putting their tails between their legs and scampering away like scared dogs. He scratched at the fake beard again; the spirit gum Julia had used to affix it was drying, and it itched.

He poked his head around the corner again and caught the truck hooking a U-turn in front of the parked planes. Within seconds it swept past him again, heading toward the terminal and busier parts of the airfield.

It had been Julia's excitement that had hooked him. As little as he thought of her plan, he wanted to disappoint her even less. She was just so . . . darn cute. He smiled wryly. How many times had his libido led him blissfully over the cliff of bad ideas? Too many to count. And now this doozy.

In his mind's eye, he saw Julia's smile—faltering when she caught his looks of concern—as she laid it all out, grabbing things from her gym bag to show them, drawing invisible diagrams in the air with her finger.

"IF I'M READING THE GUYS WHO'RE AFTER US RIGHT, THEY'RE control freaks," she had explained as the van moved toward their first destination, S & L Law Enforcement Provisions, Inc. "Allen, they knew everything about you before Vero's body had even cooled. Your address, Stephen's. They found out who transported Goody from the bar to the hospital, who assisted you in the ER—and had them killed."

For a moment, her lips had pressed together bitterly. Not in anger, Allen thought. Not entirely. He suspected a heavy dose of sorrow motivated the gesture. She didn't even know the EMTs or the nurses, but their senseless deaths grieved her.

"The point is," she continued, "I don't think they'll be able to stand a new, unknown player in the game."

"Player? What new player?"

She cocked her head innocently. "You."

"Me?"

"You're taller than the average male Caucasian, but not remarkably so. If we disguise your features enough, they'll think you're someone who knows them, but they won't know you."

"And how will they learn about this 'new player'?" he asked, condescending.

"He's going to try to break into their jet."

"Atropos's jet?"

She nodded.

Allen crossed his legs, then his arms. "Why break in?"

"Two objectives. If no one's there, see if there's anything that'll identify who hired him."

"What do you mean, *if no one's there*? If I do this, there'd better not be anyone there."

"If Atropos or whoever he has working for him—a pilot maybe—does see you, then you want to leave this . . ."

She leaned over, rooted in her gym bag, and held up the gauntlet.

"But you can't just *leave* it," she continued. "You have to pretend to lose it accidentally, drop it while running away or something."

Allen shook his head. "Why give it to them at all? You really are an exasperating woman."

She set the gauntlet on her lap, and again she fumbled around in the gym bag. When she straightened, empty-handed, Allen presumed she'd misplaced something. Then he noticed the item resting in her upturned palm. It was about the size of a dime, but several times thicker, black. He leaned closer.

"A satellite-assisted tracking device," she announced. "Goody was going to place it on Vero so we wouldn't lose him. I have the equipment to track this puppy to hell and back. It's a beacon of the gods—as close to omniscience as we'll ever get."

She examined the device, used her fingernail to rotate an almost invisible switch set into its case. Then, picking up the gauntlet, black and muscular and hideous, she carefully slipped in her hand, the tracking device on a fingertip.

"I'm going to put the SATD into one of the fingers. If I've guessed right, Atropos will want to find out who was walking around with one of his own special weapons and who made an attempt to breach his plane." She withdrew her arm, then shook the gauntlet a few times to make sure the device wouldn't fall out. "The only clue he'll have is the gauntlet."

Allen nodded. "He'll have it examined it for fingerprints."

"I'm counting on that to keep him from finding the SATD too soon. He'll want to preserve any fingerprints that may be inside. Kendrick said Atropos is freelance; he goes where the jobs and the money are. I think he'll turn to his current employer for help in finding out who this new guy is.

And I bet Litt has the means to lift and analyze a fingerprint. By the time they discover the tracking device, I'm praying that it's smack in the middle of their home base."

"So he takes it to them, and we find out where they are," Stephen said from the driver's seat. His deep voice was frigid, all business.

"Wait a sec," Allen said. "Why can't we simply attach it to their plane? Wouldn't that be safer?"

"We can't be sure the Citation will go all the way to their base. What if they land at a major airport and take another form of transportation to their final destination?"

"And even if they don't use the plane," Stephen said, "if they send it by courier or something, we'll still find out where they are."

Despite himself, Allen felt excitement lift his mood. "Want to bet it ends up at whatever swank address Kendrick Reynolds calls home?" he asked. "Or at one of the agencies he controls?"

Stephen cranked the wheel, jostling the van over what felt like a canyon wall. Allen turned to see the cop supply store's front window looming large in the windshield.

"First, Allen, we make sure you're well protected," Julia said behind him. "Then we make you look like someone Atropos doesn't know."

sixty-three

Now, disguised as Julia's "new player," Allen tried not to think of how completely alone he was. Julia and Stephen were waiting in the hangar, in the comfort of a Learjet they'd secured as a staging area for this "operation," as Julia called it. He mustered his courage and edged to the corner of the hangar. He peered first left, at the parked planes, then right, toward the distant terminal.

All clear.

He stepped out of the shadowy alley and into the waning light, heading toward Atropos's Cessna. He walked along the front of a hangar, past the huge closed doors, moving fast. At the last hangar before a long stretch of tarmac, he heard music and saw that the sliding doors stood about five feet apart. As he approached, Freddie Mercury's mournful vocals swelled:

Mama, just killed a man

Put a gun against his head
Pulled my trigger, now he's dead . . .

A loud clang, followed by a string of expletives, slipped out the door. Allen hurried past the opening without looking. A sign jutted from the corner of the hangar: CAUTION—AIRPLANE CROSSING. He walked under it, casting a furtive glance to the left at an abandoned-looking building fifty yards beyond the end of the hangar. Wooden crates, oil drums, and tires formed a huge wedge against one side.

For about sixty seconds he felt utterly exposed—empty tarmac stretching away to a runway on his right; on his left, only crumbling asphalt, followed by a field of dry weeds for a hundred yards to the perimeter fence. Behind him lay the hangars, and way past them, the terminal. He resisted the urge to look over his shoulder. Instead, he tried to identify the planes he was approaching: a Beechcraft Bonanza, a Piper Cherokee, a Gulfstream IV—sweet. Then he was among the planes and felt the burden of exposure fade away like the remaining light.

The Cessna loomed larger with each plane he passed. It was parked at least fifty paces from the last plane. Worse, it was canted toward the terminal, toward *him*. A person sitting in the cockpit would have to be blind to miss his approach. But he needed to get right on top of the thing for Julia's scheme to work. To get there, he hoped to come off as an aviation geek with a weakness for big-ticket jets; later he'd be the menace Julia thought the assailants would respond to.

He stepped up to the last plane before the Cessna, putting it between himself and his target. It was a Piper Saratoga, the model that carried John F. Kennedy Jr., his wife, and his sister-in-law to the bottom of the Atlantic. He pretended to examine the nose propeller but was actually scrutinizing the

Cessna. The cockpit windows were too high, the interior too dark to know whether he was being watched in return. Through the six oval port windows on this side, he caught movement, a flicker as though someone had walked past all of them. Again light flickered against them, and he realized something inside was strobing softly, a television or computer screen, or maybe a security device.

The sun had traveled beyond the horizon now, pulling the last glow of solar radiance from the sky. Twilight began its brief presentation, with the scent of night close behind. The jet appeared more ominous in this light, more like a living thing that killed to survive.

Absently keeping his hand on the prop's nose cone, Allen maneuvered to the other side of the Piper, made an insincere attempt to examine a propeller, then broke away and strode for the Cessna. He tried to appear casual—just a fellow pilot admiring a beautiful flying machine, or airport security ensuring satisfaction with the accommodations. He'd have to decide which he was if he happened to be challenged before he could tamper with the jet's entry door—thereby becoming a threat, aka the new player. He pulled the gauntlet from under his Windbreaker and held it against the side of his upper leg. He cringed at the gravel crunching loudly under his feet.

Now that he was close, he tried to appear "sneaky, malicious, and knowledgeable"—Julia's words again. He bent his knees a bit and glanced around quickly, thinking these things fell under the "sneaky" category. He hoped he'd only have to rattle the door latch and run; no problem—what ten-year-old hadn't done that? If that didn't stir whoever was inside— *Oh Lord, let it be a pilot, not Atropos*—he wasn't sure what he'd do. Rattle-and-run was one thing; it was something altogether different to slap on a deer suit and tromp down to the watering hole during hunting season. He tucked the gauntlet back inside his Windbreaker. Nerves would have him extracting and replacing it every ten seconds if he let them.

He skirted around the jet's fiercely pointed nose and found himself standing in front of the closed door. He turned the latch, and the door sprang open, a portion hinging up, a section with built-in steps coming down. An air-conditioned breeze blew past him, tinged with a faint sweet fragrance— aftershave or overripe fruit. The interior was dark except for the grayish-blue strobing he'd seen through the windows. He leaned in. A galley with sink and cupboards sat opposite the door. The cockpit to the left. Leaning farther, he saw the cabin was set up like a studio apartment. He took a step up. The strobe came from a big plasma TV on the back wall. It was flashing through channel after channel, waiting for just the right show to appear, but no one was watching it. The plane was too small for hiding places. Allen knew that some pilots turned on lights or radios or other electronics when they left their unhangared planes to give the appearance of occupancy. A channel-changing plasma was something new, but he supposed it was effective. But why would a security-minded person leave the door unlocked? Only one reason came to mind: because he had stepped out for only a moment, maybe just to the GA building for a vending machine snack or newspaper.

He backed off the step and crouched to look under the plane toward the general aviation building and terminal. No one in sight.

He stood and went into the plane. The light from the TV was enough to guide him to a small desk, where a laptop computer, a printer, and scattered papers lay. His heart shrank in his chest, a painful movement that left him hyperventilating. Printed on the top page was a picture of Julia, a brief description printed underneath. Scratchy, handwritten notes in the margin: *pistol—under left arm, tactically evasive, carries duffel—why?* He pushed it aside and saw his own picture, from his driver's license. *Dr.—will mend wounds? Major ties to Chatt.* Next: a picture of Steven. *Big, strong—tae kwon do? Hesitant—weakness?* The next page appeared to be a work order or invoice. Under the word *Objectives*, their names and one item were listed numerically:

1. *Julia Matheson*
2. *Allen Parker*
3. *Stephen Parker*
4. *Memory chip (see desc.) and any known copies*

Then:

Package price, $500,000. All or none.

Warning: Other teams involved; well trained, well armed. Bonus, $20,000/per.

Next to the last line was a handwritten notation: *Kendrick Reynolds.*

Kendrick Reynolds. Maybe the old man was right—a shared enemy made him a friend. Kendrick had "teams" involved. To find Julia, Allen, and Stephen? To stop Atropos? He scanned the sheet. No addressee. This plane could belong to Atropos or another of Litt's hit teams, or both. One thing was clear: someone other than Kendrick Reynolds wanted them dead.

A toilet flushed.

That mini jet-engine sound familiar to every postdiaper human in the developed world.

He looked back toward the plasma, past it to a small alcove, where a door opened.

He grabbed a handful of papers and bolted for the exit. Something crashed behind him, then something else. His head cracked against the top frame of the opening. He ducked under, fell, missed the steps completely, and landed on the tarmac, wrenching his shoulder, pulling muscles in his back. The papers blew out of his hand and whipped away. He scrambled under the plane, came to his feet, and ran.

Like an auditory shadow of his own footsteps came the rhythmic footfalls of his pursuer, close. He bolted past the Piper Saratoga. He swerved around another plane and sprinted with all his might toward the third hangar. It sounded as if the man behind him slammed into a plane, crashed to the ground, and returned to the pursuit, all in the space of four seconds.

Allen flashed under the AIRPLANE CROSSING sign and promptly crashed into a mechanic who'd stepped into his path from between the hangar doors. Before he was ever really down, he was back up again, the mechanic still rolling and hollering.

Past the first hangar.

One more and he'd—

A bullet slammed into him. No noise—just the pinpoint force of a locomotive. He went down, hitting a patch of oily tarmac face-first, feeling gravel bite into his flesh, gouging deep furrows and ripping away a two-inch slice of beard.

I'm shot! shot! shot!—the only thought wailing through his head like a siren.

His lungs burned for air; his mouth gasped in vain. Finally a dusty cloud roiled in, at once relieving and torturing his lungs. His spine felt crushed. He tried to move, and did—but not well and not without a giant's hand painfully squeezing his torso.

He cursed the bulky Kevlar vest under his clothing.

This thing doesn't work!

He screamed and got his legs under him. He leaped forward. The gauntlet spilled out, and he knocked it aside in a mad scurry to put distance between him and his would-be killer. Fire radiated between his shoulder blades, but he pushed it aside.

Run! Just run!

Pounding behind him . . .

Then nothing.

The gauntlet must have slowed him. *Yes!*

Then he realized: his pursuer had stopped to aim. Allen zagged to the right, then veered left. He heard a plunk against the hangar by his shoulder, like a rock tossed at it. Not a rock, he knew: a bullet. He was almost at the alleyway between the hangars, wondering if he'd make it down the narrow corridor without being picked off, when he saw light slicing the twilight from an opening in the hangar doors. That was the way. Shut the doors behind him. Of course, it would have a lock or latch or *something* . . .

He made for the opening.

Almost there . . .

Another bullet punched him in the back. His face hit the edge of the door. He bounced off, hit the ground, rolled to push himself up.

The impenetrable bulk of a gauntleted arm encircled his throat and yanked him up.

sixty-four

JULIA HEARD A SCREAM AND HAD JUST FOLLOWED STEPHEN into the alley through the hangar's side entrance when the big sliding door in front clattered as if someone were pushing it open. She stopped in her tracks, holding on to the door.

"Stephen!" she called. "He's in here!"

Then she was back inside, dodging around planes and taking an infuriatingly circuitous path toward the front.

He's all right, she thought. *He made it back.*

Shortly after Allen had left, it became too dark to maneuver safely through the hangar, so she had flicked on the overhead lights. Now she watched for approaching shadows on the painted gray floors. She expected to collide with Allen at any moment. She cleared the last plane and froze solid.

Outside the big doors, illuminated only by a strip of pale light, Atropos held Allen in a death grip. Allen's head was yanked backward, his arm twisted grotesquely around his back, where Atropos gripped his wrist and hair in one black fist. The killer spun to glare inside, jerking Allen around like a doll. His other hand clutched Allen's exposed neck.

Dressed in black that faded into the darkening night, his skin white in the hangar's glow, Atropos resembled Julia's nightmare vision of Dracula—if Dracula needed vision correction and a comb. He smiled at her, a victorious grin. She fought the urge to back away.

Then he moved—maybe it was no more than a twitch— and she knew he was about to make his escape.

She raised her gun, centering the sights on his forehead. He stared back into her eyes.

Allen was gagging, strangled. He rolled his eyes toward her, and she realized that he was not gasping for air; he was trying to speak. He mouthed the words silently.

Stephen ran up behind her.

"Stay back," she told him.

His heavy breathing seemed right at her ear.

Movement—Atropos's arm shot out and pulled the hangar door shut.

She couldn't fire, not with Allen out there. She ran to the door. Sounds came from the other side. The squeal of a hinge, rattling metal. A lock! She pulled at the door. It wouldn't budge. She listened. Silence. She backed away, aimed at where she thought the lock was, fired. A second later, two holes ripped through the sheet metal. Atropos was shooting through the door. She spun away.

"This way!" Julia shouted, retracing her route to the side entrance. She pushed through into the alley beyond. She was on her second bounding stride when muzzle flashes erupted from the front of the alley. Bullets zinged past, rattling the metal walls as they struck. No gunfire. He was using a sound suppressor and subsonic rounds, the same rig he had the night before. If it was outfitted with a laser sight, he hadn't turned it on.

She returned fire, aiming high. She wanted Atropos to think twice about shooting at them, but she couldn't risk hitting Allen.

Stephen crashed through the door.

"Down! Down! Down!" she yelled.

More flashes and explosions as their enemy shot at Stephen. He bounded off a wall, landing heavily on the ground.

She laid down cover fire, hoping Atropos would believe he was in jeopardy of being hit. She looked back and saw, in the brief light of the closing door, Stephen sprawled in the dead center of the alley. He wasn't moving.

"Stephen?" she growled, panic cinching her throat.

"Yeah?" Low, quiet.

"You hit? You all right?"

"We can't just lie here. He's got Allen. We gotta—"

He didn't finish. She heard scraping against the concrete, the faint rustle of clothes. A shadow shifted to her right, moving past.

"Stephen—!"

Thu! Thu! Silenced gunfire.

Bullets sailed around them, punching holes in the metal walls, tearing chunks out of the wood fencing that sealed the alley behind them. The deafening reverberations seemed to last forever.

Finally Stephen whispered, "I'm okay." He was just ahead of her, on the ground. "He's trying to pick us off."

"We can go over that fence behind us, try to come circle him."

"He'll see us."

She thought about their options. She ejected her spent magazine and replaced it with the one she kept with her shoulder holster.

"Why isn't Allen fighting?" he asked.

"Atropos had him in a death grip," she said. "He may have passed out."

"Or he's already dead." Stephen's distress was obvious. He was on the verge of doing something rash.

"If we rush him, then we all die."

He said nothing, then: "I'm going over that fence. You stay here. He can't cover us both."

"Wait a minute." She watched the disappearing rectangle of near-black at the head of the alley.

"What?"

"Just a sec." She tossed the empty magazine against the opposite wall, fifteen feet in front of their position. There was no response from their attacker. She stood and began walking slowly forward, keeping to one side. "Keep your eye on that door," she whispered, indicating the hangar's side entrance. She moved faster up the alley.

Near the end of the alley, she moved out from the wall in a wide arc. She pictured the area to her left: the tarmac in front of the last hangar, an open space leading up to the parked planes, then the jet. To her right, far past the hangar she'd just exited, were the terminal buildings and . . . She didn't want to think about what else they might find crumpled on the ground before the hangar doors. Atropos would be on the left. She braced herself for action as more and more of the area on the left side of the opening came into view.

Fully expecting to find the assassin pressed like a malicious shadow against the hangar wall, she poked her head out of the alley, drew it back in fast. Clear. Hesitating only slightly, she glanced in the other direction. Despite their situation, some of the tension she'd been holding in her neck and shoulders drained away—Atropos had not deposited Allen's twisted body on the tarmac. She found hope in that.

She signaled for Stephen to join her. When he had, they stepped into the open together. They saw it at the same time—

The Cessna.

Beyond the parked planes, it was taxiing over to the runway.

"Oh no!" She was too shocked to say anything else.

Stephen said it for her: "Allen! Atropos is taking him!"

She ran—not directly for the plane, but straight out from the alley, parallel to the jet. She would cross the tarmac and meet up with it at the runway. Far off to her left now, it would have to come back in her direction to take off. She tried not to think, only to run.

Amazingly, Stephen kept pace, then actually pulled ahead. The jet's speed increased as it turned onto the runway. Neither of them saw the wide expanse of grass that separated the parking and maintenance tarmac from the runway. Stephen hit the edge of it first and went down in a tumbling mass of dirt and grass and groans. Julia hurdled him and pushed harder. She was on a direct trajectory to intercept the plane in about twenty seconds.

She squeezed her fist, feeling the gun. The jet picked up speed fast. She wasn't going to make it. She leaped over a runway light and hit the pavement just ahead of the jet. In seconds it would pass.

Do something!

She leveled her pistol and sent a volley of lead into the cockpit windshield. Little plumes of glass dust marked her direct hits—

Then it streaked by: whining jet engines piercing her skull, gusts of turbulence slapping her face.

She ran after it . . . ten yards . . . twenty . . . No use.

"Nooooo!" she wailed. She watched it become airborne, grow smaller, and disappear.

sixty-five

PAIN ... BLINDING ... SCREECHING ...

Unbearable.

Allen's right shoulder felt as though a knife had been plunged into it. Flames of agony fanned out from it in hot waves, causing perspiration to erupt from his pores, drenching his hair, stinging his eyes.

He slowly swung with the movement of the jet. Handcuffs ripped into the flesh of his wrists and lower hands as the weight of his body attempted to slip his hands through the cuffs, slung over a hook in the cabin's ceiling. Streaks of blood ran down his arms. He would have used his legs to support himself had they not been hog-tied and pulled backward by a rope that looped around his neck. Relaxing his legs, allowing them to droop, pulled the noose tight against his trachea. So, through the maddening pain, through the bouts of light-headedness, he held up his legs.

But nothing compared to the excruciating pain in his shoulder. Atropos had nearly wrenched his arm off when he'd seized him outside the hangar, yanking and twisting it high behind his head. Certainly, he had torn it from its socket. Delirious, Allen pictured an anatomical chart showing the head of the humerus pulled free of the glenoid cavity, the rotator cuff crushed, the coracohumeral ligament snapped. Meticulously detailed, those charts were coldly indifferent to the suffering they described. Dangling by his arms now was like probing a gunshot wound with a shovel.

The heavy punching bag Atropos had knocked from its hook in order to hang Allen like a side of beef rolled lazily across the carpeted floor toward him. He squeezed his eyes shut and gritted his teeth. He braced himself for the jolt of fresh pain that would ignite within his shoulder when the bag bumped his knees, which were, he guessed, about six inches off the floor. After a minute, he opened his eyes to see that the bag had reversed directions and was resting against what looked like a black body bag. Vero, Allen thought. He remembered hearing that the assassin had taken the corpse.

His abduction and bondage had been a blur of murky images, viewed through ripples of pain and fear and confusion. Atropos's iron stranglehold had discouraged, through immediate piercing agony, all attempts to break free and rendered him a puppet under the assassin's control. He'd heard the hangar door slam . . . gunshots . . . then nothing. Atropos must have knocked him unconscious, for the next thing he knew he was flying through the plane's portal like a piece of luggage . . . Time stuttered . . . then a body fell to the floor beside him: no, it was a punching bag . . . Cuffs sharp against his wrist, feet tied . . .

Can't breathe!

. . . a noose! How long had it taken for him to realize that it was the weight of his own legs strangling him? It had finally dawned on him, even before full consciousness. When his head had cleared, it throbbed—and told him he was in big trouble.

He didn't recall the takeoff, but that the jet was now airborne was indisputable.

He was alone in the cabin. Recessed spotlights in the arched ceiling cast hard white circles on a chair, a countertop, the floor, and diffused an eerie glow throughout the cabin. Though Allen had flown in a number of private jets—Lears, Hawkers, Gulfstreams—he'd seen none quite like this. The cabin resembled a living room with all the accoutrements of a modern, expensive bachelor pad: The laptop and printer he'd seen earlier. The plasma—now off. DVD player, stereo components. Weights. An extremely comfortable-looking leather chair.

All the comforts of home, with a cruising speed of five hundred miles per hour.

But it was not a home, Allen felt, as much as it was a *lair*. And he was the hapless victim, waiting for a creature to return for its feast of human flesh.

The cockpit door opened behind him, then clicked shut. An inky shadow fell over him, and Atropos stepped into view. His Windbreaker removed, a dark green T-shirt clung to the ripples and bulges of his torso and biceps. His face was so taut it might have been forged in steel. He glared at Allen with eyes that revealed nothing but hate.

A cold pressure gripped Allen's jaw. Atropos had seized him, so blindingly fast that Allen wondered if he'd blacked out for a moment. The pressure increased until Allen thought his oral cavity would implode. Atropos slowly pulled his hand back. The fake beard peeled away from Allen's cheeks, breaking free of the spirit gum. The adhesive stretched and snapped like skin. Atropos tossed the hair aside.

Allen tasted blood, salty, coppery. His teeth had lacerated the insides of his cheeks. A gentle probe with his tongue hinted that a few molars may have buckled under the pressure as well.

No words passed between them. The other's cool application of pain, his own refusal to acknowledge it, conveyed mutual disrespect. Beyond that, Allen had nothing to say. Would he plead for life? He'd have better luck negotiating with a frenzied shark. Would he threaten the man, something along the lines of "You won't get away with this!" Frankly, Allen suspected that Atropos *would* get away with murdering him, just as he had gotten away with it before. And more important, Atropos *believed* he'd get away with it, so saying otherwise amounted to groveling. And groveling was something Allen would not do.

Atropos turned. He rolled away the punching bag and gripped the body bag in two hands, then dragged it to within three feet of Allen. Crouching, he unzipped the bag and spread it open.

Allen's breath went away. He wanted to scream but found nothing in him to let out. The plane seemed to plunge a thousand feet, spinning, spinning . . . Colors washed away. The pain brought him back. He studied the mess in the bag and raised his eyes to Atropos. He knew then that this went beyond Karl Litt, beyond his virus, beyond anything so . . . *widespread.*

This was personal.

sixty-six

FROM WHERE STEPHEN AND JULIA WATCHED, THE AIRPORT security's search resembled a nocturnal sweep of still waters for a drowning victim. Spotlights cut through the black night to pan the tarmac in looping circles. Trucks trolleyed between the parked planes, invisible except for their amber flashers and the cone-shaped projections of searchlights.

Across an untamed field, beyond perimeter fencing and an unlighted street, the van sat unnoticed, positioned so both occupants could observe the airport grounds through the windshield. Inside, Julia used binoculars to track the trucks' activity. The short nail of her right index finger scraped nervously up and down the binoculars' pebbled surface. She panned right, to where two Chattanooga police cruisers formed a crude *V* in front of the last hangar. Their headlamps illuminated a man dressed in mechanic's overalls. He seemed to be pantomiming the entire gun battle with wildly exaggerated arm movements.

"A witness," she said coolly.

Though she hadn't realized it at the time, the sound of Allen's scream outside the hangar had propelled her into what Donnelley used to call Full Battle Mode. It was a state of heightened awareness, when every synapse sparked for only one purpose: to survive. Muscles moved, seemingly on their own and aided by healthy doses of adrenaline, to aim a firearm with point-blank accuracy or move her out of harm's way. It was like a drug, and coming down was hard. After having functioned at 200 percent, even briefly, both mind and body plunged into exhaustion. Soldiers knew it. And cops. Donnelley had been both, and he'd taught Julia how to control the descent, to keep the specter of danger alive in her mind even after its white-hot breath had cooled from her skin, until she was truly safe and ready to rest. Such thoughts fooled the body to attentiveness and tricked the adrenal gland into doling out enough superjuice to keep the mind alert. By giving that specter the cold, impassive face of Atropos, she now found keeping it alive disturbingly easy.

Stephen said nothing. His attention was riveted on the trucks and their lights. If, by chance, Allen wasn't on the Cessna, Atropos would have dumped his body somewhere between the hangars and his jet—precisely where the searchers were looking now.

After the jet took off, Stephen and Julia had no time to scout the area. On the other side of the terminal, three trucks had converged from various points and sped toward them. They'd barely made it to the alley ahead of the trucks, and through the hangar to the van in the parking lot ahead of the men who'd clambered from them.

Julia lowered the binoculars and went to a memory: Allen's attempt to speak while Atropos was gripping his neck. What had he tried to say? She moved her mouth silently, visualizing Allen's face. He had been grimacing in pain. Would that have distorted his lip movements enough to prevent her from deciphering his words? His jaw had moved twice, indicating a two-syllable word or two monosyllabic words. She went through the alphabet, comparing the movements of her mouth to his.

She was thinking of words that started with *s* when she felt a tug at the binoculars. She let Stephen take them. Stress etched furrows into the flesh around his eyes, on his cheeks above the beard, on his forehead.

She touched his arm. "We'll get him back."

His eyes remained glued to the search area. One of the cops had broken away from the illuminated witness to wave his flashlight beam over the tarmac behind the cars.

"That's what I'm afraid of."

"Alive."

He lowered the binoculars to glare at her. "You don't know that." Cold. Angry. He lifted the binoculars again and scanned out the windshield.

"They *took* him, Stephen. They took him for a reason. They'll ransom him for the chip. They'll keep him alive until they have it in their hands. That buys us time to figure out a way to get him back."

They watched as the cops climbed into their cruisers and drove single file toward the terminal. The search trucks switched off their lights and followed, leaving the area dark except for a bold strip of light falling from the slightly open hangar doors, through which the dungareed mechanic disappeared. In another minute, that light also winked out.

"Why don't we just turn over the chip?" Stephen asked, surveying the darkness outside.

"Because that won't save him." Julia shifted in her chair so she was fully facing him, one leg tucked under herself. "That chip is evidence of something. I wish I knew what, exactly. But I'll bet it's not something these guys *need* to complete whatever it is they're doing. They want the chip only because it's evidence they don't want getting in the wrong hands. We've seen it. We've seen *them*. At least, some of them. We're as much a liability as the chip is. They're out to destroy us and the chip. They think they're going to use Allen to get the three of us and the chip all at once."

"So we're *all* dead." Stephen's deep, unwavering voice made the proclamation sound as though it had already happened.

"No," she said. She tried to back it up with a powerful fact. All she could say was, "Just . . . no."

A wry smile bent the hair around his mouth. "You have another plan, I suppose?"

"Look, they took the gauntlet too," she said. "It's on the plane, has to be. That means we can track it."

"Then what?"

"We go get Allen." This time she did sound certain.

Stephen looked out the windshield at the dark airport. He closed his eyes. His lips moved in silent prayer. She thought he'd fallen into a kind of trance and would be like that for some time; then he looked at her again. His face still harbored searing concern, but a measure of peace had returned to his eyes.

"Let's get to it, then," he said, keying the van to life and slamming it into gear.

sixty-seven

"HE'S COMING HERE?" LITT POINTED THE DOUBLE LENSES of his sunglasses at Gregor. His high forehead crinkled as he raised what would have been his eyebrows had they not fallen out years ago.

"Should be in tomorrow," Gregor confirmed.

"But . . . *why?*"

"He said these targets injured him."

"Injured *him?* How?"

"He didn't say."

They were standing in one of the base's former hangars; like the others, it had been converted into a climate-controlled warehouse. A completely new building had been constructed within the interior walls of the fabricated steel hangar, leaving a rusty shell over a clean, poured-cement structure. The low hum of air conditioners filled the air and never ceased. An overhead door built into a hangar door rattled open, and an electric forklift glided in, carrying a pallet of boxes. On each were labels bearing a bar code, the name and address of a hospital or clinical laboratory, and several bio-hazard stickers. Litt watched the driver deposit the pallet and back through the door. A man approached the pallet and began cutting away a membrane of clear plastic that encased the boxes.

Litt spoke without looking away from the worker. "Why here, Gregor? We don't invite people here."

"I'm going to tell Atropos no? If you are worried about confidentiality, Karl, don't be. His reputation is everything he has, and it's impeccable. He doesn't divulge targets or clients, let alone anything about his clients. And my job has always been to protect this compound. You know I take that seriously. I would never have agreed to his coming if I thought it would jeopardize us in any way."

Litt still looked unsure.

Gregor continued, "People do come here, suppliers, workers. We have to trust some people, hoping none do what Despesorio did. Atropos is more trustworthy than any of these others, I promise."

He could not tell Karl that it had been he, Gregor, who had first broached the idea of Atropos's bringing Allen Parker to them. Parker was meaningless to Gregor, but an opportunity to meet the renowned Atropos? He fought to keep the smile off his face. He had brilliantly convinced Atropos that making Parker pay horribly for the injury he had inflicted was a matter of personal integrity and restitution.

Gregor wondered what sort of harm Atropos had suffered—he sounded fine; but the fact that he possessed a deep hatred for his targets was clear. Ah, the injury did not matter.

The important thing was that Gregor was going to meet the man himself.

He remembered when Karl had once, out of curiosity, examined his bedroom, gazing at his images of assassins like Richard "The Iceman" Kuklinski and Joseph Testa and brutal warlords like Genghis Kahn and Stalin; touching his replica of the rifle that had killed JFK; looking over his bookcase of the underground series How to Kill and biographies of spies and military titans. Karl had dubbed him a "death groupie," and Gregor had taken offense. It was simply that he appreciated the skills required to take a life and get away with it.

However, he was hoping Atropos would allow a photograph of the two together. Maybe that did make him a groupie.

Litt interrupted his thoughts. "Atropos has one of the targets?"

"Dr. Parker, apparently."

"Alive?"

"For now."

Litt watched the worker pull a box off the top and walk it over to a counter. A woman sitting at a computer monitor scanned the bar code and stared intently at the information that popped onto her screen. Her fingers flittered over a keyboard, and she reassessed the monitor's information. The worker strode back toward the mound.

"What do you think he wants from us?"

"We did explain a little about Despesorio's condition, just so he was prepared," Gregor ventured. "He knows the kind of work we do."

The employee started to pull down another box. Litt raised his hand and snapped his fingers. It was a fleshless sound, like striking bone against bone. The man looked. Litt waved him over.

"You think he wants a demonstration?"

"I'm guessing he wants Parker to get the same treatment. Maybe then he'll take him back and exchange him for the memory chip."

The worker approached with the box. He set it at Litt's feet and used a box cutter to open it. Litt crouched, opened the flaps, and extracted a clear plastic envelope. Inside was a card stained with three circles of brownish blood. Information on the card identified the blood's donor: a newborn boy named Joseph. His mother's name, address, and social security number. Litt nodded.

"Every year, these Guthrie cards become more uniform," he said. "Another few years, not only every state but every country will use the same blood spot forms. Makes our job much easier." He slipped the card back among the hundreds of others in the box, then nodded at the worker, who hoisted it up and carried it toward the counter and the woman.

Litt stood, stretched his back, and looked at Gregor. "So one more field test?"

"Looks that way."

"Since you invited him, you do the honors."

Gregor sniffed and wiped at his nose. "I was just getting over the last one."

Litt ignored him. "Are you familiar with the Balinese tiger?" he asked.

Gregor shook his head.

"It was a phenomenal creature. Quite similar to Siberians and Bengals. Fewer stripes, darker in color. But the most impressive distinction of the Balinese was the way it dispatched its foes. Not its prey, you understand—its *enemies*, such as other tigers encroaching on its territory, depleting its food supply, flirting with its ladies, that sort of thing." He tugged away a wrinkle in his pant leg, then began chafing the backs of his hands. "After roaring its displeasure, the thing would attack the intruder. An opponent who fell without inflicting serious injury was allowed to die swiftly, usually by having its throat torn out." He smiled, a lipless upturning of the dark line that was his mouth. "On the other hand, an opponent that fought well, perhaps even injuring the resident tiger but not besting it, was fated to a slow, excruciating death. Purely punitive."

He pushed an errant length of hair back off his face. His narrow fingertips found something on his scalp to scratch at while he talked. "After incapacitating its rival, the victor would back off, sometimes for days. When the loser seemed to gain some strength, the victor swept in, slashed at it, mauled it further—then moved away again. Often, the superior tiger would wait until its foe had recouped most of its strength before moving in to cut it down again. This amusement could last for weeks. The defeated tiger eventually starved or bled to death. Or grew too weak to fight off the scavengers vying for its flesh, and gave itself over to them. An ignominious end to the noblest of creatures."

Gregor frowned at the abrasion Litt's fingers had caused on his scalp. It looked ready to bleed. He patted the pockets of his camo outfit, looking for a cigarette. "Atropos is a Balinese tiger," he said. "Is that it?"

Litt shrugged. "Him, you, me. The desire for revenge is common to man. The harder the payback the better. But for an animal . . . That's what makes the Balinese so fascinating."

Gregor found a nearly empty pack of cigarettes in a pocket by his knee. He fiddled with it, anxious to leave the smoke-free warehouse. "You think Atropos is playing with Parker?"

"Of course. It's what I would do." He looked at his fingers and wiped them on his lab coat, leaving faint red streaks.

"Will we be ready for him?"

"What do you have on Parker?"

Sticking the crumpled pack of cigarettes in his breast pocket, Gregor pulled out his BlackBerry. He tapped the screen and used his thumbs to key something in, then handed it to Litt. Litt looked at it, and together they walked to the woman at the monitor. Litt showed her the screen. She squinted at it, typed, squinted, typed. She waited, then nodded.

"Get it," Litt instructed. To Gregor, he said, "Like ordering up a chocolate malt."

Gregor patted him on the back. "Years of hard work, my friend."

"Who'd have thought, huh?"

"I never doubted."

"Never?"

"Why do you think I gave you my shoes?" He winked and started for the exit, patting his pockets again. Halfway there, he stopped. "Karl . . . why past tense? What became of the Balinese tiger?"

"The last one was shot in 1937."

Gregor was thinking about that when Litt added, "I didn't do it."

sixty-eight

JULIA CLIMBED INTO THE BACK OF THE VAN TO SET UP THE
satellite-tracking device, and Stephen drove slowly away from
the airport. At her direction, he maneuvered the van erratically
from lane to lane, down alleyways and in looping patterns
around blocks. She called it dry cleaning, designed to spot and
shake any tails they may have picked up at the airport.

She let out a heavy groan, and his stomach tightened.
"What is it?"

"I was able to tap into a satellite, no problem. But the
plane's altitude is throwing everything off. Maps are scrolling
into place, but I can't get a lock on the device itself."

"You can't track it?"

"I can, but I'll have only a general idea of where it is until
it lands again. My laptop is only loaded with software for
land-based operations."

"Is there software for tracking planes? Can you get it?"

"I don't dare try, after what Kendrick Reynolds did. Accessing the Bureau's system might bring half the force down on us."

She made it sound as certain as skipping into the FBI's headquarters in Quantico. It was a different world, when you had to be as cautious electronically as you were physically. Crossing the road without looking could get you killed in either world.

"But you can tell they're moving? What direction?"

"South. Over Florida right now."

Stephen nodded, picturing the plane cutting through the night sky, Allen inside, hurt, scared. The gravity in the van grew heavier, pulling his face down, adding weight to his internal organs. His insides hurt.

After an hour of aimless wandering, he began feeling the weight of Allen's absence. It radiated from the blackness beside him, where Allen should have been sitting: a nothingness so great it threatened to swallow him whole and leave nothing but an aching heart as a testament to his inability to protect his brother . . .

"Julia?" he said, making his voice sound strong.

"Hmmm?"

"Could you come sit up here? For a few minutes?"

"I really want to keep my eye on this."

"I'd appreciate it."

The briefest pause.

"Sure," she said pleasantly, as if it had been her idea.

He heard what he imagined were the sounds of a woman extricating herself from a tangle of wires. Then she slipped under the table and popped up next to him. She placed a hand on his forearm, squeezed it, then slid back into the other captain's chair.

Stephen didn't look at her but stared straight ahead, trying to gauge the void. It was still there, but weaker. Like smoke, it had swirled away when her body had moved into its space. He felt that none of it had actually dissipated; it was simply less threatening, not all gathered in one spot.

He also felt foolish. He supposed she was used to working with professional investigators who didn't need hand-holding, who didn't let things like despair and regret interfere with getting the job done, who'd rather hear the ratcheting lock of handcuffs than a comforting word. But that wasn't him. His practical side insisted that she continue setting up the equipment needed to find Allen. But he also had to contend with his emotional side, which still felt the warmth of her hand on his arm and felt as good about that as an investigator would about a break in a case. He could not erect a wall between these sides.

Yes, they would find Allen and rescue him. His determination to do so was solid and big, a mountain that could not be moved. But they would have to do it as themselves, with only the gifts God had given each of them. With her technical brilliance, knowledge of the criminal mind, and prowess at executing covert operations and tracking people, Julia obviously held the greater advantage to accomplish their goal. They'd simply have to find a way to utilize his skills as well. Which were what, precisely? Physical strength. *Okay, good, that's one.* What else? Friends in high places? *Definitely.* But there had to be something else . . .

"Something else?" she said, startling him.

"Just thinking out loud, I guess. Thanks for coming up front."

They traveled in silence awhile, Stephen taking comfort from the splashes of light against Julia's face in his peripheral vision. He kept expecting her to suggest finding a motel or at least a place where they could park the van for the night, but she never did. She seemed to be thinking, working things out, and the impermanence of the view outside helped her do that. Finally he said, "How about a restaurant?" A glowing orange sign was approaching on the right.

She hesitated. "I really should get back to . . ."

Her voice trailed off, and he felt her gaze. He wondered how much of his urgency to get away from the van, from its muted shadows and its smell of Allen's cigarettes, showed.

"You know, I could eat," she said.

They rejected the first table to which the waitress led them, a cramped two-top, and settled for a big round booth in the corner. The fluorescent lights that cast the place in an unnatural, sterile luminance were bright in Stephen's eyes, a welcome change from the gloom of the van. Something about the artificiality of the place—its orange Formica tabletops, brick veneer wall, plastic plants, Naugahyde seat covers—made the harsh reality of life seem very far away.

Julia scanned the décor, examined her hands, rearranged the napkin dispenser, salt and pepper shakers, sugar packets, and small decanter of maple syrup.

"I'll be right back," she said.

For twenty minutes, he turned away an ancient waitress trying to take his order, her lipsticked smile failing to hide her boredom. Finally Julia returned, an extra wrinkle or two around her eyes.

"Trouble?" he asked. "Or should I say, what now?"

"My mother. She has MS. Most times, she's fine; I mean it hasn't gotten really bad yet. But you never know when she'll get an attack. They can be debilitating and pretty scary. She gets trigeminal neuralgia, these stabbing pains in her face." Her eyes moistened, and he handed her a napkin. "Sometimes she can't move, can't feed herself or go to the bathroom or pick up the phone. I bought her a medical alarm she's supposed to wear around her neck, but she says she's too young for 'one of those I've-fallen-and-can't-get-up things.' She keeps it on her nightstand." Julia touched the napkin to her eyes.

"Did you call her?"

"I went across the street and up the block, in case they trace the calling card. No answer. She might be sleeping. I asked a home health agency to check in on her. I got their answering service. I left the pay phone number and waited, but I didn't want to stand around too long. Maybe the wrong people would show up."

"I'm sure she's fine."

"I don't like to leave her for long." She laughed humorlessly. "Picked up my messages. Nothing from Mom or the health agency, but a bunch of calls from my boss. I forgot I was supposed to meet him this morning. I lost all track of time. Not that I'd have gone in, but I can't believe it's been two days."

"Allen called me to get him about this time last night." He shook his head. "All that's happened."

The waitress appeared at the table. Talking to the pad and pencil in her hands, she said, "Ready?"

Julia sniffed, squared her shoulders, took a deep breath, and smiled. Stephen realized she had put her mother worries in a box. Allen had always been good at that, compartmentalizing. Stephen, on the other hand, tended to trip over every little concern until he addressed it.

Julia said, "Short stack, one egg over easy, two strips of bacon, coffee."

Stephen ordered just coffee, thanks, and relinquished the menus.

"You should eat," she said. "Soldiers are taught, 'Eat when you can, sleep when you can. You never know when you'll get the chance again.'"

"You were in the military?" He couldn't quite see her with a helmet on her head, blasting an M16 at a beat-up car that had run a roadblock.

"Goody was. He used to regale me with words of wisdom from his time in the Marines. 'A good plan today is better than a perfect one tomorrow.' 'Freedom is the right to be wrong, not the right to do wrong.'"

"He meant a lot to you."

"The world."

"I'm sorry." It was his turn to squeeze her arm.

She smiled away a frown, shook her head, said, "So eat."

"I'll grab something later. If my stomach settles."

The waitress returned with a carafe of coffee. She filled two cups and sauntered to a table with four men chatting half a room away. They were dressed in dirty coveralls, and two of them still wore the orange vests of the city's road-work crew. Only irregular snatches of conversation drifted to Stephen's ears, but Julia acted as though she could hear every word—and it fascinated her.

"Julia?" he whispered, leaning toward her. "What are you—?"

She held up her hand: *Hold on.* Concentration furled her brow; her lips moved in silent conversation.

"I know what Allen said in the hangar," she said. "I know what he wants us to do."

sixty-nine

LYING ON HIS STOMACH, HIS FACE SUBMERGED IN A DOWN pillow, Kendrick Reynolds once again could not sleep. Every time the stage of his mind grew dim, a memory would dance on and the lights would come up. He raised his head, turned it the other direction, and plopped it down, letting the pillow slowly engulf it. His hand snaked out to the other side of the bed—years after her passing, the instinct to touch his wife was still strong. He rubbed his palm on the smooth bottom sheet where she should have been. It felt cold.

Nine years. She was nine years gone. It seemed only days ago she was chiding him for being gruff with the staff the defense department provided. She had always brought them fresh-baked cookies and lemonade: quaint and clichéd and absolutely adorable. The staff had been more relaxed when she was there; as efficient, but not as tense. That defined him as well. Since her passing, he'd felt an ache right at the center of his torso, as if he were late for an appointment, but he didn't know where he was supposed to go.

As a young man, new to the state department and just starting to make real money, he'd purchased an MG TC roadster. He'd driven to Norfolk, taking the winding roads fast and hard. Several times he felt the rear end wanting to slide out from under him, inching toward an embankment; more than once he edged around a vehicle, barely missing a swerving, horn-blaring car coming the other direction. Afterward, alone with a bottle in his father's vacation chalet, his hands shook; his heart raced. He had the sense that Death's fingers had brushed his neck and he'd slipped away, and he was waiting for the Reaper's knock at the door. He felt like that all the time now. He suspected that Death had returned for him nine years ago, had reached and grabbed Elizabeth in error.

She had been a wonderful woman, tolerant of his many faults, his arrogance, his absences, his betrayals.

He missed her terribly.

Not for the first time, he wondered how his grief, his yearning to have her back, differed from Karl's feelings for his lost family. He was certain there was a difference, given how the two men reacted to their loss. Kendrick grieved quietly and moved on. Karl had— The only way Kendrick could describe it was that Karl had gone mad. And maybe Kendrick would have too, under the circumstances.

What had Karl said—that Kendrick had wanted Rebecca and Jessica and Joe out of the picture? It was true that Kendrick believed Litt's family was a distraction, that his life as head biologist of a covert lab was incongruous with tending to a wife and rearing children. When he'd first conceived of staffing a secret lab with the German children, for whom there were no official records of their existence, he thought he could keep them unofficial and nonexistent. Soon he realized all life left footprints—there was simply no way to keep thirty-five children off the books indefinitely. They needed caregivers and tutors, food and sunshine. He'd wanted a secret staff of scientists, but not scientists who functioned in reality.

After many of Kendrick's staff became the children's foster parents and he and Elizabeth adopted Karl, they had seemed like a normal family.

He smiled at the memory of Elizabeth's giddiness over having the boy in their house, falling into the rhythms of maternal servitude, incessantly checking on him in bed those first weeks. For his part, Karl had been moody but had slowly warmed to Elizabeth's charms. How could he not?

All of the children were taught at a very private school consisting of only them and a handful of academics on the government payroll. As Joseph Litt had promised, the children's scientific acuity proved well beyond their years. When Karl was twelve, Kendrick moved all the children and their families to Elk Mountain, Wyoming. At the time, it was a small town of seventy people. The Department of Defense owned much of the surrounding land, originally intended for missile silos and never developed. Kendrick had one of the nearby hills hollowed out and turned into a laboratory. A fence went up, enclosing dorms, a playground, a cafeteria, and other assorted necessities. The whole thing was billed as a weather-monitoring station and education center, governed by the National Oceanic and Atmospheric Administration and Harvard University.

Of course, he and Elizabeth could not relocate. They tried to visit at least once a month, but still her heart ached;

twelve was too young for a child to move out. She once told Kendrick that she coped by pretending they'd divorced and he had gotten custody. He suspected that in her heart she had indeed divorced herself from him for sending Karl away.

However, the wisdom of giving the children their own lab soon became apparent. At fourteen, Karl developed an aerosol strain of the *Clostridium botulinum* bacterium—botulism. He even provided the plans for a delivery system using a V-2 rocket. As the children developed, it was clear they needed advanced education and social experience. In groups of three and four, they attended top-ranked universities.

It was there that Karl met Rebecca. Kendrick discouraged the relationship, but his efforts went wherever it is that common sense hides in the face of young love. He knew Karl enough to understand that blocking his romantic pursuits would result in Karl's determination to never again provide what Kendrick wanted from the lab. A dozen years later, the union produced a baby boy, named Joseph, after Karl's father. Baby Jessica came when Joe was six. Kendrick learned to loosen his grip, and the family seemed content in their small compound outside Elk Mountain.

Until the accident.

Kendrick pushed himself up from the pillow, rolled, and collapsed on his back. The room was so dark, nothing was visible. His eyes ached. He closed them.

Karl and his team had developed a virulent, airborne strain of rabies—a Level 4 biohazard—a dozen years before the CDC developed the four-level biosafety designations, and well before the techniques and equipment currently in use to safely handle and contain them. An aerosol canister fell over, and its valve broke off, releasing the virus and triggering an emergency evacuation. Security immediately airlifted lab scientists and staff to a site sixty miles away. There had been no evac plans for civilians, who were in or around the surface buildings. When Karl learned this, he frantically pleaded and threatened the security officers to return for them. He called Kendrick, who stressed the importance of following established procedures.

"There is the general public to think about," he told Karl.

"I don't care about them! Rebecca! The kids! Kendrick, you can circumvent procedures. Do it!"

"Put Major McCafferty on the line."

Kendrick had been told the hot zone was limited to a relatively small teardrop-shaped area around the facility, the shape a result of prevailing winds. There was an 88 percent chance family members in the dorms were already exposed; a 15 percent chance that Elk Mountain townsfolk were exposed. Kendrick could not risk pulling the infected people out of the quarantined area. He told Major McCafferty to act as though Kendrick had ordered him to retrieve the families at all cost. His true orders had been to stay clear of the compound.

When the helicopter sent to get the families never returned, Karl became a demon fighting to get out of hell. He tried to wrangle the sidearm away from one of the security officers and was about to be restrained to a cot when he settled down. Two hours later, he was gone. They stopped him at a roadblock, his desperately ill family with him. Their deaths were slow and excruciating. The baby succumbed on day four. Joe, day thirteen. Rebecca lasted nearly three weeks.

Kendrick threw off the bedcovers. He turned to sit on the edge of the bed. His fingers found a water glass on the nightstand, and he raised it to his lips. The water was tepid and smelled metallic. He set it down and missed, and it tumbled off. The room's thick carpet saved it from breaking; its contents splashed up his pajama legs and over his feet. He hardly noticed.

Karl had been infected as well. His symptoms matched his family's; however, where theirs pulled them into the grave, his lessened and reversed. The physicians could not say he'd recovered fully, but that he did at all had shocked them. His respiration was weakened, his eyesight noticeably diminished. The pallor of death on his skin never fully retreated.

"You're a lucky man," Kendrick had said, embracing him on the day he grew strong enough to step away from the hospital bed.

"You think so?" His voice was thin, raspy.

"You almost died."

"I wish I had."

Mumbled so quietly, Kendrick later wondered if Karl had really spoken. He squeezed Karl's shoulder.

"I won't pretend to fully grasp the extent of your pain, Karl, but I believe you'll learn to live again. Maybe even to love again."

Karl shuffled away. At the door, he leaned on the jamb and looked back. "You could have saved them."

Six weeks later he was back to work. Two weeks after that he disappeared.

Kendrick pushed his wet feet under the sheets and flipped the covers back over his body. Maybe he needed noise to lull him to sleep, to distract his mind. One of those sound boxes that imitated rain or a brook or a fan. Anything was better than counting his own heartbeat as the blood pulsed past his eardrums. Absently, he rubbed his feet against the sheets to dry them.

He'd heard nothing from or about Karl for years. He had

assumed he'd taken his life, as his father had done. Then reports filtered in about a new dealer on the global bioweapons market. His scientists analyzed a culture of what he recognized as the *Zorn* virus from an outbreak in Africa, and he knew.

Karl was back.

seventy

"SEND WHAT?" STEPHEN LOOKED AT HER IN UTTER CONFUSION.

"The data from the memory chip. We talked about sending the chip to Reynolds. That has to be what Allen meant."

"But he was against the idea," Stephen said.

"He must have seen or heard something that convinced him Kendrick can help." She glanced at the talkative road crew. Their mouths, framing the sounds she could barely hear, had acted like a lip-reading primer for her eager mind. They had given her the key. "He used what could have been his last breath . . ."

Stephen flinched.

"But wasn't," she added quickly. "At the time, he was in big trouble. A world-class assassin had him by the neck. He was turning blue. Yet he chose then to try to communicate that we should send the data. That's serious. That's important."

"'Send it.' You're sure that's what he said?"

"When *you* say it, I can see the movements of Allen's mouth exactly. Now that I know what he said, it's impossible to imagine that I didn't pick up on it immediately."

"But if it's Reynolds these people are trying to keep the chip from," Stephen said slowly, articulating newborn thoughts, "then we'd be destroying any reason they would have to ransom Allen."

"We have to weigh that with the possibility that Reynolds can help get Allen back if he knows the contents of the chip."

They looked at each other. They were at an impasse, not a place you wanted to be when kidnappers had your brother, killers were on your tail, and some mad scientist was pointing a virus-cannon at your country.

Stephen ran his tongue over his lips. His mouth was so dry, it was like rubbing two sticks together. He took a sip of coffee, then said, "What do they expect us to do?"

"The people who took Allen? They expect us to sit tight, do nothing until they contact us."

"Then let's do the opposite. Let's send Reynolds the contents."

She smiled.

"And let's go get Allen."

The waitress approached with a tray of plates.

"To go, sorry, thanks," Julia said. To Stephen, she said, "I'll share with you." She slid out of the booth.

He watched her in wonder.

"We have a plan now," she said. "We can't just sit around."

"What's our plan?"

"Share what we know with Kendrick and go get Allen."

"Those are objectives, not a plan."

"Oh, come on." She held her hand out. "Gimme the keys.

I want to see where they are. Can you get the food and pay?" She took a couple of steps, then turned back. "You're okay?"

"Yeah, I'm okay." He smiled, and she strode off. He guessed he was okay. It was either be okay or be useless—and he didn't want to be *that*.

He had opened the driver's door and leaned in to deposit the bag of food on the passenger's seat when, from the rear seat, Julia spoke.

"We got a problem."

"What?"

"They're over the Atlantic, heading south."

"Yeah?"

"A few hundred miles southeast of Nassau."

"Heading for Cuba?" His mind tried to grasp the meaning of the jet's leaving the United States. How would that hinder their pursuit?

"I don't think Cuba. Haiti maybe. They've already flown outside the boundaries of the detailed maps hardwired into this laptop. Unless they sweep back into U.S. airspace, I'll only be able to pinpoint the transmitter to the nearest city, but no better."

"I'm not *believing* this," he said. "We lost him?"

"Absolutely not. If we can get to within a hundred miles of wherever they take him, we can still track them down. Every activity leaves a trail, and I know how to find it and follow it."

The road workers exited the restaurant, talking and laughing. Stephen climbed in and shut the door. He hitched an arm around his seat back, turning to address her.

"Foreign soil," he said. "If the cards were stacked against us before, think how much more difficult getting to Allen will be in another country. Where would we go for help? The language barrier alone—"

"Stephen!" It was a verbal slap and quieted him as effectively as a palm upside the head. When she was sure he was listening, she said, "I'm telling you we can do this—we can find and rescue your brother. I don't care if they take him to Antarctica." As firm as her countenance had been, it somehow hardened even further. "We *will* get him back."

She made him feel hope—insane and untenable maybe, but hope all the same.

He glanced away, at the men getting into a sedan across the parking lot, at the darkness of the night beyond. Did he believe her when he wasn't pinned by her determined eyes? Incredibly, he did. He believed in his heart she could do what she said.

That's all he needed.

He rolled his head in a muscle-stretching circle and let out a long, deep sigh. His heavy beard parted in a smile. "Have you ever thought of selling cars?"

"I'm pretty good at wrecking them." She checked her watch. "Now get this thing moving. We've gotta get to Atlanta before the man we need to see gets too plastered to help us."

seventy-one

THE STACCATO POPS OF GUNFIRE WOKE ALLEN FROM A FIT-
ful slumber. Before his eyes opened, pain from his shoulder
and wrists welcomed him to consciousness. Nearby, a man
spoke, something about a conference in Geneva. Music
came on. One eye opened; the other was crusted shut.
Light, shadows flickering over it. He remembered the
plasma TV, rolled his head to see it. He forced open his
other eye. A news commentator was replaced by a black-
and-white western was replaced by a commercial for car
wax was replaced by a televangelist . . . For a moment, he
imagined that these images were not coming to him, but he
was going to them: bouncing around through time and
space, appearing and disappearing, a soul caught in the cos-
mic equivalent of a tornado. He wondered if the people he
saw, saw him back, a flicker of a ghost, here and gone, swept

off to the next sight and sound before surprise registered on the faces.

He experienced a sense of weightlessness as the plane bobbed gently over air currents and he swayed, handcuffed to the hook in the ceiling.

He swung his head the other direction. The cockpit door was open. Atropos sitting at the controls, seemingly staring at the stars beyond the glass.

He tried to think of something to say. He was thirsty. He had to use the restroom. He became aware of a cold pressure on his leg and crotch, the stench of ammonia, and realized he had already wet himself.

Explosions came from the television . . . canned laughter . . . A woman's screams followed Allen back into unconsciousness.

SHADOWS TUMBLED IN THE GUSTY WIND AS STEPHEN WAITED for Julia outside a windowless tavern on one of downtown Atlanta's rattier streets. He knew it must have been a trick of his eyes or faulty electrical currents that fed the anemic yellow light on the corner a half block away, but the illumination undulated intermittently, as though something unimaginable kept fluttering past—the spirit of despair or desperation, he thought, looking around.

On the other side of the street, outside another "lounge," a loud argument escalated into a shoving contest. Stephen sighed, pushing his hands deeper into his pants pockets. Darkness shifted silently in a recessed doorway not far away. He had the uneasy feeling of being watched but had no desire to investigate. Instead, he turned away.

Staring at the streetlamp, trying to catch its flicker, he hoped she would hurry up. On the way over, she had explained that Sweaty Dave was an "identity broker," someone who arranged the acquisition of false identity documents. He would gather the raw materials like signatures and photographs and send them to someone more specialized to turn into official-looking IDs.

Husbands wanting hassle-free relief from nagging wives or greedy exes; militants looking to distance themselves from governmental scrutiny; debtors desperate for a fresh start; but mostly, it was criminals on the run who made up Sweaty Dave's client roster. They all thought they were buying a permanent escape from the mistakes of their past. But only one in ten succeeded in vanishing for good. The other nine eventually gave themselves away by slipping back into the grooves cut by their old habits and penchants.

Then again, some bad guys simply chose the wrong false-document handler, such as Sweaty Dave. The Bureau busted him several years ago, Julia explained, leading to a Faustian bargain for his freedom: he would continue his illicit brokering activities in exchange for timely tips on who was using his services. The Bureau would then wait months, even years, to collar certain fugitives, taking great pains to falsify the means of their detection. Sweaty Dave's operation was simply too sweet to risk causing criminals to cast a suspicious eye at it.

Julia had said she wasn't worried about using an FBI informant. They needed the temporary ability to leave the country undetected, and by the time their patronage found its way to someone who mattered, they'd be long gone.

The tavern door behind him crashed open. Julia backed out, tugging on the arm of a man who obviously had no desire to be with her.

"Lady, you're really starting to tick me off!" the guy yelled, craning his head back toward the dark refuge of the lounge.

As soon as he cleared the door, a heavy spring started pulling the door shut.

Someone inside called out, "You tell 'em, Sweaty!" and two or three people howled in laughter. The door slammed closed, cutting off the noise.

"Now look—!" the man said and swung around to face Julia. Instead, he flattened into Stephen. He took a shaky step back, eyeing Stephen up and down. He turned to Julia. "What's this! You going to rough me up?" To Stephen: "Well, do it, big man. Whadda I care?" Defiantly, he pushed a greasy lock of black hair off his forehead.

Stephen rolled his eyes toward Julia, who made an exasperated expression and said, "Stephen, meet Sweaty Dave."

The man glaring at Stephen had a severely bloated face: chipmunk cheeks, tennis-ball chin—complete with fuzz—and rolls of fat on his forehead. Within this soft terrain, beady eyes sat too close together, molelike. His lips were fat and puckered, not unlike two wet worms writhing over each other. And indeed he was sweaty. A thin sheen of moisture that looked more akin to oil than perspiration covered every inch of his pasty flesh. He was about five eight and as similar to the Pillsbury Doughboy as anyone Stephen had ever seen.

"Dave, can you help us?" Stephen asked, kind, composed. His tender manner appeared to soothe Sweaty Dave's wrath. The identity broker's shoulders slumped.

"This ain't the way it's done," he said to Stephen. He turned to Julia. "This ain't the way it's done."

"I'm sorry," she said.

"Two Gs before I even look at you again," Sweaty Dave said, holding up his palm and actually turning his head away from them.

She nodded. After a quick scan for nearby predators,

Stephen pulled a wad of cash from his back pocket. He quickly peeled away twenty hundred-dollar bills and set them into the man's upturned hand.

Sweaty Dave pushed the cash into a front pocket of his jeans. Then he shoved past Julia and Stephen and shuffled away, mumbling. "Can't even have a drink in peace anymore . . . I'm telling ya . . . Next time I'm not gonna be so nice . . ."

She raised her eyebrows at Stephen, and the two followed Sweaty Dave down the street. Before reaching the end of the block, he turned into a dark portico. Keys rattled. Posters of comic-book heroes covered the inside of the store's display windows. A sign ran the width of the store above the door and window: Dave's Comix Trove.

A bell jangled as Sweaty Dave pushed the door open and snapped on the lights. He called back, "Either of you comic heads? The Dark Knight? Strangers in Paradise? The Sandman? Gone but not forgotten. Lock that behind you."

Stephen pulled the door shut and thumbed a dead bolt. Piles of comic books rose like skyscrapers everywhere. With practiced agility, Sweaty Dave negotiated a narrow path toward the rear of the store. Julia followed, then Stephen, who had to walk sideways to avoid knocking over the piles.

Sweaty Dave stopped at a door on which someone had painted a horrendously bad rendition of Superman spreading open his shirt to reveal the S emblem underneath. He snatched a comic off a nearby pile and held it up to them. "Wolverine? Either of you a Wolvie fan?"

"Sorry," she said.

Sweaty Dave shook his head, disgusted, and tossed the comic down. "'Course, it's gone downhill since Larry Hama stopped writing it, but—"

Stephen tuned him out.

They stepped into the back room. Here, too, stacks of comics rose from every surface. The room was indistinguishable from the storefront, except for an old wooden desk and a bookcase behind it, both buried under mounds of comic books. Stephen looked for something, anything, that would give away Sweaty Dave's secret trade. Nothing did. He turned to see Sweaty Dave staring at him.

"Yes, you, tough guy," Sweaty Dave said. He pointed to the bookcase.

Stephen stepped around the desk and noticed that the piles of comics to the left of the bookcase were about six inches away from the wall—just enough to slide the bookcase along the wall behind them. Sweaty Dave nodded, and Stephen leaned into the right side of the bookcase. It slid easily, revealing a hidden portal of pitch blackness.

"Light switch on the right," said Sweaty Dave. "Think you can handle that?"

Stephen turned on the light and gasped at the room beyond. It was about twenty feet square and immaculate. White walls, aluminum countertops, an expensive-looking camera on a tripod facing a curtained wall. A huge bookcase dominated the opposite wall and was partitioned into hundreds of cubbyholes, each holding a stack of forms or documents or cards.

Sweaty Dave ushered them in. He stepped in front of the bookcase of forms, seeming to survey it with great pride. When he turned to face them, he was smiling. He clapped his hands together and said, "Now. What can I do you for?"

Two hours later, the two walked back to the van several blocks away.

"How many times did we sign our new names?" Stephen complained, shaking his right hand.

"Enough times to be able to duplicate it flawlessly, without hesitation. It didn't take me so long."

"Oh yeah. Jane Ivy. I got stuck with George Van Dorgenstien. I had the *i* and the *e* mixed up for the first twenty signatures."

"It all has to do with matching your age and nationality to people with similar profiles who are already dead."

"You mean there really is a George Van Dorgenstien?" He shivered.

"Was. He's dead. Plus, it didn't help that we needed a rush Job. That meant we had to find a match among the birth certificates Sweaty already had on file." She sounded beat.

They arrived at the van, and he opened the passenger's door for her.

She climbed in, turned to him. "We have to be back here to pick up the new documents in"—she checked her Timex—"six hours."

"Got it." He walked around to the driver's door. He started the car and pulled away from the curb, glad to be leaving the neighborhood, at least for a while. They traveled in silence.

Finally Stephen said, "You must be pretty whipped, huh?"

When she didn't reply, he turned to see her slumped against the door. Her face was turned away, but in the fractured glow of passing streetlights, he could make out the slow rise and fall of her chest. A gray spot of fog appeared on the glass near her nose, then faded away before her soft breathing replaced it again, like a beacon quietly proclaiming her existence. Stephen supposed that even life-threatening excitement could stave off sleep for only so long.

"Sweet dreams," he whispered and started looking for a place to hide the van and rest his own increasingly heavy eyes.

seventy-two

ALLEN'S HEAD SLAMMED PAINFULLY AGAINST THE CAGE'S iron bars. A fresh ribbon of blood broke from his brow and ran into his eye. Ignoring the pain, he spun around to defend himself, only to find the cage door closed and the men who'd taken him from the plane walking away. He slumped against the back bars. Everything hurt: his shoulder throbbed; his face ached as though it had been used as a punching bag, which, essentially, it had; his throat felt raw; the other assorted aches in his legs, back, and arms were less severe but added up to a whole lot of misery.

He wiped the blood away and tried to look around. Spikes of pain pushed through the backs of his eyes—the one swollen shut, as well as the one he laughably thought of as his good eye. Rotating his neck instead of his eye produced a pulsing ache that was much more tolerable. He appeared to be in an animal cage, probably designed for a lion or tiger, judging by the size. Bars ran on all sides, including the floor. At about four feet tall, the cage discouraged standing altogether. The sky spanned from orange to blue, the colors of morning. Through his light Windbreaker, he rubbed his arms against a nip in the air.

He shifted into a slightly less uncomfortable position. To his right, close enough to touch, the corrugated metal of a Quonset hut arched up and out of sight. Directly ahead of him, past a red dirt runway, metal hangars, and an unkempt field, a tall chain-link and-concertina fence seemed to mark the compound's boundaries. Beyond it, a lush jungle rode steep green hills to a crest of red-rock cliffs. Around him lay more Quonsets and fields, one bearing a flagpole, bent and rusted.

He'd seen it all before; it was the old air base on the video he'd viewed on Julia's computer. Somewhere was a labyrinth of hallways, made that much grungier looking by the proximity of sterile laboratories. Considering what else that memory chip revealed, this backwater arrangement of old barracks and hangars hid secrets that could very well affect the planet's entire population.

The fragrances that hung in the humid atmosphere affirmed the vitality of the jungle on the other side of the fence. They were sweet and woodsy and wet. He could smell the earth, and it smelled somehow different from the earth of Tennessee, more ancient.

He noticed the birds now, their caws and calls, chirps and whistles. The musical sound reinforced Allen's already overwhelmed sense of surrealism. He rested his elbows on his knees and buried his face in his hands. Exhaustion and anxiety swirled like colored oils through his confused brain. Countless questions presented themselves—*Is escape possible?*

What are Stephen and Julia doing? Are any of my injuries life-threatening or incapacitating if they remain untreated?—and were pushed aside by a mind too overworked to grapple with any of them.

Think! he admonished himself, but the word held no meaning. He repeated it until repeating it was all he could do.

He must have dozed off; he came sharply awake when something struck the cage. Crouched beside the cage, looking at him through the bars, was a man who appeared to be in his midfifties, handsome and regal looking despite his clothes. He was wearing a camouflage jumpsuit covered with pockets and a matching beret.

The man smiled. "You look battle-worn, my friend." His voice was gruff and laced with Teutonic sharpness. When Allen did not respond, he rapped an object against the bars; it made the sound that had awakened him.

Allen saw it was the gauntlet Julia had given him to deliver. His stomach tumbled at the thought of the tracking device wedged into one of the fingers. Would rescuers be able to find him if it were destroyed or turned off? Would his captors punish him for bringing it? He didn't know the answers and didn't want to find out. He glared into the man's piercing eyes.

The man laughed, which became a cough, a phlegmy, painful sound. "I have found that when people are caged, either they fight and scream and lunge at the bars, or, like you, they become sullen."

"Would fighting get me out of here?" Allen asked, more quietly than he had intended. His parched throat was uncooperative.

"Not at all, but it does provide some entertainment."

The man balanced the gauntlet on his lap and pulled a

PDA from a holster on his belt, similar to the Palm Pilot Allen used. He tapped the screen a couple of times with a fingertip. "Now let's see . . ."

He looked around, up at the sky. "Slight breeze, wouldn't you say? Not much, though." *Tap, tap, tap.* "Okay. And I'll just put we spoke for two minutes, but I think it was less." More taps.

He replaced the device, positioned the gauntlet under one arm, and stood. He sniffed and used the back of his hand to wipe his nose.

"What's your name?" Allen asked. He didn't know why it mattered, but it did. Maybe it was something human he could connect to.

The man gazed down at him. He rummaged through a pocket and pulled out a crumpled pack of cigarettes. He extracted one and stuck it in the corner of his mouth and lit it with a lighter he had pulled from another pocket. "Gregor," he answered. The word came out in a plume of smoke.

"Care to share?" Allen indicated the pack of cigarettes.

"They're German. Perhaps not to your taste."

"I'll take anything right now."

Gregor shook one out and handed it to Allen, who put it in his mouth and brought his face close to the bars. Gregor lit the cigarette. It smelled like burning manure.

Allen filled his lungs with the bitter, biting smoke. He coughed it out raggedly. "You're right," he hacked. "This is wretched stuff." He took another drag, wiping a tear from his eye.

Gregor nodded at something. Allen followed his gaze to the Cessna at the far end of the runway.

"He is quite extraordinary, yes?" Gregor sucked on the cigarette and let the smoke drift lazily out of his mouth and nostrils. "He said he needed sleep, but we talked for ten minutes. Fascinating man."

"One in a million."

Gregor looked down with a mild expression of surprise, as though he'd forgotten he wasn't alone. "Soon we will get you out of this sun and into your own bed. If you are fortunate, we may find you a private room." He shrugged. "But no matter, the ward can be pleasant at times. We do try to keep our patients comfortable."

"Why patch me up? What do you care?" Allen gently touched his swollen eye.

Gregor grunted. "Your injuries do not concern us."

"Then what makes me a 'patient'? I'm . . . not sick." Something in his chest shifted. He noted the snot crusting around Gregor's nostrils and suspected his own health had just taken a turn for the worse.

Gregor looked over the compound's seemingly abandoned fields and buildings. He pulled on the cigarette and shot a stream of smoke into the air, then coughed. "We think you are, Dr. Parker. If you are not, then our scientists have failed to do their jobs, and I will suffer this congestion for nothing." He squatted again and squinted at Allen. "And anyway, we promised Atropos a bonus for bringing you here."

"Bonus?"

Gregor waved a hand at him and made a face as though the details were beneath him. "Karl will cover all that with you. After you get settled." He tossed away his cigarette and held the gauntlet in both hands, appraising it.

"This, my friend, is legendary," he said. "The Atropos gauntlet." He turned it to appreciate it from different angles.

"I suppose you vacation at Auschwitz."

Gregor rapped the gauntlet hard against the bars.

Allen watched the tracking device fall from its armhole. It took every bit of self-control he could muster not to follow its trajectory to the ground. Instead, he locked his eyes on Gregor's face.

The German had not noticed. Yet.

JULIA WOKE TO FIND STEPHEN'S YETI-LIKE MUG FILLING HER vision. He was shaking her lightly and whispering.

"What?" she said, reaching for her pistol.

"It's beeping. The laptop."

She propped herself up with an elbow and saw she was in the van's rear bed. "How'd I get back here?" Her voice was thick with sleep. She remembered getting into the passenger's seat—and that was all.

"You fell asleep. I moved you."

Without waking her? She must have been exhausted. And he must have been very gentle. Still, it bothered her to know she could be manhandled without her knowledge. She was glad it was Stephen who had observed this weakness in her and not someone else. Like Allen. Behind him, the driver's seat was again flattened into a narrow bed.

"What time is it?" She raised her head to catch a glimpse out the window. She felt every muscle, every tendon. They were in the parking lot of what appeared to be a luxury hotel. Behind its tall facade, the sky was lightening. The laptop, programmed to continuously monitor the SATD transmitter, sat in the captain's chair behind the front passenger seat. And sure enough, it was beeping.

"5:38."

"Oh, man." She dropped back onto the bare mattress,

closed her eyes. But the laptop's alarm was going off . . . She had to check into it . . . She had to . . .

Stephen was shaking her again.

"Okay, okay," she said, swinging her legs off the bed and sitting. She moved forward and knelt in front of the laptop as if at an altar. She supposed some people would think it an appropriate analogy, considering her dependence on the fool piece of technology. She forced her eyes to focus on the screen.

"The transmitter has stopped," she said.

"Stopped *working*?"

"No, I mean they aren't moving anymore. They've reached their destination."

"Where?"

She willed her sluggish fingers to type, instructing the SATD program to fine-tune its calculations, to triangulate the signal with area Global Positioning satellites, to cross-reference the information with every map held in its databases. The entire process took roughly fifteen seconds. She was pleasantly surprised by the SATD's precision, given her lack of detailed international maps.

"They appear to be . . . just northwest of . . . Pedro Juan Caballero, Paraguay."

"*Paraguay?* What's in Paraguay?"

"Apparently, Allen is. Does what you know about Paraguay jibe with anything we saw on the videos?"

"I have no idea. I suppose eastern Paraguay could be sub-tropical. Is that where this Pedro Juan town is?"

She checked the computer map. "Right on the Brazilian border."

"That abandoned base on the video had airstrips."

"There's a town here, almost touching Pedro Juan

Caballero, on the Brazilian side . . ." She spoke slowly, leaning close to the screen.

"Yeah?"

"Ponta Pora. Allen said Goody mentioned something with 'pora' at the end of it. He said he thought maybe it was . . . something that had to do with internal bleeding, a rash . . ."

"Purpora."

"What if Goody had learned about Ponta Pora from Vero, and that's what he was trying to tell Allen?" She nodded and crawled back onto the mattress. "We're not due back at Sweaty's for a couple hours. Go back to sleep." When she opened an eye a minute later, Stephen was sitting on the driver's folded-down seat back, staring at her.

"What?" she asked.

"Isn't there something else we can do?"

She thought for a moment. "Call the airport. Find out which flight will get us closest to that town. Use a pay phone up the street, not in the hotel."

"Pedro Juan . . . ?"

"Caballero," she said, rolling over, pulling herself into a ball. "Wake me at eight."

seventy-three

STEPHEN WOKE HER PRECISELY AT EIGHT, ANXIOUS TO DO something—anything—that brought them closer to their goal of getting Allen back. By 8:20, they were sitting in the restaurant of the hotel in whose parking lot they'd spent the night. They'd washed up in the restrooms off the lobby, and now Julia used a cloth napkin to finish drying the nape of her neck and behind her ears. She'd ordered a breakfast similar to the one she'd had nine hours earlier in Chattanooga. This time Stephen had also ordered a substantial meal.

"It's a long way from here to there," he said, unfolding a map of the Western Hemisphere he had purchased in the gift shop while Julia was catching a few extra winks. He arranged the map so the eastern seaboard down through South America was centered on the table, and tapped the tip of his forefinger on Atlanta. "We have to be at the airport at 11:50 this morning."

"That's cutting it close." She'd woken with the skeleton of a plan rattling around in her head. They'd have to move quickly to get everything done in time.

"That's the last flight of the day for any airline." He ran his finger south to São Paulo, Brazil. "As it is, we don't get in till after midnight. Tomorrow morning, we catch a commuter flight into Pedro Juan Caballero. Be there 'bout noon. Then we'll have to travel to wherever it is they took Allen." He shook his head, discouraged. "That's a long time for them to have him. According to the SATD, Atropos's plane made it in under ten hours. If it takes us half a day to find him, he'll have been there almost two days."

Julia frowned. "Half a day to find him may be optimistic."

"But you said—"

"We'll find him. It just won't be easy." She examined the map. It really was a long way. Farther, even, than Europe, though she'd always thought of South America as a near neighbor.

The waitress came and left, leaving their breakfast plates scattered across the Caribbean and Venezuela.

"How about chartering a jet?" Stephen suggested.

"The passports Sweaty's getting us will look great. They'll get us past busy airline clerks who are really checking for the destination country, but charter companies are very careful. They have to be, with pirates out there wanting to take their planes and terrorists looking to bypass airport security. I don't think our passports will work with them, and then we'd really be up the creek."

He nodded, solemn. "We're not going to miss that flight," he said firmly. He scooped an entire fried egg into his mouth and still had room to say, "So what's your plan?"

ALLEN LAY ON HIS SIDE, HIS KNEES PULLED TO HIS CHEST, HIS arms hugging his legs. A metal crossbar pushed up through the green canvas of his cot, making his ribs ache. It was the least of his problems. A long time ago—hours? days?—when the sun had been high and hot, the guards who'd thrown him in the cage returned. They'd dragged him out, hauled him into a Quonset hut and down several flights of stairs, through dingy corridors to this room, this cell. Eight feet by eight feet, at best. The cot was bolted to the floor. A plastic wash bucket was his toilet. Wire mesh protected fluorescent tubes in the ceiling. There was no light switch; the tubes had burned bright white since his arrival.

The guards had stripped off his soiled clothes and left a khaki jumpsuit. People had peered through the window in the door and occasionally brought in water or a plate of inedible slop.

The first unattributable pain he noticed was in his eyes. They felt swollen, the eyeballs themselves stretching and pushing against the ocular sockets. The headache came next, a throbbing that picked up pace until it became a never-ending pressure. His vision blurred. His bowels cramped. His muscles arched. His *fingernails* hurt.

When two guards had pulled him from the cage, they might as well have worked a knife blade into his shoulder socket, the pain had been so great. Regardless, he had writhed around as if in the throes of a panicked escape attempt. Unable to break free, he had lunged for the ground, pulling his escorts with him. His face had struck the dirt. He found the tracking device with his lips and pulled it into his mouth. As the soldiers had forced him up, he swallowed.

It was still inside him, and he wondered if it was working. Certainly, the thing wasn't designed for such abuse. He had thought about what to do later and decided he couldn't risk being separated from it. He would have to swallow it again.

He thought about Stephen. He'd be hounding Julia to find him. He hoped she had understood his message and followed through with sending the data to Kendrick Reynolds. They would need all the help they could get to rescue him.

If it isn't too late.

Nix that. Think of something else. Julia. He did like the way she looked. He liked that she was tough too. And smart. Somebody he could get to know.

He thought of all the women he'd known, the ones he could remember. One by one, he counted through them, tried to recall how they'd met, what they'd done on their first date, their names.

He entertained any thought that entered his mind, anything but the most pressing, the most insistent. He didn't want to think about it. He didn't want to know—

Why am I feeling these pains? What have they done to me?

—Angelina. Pretty blonde. Senior prom. No, he'd taken Robin. Brunette. So how had he known Angelina? Homecoming?

The dead bolt rattled, thunked. The door cracked open. A face peered in, then bent low. A water bottle rolled in. The door shut; the lock thunked.

He was thirsty. He willed himself up to get the bottle. Didn't move. He watched the bottle, on its side, unmoving.

Reminded him of Patty. She loved water, wouldn't drink anything else. Drove him nuts, that girl.

WHEN HE RETURNED TO THE COMIC SHOP, STEPHEN PAID Sweaty Dave the balance owed by purchasing a cellophane-sealed comic book with a thick stack of hundreds. The book itself was a new issue of an unpopular comic, worth a few bucks at best. The documents it hid, however, were invaluable.

Back in the van, he and Julia inspected the bogus identifications, stunned by their perfection. The passports possessed stamps from other countries, dating back half a dozen years. Some of the pages were dog-eared, and Stephen's had a coffee-cup circle stained into the front cover. The driver's licenses also showed signs of wear, but not to the extent that the numbers were illegible or the pictures hard to see. Sweaty or one of his cohorts had digitally removed his beard but left him with a mustache, so it appeared that it had been taken at a different time from the passport photo. Their new birth certificates appeared to be yellowing and slightly brittle from age. Julia said that the effect was achieved by immersing the paper in weak tea, then warming it in an oven at low temperature. As a final touch, Sweaty Dave had given each of them several major credit cards, complete with a few hundred dollars of available credit. Julia got a Sears card embossed with her new name.

"You have to shave," she told him, "or at least take a trimmer to it."

"I won't look like my photo."

"That's okay," she assured him. "People who check IDs expect appearances to change. They get suspicious when you look too much like your photo. They're trained to compare the nose, eyes, size of the ears, shape of the face, things that don't change. They'll know it's you, don't worry."

seventy-four

GREGOR BURST FROM THE QUONSET HUT DOOR, PISTOL drawn. Making his way toward the airstrip, he grimaced at the sky. Guards, two with rifles, two with Uzis, were already there, looking off toward the distant Amambay mesas to the south. The jet seemed to rise up from the treetops. It sailed overhead, low and loud.

At the end of the runway, the parked Cessna's door opened, and Atropos came out, stopping on the steps. He glared up, blocking the sun with his hand.

Gregor ran all out for him.

Atropos saw Gregor and pulled his gun.

Gregor stopped. He realized Atropos was responding to his own drawn weapon. He holstered it and jogged the rest of the distance.

Atropos's big pistol remained in his hand, pointed at the

runway. His thick black hair was even messier than it had been when he arrived. His clothes were wrinkled, as though he'd slept in them.

"Another plane!" Gregor called. "One of yours?" He knew it had to be. It was the same model as the one Atropos flew.

"Have you taken care of Parker?" He saw Gregor's confusion and said, "Allen Parker. When can I take him?"

"Soon. We just want to make sure—do you know anything about that plane?"

Atropos stepped onto the packed-dirt airstrip. He strode past Gregor, heading for the four guards. Karl Litt appeared from behind the Quonsets. He scanned the sky as he moved slowly toward the guards.

"Atropos," Gregor pleaded. "I need to know—"

"Yes, that's me."

"You weren't supposed to tell others. I invited only you."

"I know."

They were almost within earshot of Karl. His scowl was already visible.

"This is a problem," Gregor said. "I told Karl you were coming alone."

Karl stepped toward them. "What's going on?" he asked loudly.

Gregor trotted ahead of Atropos, holding his palms up. "I was told—"

The jet roared up from the east, over the trees, and dropped down onto the runway. Its engines whined as its reverse thrusters kicked in. It taxied past the men at more than a hundred miles per hour. Slowing quickly, the sound ramped down. The plane reached the end of the airstrip, near the other Cessna, turned around, and approached them at a slow clip.

The guards brought up their weapons. Gregor felt Atropos's pistol push into his temple.

"Tell them to drop their weapons."

Gregor did, and the rifles and Uzis clattered to the ground.

Atropos lowered his pistol. He said, "Stay calm. Nothing is wrong." He looked at the guards, at Karl. He repeated, "Nothing is wrong."

The jet coasted up to them, stopped. A long moment later, the engines died, winding down like a dying breath.

Gregor saw movement in the cockpit, shadows, an indistinguishable face. He glanced at Atropos; he was smiling, looking pleased and relaxed.

The door clamshelled out, one half rising up, the other dropping to the ground. A man stepped out.

Gregor blinked, confused.

The man was identical to Atropos: same height and build, same thick-framed glasses, same mussed-up hair.

The guards hitched in their breath, uttered the first syllables of questions or exclamations; Gregor remained silent, gap-mouthed.

Atropos stepped forward. The other one came down from the jet's steps, and they embraced.

The assassin Gregor had met the day before turned. He touched his chest with four fingers and said, "Atropos." He tapped the chest of the new arrival with the same four fingers. He said, "Atropos."

"You—you're both Atropos?"

He nodded.

A sound reached Gregor's ears. Quiet, growing louder. The scream of twin jet engines, rolling in over the tops of trees.

HIS HEART LEAPED AT THE SIGHT OF HIS BROTHERS. THEY WERE standing on the packed-dirt runway, watching him bring the plane in. How long since they'd all been together? Two, three months, at least. Each had his own territory, his own quarter of the globe to administer his services. On rare occasions, when demand exceeded their expediency, they would share a continent or—very seldom—a job.

But a few times a year, they came together, not as colleagues, but as family. A chartered yacht out of Cuba. A hunting cabin in Bavaria's Hanau forest. A scuba adventure in the Andaman Sea of Thailand. Their time together was always relaxing and invigorating and, above all, fulfilling. They were the only times any of them felt whole.

Atropos had heard of long-married couples who ached when the other wasn't around; they'd been together so long and had ceded so many intellectual and emotional roles to the other, even sociologists conceded that these people were *incomplete* without their mate. That was *them*, Atropos, for months at a time, until they reunited and became one again.

Their father was a great assassin, also named Atropos, as his father was and *his* father before him. Their father had realized the potential profit in bearing twins—financially and to the reputation of his name. The new science of artificial insemination had yielded high success rates. At the time, the process had involved fertilizing three to four eggs; typically, only one survived to birth. He had convinced a doctor to fertilize eight eggs. Half had lived.

He had taught them the ways of the assassin and allowed them to experience their craft firsthand, on his jobs. Then later he had sent each of them to a different master: stealth and entry, escape and evasion, martial arts and close-quarter combat, weaponry.

Instruct one another, he had said. *Become experts in one skill, then experts in all.*

Only later they realized his wisdom. Not only did their talents surge, but the bond between them became as essential, as organic as the valves between the chambers of a single heart.

Their father had also instilled in them pride in the Atropos tradition. They understood their vocation, their role in affirming and growing their heritage. They were the first Atropos who could turn their family's myth into reality. Their forefathers had built the skeleton; they were the muscle and flesh. And so they had spread out, for the sake of their name.

The tires touched down, bounced up, then came down again and rolled. Atropos tore past the Cessna that was parked near the cluster of spectators and aimed for the other one at the far end of the airstrip. He noted the soldiers, their weapons on the ground.

His brothers had done that, made sure he was safe.

He tried to avoid the reason for this impromptu meeting, but he felt his throat tighten, his stomach cramp. Coming alongside the other Cessna, he turned and nudged the throttle. The jet taxied toward his brothers.

He stopped the plane, turned off the engines, and rolled out of the pilot's seat. He paused in the cabin to run his fingers back through his hair. It was thick and needed a cut. He took deep breaths, wondering where their other brother was, in one of the planes or someplace cooler, a morgue or refrigerator.

Hate made his chest feel hot. He diverted his attention to the television, flipping through channel after channel. After a few seconds, he was *there*, catching all the dialogue, every nuance the actors tried.

Okay.

He turned the heavy bolt on the door and pushed it open. Anxious hands from the outside gripped it, helping it along. His lips formed a smile, but he saw his brothers' faces, and it fell away like dried clay.

He nearly fell out of the plane, into arms that welcomed him, needed him. He pulled them close. Their heads touched. He felt their strength. But more, he felt their grief. He wasn't whole. They were all together—all who remained—and they were not whole. He realized this hollowness would never go away.

seventy-five

WHILE STEPHEN DROVE, JULIA STAYED IN THE BACK, CLICK-ing away on the laptop.

"We have to be at the airport at least an hour early, you know?" he said.

"No problem."

Five minutes later he pulled to a stop. "Make it fast."

They were at the curb in front of an electronics store. She hopped out and returned after a few minutes, bag in hand.

"The sales clerk said there's a bowling alley up the street about ten minutes." She handed him scribbled directions on the back of a sales receipt. "It'll take me longer than that to transfer everything, so no hurry."

He checked the directions and got the van moving.

"MR. REYNOLDS?"

Someone was gently shaking his shoulder. He felt the heat of the fire from the hearth on the right side of his face, then the weight of the binder in his lap. He had been reviewing security briefs from the various agencies that reported to the NSA when he'd drifted off. His eyes fluttered open to a blurry face in front of him. He'd found that coming out of sleep slowed with age. Now it was a struggle, like rising through water, wondering why the surface wasn't where you thought it would be. He suspected that the easier endeavor would be to simply stop struggling and let himself sink away. He'd never had the courage to try it.

One of Captain Landon's lieutenants smiled at him, a patronizing smile that irritated him.

"What do you want?" He straightened in his chair, folded the binder, and held it out to the kid. "Put this on the table there."

"A call, sir. Julia Matheson."

Kendrick noticed the cordless encryption phone in his hand. He snatched at it, feeling some resistance until the man let go.

"Get out of here."

When the lieutenant was gone, he spoke into the phone. "Ms. Matheson? How good of you to call."

"Atropos took Allen Parker."

"Took?"

"He flew away with him in his jet. Took."

"I've never heard of him doing anything like that. He's a killer. He kills. What does he want with your friend?"

"Ransom? The evidence?"

"You still have it?"

"And more. We know where he went. You said you wanted to find Karl Litt?"

Kendrick leaned off the back of the chair. He felt an old, familiar pang in his chest, the anticipation of reaching a long-desired goal.

"You know where he is?" His voice was almost a whisper.

"We want Allen back. Will you help us get him?"

"Yes, of course. Where?"

"You'll help us rescue Allen? I have your word?"

"I will use every resource at my disposal, and I think you know my resources are considerable. Now, *where*?"

"Can you trace this call?"

"It's already done. Tell me where Karl Litt is, Ms. Matheson, and you will have your friend back before nightfall."

Silence.

"Ms. Matheson? Hello?"

He pushed himself out of the chair, grabbing the cane beside it. He stumbled and caught himself as he made his way to the door, faster than he had moved in a long time.

"Landon!" he called. "Somebody!"

He yanked open the door, startling the lieutenant on the other side. He held out the phone, like a tired and injured runner passing off a baton.

"Trace this. Hurry!"

JULIA CLOSED THE CELL PHONE AND HARD DRIVE INSIDE THE locker and pulled out the key. She looked around at the bowlers and spectators, the few people at the snack bar. No one was paying attention to her. The air was ripe with beer and sweat and something like talcum powder. She imagined the people Kendrick would send, ripping open locker after locker until they found the right one. Something these regular folks would talk about for a while, then forget.

She didn't know if Kendrick would care what she and Stephen did after he got what he wanted, but she wasn't taking any chances. She wanted to be on the plane before he saw the data Vero had delivered. Nothing would stop them from getting Allen back. She only hoped Kendrick was good for his word.

On the way out to the van, she dropped the key in the trash.

ON THE 767, OVER THE CARIBBEAN, STEPHEN ASKED TO watch Vero's video again. Julia set the laptop on his tray table and told him how to access it. His big fingertips hovered over the keyboard like fat birds trying to land on tiny perches. He brought an index finger down, depressing several keys at once.

"Ah!" he said and carefully tapped the right key. "The world wasn't made for big guys."

"I can't say I relate." She glanced at the monitor but saw nothing but the privacy screen she'd slipped on before arriving at the airport. Only the person sitting directly in front of the screen could see the images it showed.

"Stephen," she said slowly, thinking about what she wanted to say. "A couple times Allen started to say something about why you left medicine and became a pastor. You stopped him. Can you tell me now? I'm just curious." She reached out and laid her hand on his.

He stared at it, expressionless.

"I killed a man," he said. "I murdered him."

Her hand jumped slightly. She hoped he didn't notice.

He shifted his gaze to the window. "Back then—this was a few months before completing my MD—I was pretty cocky. Respected, wealthy family. No problem getting dates. Had a residency lined up at Boston's Massachusetts General. 'Course, med school is vicious. On the rare evening I didn't have night courses and wasn't studying or doing volunteer work at the local clinic, I hit the bars. Hard. Most of us did. We'd try to get two months of high tension out of our systems in one night."

He paused, shifted in the seat.

"We were in a sports bar, Malone's. Celtics and Bucks on all the TVs. We'd gotten pretty rowdy, a few of us."

He turned to Julia and leaned closer.

"Some guy at the bar told us to shut up. Jeff—a friend of mine—he got into a yelling match with him. The guy came over, all in-your-face, and dumped a plate of potato skins in Jeff's lap. Jeff was a wiry little guy, feisty like a Chihuahua. He just about jumped over the table to get at him. I put my arm out and stopped him. So the guy who'd come over starts saying, 'This your babysitter, that it? Doesn't want Jeffy to get hurt.' Stuff like that."

Stephen was looking past Julia, completely there, back in that bar.

"Jeff picks up a saltshaker and beans the guy right in the forehead. Now they're both trying to get over the table. I had to stand up to hold them back. The guy sees me rising up and thinks I'm coming at him. He gives me a shove. And of course I shove him back, which puts him on his butt, sliding across the floor. He's up in a heartbeat, ready to dive at me. He stops and sizes me up. I got a hundred pounds and eight inches on him. He reaches round his back and pulls out a knife, starts carving little circles in the air, you know? I'm like, 'Whoa, buddy,' but now I'm really ticked off. I mean, the guy pulls a *knife*? He kind of lunges, and I haul off and plant my fist right in the side of his head."

He stopped, thinking. His face seemed to have slackened, like a candle just starting to feel the effects of its own burning wick.

"He went down and never got up. Ever. My punch fractured his skull and ruptured a middle meningeal artery. They arrested me for manslaughter, then eventually determined I'd acted in self-defense."

"Sounds right to me," Julia said.

He shook his head. "I was never in danger. That lunge was a halfhearted attempt to save face. It didn't come close. I saw it in his eyes. He was scared. He wasn't going to take us on, with or without a knife."

She patted his hand. "Law enforcement has what's called the twenty-one-foot rule. It says that a suspect with an edged weapon is a deadly threat within twenty-one feet. It takes one and a half seconds for a person to close that distance, about the same time a quick-thinking cop can draw and fire his weapon. And our society's infatuation with firearms has dulled us to the dangers of knives, which can kill with one puncture, one slash. In the situation you were in, any cop worth his spit would have shot that guy. Including me."

He studied her face, said nothing.

"He was freaking out, angry, probably had a few drinks. There's no way you could have been sure he wouldn't have attacked you. *He* didn't even know, most likely."

She saw in his face that Stephen had long ago made up his mind: he'd killed an innocent man.

She said, "So that shocked you into dropping out of college, finding God?"

"The guy—his name was Wayne Reitz. Only twenty-two. His father came to see me. He was a pastor of a big church. He wept for his son; then he told me to get on with my life, not to let what happened crush me." He found her eyes. "Not to let it crush *me*. Well, I did feel crushed that I could do such a thing with my bare hands. A soon-to-be healer, practitioner of the Hippocratic oath to do no harm. There was this pressing weight on my chest."

He took a deep breath and let it out slowly.

"CliffsNotes version: I went to Pastor Reitz's church. I wanted to know if he really meant his kind words. How could he not hate me? He explained God's will and forgiveness. It took a long time, but I started to breathe again. I did some work around the church, went to seminary . . . didn't become a physician."

In his eyes she saw the pain, still there like the ghost sensations amputees experience. There was also compassion and caring. It all added up to a reluctance to do physical harm.

"As a pastor, as a compassionate man," she said, "you believe in fighting evil, right?"

He nodded.

She let the thought hang there. She smiled and slouched against the curving wall of the plane, pushed a small blue pillow behind her head, and closed her eyes. After a few moments, she heard Stephen fiddling with the laptop.

She opened one eye. "Get it?"

"I just want to watch those videos again," he said, slipping a pair of headphones over his ears. "We're missing something. I know it."

She closed her eye. "Let me know if you need a hand."

JULIA USED HER FORK TO NUDGE THE SHRIVELED CHICKEN
breast on Stephen's plastic dinner tray.

"Aren't you going to eat?" she asked around a mouthful of
something that looked like string beans.

"Huh?" he said, pulling his eyes from the laptop's monitor. Her fork was still resting on his meal, which shared
her fold-down tray since the laptop occupied his own. "Go
ahead. I'm not hungry."

She craned around to get a look at the monitor. It was
replaying the video of the man's violent death in the hospital.
She swallowed hard. "Trouble?"

He leaned back, shaking his head. "I've watched the
videos a dozen times, scrolled through the list of names, studied the map. I've got to believe they're all components of a
plan to invade the U.S., but I get the feeling I'm missing
something." He struggled to put his thoughts into words. "It's
like standing too close to a mosaic: I can't see the big picture."

"The camera dwells on the victim," Julia said. "He has to
be someone important."

"That's just it. He's nobody. Just some poor joe who con-
tracts—" His face lost its color.

"Stephen? What is it?"

"It's so *obvious*," he said slowly, his eyes chasing erratic
thoughts. "When did the man contract Ebola?"

"We assumed it was when the crop duster flew over, that
it was in the powder it dumped on them."

"Them?"

"The men having lunch, our victim among them."

"When did the camera start following him?"

"Judging by the times and date on the screen, the filming
began on the morning of the same day."

"That's it. Watch all the scenes; study them. Almost every

one of the men eating lunch with the victim—maybe *every* one, I'll have to check again—attended his funeral. They're there, mourning, dancing, watching."

"So . . . ?" Julia said, drawing the word out as she shook her head.

"So," he said. His eyes were wide and frightened. "How did the camera operator know *which* man would contract Ebola from the powder dumped on a group of twenty?"

seventy-six

KENDRICK REYNOLDS LEANED ON HIS CANE IN A ROOM FEW people knew existed and fewer had ever seen. Egg-shaped, like the three more famous rooms above it, this one lay forty feet below the bottom floor of the White House proper. Spartan by Pennsylvania Avenue standards, it resembled a reading room in a men's club, with dark leather wing chairs and ottomans arranged in conversation-conducive clusters. A Biedermeier sofa and a simple coffee table dominated the center of the room. Having escaped the decorating budgets of a succession of First Ladies, its walls were white; the two dozen or so original paintings that hung from them represented little-known experiments of brutal gore or obscene sexuality by such modern masters as Eakins, Rodin, and de Kooning. If she could have laid eyes on the room, Reynolds's wife would have proclaimed it evidence of the male gender's inability to reconcile masculinity and culture.

More important than the room's aesthetics, thought Reynolds, was its security. A grid of fine wires embedded in the walls, ceiling, floor, and single door completely enveloped the room with an electromagnetic field. The air itself, pushed in and pulled out of two large vents in the ceiling, went through filters charged with the same electromagnetic field. No signal of any kind—from the timbre of the human voice to the most sophisticated electronic data pulses—penetrated this barrier. It was one of perhaps a half dozen rooms in the world absolutely impervious to eavesdropping. There were no phone lines, no permanent computers, no power outlets or electric wiring to transmit signals to the outside world—a method of eavesdropping known as "carrier current." The same type of power cells submarines used energized the room's lights and needed replacing only once a year. Though visitors navigated a battery of X-ray machines and ohm detectors, the guards manning these machines looked for recording devices, not bugs, which the electromagnetic field would render useless. Computers brought into the room had to be TEMPEST certified, meaning the transient electromagnetic pulses they emanated were too low to be detected by devices designed to capture them from the atmosphere and re-create the data they represented.

Reynolds turned from a disturbingly violent monochrome by H. R. Giger and hobbled to a rectory table where his laptop waited with more patience than he himself could manage. Reaching to touch the closed lid, he caught a slight tremble in his hand. He clamped it into a fist and watched it as he might a supposedly dead snake.

He heard the door open and looked up to see John

Franklin stepping through the threshold, a guard leaning in behind him to pull the door closed again.

"Kendrick, what is it?" the president asked. In his late forties, square-jawed and blue-eyed, he was an aging golden boy whose stature and refinement reflected a life of privilege and spoils. The man's thick hair was artificially silvered, because an image consultant had told him it would suggest experience and wisdom.

Kendrick listened for the *click* of the door's latch and the hydraulic swelling of its seal, which gave the room its Zero Acoustic Leakage rating. When he heard it, he said, "We have a problem. Not a little one."

One of the president's eyebrows rose slightly, a practiced maneuver.

Kendrick continued, "As you know, one of my projects has been looking for a man named Karl Litt."

The president sat on the sofa, crossed a leg over his knee. He searched his memory. "The scientist who disappeared . . ."

"Yes. Almost thirty years ago. But, Jack, there are some things about him I never told you." To the president's furrowed brow, Kendrick shrugged and added casually, "Plausible denial and all that."

That got his attention, Kendrick noticed. He pushed his fingers under the laptop, thought about his cane and tripping and the thing crashing to the floor, and said, "I'm sorry . . . Could you?"

The president hopped up and moved the computer to the coffee table. They both sat. Kendrick opened the laptop and pushed its power button.

"I'm not going to bore you with details you've probably heard a hundred times. The preliminaries are simple. Around the end of World War II, the U.S. recruited hundreds of

German scientists. Many of them we brought in covertly, so other countries didn't know who we had or what we were doing. Almost every case proved invaluable to our technological advancement, to our ability to defend this country. Physicists like Wernher von Braun and Otto Hahn *made* the atomic energy program in Las Cruces. Hubertus Strughold went to the School of Aviation Medicine at Randolph, where he continued his human experiments in radiation warfare. Gerhard Schrader, who developed the nerve gas called tabun, went to the CIA's Chemical Biological Warfare program. They were everywhere, working on everything from jet propulsion to mind-control techniques."

He glanced at the computer monitor. It was cycling up.

"I worked primarily with biologists. I met Karl Litt when his father sent him and thirty-four other gifted children to us instead of sending the scientists we were expecting. Long story short, my bioweapons program was at least as successful as the other programs. Ours was the most secret. Nobody likes the idea of intentionally using germs to kill people. They're too unpredictable, too mutable. Nuclear power is limited. If every bomb in existence ignited, they'd destroy the world. But if one or ten or a hundred went off, it'd be awful, absolutely, but most of the population would survive.

"On the other hand, one very aggressive germ could go on forever, killing its host, moving to the next person and the next, exponentially, mutating to defeat our attempts to stop it. Where a bomb kills quickly, death by virus can be horrendously slow, unimaginably painful. Plus, as we disintegrated from the inside out, we'd get the added pleasure of watching our loved ones bleeding out around us."

The president's face registered his disgust. He rose,

walked to a credenza, and lifted a portion of its top. He removed a decanter and two crystal glasses.

"Glenlivet?" he asked.

"Thank you." Kendrick looked across the room at a vividly rendered oil painting of David's triumph over Goliath, in which the boy warrior had not only decapitated the giant but proceeded to devour his oversized heart.

The president returned to the couch, arrayed the glasses on the table beside the laptop, and poured in two fingers. He thought a moment, then doubled the volume in each glass. He handed Kendrick one and sipped from the other.

Kendrick pulled in a mouthful, savored it, swallowed. Holding the glass just under his chin, he said, "At the end of World War II, the Soviet army discovered a biowarfare factory at Dyhernfurth, Germany. The idea that the Nazis were making such things infuriated the world even more than their conventional war machine did. In 1979, an outbreak of anthrax poisoning in Sverdlovsk, USSR, was attributed to an accident at a Soviet germ-warfare factory. Soviet citizens and people worldwide were outraged. The incident sowed the seeds that eventually strangled Communism." He sipped. "People don't like that stuff."

The president nodded. "That's the reason we've stopped pursuing it."

Kendrick smiled. "Not completely. As a nation, we can't let other countries advance beyond us in this field, if for no other purpose than to understand what's possible and develop defenses against it."

"The Geneva Protocol."

Kendrick bowed his head in respect, surprised that Jack Franklin knew the citation. The Geneva Protocol of 1925, a treaty among the League of Nations, outlawed the *offensive* use of chemical and biological warfare agents but allowed their use to *defend* against attack. The treaty was still in effect.

He said, "In '69, Nixon proclaimed that the U.S. uni- laterally renounced any use of biological and toxin weapons, and ordered the destruction of all of the country's biological warfare stockpiles. His administration then made quite a show of converting the biological warfare research facility at Fort Detrick to a cancer research laboratory. Other facilities suffered similar fates."

The president scowled, serious. "I am aware that several facilities survived and continued . . . experimenting, develop- ing, whatever it is they do."

"In the spirit of the Geneva Protocol, the ultrasecret nature of our germ program allowed us to keep a few facili- ties up and running, the most clandestine labs."

The president nodded.

"What you don't know is that Karl Litt had a particular interest in developing race-specific diseases."

"Race-specific? You mean—"

"He wanted to target particular people groups and anni- hilate them."

The president started to speak, then chose instead to empty his glass into his mouth.

Kendrick said, "I think it was a remnant of his father's influence, his father's work. Josef Litt taught his son extra- ordinary things in the field of science. He may have instilled a distaste for Jews as well. If so, he hid it well. I never saw it overtly displayed." He shrugged. "Or it was something Karl wanted to do in honor of his father. He loved him very much, and over the years, I think he came to idolize him."

"You're talking about the Final Solution." The president shook his head. "Jews are not a race."

"Most Jews trace their lineage back to a group of Semitic, nomadic tribes dwelling in the eastern Mediterranean area before 1300 BC—the Hebrews. That gives them an ethnicity that population geneticists can identify. For years, biologists have possessed the technology to discern between ethnically defined populations. The same way we can identify certain physical traits commonly attributed to people of a particular heritage, biologists can examine DNA for ethnic traits. Litt focused his efforts on aligning pathogens with these ethnic markers."

Kendrick fell quiet a moment, remembering. "Litt told me once that he'd found a DNA characteristic unique to Ashkenazi Jews, those who settled in central and eastern Europe, and whose members include most American Jews. For some evolutionary reason, Ashkenazim are prone to ten inherited disorders—Tay-Sachs, ulcerative colitis, Gaucher's disease, I forget what else. Most of them are caused by recessive genes, meaning that symptoms appear only if two copies of the mutant gene are inherited, one from each parent. Litt was trying to mutate the second gene in people who had inherited only one. He abandoned the idea when he couldn't figure out how to accelerate the disease's effects once the mutation occurred. Victims simply took too long to succumb."

"That's insane," the president said quietly. "We supported this research?"

"Of course. Think of the applications of a substance that could instantly incapacitate an enemy while leaving our own men unaffected. Vietnam, Desert Storm—in both cases, our troops were in close combat with an army ethnically distinct from most Americans."

"So much for the melting pot."

"Some of our men would, no doubt, carry the ethnic

markers of the enemy, and they would die. There's no way around that, at least for now. But the losses on our side would be insignificant compared to the losses incurred during conventional war."

Kendrick watched the president absorb this. He felt the presence of the room's vile artwork pressing in on him. The collection, which he'd always suspected was an attempt to muster courage and aggression in the men who would gather here to decide on issues of war, seemed merely repugnant in light of the current conversation.

"But . . . *genocide?*" the president said finally.

"Genocide would occur if the virus was used indiscriminately or maliciously, yes," Kendrick agreed. "But that would never be *our* intention."

"Is it Litt's intention?" Something occurred to him, and he squared his shoulders at Kendrick. "Are you saying Litt has perfected this . . . this Jew-killing virus? Kendrick, is he planning an attack on the Jews?"

Kendrick suppressed an urge to lower his head. Instead, he leaned forward. "It's much worse than that, Jack. Much worse."

seventy-seven

THE LAPTOP DISPLAYED A MENU OF THE FILES JULIA Matheson had sent him. Kendrick reached for the track pad. He said, "Watch these videos closely. The first one shows a field test of a virus—Ebola." A village with dirt roads appeared on the screen. As a black man stepped out from one of the shacks, Kendrick continued. "Ebola is very similar to the rabies virus. In fact, it was created in the Elk Mountain lab during Litt's tenure."

Jack Franklin nodded; then his brows came together. "Whoa, what?"

Kendrick tapped a key to make the video pause.

"Litt *created* Ebola?"

"All his fiddling with the rabies virus," Kendrick confirmed. "Trying to make it more virulent, more lethal, faster acting. Before we knew it, it wasn't rabies anymore. It was something new."

"But the outbreaks in . . . uh . . ."

"The first one occurred in Sudan in 1976, after Litt disappeared. Of course, it wasn't called Ebola when it was in our lab. He called it *Zorn*, or *Zorn des Gottes*—wrath of God. It wasn't until I saw a slide of Ebola, like an ampersand or G clef in music with a long tail, that I knew Karl was out there somewhere, perfecting his creation, field-testing it."

The president stared vacantly into a dark corner of the room. He had been jarred out of his presidential persona; it was as a member of the human race that he was considering what Karl had done. Kendrick hoped to keep him in that frame of mind, at least until his presentation's coup d'état. He lifted the decanter and refilled their glasses. The president gazed down at the swirling amber, then brought the glass to his lips. He nodded at the laptop. Kendrick restarted the video.

As Jack Franklin watched the man on the screen succumb to Ebola, a thin film of perspiration broke out on the chief executive's upper lip and forehead. Several times he glanced over at Kendrick, who would nod grimly. The second video began right after the first ended.

Kendrick tilted to one side and fished the meerschaum pipe out of his right jacket pocket. Then he leaned the other way and pulled a small leather pouch out of the opposite pocket. He packed a wad of tobacco from the pouch into the top of God's head, taking great care in tucking straggly strands into the mound. He stuck the pipe between his teeth. He stashed the pouch, withdrew a lighter from the same pocket, and waved a two-inch flame over the bowl.

The video wound to its conclusion, and the menu screen took its place.

"The man at the end?"

The president nodded.

"Karl Litt."

"What happened to him?"

"He was exposed to an early strain of *Zorn*. It . . . *changed* him. Whatever it did, it must have been wearing away at his body all these years." He pulled on the pipe, then blew out a billow of smoke, which vanished into an air vent. "We identified the abandoned air base from the second video. And this . . ."

He selected a file. The screen filled with a map of the eastern seaboard, the Caribbean, and South America. He pointed at a red dot blinking over Chattanooga.

"This is a real-time recording of a satellite tracking operation. It's a plane that eventually lands on that airstrip."

"You know where he is."

"One more thing." He called up a map of the United States. A dozen or so areas glowed red. He zoomed in on one of them, which resolved itself into a distinct egg-shaped pattern with map markings in blue under it. "What does this look like?"

"Chicago."

"Look at the red superimposed over it."

The president studied it. The color was bloodred near its center and faded irregularly to a light pink. Freckles of white permeated the entire colored area. The president's eyes flared wider. "It's a . . . *blast pattern*."

"Except less round."

"Yes . . . yes . . ." He seemed to be having trouble breathing.

"It's a biochemical disbursement pattern," Kendrick said. "The dark red shows the vicinity of the initial release." He touched the mouthpiece of his pipe to the screen. "The shape is defined by estimating wind direction and speed, humidity, obstructions, vector weight, and so on."

The president nodded. Kendrick knew he'd seen such diagrams before, attached to defense budgets, showing hypothetical terrorism scenarios. But one thing was new.

"What are the white dots?"

"Targets," Kendrick answered simply. "Specific targets, specific addresses. Look here." Clicking on the keyboard, he brought up the list of names, addresses, and medical procedures. The data began scrolling like movie credits. Name after name flashed past. "Every white dot on the map represents one of these names. They all fall within twenty geographic areas of the United States."

"I don't understand," the president said, watching the names blur by. "Litt identified his victims by name? Why?"

"To prove he could." He jabbed the pipe between his lips and immediately spat out a short stream of smoke.

"So many . . ."

"Ten thousand. Twenty sites, five hundred per site."

The president jerked his head up as though he'd been slapped. A fiery redness rimmed his eyes. "All Jews?"

Kendrick shrugged. "Could be anyone. Jews, African-Americans, Asians, Caucasians. I guess you can say Litt's become less discriminating with age."

The president looked from Kendrick back to the flowing data on the screen. He reached out and, using a finger from each hand, jabbed key after key, apparently at random. "Stop this thing! Stop it—!"

Kendrick hit the space bar. The names froze in place.

"This is *obscene*," the president said, angry, disgusted. He stood, stepped purposely for the door, stopped. He studied the glass in his hand, drained it. Without turning, he said, "Your assessment can't be right. A biological attack with a pathogen that affects everybody? White dots would cover the entire red

pattern. Everyone would succumb. Imprecision and mass casualties are the hallmark of biochemical weapons. What's the
point in identifying a thousand victims out of millions?"

"I said it could be *anyone*, not *everyone*. Litt knows who
his virus will kill. He chose them."

The president turned. "Chose them?"

Kendrick reclined back into the sofa, draping one arm
across the seat back, the other raised to pull the pipe from his
mouth. "Apparently Litt has designed a strain of the Ebola
virus that seeks out specific individuals through their DNA.
Once released into the atmosphere, the virus probably travels
from host to host like a flu bug, but harmless. It checks the
DNA of each host, comparing it to some set of instructions
he has encoded within the virus. If it matches, it turns into
full-blown Ebola; if it doesn't, it moves on to another host . . .
until it finds a match."

Kendrick was calm, relaxed. He knew Jack Franklin. The
man had not reached the pinnacle by following anyone's lead,
by drinking anyone's Kool-Aid. He had a habit of responding differently from the people around him. If you wanted
him to remain calm, you came at him in a tizzy; if you
wanted him worked up—

Kendrick sighed. His eyes fluttered. He appeared ready to
fall asleep. "Jack," he said, "Karl Litt has created a program-
mable virus. A fatal virus. No one has to get near the target.
The assassin is the virus: invisible, silent, unstoppable. If you
breathe, it will find you."

The president picked up the decanter. His arms lowered
to hang at his sides, empty glass in one hand, whiskey in
the other. He made no move to unite the two. He walked
around the coffee table and dropped onto the sofa, his features drawn tight.

"Where'd the DNA come from?"

"You name it. We leave our DNA everywhere. If hospitals aren't drawing it out of our veins, we're leaving it in the combs we use, the clothes we wear, the envelopes we lick . . . Doesn't matter. Somehow, he got it. At least enough to slaughter ten thousand men, women, and children."

"Are these people he knows? Personally?"

"Not likely."

"Then why? Why do such a thing?"

"Because he can. Once the world believes he can select people at random to die so brutally, and that he's willing to do so with impunity, don't you think they will do anything to appease him? He can hold whole countries hostage. Demand anything: a hundred billion dollars, a million people for slave labor. Anything. Random, selective death. Anyone, anywhere. It's the power of God."

The president shook his head dismally. "Ten thousand American citizens?"

"For a start."

"God have mercy."

"Mmmm." He pulled once on the pipe, then turned it around to study the meerschaum rendition of Michelangelo's God, letting tendrils of smoke drift lazily out of his slightly parted lips. After a minute, he leaned over and carefully placed it on the table. "But *we* should not have such mercy."

"What do you mean?"

"I have one more thing to show you." He moved his finger over the laptop's track pad, grateful his hand had stopped shaking. The names scrolled.

The president moved to the edge of the sofa, leaning to watch. Kendrick caused the names to slow, then stop, then reverse. Then stopped again.

The president made a sharp noise, the way one would upon witnessing an accident. He grasped the laptop's monitor. The plastic made a popping noise as his knuckles burned white from the force of his grip. Kendrick could almost feel the air around him heat up.

Three names glowed on the screen, white letters on a black background. In format and content, they were similar to the other 9,997 names. But these and these alone would seal Litt's fate.

Kendrick suspected that the top one—John Thorogood Franklin of 1600 Pennsylvania Avenue, Washington DC— by itself meant little to this man; he was strong enough to give his life if necessary. It was the next two that cinched it: the First Lady and their eleven-year-old son, a boy so loved and doted upon by his father that the media had—not so inaccurately—credited him with inspiring a familial inclination not seen in a chief executive for decades, and in so doing carrying the election for his dad.

The president glared at the screen for a long time. Except for the rise and fall of his shoulders as he breathed heavily, he might have been made of stone—frozen by a sight as hideous as Medusa and her serpentine locks. When he finally turned, gone were the fear and disgust that had marked his countenance since the first video began. The emotions that replaced them were unmistakable: righteous indignation and fierce determination.

Kendrick matched the expression with a scowl.

"Tell me," the president said in a voice of granite, "what do we do to stop this thing?"

seventy-eight

To distract her mind from the aches and stiffness of her body so sleep would come, Julia looked for familiar images in the intricate shadows on the ceiling. They were cast by the streetlamp shining through the lace curtains over their hotel room's window. Slowly her imagination turned the dappled pattern into figures: a grinning devil's face . . . a butcher's knife . . . a fat snake, poised to strike . . . flames . . . A slight flutter of the gossamer curtains gave these last two images eerie movement. She closed her eyes.

Their plane from Atlanta had landed at São Paulo's Guarulhos Airport shortly before midnight. By half past, they had taken a cab to one of the glitzy hotels on Paulista Avenue, walked a dozen blocks into seedier streets, and found a small hotel more suitable for vagrants than vacationers. She liked that the cabbie couldn't lead pursuers to them and that the hotel's night clerk was more interested in the tattered girlie magazine on the counter than in who was checking in.

She had calculated the odds of someone being able to track them down along their route to find Allen. It wouldn't be difficult. She had to assume Karl Litt had discovered the tracking device, which meant his people would be laying an ambush for them somewhere between Atlanta and their destination. It made more sense to trap them closer to Litt's headquarters, where his influence and familiarity presumably were greatest. Still, he might expect them to think that way and make his move farther from his home base, hoping to catch them off guard. She was determined not to let that happen. Even here, where it would be easy to let the sprawling Brazilian capital—with eleven hundred square miles and sixteen million inhabitants—lull her into a false sense of anonymity, she had to be on her toes.

Then there was Kendrick. He knew precisely where she and Stephen were heading, and if his purpose for wanting Vero's data was to conceal it instead of to find out what Litt was up to, as he claimed, he would be after them as well. She'd risked everything to ask for his help. She didn't want to admit it to Stephen, but she figured they had a slingshot's chance in a gunfight of rescuing Allen without the firepower Kendrick could bring to the table. If he was one of the good guys, she wasn't sure what to expect. Would he threaten Litt into releasing Allen and use diplomatic channels to defeat him?

Litt wasn't a country, though, so what kind of pressure could the United States apply to him and his organization? She recalled a seminar at which the lecturer had pushed the notion that major corporations were the "countries" of the future. As technology made geographical, cultural, and linguistic boundaries obsolete, the seat of global power would shift from governments to boards of directors. Withholding innovations or using them to gain leverage over others would be the new way of demonstrating might.

By combining the nongeographical and apolitical aspects of a private organization and the militaristic might of a nation, Litt's plans might prove to be a sort of evolutionary bridge to a civilization where the Microsofts and ExxonMobils of the world dictated social policy and law.

She realized her mind had wandered and squeezed her eyelids tighter, until little plumes of red burst forth from the blackness. If beating the bush of hypothesis scared up anything, it was the fact that she knew almost nothing about Litt. Like a child making a monster out of a pile of laundry in the dark corner of her room, she had allowed the mystery of her enemy to grow into an omniscient, indestructible beast. Most likely he was some pathetic terrorist Kendrick Reynolds could squash with one strike from a team of commandos. It was this kind of action she had in mind when she sent Kendrick the chip data.

In a perfect world, she and Stephen would arrive at Litt's headquarters after Kendrick's men had done their thing. She and Stephen would find Allen in a jury-rigged medical tent getting a cursory physical or in some mobile command center being debriefed. They'd be commended for alerting the U.S. government about the terrorist danger; told to forget everything they knew about Litt, Ebola, and rumors of invasion in the interest of national security; and sent home in the belly of a C-130 to get on with their lives.

She opened her eyes, looking for the devil's head in the shadows above. Optimism was the last thing she needed right now. It would turn to disappointment when Kendrick's help turned out to be insufficient or nonexistent. The disappointment would turn to depression, which would make her indecisive and reactive. And that would get them all killed. Better to go into this on a foundation of reality. Rescuing Allen was going to be the toughest thing she'd ever attempted, and success was far from assured.

Determination surged into her chest at the challenge. In the dark, her lips formed a kind of steely smile.

They had entered the room exhausted and had fallen into their separate beds without bothering to undress or even visit the communal bathroom down the hall. A window air conditioner had been on, filling the room with a horrendous combination of humming, ticking, and tepid wind. After a minute, Stephen had grunted out of bed and switched it off. After that, the curtain had settled, and the shadows had congealed into the spiderweb pattern she now perused.

Julia listened and heard Stephen's slow, deep breaths. She was considering waking him to discuss Litt's germ or their plan of attack or anything that might help her not feel so small and alone . . . when she fell asleep.

seventy-nine

ALLEN COULD NOT HELP HIMSELF. HIS MIND KEPT RETURN-
ing to the video on Julia's computer of the man succumbing
to Ebola, or what they had assumed was Ebola. The pain, the
bleeding out, the convulsions. He remembered the way he
had described it to Julia: "Internal organs start to decay as
though you're already dead, but you're not. Your blood loses
its ability to clot; then your endothelial cells, which form the
lining of the blood vessels, fail to function, so blood leaks
through. Soon it oozes from every orifice—even from your
eyes, pores, and under your fingernails. Then you die."

He felt it in him, dissolving his tissues like acid.

He wished he were imagining it. Eighty percent of med
school students experience some form of hypochondriasis—
their detailed study of serious illnesses plants the seeds that
blossom into psychosomatic symptoms. His roommate had

suffered from it so badly, he'd dropped out. Allen wasn't prone to that; even if he were, he thought he'd recognize the difference between made-up pain and real, my-guts-are-disintegrating pain. What he felt was the latter.

The cot's crossbar still pushed into his ribs, but now he imagined his ribs bending softly under the pressure, his liver and kidneys and lungs oozing around it, dripping to the floor.

He opened his eyes. The bright fluorescents jabbed at them. The wall four inches from his nose was painted white. The roller had textured it with fine dimples. A faint brown smudge had remained after the last cleaning. He rolled over, folding the thin pillow to give his head more support.

Someone was standing in his room, leaning into the corner opposite the cot. *An angel,* he thought. White skin against the white walls. A white tunic draped over the white skin. But no, wouldn't an angel be beautiful? Perhaps not. This one was gaunt, skeletal, its head bald and bulbous. It wore sunglasses.

Allen raised his head, squinted at the figure. It was a man. The tunic was a lab coat, but the distressing angularity of his face and the paleness of his skin were just as Allen had first perceived. He'd seen the face before. The video: he was the man who had approached the camera at the end of the second clip, when Vero was filming the air base and laboratories. Allen propped himself up on an elbow.

The man smiled. "Good morning, Doctor," he said.

"What . . ." His throat was raw. He tasted blood. His voice was weak and gravelly. "What have you done to me?"

"I believe you know."

"I know . . ." He swallowed dryly. "You're Karl Litt."

The man pushed off the wall and stepped closer. His hands came together. With long fingernails he began scraping the back of one hand, then the other. "How do you recognize me?"

Didn't Litt know what was on Vero's chip? If not, Allen wasn't sure he wanted to tell him. He changed the subject.

"Is this . . . Ebola?"

"Did you determine that from your symptoms? I hope my specialty isn't also getting around."

"How? How was I infected?" They may have injected him when he was unconscious, but he didn't think so. If it was an airborne strain, then . . . "Why not you or the other guy . . . Gregor? Why not everyone here?"

"So you *don't* know it all." He looked around the room, then sat on the edge of the cot. "How much do you know about DNA?"

Allen raised his body into a sitting position. He felt his organs shifting and sloshing inside. He scooted back, slowly, painfully, until his shoulder blades were against the wall. "Not my field."

"As a physician, I'm sure you know more than an auto mechanic. But I'd hate for you to miss the punch line because the rudiments bogged you down. Oh . . ." He tugged a white handkerchief from his breast pocket and held it up to Allen.

Allen looked down. Blood had drizzled down his chest. He touched his fingers to his face. Lots of blood. He felt his cheeks, hoping it wasn't coming from his eyes.

"You have a nosebleed," Litt said. "It happens."

Allen took the handkerchief, wiped his hands and his face, and held it firmly to his nostrils.

"DNA," Litt said. "The complex molecule is a hereditary blueprint that defines a person's skin pigment, eye color and shape, hair color and texture, height, bone structure—every physical trait, including genetic diseases. Each DNA strand is

made up of six billion repeating chemical units called nucleo-
tides, consisting of one of four different kinds of chemicals
called bases—A for adenine, C for cytosine, G for guanine,
and T for thymine. So an individual's genome could be expressed GTTCGTCAAATTG . . . and so on for six billion
letters. No two people share the exact same sequence. Twins
are close, but still unique. Interestingly, nature—" He held a
up a conciliatory hand. "Or God. I understand your brother
is a priest."

"A pastor," Allen said flatly.

"Well, then . . . God put markers in generally the same
spots on our DNA strands. These markers are the same in
everybody. They're like road signs that tell us what the sub-
sequent DNA codes are for—height, hair color, Huntington's
disease, obesity. These markers simplify the process of finding sequences unique to specific individuals. How many
thugs are doing time because they left a bit of their DNA at
a crime scene—blood, semen, skin, hair roots?"

"All right," Allen said. "DNA is unique and identifiable.
That doesn't explain—"

"Now, now, Dr. Parker. This is fascinating stuff, if you
hear me out." He cleared his throat. "I'm sure you're more
versed in the ways of viruses. To refresh: A virus is designed
to survive. Whatever it needs to replicate itself—to propagate
the species, if you will—it will do. That may mean mutating
to avoid a threat, such as an antibody, or to avoid competi-
tion from a stronger virus. That's why we have so many different ones. Herpes viruses seek out the cells of nerve tissue,
the avian flu virus goes right for the alveoli cells, deep in the
lungs. A virus is like a key looking for the cell with a matching lock. When it finds the right cell, it unlocks it and strolls
on in, a thief with a key to the jewelry store. The virus tells

the cell's DNA to stop what it's doing and focus on replicating the virus. So now a cell is destroyed, and the virus multiplies. In Ebola's case, the cells it commandeers happen to be the ones that hold together blood vessels and organs.

"Since we know that a virus has the ability to *find* what it needs, why not *tell* it what it needs? Gene splicing is a fairly simple matter these days. The technology exists, for instance, to take out the gene that codes for brown eyes and literally stick in the gene that codes for blue eyes. However, I did not change what the Ebola virus looks for—the lock that fits it. I simply *added* another lock. When Ebola finds a tissue cell it would normally unlock, it encounters a *second* lock and can't get in. That other lock is a specific individual's DNA, just enough of a sequence to differentiate that person from all but a few other people in the world. I splice that sequence into the section of the Ebola DNA that tells it what to look for, part of its glycoprotein gene. Now, it looks for only the endothelial cells of the person I told it to find. When both keys match, it takes over the cells, replicates, and essentially becomes full-blown Ebola. Or, more precisely, Ebola *Kugel*. *Kugel* means "bullet" in my native tongue. A bullet instead of a bomb." His lipless mouth bent upward.

Allen thought a moment. "You've got Ebola piggybacking on a common cold virus?"

Litt nodded. "Rhinovirus. It can move across the country in twenty-four hours. But Ebola is not so much hitching a ride as it is spliced into it. That way it replicates with the cold virus. I'm making it all sound very easy," he said with a wave of his hand, "but it's infinitely complicated, I assure you. If it weren't, someone else would have already done it." He slapped Allen's leg with his skeletal hand. "Now then. Why am I telling you all this?"

When Allen said nothing, he continued. "To convince you I know what I'm doing. None of this is an accident. I am in complete control. So believe what I say now." He bowed his head closer to Allen and whispered, "I have the cure."

Hope moved through Allen like adrenaline. He tried to suppress it, hold it down, but his heart thumped faster, his stomach tightened in anticipation.

"There is no cure for Ebola," he said.

Litt rolled his head, exasperated. "Have you heard a word I've said? Ebola also doesn't seek out specific individuals—but look at *you.* In fact, Ebola did not exist at all until I created it. Since I intend to use it against my enemies, would knowledge of a cure be something I shared?"

"So why tell me?"

"You have something I want. I'm negotiating."

"Vero's memory chip."

"And information: who knows what."

"Julia and I, we looked at the chip data. That's all."

"Your brother?"

Allen rolled the back of his head against the wall: no.

"See? You're lying. How can I trust you now?"

"What do you *want?*"

"Kendrick Reynolds. You know him?"

"The billionaire?"

"Have you spoken to him or his people? He would not have hidden behind anybody, not for something this precious to him. He would have enticed you with his fame. Did he contact you?"

Allen waited to answer, then said, "I don't know what you're talking about."

"Did he get the chip?"

Allen did not reply.

Litt's voice rose. "Does he know where I am?"

Allen held on to his deadpan expression. *Did* Kendrick know? It wasn't part of Vero's data, except the few scenes of the air base and the jungle beyond, and to Allen they'd seemed anonymous and ambiguous. If the tracking device was working, Julia and Stephen knew where he was, but did Kendrick?

Litt said, "I could care less what else he knows. If he's not already aware of Ebola Kugel, he will be soon. If he's not already aware of my plan to use it on American soil, he will be soon. All I need to know is: does he know where I am? That's all. Whatever your answer is, convince me it's true, and the Ebola virus eating your insides will go away."

"I don't know."

"Does the chip reveal my location?"

He did not reply.

Litt stood quickly. He brushed off his lab coat. "Think about it, Dr. Parker. Your pain can end whenever you want." He rapped on the window panel in the door.

"Litt," Allen said.

The sunglasses rotated toward him.

"If there's any chance this Kendrick guy has found out where you are, why don't you leave?"

"I need to *know*, Dr. Parker. This is my home, my laboratory, everything to me. You understand?"

Allen remembered the list from Vero's data chip, and he finally understood its terrible implications. He wondered if all those people were already infected. Were they only now starting to feel not quite right, or did they feel the pain he did? Were they frightened, as he was? They were husbands, wives, and children. Brothers, sisters, parents. So many people affected. So much grief.

He said, "I saw your list of names." He tried to look hard, challenging. He suspected the only thing he conveyed was illness. "Why so many?"

The door rattled and opened. Litt gripped the edge. "Movies," he said.

"Movies?"

"They've desensitized us. One death, ten deaths are no longer interesting. Ten *thousand* deaths will get their attention."

"You've never studied Stalin?"

Litt raised his chin.

"'When one person dies, it's a tragedy. When a million people die, it's a statistic.'"

"Dr. Parker, I don't think any parent will think of the death of his or her child as a statistic, do you?"

After a moment, he gave a satisfied nod and left.

eighty

THE FIVE-HUNDRED-MILE TRIP FROM SÃO PAULO TO PONTA
Pora took more than six hours, thanks to TAM Transportes
Aéreos's scheduled stops in the backwater towns of Mailia,
Presenente Prudenti, and Dourados. At each tiny airport, the
pilot and one flight attendant would disembark to share a
soda and a few apparently hilarious jokes with the ground
crew, while the copilot hurled rocks at mangy dogs. A handful of Brazilians, most looking tired or drunk, would shuffle
off as their indistinguishable replacements shuffled on. At
any given time, the thirty-passenger turboprop boasted a
manifest of half that number.

The sky grew grayer with each stop, and each time the
plane was in the air, the attendant would give a dramatic
presentation describing the deluge assaulting the western
edge of the state, where Ponta Pora lay. Upon leaving

Dourados on the last leg of the trip, the weather outside the plane made her warnings superfluous. The plane pitched and rolled like a kite caught in a blustery wind. Two passengers became sick, filling the cabin with the pungent odor of illness. Julia and Stephen closed their eyes, gripped the cracked vinyl armrests and each other's free hand between them.

When they finally landed in Ponta Pora, the early afternoon sky was as dark as dusk. Sheets of heavy rain sliced down at an angle, seeming to undulate in the waning light. It beat so fiercely against the metal skin of the plane, Julia knew the engines had stopped only when she saw the propellers winding to a rest and the other passengers standing and gathering their belongings. As the cabin lights came on, Stephen's reflection appeared behind hers in the Plexiglas window.

"Wouldn't you know," she said to his reflection.

Before leaving Atlanta they had transferred their belongings—a change of clothes for each, light jackets, toiletries, Julia's computer gear—into two JanSport daypacks, khaki for him, olive for her. They'd stuffed the remainder of the cash into the padded shoulder straps. That turned out to be an unnecessary caution; customs officials in São Paulo were beyond lax. They gave the packs nothing more than a heft, as if they were so attuned to contraband, they could recognize it by weight alone. Julia wished she'd brought her gun.

Stephen pulled the packs out of the small overhead compartments above their seats and started forward.

Julia reached for hers. "We're going to have to pull our own weight. Starting now."

"So don't let me be gentlemanly." He winked and relinquished his grip.

The attendant was having a hard time holding a grin as rain blew through the door, soaking her uniform and plastering her bangs to her forehead. She swung a hand toward the open door, hurrying them along. *"Adeus. Por favor, va depressa."*

"Adeus. Obrigado," Stephen answered. He caught Julia's bemused stare. "There was a language card in the seat-back pocket."

He ducked through the portal and started down a short flight of rolling metal stairs to the water-covered tarmac and was immediately drenched. Blinking rain out of his eyes, he turned back to see how Julia was faring. She skipped the last step, hopping past him, and darted for the airport door—a lighted rectangle in an otherwise black silhouette of a building.

Inside, she bent at the waist and briskly fanned her fingers through her hair. Big plumes of droplets burst from her head. She said, "Can you believe this?"

"Can we use it in our favor?" He was appraising the small airport, giving each person a few seconds of scrutiny.

Julia slapped him on the back. "Now you're thinking."

He handed her a jacket from his pack, slipping an arm into his own. In the high heat of mid-May Atlanta, they hadn't remembered that it was late fall here. Subtropical though it was, the temperature was in the brisk fifties. The rain made it feel even cooler.

They pushed through big glass doors and found themselves protected from the rain by a deep portico. At least ten cars were parked at the curb, none of them cabs. Right in front of them, an old Ford station wagon began chirping something melodious from a modified horn. A man behind the wheel leaned toward the passenger-side window and waved them over. He had long black hair and cocoa skin, and appeared more Indian than Latin.

"Para onde quer ir?"

Stephen shook his head. "I'm sorry . . ."

"Oh, ha-ha! Where to? You need hotel? I know good hotel."

"No," Julia said behind him. "We'd like to eat. Do you know a decent restaurant?"

"*O restaurante?* Sure, sure! Come inside."

Stephen pulled a ten-dollar bill from his breast pocket. He showed the driver. "American?"

"Sure, sure!"

They climbed into the backseat, which was like a carcass, its skin stripped and picked away, and sat on wiry stuffing. Stephen shifted and settled into the least uncomfortable position, with a coiled spring pushing up into his thigh.

Julia asked, "Can you get us to Pedro Juan Caballero? Is it a problem getting across the border?"

"PJC. No problem. Open borders. No one cares." He ground the transmission into gear and swerved away from the curb without checking for oncoming traffic.

Thinking of the tracking device's position outside of town, Stephen leaned forward and asked, "Do you know, is there another town or an estate or something about ten miles northwest?"

Julia touched his arm. When he looked, she gently shook her head: *Don't talk about it.*

"Northwest?" the driver said.

"Never mind. It's okay."

"Nothing that way," the driver said. "Just forest. Trees."

"We'll do our own recon," Julia whispered.

"I figured knowing what we're going into couldn't hurt."

"We don't know who we can trust."

Stephen caught the cabbie scowling in the rearview mirror. South Americans were known for their exceedingly good manners toward strangers. He'd heard that they'd rather suffer an indignity than offend with a retort. But then, they were only human. He supposed the cabbie didn't appreciate his passengers whispering secrets.

"I'm sure there are plenty of good restaurants around here," Stephen said to the driver, trying to make amends by pulling the man into a conversation.

"Yes," he replied, curt.

"Almost there," Julia said and squeezed Stephen's hand.

He looked out at the dark, wet day. "I only pray we're not too late."

The downpour robbed the Siamese-twin towns of Ponta Pora, Brazil, and Pedro Juan Caballero, Paraguay, of any personality they may have possessed. Everything appeared flat and gray. Lights burned in store windows. Empty chairs and benches squatted on the sidewalks. The storefronts were all narrow. The signs above them appeared amateurishly hand-lettered and in several languages, rarely English—except for a profusion of Coca-Cola and Marlboro signs. In the three blocks they watched, the wagon passed four, maybe five drugstores, their busy windows marked with an odd assortment of symbols: the familiar pestle and mortar, the caduceus, large capsules and tablets, test tubes, even skulls and crossbones.

A steady vibration coming up through the seat and a particular sound told Julia and Stephen what their eyes could not detect: the streets were cobblestone. When tires are on wet pavement, they hiss, like the air is coming out of the world. These tires made a gentle, rhythmic *sha-sha-sha*—the beat of a snare drum.

"Are we in Paraguay?" Julia asked.

"Oh, yes."

"How far back was the border?"

"Minutes. Just minutes. The big street, Avenida Internacional. Did you see it?" He motioned behind them.

Stephen remembered a street that was slightly wider than the others, a few blocks back.

"That was border. Nothing. I told you."

"I can't see the difference," Julia said.

"The signs. Guarani and Spanish here, mostly Portuguese there. When no rain, PJC has lots more vendors in the street, no restrictions like Pora."

"So really it's one big town, shared by two countries."

"Eh, not so big."

They wound through the deserted streets for another few minutes; then the driver pulled over. "Good food here."

"Looks like a bar," Stephen said.

Julia opened the door. "It'll do."

Stephen handed the driver the ten and slid out with the daypacks.

The station wagon coasted away, rain making it fuzzy and ethereal. As it began rounding a corner, a gust of wind rippled the rain, and the car vanished.

Stephen smiled at Julia's wet-dog look. "We hoofing it somewhere else?" he asked.

"You got it."

"First hotel?"

"First restaurant, deli, or bar, not counting this one. I really am starving." She took the pack from him and hoisted a strap over her shoulder.

He looked one way, then the other. Both directions looked bleak, abandoned. He lowered his head against the driving rain and started walking.

eighty-one

THE CALL CAME IN ON WHAT GREGOR THOUGHT OF AS HIS "informants' line." It was the number he'd given out to airport personnel, cabbies, hoteliers, and restaurateurs in Pedro Juan Caballero and Ponta Pora to report on people asking about Karl, the compound, or missing persons. Most of the calls had been false alarms, the result of overactive imaginations and underfunded bank accounts. He paid a few of these anyway, simply to encourage watchful eyes and loose lips.

This call was different. He realized it as soon as he heard the description of the man and woman. Steven Parker and Julia Matheson. Here. They'd somehow followed Allen Parker. No doubt it was the Matheson woman's doing. FBI. CDC. Whatever. Probably a homing device on the plane.

He thought a moment. "Give me your number." He entered it into his BlackBerry. The government-run phone system was so undependable, it seemed everybody in the region had a mobile phone. Maybe no pot to pee in, but definitely a flip phone. He told the cabbie to keep an eye on the visitors and promised him a big bonus.

He hurried down one of the complex's dim, dank-smelling corridors, passed his face in front of a thermal reader, and entered the laboratory wing. He stood for a moment, letting his eyes acclimate to the area's bright fluorescents. Karl would have his head. What was Gregor thinking, inviting Atropos to the compound? It had exposed them to discovery by people they *didn't* want visiting. The arrival of Matheson and the brother made that clear. If Karl shot him on the spot, he'd deserve it.

Shoot? Karl wouldn't shoot him; he'd extract his revenge in a more poetic, nastier way. It didn't matter that they'd known each other since childhood. Gregor had jeopardized Karl's life's work. And for what? To meet Atropos. One of the great hit men of the world. Correction—*several* of the great hit men of the world.

Despite the dire situation, Gregor smiled. What a revelation. To be one of a handful of people who knew Atropos's secret. No wonder he was so prolific, so omniscient. Atropos was not one man but *four*.

Three now, Gregor thought. The three brothers had asked to be taken to the compound's morgue. Before Gregor had left, he witnessed the opening of the body bag the first Atropos had brought. Inside was another Atropos, grotesquely wounded.

Their grief had been great and wretched.

He understood now how Matheson and the Parker brothers had hurt them . . . *him.* They referred to themselves in the singular, as though, like their name and appearance, they shared one mind, one personality, one soul. If giving them the same name and treating them as one had been their father's way of making the world think one person was as powerful as four, he had succeeded; but in so doing, he had also made his sons completely dependent on one another, like one person split into four.

They wanted revenge. They wanted to see Allen Parker suffer and beg for death, a torture Karl's germ provided in spades.

And now the other two responsible for Atropos's loss were within striking distance.

Why did Karl even have to know they had arrived? That was a can of worms he didn't want to open. And Atropos would gladly remedy this problem.

They were back out at the planes, waiting for Allen to manifest the virus, waiting to torment him as he died. Gregor would tell them he had arranged for the arrival of their brother's other two killers. His gift to them.

He showed his face to the black tile next to the door, which opened. As he stepped though, heading for the stairs that would take him topside, he marveled at his skill at turning complications into advantages.

Karl's microscopic bugs may be the future of assassination, he thought. *But I've got today's model right here, right now. Times three.*

eighty-two

JULIA AND STEPHEN STEPPED OUT OF *AKÃ HARUJA*—THE Pig's Eye Tavern, the owner/waiter/barkeep had told them. Their bellies were full, and a mug of homemade beer had taken the edge off Julia's nerves. From their table near the front window, they had watched the rain abate and then ramp up again as they paid the check.

The streets were still empty. The sky was still black, a swirling cauldron of low clouds.

Julia nudged him. She was looking at a station wagon on a side street a block away. It was parked, its headlamps and cabin dark.

"Is that the cab?" Stephen asked.

While they watched, the tailpipe burped out a puff of exhaust. The downpour muffled the engine noise. The head-lights came on, dim cones of light catching the drops passing through them. The vehicle rolled forward and turned onto their street, heading for them.

Stephen angled his arm across Julia, gently pushing her back an inch.

"It is," she said.

He looked back at the tavern's door. He could grab Julia and be through it in three seconds.

The station wagon approached slowly. Its right front tire dropped into a pothole, splashing out muddy water. Stephen sensed the headlamps illuminating his legs, then his chest, then his face, growing brighter. He took a step back, forcing Julia to do the same.

"Let's see what he wants," she said.

"How could this be good?"

"We're not going to get anywhere if we don't take chances."

"Didn't you say we can't trust anyone?"

"He already knows our business. Maybe he's thought about it and wants to sell us some information."

Stephen expected the car to make a roaring lunge at them, but it simply coasted alongside and stopped. He could see the cabbie's smile as he leaned to roll down the window.

"Hey!" the cabbie said. "Other place food no good?" Acting natural.

Julia leaned around Stephen. "What do you want?" she asked.

"Get in. Rain no good."

"Come on," Stephen said and took a step toward the tavern.

"I have news," the cabbie called. "Good news for you."

"Like what?" Julia said.

The driver's smile faltered. "My mind came back. You asked about place in the northwest, yes? There is something."

"What?"

"Get in." He read their expressions. "Is okay. Look, I have nothing."

Stephen leaned closer. On the passenger side of the bench seat were loose papers, a tattered magazine, and a mobile phone, a brick-sized thing from a decade ago.

Julia stepped past him and tugged on his shirt. She opened the back door and climbed in. Stephen followed. The heater was blasting out scalding air; it smelled like burning plastic.

The car started moving.

"We'll talk here," Stephen said.

"This street no good. Bad . . . uh . . . element . . . kids." He turned a corner.

Stephen looked at Julia. She lowered her head, whispered, "If this turns bad, jump out your side. Don't worry about me."

He nodded. "Are you buying any of this?"

"If nothing else, it's a lead; it's something."

The car made another turn. All the streets looked alike: empty, dark, and wet.

Julia poked him in the thigh. "Listen. If something happens to me, go to the American Consulate. It's probably in Asunción."

"Nothing's going to—"

The car braked hard, throwing the two of them into the seat in front of them. Rain hit Stephen's face. The driver's door stood open. The driver was gone, three quick, splashing footsteps, then nothing.

Stephen jerked his door handle up. Julia grabbed his arm. Blood was smeared on her upper lip, leaking out her nose. She was peering over the front seat, through the windshield.

He looked. There was nothing out there but a disappearing

red dirt road, rust-colored puddles, millions of little stalag-mites of water pinging upward, wavering sheets of heavy, dark rain . . .

And a man.

Walking toward them in the center of the street. Just a sil-houette. Rising and falling with each step. Gone now, lost among the cascading beads. There! Closer! Broad shoulders. Tall. Wearing a . . . *cape*? No, a long coat, an oilskin slicker. It took a few seconds to realize the figure had stopped mov-ing; the rain maintained the illusion of movement. Then it slacked.

"The Warrior," Stephen said. The wound in his side seemed to throb, as though confirming the killer's presence. He became aware of the dome light, making their faces vis-ible to the man outside. Atropos waited at the far edge of the headlights, appearing blurry and grainy, a 1970s eight-millimeter version of himself.

"He knows where Allen is," Stephen said.

"We're not ready," she said. "He'll kill us. We need to do this differently."

"Like how?"

"We need to be the ones surprising him, not the other way around."

"Too late."

"Why's he just standing there?"

"He's *grinning*," Stephen said. He felt his muscles tighten with anger.

Atropos swung his arm up. A red light glimmered; then his hand appeared to explode in white light. Windshield glass shattered over them. Then again. Stephen turned to cover Julia, but she was already falling out of her open door. He shouldered open his own door and tumbled out into the mud. He rolled to the rear and fell into Julia, crouched at the bumper. The back window ruptured; glass pellets washed over them.

He looked at her hard. "You run," he said. "I'll distract him." He started to rise. She lunged at him, encircling his neck with her arm. Her face, mud peeling off it with each strike of raindrop, was all he could see.

"You're not doing that!" she said. "You didn't come this far to die in the mud. I can't save Allen alone. I need you."

"You need me *right now*," he said. "Let me get you out of here."

"Not like this. We both go or neither of us does."

He saw in her eyes she was serious.

She uncoiled her arm and took his hands. She moved them to the bumper. "Hold on," she said. Then she rolled away, back around the side of the station wagon.

"Wait—!"

He peered through the windowless back. Through cantaloupe-sized holes in the windshield, he watched Atropos approach, slowly, with confidence. He saw Julia's hand come up by the steering wheel and grab the shifter. She yanked it down. The engine gunned, and the station wagon fishtailed and shot forward.

The tires slung mud into Stephen's face, blinding him. He pinched his eyes closed, held his breath, and tightened his grip on the bumper. The road played out under him, jostling him over ruts and potholes. A hundred tiny fists beat his chest, stomach, legs. Their speed seemed tremendous, and the ride went on and on. The hidden edge of the bumper cut into his fingers. Mud pushed under his grip, slick as soap. He turned his hands to stone, but he couldn't hold on much longer.

The wagon crashed into something. His body lifted and

his head cracked against the tailgate. He released the bumper. His face dropped into a puddle. He used it to splash the mud out of his eyes, his nose, his mouth. He rolled onto his back, raised his head, and looked. They had traveled only about three blocks.

How could that be?

Atropos was back there, not as far away as Stephen would have thought . . . or wished. Red mud coated the killer's right side, as though he had hit the road to avoid the station wagon. The rain was washing him clean again, as it was Stephen.

Julia appeared at his side, a fresh gash in her forehead.

"I'm all right," she said before he could ask. "Come on."

She tugged on him, and they both rose. They passed the station wagon, which had struck a large wooden cart. Crates of oranges had tumbled onto the hood and road.

At the first street, they turned right. Stephen looked back, slipped in the mud, and fell hard. Julia pulled him up. Stephen wiped his eyes and peered around.

They were on a street mixed with storefronts and small houses that appeared to be cobbled together from old signs and corrugated metal. The rain and false dusk cut visibility to roughly two blocks; any direction could lead to a dead end or to the relative safety of a crowded indoor market—there was no way of knowing.

"This way," she said, heading up the street.

Stephen took the lead. They sloshed through rust-red torrents, blinking at the pelting rain. The water was cold; Stephen's toes went from frigid to sore to numb. At each cross street, they scanned for signs of people or police or shelter. Stephen continually veered to one side of the street, then the other, rattling door handles, rapping at doors. Pedro Juan Caballero could have been a ghost town.

At an intersection, a cutting wind hurled beads of water at them with the force of a shotgun blast. They stepped out of the crosscurrent, and Julia stopped as fast her feet slipped out from under her. She clung to Stephen's arm, managing to stay up only after planting one knee in the mud.

Atropos was coming toward them. Somehow he had overtaken them, or they had gotten turned around in the storm. Julia kept her eyes on the killer as she regained her footing. The wind had caught the man's long coat, causing the sides to flap behind him like leathery wings. She saw a flicker of red dancing at his side: his pistol like an extension of his arm.

Lightning burst across the sky, illuminating a million raindrops as if they were tiny mirrors. It blinded Stephen for a sheer moment. In that time, Atropos halved the distance between them. Clear, now, was the look of grim determination on his face. His right arm rose stiffly, pivoting at the shoulder. The laser drew a glittering arc toward them.

"Move!" Julia yelled. She shoved her weight into Stephen. The two splashed down in a stream of rushing water at a point in the street where a curb would have been, had these back roads possessed them.

He didn't hear the spit of the silenced gun, but a nearby window shattered like a melodic counterpoint to the rain's ceaseless pounding.

"Move! Move!" she screamed. They tumbled over each other, gaining their feet. He pulled her up and pushed her forward, back the way they'd come. She stumbled again, splashing down in the mud. He leaped over her, his momentum making a sudden stop impossible. He turned and was blinded by Atropos's red laser. He snapped his head away and felt the hot-piercing impact of a bullet.

eighty-three

THE RED DOT OF ATROPOS'S GUN FLICKERED THROUGH THE beads of falling water and touched Stephen's face like the finger of fate. He flew back, crashing through the door of a shop, its glass pane bursting into slivers, for a second becoming indistinguishable from the rain.

"Stephen!" A drenched rope of hair fell into her face. She swatted at it, flipping it away. "Stephen!"

She rose from the mud and swung around toward Atropos. He stood dark and solid in the center of the road, fifty feet away. The gun was at his side again, and he was simply watching. Slowly, watching him, but anxious for Stephen, she stepped to the shop door. The Warrior made no advance, no move intended to stop her. He seemed to be communicating his understanding of the situation: she and Stephen were his to kill at his leisure; nothing they did could prevent him from acquiring his trophies.

Stephen was lying inside the store, his feet protruding over the bottom wood slat of the door. His head was thrown back so only his hairy chin and neck were visible beyond his chest. Did she really want to see his face, the damage a 9mm could do to it? But if he were alive, could she deny him the chance to behold a friendly face before dying?

Then his chest heaved, and he raised his head. His eyes found her and his lips tried to form a smile, but settled on a grimace.

"Stephen?" She felt disoriented, dreamy.

"I think he shot me." He crossed his right arm over his chest and gripped his shoulder. She saw where the jacket was torn and soaked in blood.

She stepped through the broken door and crouched at his side. "I thought . . ." She smiled, and he took it in; the healing touch of an angel—or a shot of morphine—could not have effected such a positive change to his expression. He grinned, reminding her of when they met, only a few days ago; she'd felt an instant kinship with him and had hoped she wasn't being naïve. Her chest tightened as she realized now he was one of the few genuine good guys—as Goody had been. Her heart ached to see him hurt.

She stuck her finger in the bullet hole in his jacket and felt for the wound. He winced.

"High on the shoulder," she said. "Not too bad."

His eyes widened. "Where is he?"

She looked out through the destroyed door. "He's just standing there, watching. I think he's toying with us."

At that moment Atropos's rain-blurred figure took a step toward them, then another.

"Stephen, you have to get up." She got her arms under him and helped him up. Atropos was forty feet away and closing in fast. They stumbled around displays of pottery and handmade ceramic picture frames, heading for the back of the store. They plowed through a closed door into a living room, where a family huddled together on a threadbare sofa. The mother, a teenage daughter, and two school-age boys were making an admirable attempt to disappear into the father's embrace. They all looked healthy and loving. And utterly terrified, Julia thought.

"I'm sorry," she said. She pointed toward another door that was ajar and seemed to lead to more rooms. "Go in there, *please*!"

"They don't understand," Stephen said.

"Go! Go!" she yelled, waving the way. The family dislodged themselves and started to comply. Julia shot to a third door, this one metal and heavily bolted. She opened it. "Alley," she announced. They heard the crunch of glass from the store. "Come on."

The passage was narrow and dark. Slate clouds swirled in the strip of sky overhead. The rain pelted the side of one of the buildings that formed the alley and cascaded down; a fine mist descended upon them. They sprinted left. She heard Stephen's splashing footfalls and labored breathing behind her—sounds the tight alley magnified. They passed another alleyway that transected their own. Ahead, the rain at the end of the alleyway appeared to bow inward, taking the shape of a man before he actually materialized just inside the alley.

It was Atropos.

She stopped cold. Stephen huffed behind her. "I . . . don't . . . understand . . ." he managed between inhalations. "Could he . . . have . . . come around . . . that fast?"

She thought of the crunching glass they'd heard in the store. No way. "Go back," she said. The figure was moving toward them. Spinning, they dashed toward the opposite end.

Ahead of them, Atropos stepped through the door into the alley. His head snapped around to take them in.

They stopped cold. They looked from one warrior to the other. Physically, they were identical in every way. They even converged on Julia and Stephen with the same measured gait. Each held a pistol in his right hand, a little red dot dancing beneath it, reflecting off the wet surface.

"They won't shoot," she told Stephen. "They're in each other's crossfire." She inched toward the Atropos that was farthest from them, the one who had followed them through the store. She pulled Stephen along by the hand.

"When they get close enough, they will," he said.

"That's why we're going to run down this other alley. You see it?"

"Yep."

"To the left."

"Yep."

"Now!"

They bolted into the cross-alley, crashing over a garbage can. Food wrappers and bits of trash clung to their legs; the odor of rot wafted over them. Julia's stomach, already knotted by fear, contracted at this new revulsion. She knew she could vomit and run at the same time if she had to. But in the next second, she'd forgotten about corporeal grievances— her aching muscles, her cold and waterlogged flesh, nausea—and simply ran. She listened for a sound that would signal the warriors' arrival at the head of the alley. Would they try to get closer? Or would they just aim and shoot, a certain bull's-eye in this straight-as-a-shooting-range passageway? Would the spit of a silenced round be the last thing she ever heard?

They came to the end of the alley and whipped around

the corner, out of the path of any bullets sailing their way. They pressed against a stuccoed wall, panting.

"We gotta keep going," she said. Then a movement caught her eye, A block away and across the street, a stranger emerged from an alley. He was wearing a leather jacket, appearing casual with one hand in a pocket. He had stolen Indiana Jones's hat and had it cocked forward, obscuring his eyes. Rain poured off of it like a backyard water feature. He motioned to them, beckoning, then stepped out of sight.

Stephen looked at Julia.

"I don't know," she said.

A loud sound came from the alley next to them, a knocked-over-trash-can sound. That decided it for her. She ran toward where the man had stood. They curved around the corner and saw him at another intersection of alleyways. He was a black man and almost invisible against the darkness. Again he beckoned to them. He disappeared into the adjoining alley.

When they followed, they found that the alley disappeared into darkness. Behind them, footsteps echoed against the buildings. They plunged into the darkness. As a wall of brick materialized at the end of the alley, a metal door swung open. Julia crashed into it; Stephen crashed into her. Bodies rushed out of the black opening, enveloping her in unyielding, viselike arms.

She kicked out, and a pair of hands seized her foot, wrenching her leg. She was pulled into the darkness. Stephen came behind her, grunting and thrashing. The door shut, and the arms hurled her to a dirt floor she could not see. She felt Stephen land beside her. A click, and light pierced her pupils. Blinded, she heard more clicks, metal sliding on metal, mechanisms locking into place. She knew these sounds. Shielding her eyes, she looked around—

Into the black barrels of a dozen guns.

eighty-four

JULIA BLINKED. A FACE PRESENTED ITSELF OVER THE RIFLE poised directly in front of her. Crevices exaggerated the contours of the man's mouth and cheeks, the permanent twin furrows between his eyes. A spiderweb of delicate lines fanned out from his eyes, which were red and moist and slightly protuberant. Folds of flesh gave him little jowls that, coupled with an expansive mouth that God surely intended for profound utterances, made him look wise. It was a face at once friendly and sad.

It was the man who had beckoned to them.

The rifle came down—only this one—and the man pressed an index finger to his lips. "Shhhhhhh," he whispered, soft and long, as a mother to a baby. He took one step backward and leaned an ear to the metal door. Gently he laid the fingertips of his empty hand against the door, as though feeling for vibrations.

No one else in the room moved. They stood in a circle

around Julia and Stephen, leveling an arsenal of pistols, rifles, and shotguns at them. Water dripped from their clothes. The man at the door cocked his head and raised his rifle like a shaman's staff, a call for silence. Then she heard them: footsteps approaching the door, the scuff of a sole against pavement. The sound moved past without pausing.

Someone behind Julia clicked his tongue, preparing to speak. The man at the door raised the rifle higher, shook his head. The sound outside the door returned, this time stopping directly outside. Silence. There was no noise for so long, Julia wondered if the person outside had moved off undetected. There was an almost imperceptible *click*. Her eyes fell to the doorknob, which was turning slowly. After the slightest rotation, it stopped. The person outside—certainly one of the Warriors—rattled the handle, shook the door.

"Get down," Julia hissed, trying for both discretion and urgency.

Then it happened: the assailants outside fired into the door. The bullets made convex dents in the door's metal skin but did not penetrate it. Two . . . three . . . four. The man at the door moved to the side, gesturing for the others to do the same. The handle jerked violently, then again, as bullets hit its outside counterpart.

Julia noticed that a heavy bar had been braced horizontally across the door; their safety was not dependent on the handle's integrity. The handle fell away, leaving a three-inch hole straight through to the gray alley. A shadow moved over it, then an eye appeared, rolling to take in the men, locking on Julia.

A rifle cracked behind her, loud. The bullet pinged three inches from the eye, which pulled away. A sound-suppressed barrel slipped into the opening. It spat blindly, hitting the wall behind Julia.

Men yelped and bolted toward an interior exit.

The black man by the door slammed the butt of his rifle against the barrel, which spat another bullet—this one kicking up a chuck of dirt a foot from Julia's knee. She felt hands under her arms, and she rose off the ground at rocket speed. She swung through the air and landed on her feet behind the crush of men leaving the room. She looked back. Stephen's expression was firm, implacable. He pushed her forward.

The man at the door kept striking at the barrel until it retreated. At the edge of the hole, the door's metal skin exploded inward. The Warriors outside were shooting through without exposing their barrels.

She made it into the next room. The men crowded the back wall, pointing their rifles at the doorway. The black man ran in and slammed the door. He nodded, and someone hefted open a trapdoor in the floor.

The black man walked to the edge. He took in Julia and Stephen. "Come," he said.

Julia hesitated.

His expression softened. "It's not a dungeon. It's an underground passage. To a safer place. It's only a matter of time before those blokes get in." Tinged British, his voice was deep and smooth.

As if to appease her, or to indicate he was out of there, with or without her, he stepped into the hole and descended until he was gone. She peered down. A flashlight flicked on, revealing the man's face at the bottom of steep stairs. She glanced at Stephen and dropped her foot through.

The air below was moist and cool and redolent with an earthy scent that reminded Julia of clean skin. Without a word, the man turned and walked into a tunnel, carved through red dirt and clay. She followed. As they moved deeper, the sounds of the other men's boots on the steps, the creaking of leather holsters and jackets, the rattle of their weapons became ambient white noise, like the dull roar of a conch. When the man in front of her spoke again, he was a decibel shy of yelling.

"These passageways were constructed during General Stroessner's dictatorship. He had a passion for torture. Paraguay has been free of him for three decades now, but evil still haunts this little town, so the tunnels remain. The trapdoor we used has a metal core and a good lock on the underside, but even if your mates with the guns get in, they probably won't find us."

"Probably?" Julia said.

"Best we can do on short notice."

They came to a room from which a half dozen tunnels branched off. The man lit a lantern that hung from a hook in the ceiling and waited for the other men to stream in. He spoke in a foreign tongue, and someone responded.

"Everyone's here," he said. "Name's Sebastian Tate." He flashed a set of big teeth and held out his hand.

"Julia," she said. "This is Stephen."

His eyes settled on Stephen's shoulder. "You're hurt." He called to someone behind them. An old man with a mangy long beard stepped forward, pushing a huge revolver into the front of his pants. He gingerly peeled Stephen's jacket and shirt off the shoulder and prodded the wound with long, bony fingers. He waved his hand at it, as if disappointed. *"Pire erída,"* he said.

"Flesh wound," Tate interpreted. "Are you in pain?"

"I'll live."

To the old man, Tate said, *"Pohã."*

The man rummaged in a leather pouch tied around his waist, produced three white pills, and handed them to Stephen.

"Aspirin," Tate said. He turned to Julia. "You look like you can use some too."

She touched the gash in her forehead. "Yeah, thanks." She dry-swallowed the pills and asked, "How did you know to help us?"

"Those freaky triplets were shooting at you."

"*Triplets?* We only saw two. I think."

"There were three, as identical as Oreos. One of the men saw them come into town from Angra Road. Only one place those *geepas* could have come from. And if that place wants you dead, you must be worth saving."

"What place is that?"

"The old air base. Now let's get going." He strode into one of the tunnels. As they walked, he explained that he'd come to Paraguay as a journalist for the London *Times*, covering the country's escalating organized crime problem. What he found, however, was infinitely more sensational—the regular disappearance of the citizens of Ponta Pora and Pedro Juan Caballero. Men, women, and children, simply gone. One per week, on average. His editors were not interested, so he took a year-long sabbatical to investigate, try to write a book. He "came under the enchantment of a beguiling inamorata," was the way he put it—and the year stretched into two, then three. Despite the area's paltry cost of living— the typical Paraguayan pulled down less than most Americans spend on cable television—his savings eventually eroded, and he took a job as the northeastern correspondent for *ABC Color*, Paraguay's national daily newspaper.

He stopped and turned around, his hand gripping the side of a staircase leading up to a trapdoor, a thin bead of light seeping along its edges. Muted voices filtered through as well. And laughter, which made Julia smile thinly.

"We're here," Tate said.

eighty-five

JULIA AND STEPHEN FOLLOWED SEBASTIAN TATE UP FROM the tunnel into what amounted to its polar opposite: a cavernous warehouse, brightly lit by hanging metal lamps and warmed by a clanking industrial furnace. Boxes and crates lined the walls, leaving a ballroom-sized area in the middle. Like the room at the other end of the tunnel, the floor here was hard-packed earth. A fine pelt of grass had sprouted around the edges of the open area. A flea market's assortment of tattered sofas, disemboweled easy chairs, automobile seats, and lawn chairs with missing webbing appropriated half of this open area, along with a hodgepodge of shelves, tables, and dressers. The spirited conversation Julia had heard from below came from roughly two dozen people, mostly women.

One of them, a pretty woman in her thirties with flowing black hair, walked quickly toward them. *"Mba'éicha?"* she asked.

"Opavave al pelo pa," Tate answered.

She collided with him and wrapped her arm around his neck. He groaned as she squeezed him. Then they kissed, long and passionately. She broke away and studied Julia and Stephen.

Tate spoke to her, and she returned to a small group of women.

"My Rosa," he said, flashing two rows of big teeth.

Rosa returned with two other women, each trying to talk louder than the others until they were very nearly screaming.

Tate calmed them down, addressing each in turn. He grinned at Julia and Stephen. "Rosa wants to wash your clothes. She says she's never seen two dirtier people."

A young woman stepped closer. *"Jahu?"*

Tate nodded. "Ernestina will prepare baths for you in the back rooms. And Fatimá will get you drinks and *soó ha chipa*—meat and bread."

"How nice," Julia said, nodding. "I feel like I should understand them. That's not Spanish?"

"Guarani. Mostly an aboriginal tongue, with a measure of Spanish tossed in." He pointed at Stephen's side. "You've got another injury."

Through the soaked and muddy clothes seeped a basketball-sized circle of blood.

Stephen looked under his arm at the splotch. "Must have torn out the stitches."

"Roberto will see to that."

He hailed the old man who'd helped earlier. Roberto grunted off the floor, where he was removing his boots, and began a shuffling journey toward them.

Tate said, "He was trained as a vet, but he's pretty good with humans too."

Julia nudged Stephen. "I guess I get a bath first, then."

"Enjoy."

Ernestina took her hand and led her toward a door. Before stepping though, Julia looked back. Tate was kneeling by two men, showing them how to field-strip an automatic pistol.

FIFTY MINUTES LATER, STEPHEN WAS SITTING ON A SOFA, JULIA beside him in one of the formerly overstuffed chairs. Both were wrapped in heavy Indian quilts, self-consciously waiting for Rosa to return with their clothes. Whatever the temporary discomfort of sitting almost nude among strangers, Julia thought, being warm and clean was worth it. She'd had to drain the tub of its murky red water after a quick submersion and refill it to soak the rest of the grime off her body. Even so, she was still dislodging granules of cinnabar sand whenever she ran her fingertips over her scalp.

Fatimá stepped up to the low table before them, balancing three large bowls in her arms. As she set each on the table, she announced its contents. *"Yva."* She lowered a bowl of whole fruit: apples, bananas, mangos, and mostly oranges. *"Asodos."* Steaming slices of charbroiled meat.

A hearty aroma washed past Julia, and despite the meal she'd eaten at the Pig's Eye Tavern, she felt hungry again. By Stephen's rapt attention to the bowl, she guessed he was feeling the same.

"Chipa." Loaves of brioche-type bread, so hot the girl's beaming face wavered behind its steam. Fatimá straightened, planted her hands on her hips, and smiled, pleased with herself.

"Grácia," Julia said.

Ernestina had given her a cursory lesson in Guarani. So far, Julia's repertoire consisted of four words: *yes, no, thanks,* and *bathroom.* What more did anyone need?

Fatimá nodded at Julia. She swung her head around, tossing her hair over one shoulder. She flashed emerald eyes at Stephen and gave him a smile measurably bigger and brighter than the one Julia had received. *"Okaru."*

Stephen stared dumbly at her. Julia couldn't tell if it was the word or her stunning beauty, so flirtatiously displayed, that left him speechless.

"Okaru," she repeated and pretended to pick something out of one of the bowls with all five fingers and put it into her mouth. *"Okaru."*

"Eat!" Stephen said, snapping out of his daze. "Yes, thank you . . . *grácia.*"

Fatimá pursed her lips into a coy smile and sauntered off.

No chef in Paris or New York could have made a dish better tasting than the *asodos* and *chipa.* The two ate leisurely and watched their hosts move about the big room, discussing points, studying maps, cleaning and recleaning guns. A few wandered over, nodded solemn greetings, grabbed oranges, and returned to their business. Julia became aware of an almost palpable sense of apprehension hanging in the air, a musty odor of fear.

A shifting shadow caught her eye, and she spotted a man sitting high on a stack of crates, peering out one of the windows that lined the top of the twenty-foot-high walls. In the shadows, only his dark shape was visible against the dull-iron luminance of the world that lay beyond the glass, but she could clearly make out his rifle. She was scanning for other lookouts when Fatimá came by with two mugs made from bull horns.

"Tereré," she called the drink. They thanked her, and she left, swishing her simple cotton dress to and fro as she did.

Julia smelled the concoction and sipped. She made a face and set the mug on the table.

"You better like that," Tate warned, plopping down on the sofa next to Stephen. "Everybody drinks that stuff here. Everybody, all the time."

"It's bitter," she complained.

"You get used to it." He surveyed the remaining food on the table, peeled off a strip of bread, and pushed it into his mouth. Chewing slowly, he leveled his sad, perceptive eyes at her. He was not smiling.

"Wanna tell me why you're here and why *Naña-ykua* doesn't want you to be?"

"*Naña . . . ?*"

"*Naña-ykua.* It means 'Demon of the pit.' The townsfolk believe that place is evil, and for good reason. Long as most can remember, people would go out that way and never come back. Or they would—with tales of the guards shooting at them. What are you here for?"

Stephen answered. "They kidnapped my brother."

Tate nodded. "That's what they do. That bloke over there, the one with the scar on his face? That's Emilio. His papa disappeared ten years ago, right off the streets here in PJC. Emilio went to the local *tahachi*, the police. Said they'd look into it, but they didn't. One of our men, who used to be on the force, said a drive out to the gates of the air base was good for a 100,000-guarani banknote—a couple days' wages. Emilio even went to Asunción, to the *federales*. Nothing ever came of it. He got together with others who'd lost someone, a wife, a child. They'd go out and take potshots at the guards, the buildings, try to sabotage the vehicles heading out there.

Eventually *Naña-ykua* installed heavier security, some really nasty stuff, and that ended that. Emilio and his mates started patrolling the streets at night. They interrupted a couple kidnappings. Beat them good. After a few of those, the disappearances stopped. Then they began in Cerro Cora, about fifteen klicks west. We helped set up patrols there too. Then in Antônio João. Kept pushing the kidnappings farther and farther away. Where'd they get your brother?"

"Chattanooga."

"In the States?" Tate's eyes flashed wide. "Whoa."

"Not the same kind of kidnapping," Julia said. "But they have him, and we want him back."

Rosa came over and sat on Tate's lap. She spoke to him.

Tate nodded at Stephen. "Your clothes are ready. They're in the back room, where the baths are."

Stephen left, and Rosa began running her fingers over Tate's head and neck.

Julia watched for a moment, then said, "You've made this your home."

"Rosa's my home." He closed his eyes, feeling her gentle massage. Then he looked around the room. "These are wonderful people. Kindhearted. Generous. They don't deserve what's been happening to them. Husbands, wives, kids—just gone. Stolen. At first I wanted to expose the problem the only way I knew how, by writing about it. Then I found Rosa, and all these mates found me. Now I want to help in more tangible ways."

"That's admirable, fighting their cause."

"It's my cause now too." He smiled up at his lady. "Rosa won't go back to England with me. She won't leave her family. So this is my home, as long as Rosa will have me."

Rosa kissed the top of his head, then his ear.

"Looks like the feeling's mutual," Julia said. She paused a moment. "You're handy with guns."

"SAS, in a previous life."

She cocked an eyebrow at him, seeing more in his weathered face and firm body than she had before. SAS was considered the first and still the best special forces unit in the world.

"This ragtag bunch," he continued, "farmers and ranchers mostly, needed my kind of help."

"To protect themselves from the kidnappings?" A former SAS member seemed like overkill. Start taking people where she came from, and a good two-by-four would put an end to that quick enough.

"They have bigger plans, if they can ever—"

He looked up and nodded appreciatively.

Stephen was heading toward them, dressed in clean clothes and looking thoroughly pleased by the fact. As he walked past a cluster of men, the man Tate had identified as Emilio stepped up to him. The two spoke words and continued heading toward the oasis of furniture set to one side of the expansive room.

Stephen plopped down and held up something for Julia to see. It was a big revolver.

"He wants you to inspect it," explained Tate. "It was his father's."

"Yes, my papa's. A nice gun," confirmed Emilio, standing by the couch and grinning down at Stephen.

Stephen hefted the weapon and sighted down the barrel.

"Very nice," he said. He handed it back to Emilio, who lofted it proudly, then shoved it into his waistband.

"Well, look at you," Julia said, eyeing Stephen's fresh appearance.

Stephen tugged at his collar and brushed the front of his

clean and apparently ironed shirt. "Yes, yes," he said. "I am myself again." He plucked some meat out of the bowl and folded it into his mouth.

Emilio pulled a lawn chair closer and sat.

"Thank you for your hospitality," she told him.

"You feel better?"

"Much, almost human. I'll feel even better with my clothes on."

Emilio blushed, the blood giving his dark skin a cinnamon hue. "Soon, I think." He spoke to Rosa, who glanced at Julia and laughed good-naturedly. She slid off Tate's lap and walked toward the back rooms.

"I'm fine, really." Julia pulled the quilt tighter and tucked the edges under her legs. She turned to Tate. "You said they have bigger plans that could use your SAS background. What?"

"To crush *Naña-ykua!*" Emilio said. He yanked the pistol out of his waistband and pumped it in the air. *"Aikoteve peikoteve che rehe, Naña-ykua!"*

Cheers and hoots sprang from the men around the room.

"Well . . ." Tate said, patting the air to calm Emilio and urge him to put away his weapon. "Someday."

"Someday? No someday!" Emilio said. He smiled at Julia. "We get them now, no?"

Stephen was nodding. Julia didn't know how to respond. Was Emilio offering this group's help? Could they really go in, guns blazing, and get Allen?

Emilio said, "Bad people out there. Who is gone? Who they take?"

"My brother."

"Oh, *eme'êna.*" He stood and yelled at the others, an obvious rallying cry.

The other men raised their weapons over their heads. Some had to dash across the room to grab a pistol or rifle. They chanted the same phrase over and over. To Julia it sounded like the nonwords of an Ennio Morricone soundtrack, or maybe "We can fight! We can fight!"

Emilio slammed his revolver down on the wood table. He raised Julia's horn of *tereré*. "We go tomorrow," he said, showing her every tooth in his mouth. "No more! No more *Nañaykua!* Tonight we rejoice and drink." He hoisted the horn. The brown liquid splashed out, soaking his face. He laughed, and the other men joined in.

Julia grinned at Stephen. She asked, "You ready?"

"No more *Naña-ykua!*" he said, punching his fist in the air.

eighty-six

JULIA'S EYES SNAPPED OPEN. SHE GASPED FOR AIR, BUT nothing came. A palm was clasped tightly over her mouth. Her hand immediately slid under the jacket she was using as a pillow; then she remembered she did not have a pistol.

Tate's face loomed out of the darkness. He held a finger to his lips and removed his hand. He turned from her and pressed his hand over Stephen's mouth. He woke much more gracefully than she had: only his eyelids moved, sliding open like those of a restless corpse in a movie. She checked her watch: 3:40.

Tate jerked his head toward the door of the little room they occupied and started picking his way over the sleeping bodies of the men around them. Julia and Stephen followed him with their backpacks. They stepped out of the smaller room into the cavernous central room, which was nearly as dark; fat bars of moonlight fell through the high windows and streaked the floor. Tate pressed himself against the wall and looked up at those windows

The sentries, Julia thought, but could not see them.

He drifted quietly and quickly to another door and slipped through. They followed him into another room, where a flickering flame made the walls appear to fall away and leap forward. Hanging on hooks, coats, jackets, and sweaters danced in the stuttering light like nervous ghosts.

"Listen," Tate whispered, so close to their faces she could smell the bitter *tereré* drink on his breath. The candlelight illuminated the high spots of his face and filled the rest with inky shadows. The effect was beyond eerie and intensified his very presence. "I'll take you to the air base, if you still want to go. Right now, just us."

"But the men," Julia said. "They said—"

"They're not going to go. I tried to tell you last night. They're not ready, and they know it. Something will come up. The weather. A family member will get sick."

"But they were so . . . excited."

"They get like that from time to time. It's what's in their hearts. They really do want to go and bring *Naña-ykua* down. They pray that maybe all the kidnapped people are still there, alive. But they know better. They want revenge, and they want to end the disappearances and the fear."

His scowl appeared severe in the light.

"*You* got them going this time," he said, "you and those weird triplets after you. In the end, they'll remember they have families that depend on them, and they'll remember how fortified that air base is. They'll remember that they are farmers and ranchers, not soldiers. They'll go back to patrolling the streets, defending their people one threat at a time. In six months or a year, they'll get worked up again. Maybe then or the time after that, they'll go through with it, God help them. But not today."

They were quiet. Then Stephen asked, "Why are you helping us?"

"Because you don't stand a chance on your own." He moved to the wall of jackets and selected two, tossing them to Julia and Stephen. He was already wearing his own leather jacket, dark and crinkled like skin sloughed from his face. He gripped the door handle, then turned back as though he'd forgotten something crucial. "You'll probably die anyway," he said, his hushed voice velvety in the still air, "but this way I'll be able to live with myself." He opened the door and stepped into the chilly night.

JUST OUTSIDE PEDRO JUAN CABALLERO, THE DIRT ROAD became an obstacle course of deep furrows and gaping pits— all filled with opaque water and banked with slippery mud. They were traveling in the oddest vehicle Julia had ever seen: it was a flatbed pickup of sorts, with a boxy front end, high cab, and bumpers that jutted out at least three feet from both ends; they looked like guardrails welded to horizontal posts. The seat was a wooden bench, the dash an unsanded wood plank. Strangest of all was the section of school lockers mounted to the bed behind the cab and rising above the roofline like a submarine's conning tower. The thing alternately roared with unnecessary gusto and then wheezed, ticking and coughing, on the verge of death. She couldn't decide if the Mercedes-Benz symbol on the ravaged grill was authentic or a joke.

At first, she was happy to discover the heater worked.

Then, when her toes started feeling like boiling sausages and perspiration streaked her face, Tate informed them that the heater was stuck—and lowering the fan speed would cause it to overheat and break for good. He cracked the window to counter the heat, which chilled her face without helping her suffering feet one bit.

They sat in grim silence, staring through two recently cleaned spots in the bug-spattered windshield at the road's torturous topography. Tate flicked on the radio, and a stream of staticky polka music emitted from a small speaker. Barely into what Tate described as a circuitous thirty-mile, five-hour trip—the last eight miles on foot—her rear end already hurt. On top of the constant jostling on the hard bench, she suspected that a toothpick-sized splinter had embedded itself down there, but she decided the discomfort was better than the indignity of removing it. Every time Tate slammed the gearshift into the lower section of its *H*-shaped pattern, she had to push her knees to the right, into Stephen's thighs, to avoid getting them cracked by its long metal rod.

After nearly two hours, Tate said, "Now then."

She jumped a bit at his voice and was certain Stephen's head had hit the metal roof.

"The compound is under an old military airstrip in the heart of Paraguay's only jungle region."

"Under?" She'd never considered a subterranean complex.

He explained the slow process of discovering this fact through interviews with suppliers and Paraguayan officials looking for graft, and through personal reconnaissance.

"And this isn't even a jungle, really. Not in the way most people think of jungle—with a high triple canopy that keeps the sunlight out, heavy vines, fronds as thick as blankets. It's not quite that dense, despite being part of the rain forest that

spreads down from the Amazon Basin. Think of very conges-
tive woods and you'll get the idea."

"So we can reach the air base through the woods?" Stephen
asked.

"I didn't say that. *Naña-ykua* has provided for himself
what nature did not: an impenetrable fortress. Radiating out
from the compound are tree-mounted cameras, micro-
phones, microwave motion detectors, electric fences, booby
traps, mines. We learned the hard way about these devices."

"Then what are we doing?" Julia asked. She looked at
Stephen. Was he pale or was it just the way the moonlight
washed over him? She squeezed his hand reassuringly.

Tate smiled. Leaning toward them, he mock-whispered,
"I found a secret."

She waited for him to elaborate.

"An old mine. The Spaniards who settled this land didn't
find the gold and silver they had in Central America or the
northern part of South America, but they sure did look for it.
The thinnest vein got them digging, tunneling until the
thing petered out." He glanced at them, his smile broaden-
ing. "There's one that runs right into the compound."

"The opening is accessible?"

"It starts way outside, so far outside that it goes under
almost all of Litt's perimeter security."

She nodded. Could the tide really be turning in their
favor finally? "And Litt's people don't know about it?"

"Used to, I think," Tate answered. "They tapped into it
when they moved in, far as I can tell. They put in a big steel
door, an emergency exit, I think. Looks like they forgot
about it. When I stumbled onto the mine, the entrance was
completely overgrown with foliage; there were cobwebs as
thick as ropes, spiderwebs, bats, other critters."

"They must have it secured."

Tate smiled, drawing infinite pleasure from the well of their surprise. "I found all their devices and reworked them so I could trot on by without anyone the wiser. I've been running reconnaissance through there for over a year. Can't get into the underground complex. I picked the lock on the metal door, but it only opens into a long hall with a door on the other side that has an electronic lock I can't pick. I was able to sneak into the topside part of the compound and observe their comings and goings. They're so confident about the perimeter security, they pretty much ignore inside the compound. On the surface, at least." He paused. "And I know where the stairs are."

"So why haven't you used them?"

"I have no idea what to expect down below. I've never wanted to use force, because that would alert them to the security breach. Then they'd look for it until they rediscover the mine—"

"And plug it up," Stephen finished.

"I want to keep that ace up my sleeve. For when we're ready."

"Well, Stephen and I are ready." In her excitement Julia had absently reached beneath her to hunt for that obstinate splinter. She caught Stephen watching her with an amused smirk. "The seat bit me," she said.

Tate laughed, deep and loud. "Woman, I've been driving this thing so long, half my butt is wood!"

That got them laughing, and for a moment they forgot about their destination and the perils that awaited them.

eighty-seven

THE SKY HAD LIGHTENED TO A RUSSIAN BLUE BY THE TIME
Tate steered the truck off the road and into the jungle. He
plowed through fifteen feet of dense foliage, killed the engine,
and hopped out. Stephen and Julia joined him at the back.
Stephen stretched and massaged his muscles. Julia considered
rubbing the ache out of her backside but settled on rotating
her upper torso, hands on her hips. She breathed in the tropical air, felt the humidity against her skin, listened to the drips,
the rustling, the infinite stillness of the jungle around her.
Turning her thoughts to the daunting task that lay ahead, her
stomach tightened; but the rest of her felt energized, excited to
be moving toward the contest, happy to be *doing* something.

Tate gave them the once-over and shook his head. "You're
not ready for a trek through the jungle," he announced and
hoisted himself onto the flatbed. He clicked through the

combination on one of the lockers, leaning close to see in the half-light, and yanked up the handle. When he turned around, his arms were laden with an assortment of items. "Hop up here and sit down."

When they did, he jumped to the ground, losing a few items on impact. He put his goods next to them, pulled out four large Ziploc bags, and handed two to each of them. "Pull these over your socks." When they had replaced their sneakers, he lifted Julia's left foot and began mummifying it with duct tape.

"Is this necessary?" she asked impatiently.

"Depends." He continued rolling the tape around her foot, the adhesive screeching rhythmically with each pull like a bird in pain. "Are you okay with spiders and snakes?"

"Snakes?" she said weakly.

"Lots of them. False water cobras, pit vipers, more varieties of coral snakes than in any other part of the world—all very deadly. If you see something slithering, kill it or run." He ripped the tape free from its roll. He rummaged through his pile, extracted a pair of women's gardening gloves, and handed them to her. He passed two large work gloves to Stephen. "Two rights, I'm afraid."

"Whatever works," Stephen said as he began what turned out to be a long process of squeezing his monstrous hands into the gloves.

Tate used tape to connect Julia's gloves to the sleeves of the heavy leather jacket he'd given her, then examined the neck opening, hitching the zipper all the way up. "That oughta do it."

He handed her a filthy and frayed wool cap, which she held delicately away from her. "Are we trying to scare Litt to death?" she asked.

He jumped onto the flatbed and stepped to the open locker. The sky had lightened enough to reveal its contents of shovels, rakes, and hoes. These he removed, dumping them noisily on the flatbed. He hinged open a false back and pulled out two pistols.

"Sig Sauer or Beretta?" he asked, squatting by Julia.

"What, no Springfields?" she joked. She was relieved to have something more substantial than a hoe with which to face Atropos and Litt.

Tate was all business. "I think you'll like the Sig," he said, lifting one of the guns.

"I went through the Academy with one," she responded, taking it. Its heft felt good in her hand. She removed the magazine, saw that it had the maximum number of rounds—thirteen—and slammed it back into the bottom of the grip. She pulled back on the slide, ejecting a bullet.

"I always keep one chambered," Tate said.

She nodded, retrieved the round, and flicked the magazine release with her thumb.

Tate watched her, the folds of his face molded into an incredulous expression.

"What?" she said.

"You can do that with bulky gloves on."

"Funny thing. Our training at the Centers for Disease Control including handling weapons in a biosuit—you know, those floppy astronaut-looking outfits? Never thought I'd be chasing germs in a South American jungle, wearing duct tape and gardening gloves, but it doesn't feel that different from my training."

"Did you think you'd ever need that kind of training, that biocop stuff?"

She thought about it. "In this day and age? Sure. But I

pictured going into a skyscraper in Manhattan with a SWAT team and a platoon of biologists."

"And after I left the service, I thought the scariest thing I'd be doing was covering Parliament for the *Times*. Have a Charles Douglas-Home Prize on the mantel by now." He held the Beretta out to Stephen.

"No thanks."

Tate shoved the pistol into his waistband at the small of his back and began replacing the gardening tools he'd taken from the locker. He opened the one next to it and removed a safari hat, black police-issue gloves, and a web utility belt, already rigged with a holstered pistol, a knife, a flashlight, a coil of rope, and a machete. He tugged a knapsack out of the locker, checked its contents, then slung it over his shoulder. He shoved a fat cigar in his mouth, already lighting it with a match cupped in his other hand. He snorted out blue smoke, tossed the spent match over his shoulder, and spoke around the cigar: "Ready?"

Julia and Stephen looked at each other.

Tate leaped to the ground. He approached what appeared to be a solid wall of vines, branches, and leaves at the front of the truck. In one fluid motion he drew the machete and cleaved a long vertical line in the wall. He pushed himself into this opening, as though through a curtain, and disappeared.

eighty-eight

DESCENDING THE STAIRS TO THE UNDERGROUND COMPLEX, Karl Litt called to Gregor on his handheld. When he reached the anteroom at the bottom, his security chief finally answered.

"Where are you?" Litt demanded. He put his face in front of the thermal reader, and the heavy door serving the primary corridor unlocked.

"Inspecting the perimeter. What's up?"

"I had an interesting conversation with Atropos . . . one of them." Litt paused, leaning against a curving wall of rusted, corrugated metal. Ahead, the corridor came to a *T*: left to the laboratories and infirmary, right to the living quarters.

Gregor said nothing.

Litt said, "Parker's brother and Matheson, Gregor? Did you forget to tell me?"

After a moment, Gregor said, "Atropos was on it."

"That's not the point. How did they track Parker here? Who else knows?" He closed his eyes.

Gregor's incompetence had reached the pinnacle. Sixty years ago, when Gregor had failed to show an aptitude for science, Litt had convinced Kendrick to find another use for him. Gregor went away, then returned with military and security training. After Litt left Elk Mountain, he sent for Gregor, who'd come without hesitation. Even then, Litt had known Gregor's lack of intellectual acuity was not limited to science but was systemic to the man himself. Still, he was diligent and loyal; more important, he was a friend. Over the years he'd demonstrated a talent for keeping the compound secure and secret—not an easy task considering its constant need for supplies and human subjects, coupled with Kendrick's determination to find Litt.

Now, however, Gregor's efficiency had evaporated: the polygraph had failed to detect Despesorio Vero's intentions; Gregor's insistence on hiring Atropos had not resulted in Despesorio's quick capture or recovery of the evidence he had smuggled out of the compound; and now he'd allowed outsiders to find them. More than once lately, Litt had wondered if these slips were not so accidental. Perhaps, like Despesorio, Gregor had become disenchanted with life on the compound. Could Gregor be concerned that his role there would diminish with Ebola Kugel's successful launch? He should know Litt would always need security, as long as it was *good* security.

"Karl, I've got the situation under control."

"You do?" He shouldered himself off the wall and continued walking. "Do you know how they found us? Do you know who helped them? Who they've talked to about it? I don't think you have the situation under control! Find them.

Find out what they know. I shouldn't have to tell you that."
He waited for a response.

Gregor said nothing.

Litt dropped his handheld into a hip pocket and walked away, his anger growing with each strike of his heel on the dirty concrete of the corridors. By the time he opened Allen Parker's cell, he was ready to pummel the prisoner's face into a bloody mess. He stopped short.

Parker lay faceup on his cot, his mouth agape, thick saliva oozing out. His head rolled back and forth. His hands crawled like nervous spiders over his torso, clenching at his chest, then his stomach, his side, returning to his chest. A cardiac monitor had been wheeled in. It plotted the beats of Parker's lethargic heart.

"Bradycardia," a voice said.

Litt jumped. In his fury, he had not noticed the mousy Dr. Rankin standing on the other side of the room.

"His heart's beating too slowly," Rankin said. He was wearing a green surgical gown, tied at the waist, and a matching cap, which had hiked up high on his head and roosted there like a mascot. As he spoke, he poked a syringe through a medicine ampoule's rubber stopper and withdrew a careful measure of clear liquid. He turned to a wheeled cart of instruments, set down the bottle, and held up the syringe to expunge it of air. "He's developed dyspnea. BP's down to 70/50. This atropine should take care of—"

Litt rammed a bony shoulder into Rankin's back. The doctor tumbled into the cart, spilling its contents to the floor. He hit his head on the wall and sat down hard.

"Are you *mad?*" Rankin said, more shocked than angry.

"In fact, Doctor," Litt said, leaning over Allen, one knee on the cot, "I am *extremely* mad." He leaned over Allen.

"How did they know? Who told you to come? Where is the—"

"Do you have film on him?" Speaking to Dr. Rankin now. "Where is his film?"

Rising, rubbing his head, the physician pointed at a large envelope clipped to the cart.

Litt removed a thin sheaf of X-rays and held the first one up to the light. He dropped it and examined the next, then the next.

"There," he said, pointing. It was a small, crisp oval of bright white among cloudy gray shapes. "In his upper intestines." He dropped the X-rays. "Ten-to-one it's a tracking device." He bent and picked up a scalpel off the floor.

He grabbed a handful of Allen's jumpsuit at the navel and slashed at it. He pushed his fingers into the tear and ripped open the material, exposing Allen's stomach. He positioned the scalpel just below the belly button.

Hands gripped his shoulders and yanked him back. He spun to face Rankin.

"The man is almost dead. Be . . . *civil*, please!"

Litt's wrath surged over the physician like ink. "Do *not* interrupt me! Ever!" He lashed out.

Rankin stood before him, vibrating like a struck piano chord, eyes wide behind prescription glasses that reflected back the alien orbs of Litt's own black lenses. His mouth froze in the form of a perfect *O*.

Warmth over his skin caused Litt to peer down. The hand holding the scalpel was half hidden by a fold in the doctor's surgical gown. Blood formed a scarlet glove up to his wrist and poured from the bottom of his hand to the tiled floor, the first great globule landing as he watched. He had plunged the scalpel under the man's sternum, upward to his heart.

A squeal, nearly inaudible at first, issued from the little circle of mouth, rising in volume and pitch as Litt studied a magnified tear quivering on one of the doctor's bottom lids. He pushed the scalpel deeper. The tear fell. The squeal stopped. Litt released his grip, and the body crumpled to the floor. He stepped back, holding his dripping hand away from his side. His eyes rose to the body on the cot. Taking Rankin's life had drained much of the emotional frenzy out of him. What did it matter if the tracking device remained where it was? Parker's brother and the woman had already followed it here. The damage was done.

He stepped into the hall. No one was in sight. He re-entered the room and straddled the corpse, placing his feet wide to avoid the blood. He bent at the hips and knees; an observer would have thought Litt intended to kiss the dead man. Instead, he paused inches from the face. He cocked his sunglasses up to examine the now waxen visage.

The right side of Rankin's glasses had skewed upward in the fall, leaving his right eye naked. It was dark brown and nearly lashless, and Litt marveled at its glazed quality, as if dulled by the dirty thumbprint of Death. Then he realized that the glazed eyes of the dead—endowed by poets with wisdom and otherworldly sorrow—were caused by dryness, nothing more. The sparkle they lacked was moisture, not the essence of life.

Disappointed, Litt let his glasses fall back in place. He dipped his fingers into the bloody pool. He rose and moved to Allen's side. Locking his vision on the gaping face like a pickpocket watching his mark for the slightest sign of suspicion, he smeared the blood over Allen's right hand. He covered the front and back and had to return to the pool twice to complete the task. He used the limp hand like a brush to smudge the khaki prison jumpsuit. He also ran the hand down the side of Allen's face.

Allen's one useful eye fluttered open. He sucked in a wheezing breath.

"Litt," he said. "The cure."

"Who sent you? Does Kendrick know?"

"Cure . . ."

"It's here, my friend. Do you know what it is?"

Litt scanned Allen's face: sweaty skin, ash gray; quivering lips; bloody gums. The eye, though—conscious and aware. He'd seen it before, as if the mind were the last to give in to the disease.

"Me," he said. "My blood. Years ago, I was exposed to an early strain. I survived." He raised his head. "My family did not, but I did and started producing antibodies. Isn't that a cruel joke? My body created the cure for the disease that killed my wife and children. I've developed the antidote, but I've shared it with no one. And never will."

He stood. Allen's eyelid dropped.

At the door, Litt looked back. In a fit of anger or insanity, the prisoner had murdered his caregiver.

Litt shook his head and closed the door.

eighty-nine

THE TREK THROUGH PARAGUAY'S NORTHEASTERN JUNGLE was as excruciating as Tate had warned. Branches ripped at their clothes, snagged their hair. Thorns jabbed at them, and elephant grass whipped at their faces. The flickering shafts and dapples of sunlight piercing the foliage only added to the confusing array of leaves and darkness, solids and space. Tate led them in one direction, then another, sometimes hacking through layers of vegetation, sometimes following the serpentine meanders of small-game trails. They waded through narrow streams—Julia constantly anticipating the first sharp pinch of a piranha.

"Don't fret over one or two bites," Tate had said. "It's when you feel a quick half dozen that you have to get out fast."

At the next crossing, a nibble on her calf scared an audible gasp out of her, and she scrambled onto the bank a dozen feet ahead of the others. When she discovered that she had been attacked by a piece of duct tape that had come loose, she rubbed it and said nothing.

Tate dropped down beside her, taking the healthy deep breaths of an athlete in training. He checked his watch and said, "Three-minute break." He removed the knapsack from his back and withdrew a canteen, which he handed to Julia. She took a long pull of tepid water, quenching a thirst she had only vaguely acknowledged. Tate rummaged in the knapsack, then offered leathery strips of beef jerky, brightly wrapped energy bars, and the requisite oranges.

Julia squinted up at an impossibly yellow sun dancing on the treetops. For a moment, it was possible to believe she was back in Georgia, out in the Chattahoochee wilderness, her feet caressed by the waters of Holcomb Creek. Jodi would be getting on Goody for talking business, while he waved her off good-naturedly and slapped her behind. The boys would be laughing, splashing in the creek, asking, "When are we gonna eat?" The sun warmed her face, splashing red flowers against her closed eyelids. A thousand fragrances mixed on the breeze and—

"Time's up!" Tate bellowed like a football coach.

Julia gazed up at him, dazed and disappointed. He unsheathed the machete, exhaled loudly, and marched forward, leaving a smoldering cigar in the cup of a peeled orange.

After an hour, the treacheries of jungle travel became tedious, and her mind reached out to their destination: *What will we find there? What opposition? What breaks?* She wondered what Kendrick Reynolds was doing. Had he sent in a commando team? Was he, even now, negotiating for Litt's surrender? Two days had passed since she left the hard drive for him. He should have begun the operation to stop Litt immediately.

She slid down a muddy bank into yet another stream, following Tate and dimly aware of Stephen's presence behind her. She was moving mechanically now, using some primal surface consciousness to travel efficiently, grabbing a root to stabilize herself for a tricky descent or mimicking Tate's jog around a nasty thicket.

She didn't realize Tate had stopped until she walked into him. He had his forefinger pressed to his lips. She held up her palm to Stephen. Around them, trees rose like scaffoldings, holding their heavy leaves sixty feet above the ground. Smaller trees and bushes, their spindly branches and dappled leaves exploding wildly from unseen stalks, crowded like children around their parents' legs. The three humans stood in shadowy darkness, but for a single shaft of intense light that defied the canopy's protection to splash the ground at their feet.

"We're here," Tate whispered.

Julia rotated her head, saw nothing that would distinguish this spot from any other place in the jungle. As it was, she felt disoriented by the jungle's lack of a horizon or of landmarks that remained visible for longer than a few minutes. It didn't help that she had lost track of time, sensing the distance they had hiked only through her fatigued muscles.

"We will be going under much of the compound's perimeter security," Tate reminded them, waving his hand vaguely in the air behind him, "but I cannot be sure how much sound carries from the mine into the compound. I am always quiet."

He looked intently at Julia, then Stephen. They nodded. He turned, seized a tall bush, and began shaking it. He wrestled with it until it tucked in on itself, revealing a gaping black hole. Julia realized with a start that they were standing at the base of a cliff, so dark and protected she had not seen it at all. The mine opening began about four feet above the ground and rose like a screaming mouth for six feet. Irregularly elliptic, with rounded edges, it looked more like a cave than something man-made.

Tate hoisted himself into that blackness and for a moment disappeared. He reemerged, as if from a pool of ink, to offer Julia his hand. She clicked on her flashlight and saw that the mine opened up as it moved into the mountain. Rotted timbers lay on the floor, among stones, dirt, filaments of abandoned spiderwebs, and animal droppings. Stephen fell in beside her, tugging at his own flashlight, which didn't want to leave his belt.

"This is as far as I go," Tate whispered

ninety

"THE MEN NEED ME," TATE SAID. "MORE IMPORTANT, I HAVE something with Rosa I'm not ready to give up yet."

He was silhouetted in the mine's opening, hunched slightly but seeming agile and strong, ready to embark on an adventure he had already declined. Smoke swirled around his head, giving Julia the impression that it was he, not his cigar, that was burning.

"You do what you have to do," she said. "We appreciate what you've already done for us."

He squatted and motioned for them to take positions near him. He flipped up the face of his watch, revealing a compass. He tore the Velcro strap away and handed the device to Stephen. Then he shrugged off the knapsack and gave that to him as well. Retreating back through the mine was their best bet, he explained, if they could get there undetected. He would mark the way back to the truck, where he'd wait as long as possible. If they were under heavy fire, he suggested stealing one of the compound's vehicles and plowing through the front gates.

"If worse comes to worst," he continued, turning away to blow out a stream of smoke, "run like madmen into the jungle. Head south-by-southwest. When you hit water, go downstream. Before then, though, you'll encounter an electric chain-link fence. Find a tree with an overhanging branch to get past it." He thought for a moment. "Oh, and if they do chase you into the jungle, *do not* use your gun."

"Explain," Julia said.

"Emilio's men used to snipe into the compound from the jungle. They'd take someone out, then fade into the jungle. Back again to kill again, then gone again. It makes the target area virtually useless and frazzles the enemy's nerves."

"What happened?"

Tate took an angry draw on his stogie, then flicked the glowing stub into the sunlight. "They installed these anti-sniper contraptions. One shot and these things shoot back—with *lots* of firepower. I called a friend of mine, still in SAS. He said they're probably Deadeyes. They monitor the perimeter of the compound, just waiting for some fool to fire a rifle or a pistol, any small arms."

"And when someone does?"

"It's the last thing they ever do. These Deadeyes track the trajectory of the projectile, calculate it back to the point of origin, then make anything at that point of origin disappear—by way of heavy aircraft artillery—all within three seconds of the shot."

Stephen exhaled heavily.

Julia shifted her weight, thinking. "Does that mean anyone chasing us can't shoot either?"

"Not necessarily." His words came laced with the ashy odor of tobacco. "According to my mate, the Deadeyes can be programmed to monitor specific regions, so troops behind them can shoot toward an enemy without triggering the Deadeyes. Handheld remotes control them. They can be turned on and off and redirected instantly. Acoustic and electro-optical sensors identify muzzle-flash signatures, so grenades or firecrackers won't distract them. They're very sophisticated and very dangerous."

Stephen asked, "Didn't your friend wonder what this place was doing with these things?"

Tate shook his head. "I know of an oil sheik with his own fully armed Harrier jet. A Colombian drug lord has a German Leopard tank, top of the line. None of this stuff is as regulated as civilians would like to think."

Julia stood, feeling the weight of the Sig Sauer at the small of her back. "Let's do it, then."

Still crouching, Tate pointed with a chiseled arm. "Go straight back. When you think you must have gone too far, keep going. You'll see the metal door I told you about first. Little farther, you'll find rungs on the left wall. They lead to a hatch inside the compound." He described the surface topography radiating from the hatch: jungle behind, Quonsets before. He told what he knew of the surface guards, their number, stations, and routines. He gave directions to the stairs.

"Beyond that, you're on your own," he finished.

"Uncharted territory," Stephen said.

"Good lu—" He stopped, then gripped Stephen's shoulder firmly, shook his head. "To hell with luck. God be with you." He turned his eyes to her. "Both of you."

At that moment, Julia realized how intensely he wanted to

join them, to go all the way and damn the torpedoes. He'd witnessed the mournful aftermath of countless abductions, attended the funerals of people who'd gone to the air base for revenge. He'd been waiting for justice a long time. Now someone was going to try. But he knew it wasn't his time, not yet.

She nodded and turned into the black coolness of the mine. Stephen brushed past her, taking point. Ten paces in, she looked back. Tate was squatted like a guardian troll in front of the radiant mouth of the mine, his forearms resting across his knees. She stifled the urge to call out to him, to plead for him to come. She wanted to say, *How can we possibly do this without your help?* Instead, she followed Stephen deeper into darkness, wondering if this mine would prove to be their River Styx.

When she turned again, Tate was gone.

ninety-one

STEPHEN BRACED HIS FEET AND HANDS AGAINST THE RUSTY metal rungs set in the concrete tube that ascended from the mine like a chimney and pushed his shoulder into the manhole cover above him. It rose slowly, sounding like a mason jar when you unscrew the lid. Blinding light sliced into the pitch darkness of the shaft. And something else. The stench of rot—it pierced his nostrils and stung his eyes, perhaps not as effectively as the gaseous irritants cops use to incapacitate suspects, but enough to force shallow breaths and teary vision. Squinting, he made out the source—and also the reason Tate thought this was a safe entrance into the compound: he was behind a trash container roughly the size of an eighteen-wheeler. Sludge oozed down its side and through unseen holes in its bottom, forming pools that collected tissue paper and cans and other refuse the way tar pits entrap animals.

Metal wheels held the container ten inches off the ground, giving him a view of the base beyond. Straight ahead and down a grassy incline were the Quonsets Tate had described. That's where they'd find the stairs into the underground complex—and Allen, Stephen prayed. He looked off to the right, and his heart jumped. There, a hundred yards away, was the entrance gate and a guard shack. They were the first things he recognized from the home movie Despesorio Vero had smuggled out—the second video, which showed the air base. The sense of being here, of having made the journey in search of his brother, made the hair on his arms stand up.

Two guards were talking, submachine guns at their sides. A collection of battered metal trash cans next to the Dumpster nearly shielded Stephen's position. He and Julia would have to be careful when they emerged.

He eased the cover down, pinching off the light. He snapped on his flashlight. Below him, also clinging to the rungs, Julia peered up.

"Can we get to the stairs?" she asked. Her whispers sounded loud in the concrete shaft so near the enemy.

"I think I spotted the building they're in. There are guards at the front gate, within view. I don't see any way to just *slip* in. We're near a Dumpster. Maybe we can—"

The entire shaft rumbled around them. Flakes of rust rained down from the bottom of the manhole cover. Under Stephen, one end of a rung popped loose, and his foot sailed into Julia's forehead. She lost her grip. For a moment she remained suspended over the fifty-foot drop to the mine floor, her body wedged diagonally in the shaft; her cheek was pushed into the side; her feet fought for traction on the opposite side.

Stephen's flashlight struck the top of her head and tumbled

down, strobing until it hit the earth and blacked out. Julia fell and jerked to a stop as Stephen grabbed the shoulder strap of her knapsack. She flailed her arms in the dark until she found the rungs and pulled herself to them.

Above them, sirens sounded.

ninety-two

KARL LITT HAD JUST FINISHED SCOURING DR. RANKIN'S blood off his hands and arms and was watching the last pink swirl slip down the drain when the blast quavered through the bathroom. He gripped the edge of the countertop. It felt like the bumper of a very powerful car, ready to roll. The light flickered. He caught his sunglasses as they slipped off the counter. Someone screamed in the hall—impossibly loud. Then he realized it was the base's air raid siren, which Gregor had made functional shortly after they'd leased the base. He yanked his handheld out of his pocket.

"Was ist los!" he yelled. What's happening?

"Air strike!" Gregor answered. "I saw it. One of the hangars went up. A jet. Here comes—"

Another explosion. This time the thunderous sound

echoed through the handheld's speaker, breaking up into squeals and static.

Gregor cursed. "They're after the planes," he said. "I just saw Atropos—the Atroposes—heading for the Quonsets. One of the Cessnas got hit. Karl, get out of there. Get—"

The room shook. Static.

"Gregor? Gregor?"

Litt bolted from the bathroom and headed for the bedroom door. The monitor on the dresser showed several people running past in the hall. He tripped over something and fell to the floor. He got to his knees, and his handheld jangled, an incoming call. Without looking at it, he answered.

"Gregor?"

"Hello, Karl," Kendrick Reynolds said.

Litt glanced around the darkened room, half expecting to see the old man standing there, grinning down at him.

"I'm surprised how quickly we found your number," Kendrick said. "Once we knew where to look."

Litt rose to his feet. He had always believed Kendrick's assault, if ever he found Litt, would entail an elite division of commandos quietly killing its way into the compound and slipping into the subterranean complex to kidnap or murder the evil Karl Litt. Explosions didn't fit the model.

"Karl?"

"I'm here." He opened his bedroom door. The corridor fluorescents appeared unaffected. Several were out and others flickered, but they'd been like that as long as Litt could recall. Squinting against the light, he remembered the sunglasses in his hand and slipped them on. The siren blared, piercing his ears.

"You don't think you'll get away, do you?" Kendrick

asked. "The sort of air strike we have planned for you will take some time, but I assure you, it's quite comprehensive. The explosions you're feeling now are merely a prelude. My advisors thought it would be prudent to knock out any aircraft you have in the hangars. Next, we'll pelt the surface above your head with earth-penetrating tomography bombs. Those will give the Vikings flying at forty thousand feet with their ESM suites and Inverse-Synthetic Aperture Radar clear pictures of the area's subterranean architecture. We'll see your underground complex as if it were topside."

Litt stopped moving down the corridor. "How . . ."

The sirens stopped.

Kendrick said, "That's better. Did your alarms stop because of a lull in our bombing? I'm sure the next wave will commence shortly."

"How did you figure the underground part?" Litt asked. He could not imagine that Despesorio's information was so detailed.

"You got sloppy, Karl. You let a tracking device get in."

That thing inside Allen Parker. It must be more sophisticated than the devices he had surgically installed in his staff—always under the guise of repairing an "accidental" injury. His could not be detected under so much earth and concrete, and they did not provide the altitude relative to ground level. Leave it to Kendrick to have the best.

He pressed the handheld into his face until his cheek and ear hurt. It was Gregor who had become sloppy, inviting Atropos. He hoped that last interrupted transmission from him marked his death.

"After the Vikings get a handle on the layout, we'll send in the F-15s. They'll drop GBU-28 bombs. You know about those, Karl? Bunker Busters? Forty-seven hundred pounds.

Designed to punch through packed earth and twenty-two feet of reinforced concrete before exploding. Boggles my mind, the weapons we have these days. FA-18 Hornets will sweep in next. They'll cover the whole area—especially inside the smoking craters—with Maverick missiles and napalm. That stuff burns at 3,000 degrees, Karl, enough to make your germ just . . . disappear. Want to know what's next?"

Litt ran an arm over the perspiration on his forehead. All the lab doors were open, the workers gone. He went into his private lab, where he squatted in front of a cabinet and opened it, revealing a safe.

The floor shook, a prolonged vibration that cracked the tile. Explosions rumbled in the distance, deep and low. If Kendrick had faithfully described the attack, either the tomography bombing had started or they were still striking at the hangars and the assassins' Cessnas. He hoped the Hummer he had stashed in the jungle was small enough and distant enough to escape the bombing. He hoped he could get to it before the serious ordnance rained down. He hoped he wouldn't stumble into the ground troops Kendrick would surely send in last.

And while he was hoping, he hoped to someday see Kendrick feel the bite of his germ and watch him as he died.

"How can you do this?" he asked. "You're bombing a foreign country."

"Haven't you heard? You're operating the largest methamphetamine laboratory in the world there. Side things too—refined cocaine hydrochloride, heroin, marijuana, a little money laundering for the Colombian and Bolivian cartels. All kinds of nasty stuff we created the Anti-Drug Abuse Control Commission to stamp out. Considering how much anti-drug money Paraguay and Brazil get from us, they were more than happy to cooperate."

Inside the safe was a Halliburton briefcase. Litt pulled it out and stood. Its heft made him feel a little better.

"You realize," Kendrick said, "you might have gotten away if you'd have left the president's family out of your plans. Without his authorization, I would have had to send hired guns. And we've seen recently how ineffective they can be."

"*Das gebrabbel.* Make sense, Kendrick." He headed for the stairs.

"You could have targeted *me* without hearing so much as a raised voice." A pause. The clinking of ice against glass near the receiver. The old *Schlauberger* was having a cocktail. "My time's almost up anyway."

Footfalls slapping against the tile startled him. He turned as a man ran past, lab coat flapping. The man rounded the next corner, going for the exit.

Litt moved the handheld closer to his ear and heard ". . . was the only thing that allowed me to move so quickly."

"What? What was?"

"Hold on a mo—"

Litt heard him speak to someone. The background noise was a cacophony of voices, some raised in excitement, others droning out information. Litt grew incensed at the thought that Kendrick's room hummed with the activity of his, Litt's, destruction.

After a moment, Kendrick came back on. "Excuse me, Karl. We have a lot going on."

He pictured Kendrick's smug expression. He said, "*Du willst mich wohl für dumm!* This isn't over, Kendrick. You're too late."

"You mean your hit list? The people you infected? Yes, your bitterness, your vengeance, will be felt, if that pleases you. But that's where it ends, Karl. You will have killed them in vain. The media will assume some cult infected them through a contaminant in their food or drink or injected them and then sent out a list of victims. Cruel, but nothing else. They will never hear from you. They will never know *why*." He paused, then added, "We'll probably frame a militant group, take them out of the picture, and make our citizens feel safe again. In a few years, even their grief will fade."

Litt arrived at the door to the laboratory wing. He moved his face to the facial thermogram. Nothing happened. His heart wedged in his throat. He looked into the black pane again, his reflection glaring back. The door clicked open. As he started up the stairs, he said, "I'll save you a spot in hell, old man."

"You do that, Karl."

He heard a click on the line, then nothing. He growled and shoved the handheld into his pocket. At the top of the stairs, he pushed through the door into the sun and the sound of droning planes.

ninety-three

CONVINCED THEY HAD BEEN SPOTTED AND FIRED UPON BY a guard with some sort of monster-gun, Julia and Stephen scuttled back down the chimney as fast as they could. Julia anticipated her next moves: roll away from the ladder to make room for Stephen; grab the flashlight; draw the Sig Sauer; run like hares for the adit. Stephen clambered down right above her.

He was counting—"Fourteen, fifteen, sixteen."

"What's that?" she asked, breathless, thinking he somehow knew when the next assault would strike.

"Rungs," he said. "Nineteen, twenty. Trying . . . not to . . . panic. Now shhh. Twenty-three, twenty-four . . ."

Her feet touched dirt, and she rolled away.

"Thirty-one, thirty-*two*!"

She grabbed him and started tugging.

"Wait, wait, wait," Stephen said.

Julia shook the flashlight, and it lit up. She centered it on the hole in the mine's ceiling where the shaft rose to the surface.

"Shouldn't we have heard something by now if they were after us?" he said.

Overhead, the siren stopped. Then another sound, thunder-like, and the ground vibrated. Dirt sprinkled from the ceiling.

"That was an explosion," Julia said.

"Is this Kendrick Reynolds's doing?"

She shrugged.

"We gotta get Allen out of there," he said, stripping off his gloves, unraveling the tape at his ankles and wrists. Julia did the same, then yanked the beanie off her head. Stephen was already heading back up. He rammed his shoulder into the manhole cover, heaving it to the side and hoisting him-self up and out.

Julia followed, coming up behind the Dumpster. Smoke spiraled into the sky. She peered around the big trash con-tainer. A hangar was torn and smoking. It was at the far end of the airstrip near three small jets. One of the jets was miss-ing a wing and rested on its nose, its tail angling up like a sinking ship. It was leaning against one of the other planes.

A fighter roared in, dropping dozens of what looked to Julia like bowling balls. They struck the cluster of jets and another hangar, setting off a chain reaction of explosions.

"Guards," Stephen said.

He was standing behind her, looking in a different direc-tion. She followed his gaze to two guards by the gate and guard shack. They were huddled together, crouched low, cast-ing wide eyes at the plane flying away. When it disappeared, they scanned the grounds, perhaps hoping for someone to tell them how to interpret this new event. One of them held a walkie-talkie to his mouth, yelling into it. A crash of metal caught their attention.

Julia turned also. A half dozen people had come through a door at the end of a Quonset hut and were streaming toward the gate.

"That's the Quonset Tate said the stairs were in," she said.

Stephen brushed by her.

"Wait!"

But he was gone, around the container and jogging down a small hill toward the huts. She started after him, then stopped when one of the guards raised his submachine gun. She yanked her pistol out of her waistband. She had the guard's head in her sights when he slipped away. She watched him apparently decide that the fleeing workers knew something he didn't. He turned and trotted through the gate, machine gun bobbing on its strap at his side. His buddy watched him go, then followed.

Stephen intersected the group of evacuees. He reached out, grabbed two handfuls of white lab coat, and lifted its occupant off the ground. He spoke, the man shook his head no, and Stephen dropped him on his backside. He snagged another man, got another negative response. She couldn't make out his words, but she knew the theme: *Where's my brother?*

Cautious—more cautious than Stephen, at least—she started for him. She kept her gun at her side and her finger flat against the trigger guard.

His latest captive pointed and must have indicated knowledge of Allen's location; Stephen swung the hapless soul around like a doll, clasped him in a headlock, and marched him toward the Quonset door.

Julia picked up her pace.

Suddenly, from behind one of the other Quonsets stepped Atropos. He saw Stephen and his captive go through the door and started after them. Julia raised her weapon, taking aim at the killer. Another group of people came out the door, blocking her shot. Atropos was almost there. She raised her aim and shot the light fixture hanging over the door.

Atropos spun, backing away as he did, quick as a cat. He pivoted his left arm up and immediately squeezed off a round into a woman who had darted in front of Julia. The people broke into a dance of frenzied activity and hysterical screams. Two more Atroposes came around a corner. They reached their brother and advanced toward her as one. She ran to the side of the Quonset, running toward the rear with all of her strength, hoping they didn't reach the corner behind her too soon.

ninety-four

HEART BLOCKAGE IN THE EARLY STAGES OF EBOLA INFECTION
is a blessing. It saves the patient from the agony of feeling his
organs melt away, of watching his flesh blister, swell, and
split, of hearing his own screams until his throat wears out or
fills with blood and bile. It comes from the same well of good
fortune that drowns a man before he is eaten by sharks, or
poisons a spy with a capsule of strychnine under the tongue
before his enemy breaks out the tongs and cattle prods.

Allen Parker's heart was granting him this mercy—
winding down, responding to the Ebola virus, which was
attacking and short-circuiting the electrical impulses of his
atrioventricular node. His breathing became shallow and
labored. But the pain continued. His hands, which had been
roaming his body looking for a way to snuff the fires that
scorched him in a thousand places, slowed and stopped.

And with each minute, his heart dropped a few more beats, until—

No pain. Just like that, it was gone.

THE LITTLE MAN IN STEPHEN'S GRASP HAD STOPPED SQUIRMING and now walked obediently ahead of him. With each explosion—reaching them as muffled thunder and the trembling of the staircase they descended—Stephen thought he was going to bolt. But they were heading down into the subterranean complex, and the man wanted out of it—a direction Stephen blocked.

At the base of the staircase, his unwilling guide stepped up to a black tile in the wall, and the metal entry door clicked open. The man tugged at it and stepped into a poorly lighted corridor.

Stephen's nostrils flared at the redolence of earth and dust. He looked for signs that the corridor was dangerous, then stopped looking; safe or not, he was going in.

The man marched stiffly until they reached an intersection. He paused and selected the right-hand passage. They approached a door with a small square window showing brighter light on the other side. Before reaching it, they turned down another corridor.

Stephen, his big paw clamped around the back of the man's neck, gave him a shake. "No tricks."

"Please . . ." the man said. He pointed weakly in the direction they were heading. Finally he stopped in front of a door.

"Open it," Stephen commanded.

The man threw back a rusty bolt, turned the door handle, and dropped straight to the floor, out of Stephen's grasp. He rolled away, stood, and ran.

"Hey!" Stephen took two steps toward him, stopped. He looked back at the door. Light from inside sliced into the corridor from a thin breach. He pushed on the door.

A cardiac monitor's C-sharp rhythm of ventricular fibrillation struck him like a bad smell: heart failure on the brink of flatline.

And then the visual assault: a man lying in a near-black pool on the floor, a blossom of blood in the center of his torso. And Allen sprawled on a cot, mouth agape, one eye swollen shut, the other staring blindly at the ceiling.

"Oh no, no, no . . ."

Stephen's heel hit the pool and flew out from under him. His head cracked against the tile. He stared at the caged light in the ceiling, thinking for a moment that he was supposed to see something fantastic in it. Then he rolled his head backward and saw an upside-down version of the doorway and the dark corridor beyond. He rose from the gore, blood clinging to him from his armpit to his knee. He rubbed his head and went to his brother.

"Allen! *Allen!*" He shook Allen's shoulders, sickened by the way his head bounced limply and lolled to the side. "No, Allen! Not here, man! Don't give them the satisfaction!"

He aimed his fist at Allen's sternum and administered a precordial thump. The heart responded—slightly. He tilted Allen's head back, pinched the nostrils, and blew twice into his mouth, filling Allen's lungs. He found the base of the sternum and moved up two fingers. His hands nearly covered Allen's chest. He leaned over and pushed down . . . came up . . . pushed down . . . came up—pumping the heart for him. After thirty compressions, again he filled Allen's lungs.

The cardiac monitor fell silent, then beeped. Allen hitched up, gasping for breath, fighting against Stephen's hands.

"Yes!" Stephen said and threw his arms around his brother.

Allen went limp. His head flopped back, and once again, the EKG machine took over the job of screaming for help in a sporadic, weak rhythm.

Stephen gave him another precordial thump and restarted CPR . . . two breaths . . . thirty compressions . . . breathing . . . pushing . . . He had to restrain himself from frantically pumping on Allen's chest without rhythm or meter. He wanted to *force* life back into him. Tears flew from his cheeks, splattering against Allen's bloody face. He pulled in a deep breath, gritted his teeth, and *pushed*.

Allen heaved up, gasping. Stephen reached behind his head. "Allen! Stay with me."

The cardiac monitor beeped . . . beeped . . .

Allen seized Stephen's shoulders and hitched in two sharp, raspy breaths . . . then nothing . . . He fell limp again.

This time, there was no response to the precordial thump. Stephen scanned the room. No defibrillator. His eyes roamed the clutter scattered on the floor: X-ray film, surgical instruments, rolls of cloth tape . . . ampoules of medicine and syringes.

He swung off Allen's cot and dropped to his hands and knees on the floor. He snatched up an ampoule and read its label. *Magnesium sulphate 8 mmol.* Sometimes used during resuscitation, but under what conditions? He tried to remember. Administering CPR was one thing—kids learned that. Injecting drugs to restart a heart was something else completely—despite being seven credit hours away from earning an MD. Potassium chloride was a good example. Depending on the cause of the heart failure, potassium could either restart it or frustrate efforts that would otherwise work.

He kept scooping up and examining ampoules, hoping a solution would spring out at him.

Epinephrine. Adrenaline!

He found a syringe, loaded it up with the epinephrine, and gently injected the drug under Allen's tongue, which would cause it to work as quickly as an intravenous line. He breathed into him, then rose, his straight arms coming together over Allen's sternum. This time, as he pumped, he did not count. He prayed.

Acutely aware of the heart under his palms, he thought of the life that was slipping away. He remembered Allen the toddler who'd scribbled with Crayons on the walls . . . the eight-year old who had crashed his bike, knocking out a tooth, and who had run to his brother for comfort instead of to Mom . . . the new teenager who'd shyly asked Stephen what it was like to kiss a girl . . . the young man who'd performed a near-perfect backflip on the living room floor when he received his acceptance to med school—only "near perfect" because after landing he had crashed down on an antique coffee table, obliterating it. He recalled his brother's face when—

Beep. Beep. Beep.

Allen pulled in heavy gulps of air. His eyes were open, but they were focused on something distant. Tears buckled on his lids, spilled over. He reached out blindly, felt Stephen's face and shoulder, and slid his arms around his brother's body, pushing his face into his chest.

Stephen hugged him in return and watched the EKG monitor. The rate was slow but steady. His vision blurred. He blinked away his own tears; they seeped into his beard and tickled his face.

"What happened?" Allen asked, the words scraping over his vocal cords like pebbles. "Where was I?"

Stephen squeezed him tighter. His hands and arms felt too much of Allen's skeleton. He said, "Maybe heaven, little brother. But heaven can wait for you. I got you now."

Allen pushed back to look into Stephen's eyes. He touched Stephen's face, as though ensuring himself it was real.

Stephen was stunned by the way Allen's cheeks and eyes sank into his skull, accentuating his cheekbones and jaw. A large rip at the waist of his clothing showed pale skin and a shrunken stomach. He must have lost twenty pounds in the three days since his capture. Finally, Stephen's eyes broke away and settled on a bowl of water and a cloth beside the cot. He dipped the cloth into the water and dabbed at Allen's face. The blood washed away, but the tears—constantly replenished—seemed more permanent.

Allen returned to the comfort of his brother's chest. Stephen's arms cocooned him, warming, comforting, protecting. Allen slumped as tension waned and fatigue took hold.

"I thought we'd lost you," Stephen whispered.

An explosion rocked the room. The wire mesh over the light came loose on one side and swung down. Somewhere down the corridor, glass shattered.

Carefully he lowered Allen back onto the bed. His eyes were wide and darting. Stephen had heard that a side effect of adrenaline was short-term hyperalertness, followed by a crash that comatosed some patients. The alertness could help get Allen out of the compound; they would worry about his crashing later.

He pulled another ampoule out of his shirt pocket, one he'd found earlier: *atropine*, which would keep Allen's heart rate up and work with the adrenaline to energize him.

He scooped up another syringe, loaded it, and plunged the needle into Allen's arm.

"This'll help," he said soothingly.

Walls shattered in another part of the complex. The sound reverberated through the corridors, which were becoming thick with smoke and dust. He realized that the explosions were infrequent now and sporadically placed—if his own judgment in such matters could be trusted—as if they were *probing* for something.

"You're doing fine," Stephen said, tossing aside the syringe. He hoisted Allen up, slung him over his shoulder, and stood.

He made only one wrong turn getting back to the exit. The door was locked. Beside it, a black pane was set in the wall. The man who had led him to Allen had put his face up to one like it. He held his own face in front of it, moved it around, tried the door again. Still locked.

This far . . . for nothing.

He had not seen anyone else on this level. The chances of people hiding out here—or of his finding them if they were—were about the same as surviving the bombs pounding overhead.

Then a memory struck him—so full of potential, he held his breath while his mind gnawed on it.

It could work.

He eased Allen down next to a wall. "I'll be right back. I gave you a heavy dose of adrenaline. You all right?"

"Hmmm." Allen raised his eyebrows to show he was. "Feeling . . . a little better."

Stephen took off along the corridor, into air that had taken on the murkiness of pond water. When he returned, Allen rolled an eye at him and grimaced. Behind Stephen, dragged by one foot, came the corpse from Allen's cell. It left an intermittent swath of crimson. Stephen scooped up the body and maneuvered its face into position in front of the glass panel. He turned the head this way and that, backed it away and drew it near. The noise of the explosions escalated. The tremors became quakes. The smoke thickened and stung their eyes.

He laid the body down in frustration, not sure what else to do.

Allen spoke. "Thermal."

"What?"

He said it again.

Stephen looked down at the corpse, wondering where mere disrespect became sacrilege. He straddled the body and began rubbing the face. His hands engulfed it. He was able to stroke all of it simultaneously, from forehead to chin, ear to ear. His thumbs stayed on the bridge of the nose, moving from between the eyes to the tip. He rubbed as vigorously as he dared and tried not to think of the flesh beneath his hands: the chin scratchy with light beard stubble; the lips catching on his palms, the bottom pulling down, the top snarling up, each flipping back on the opposing stroke; the forehead sliding sickeningly over the skull.

He heaved the body up and held the face before the black pane. A bolt inside the door clicked. Gently, he lowered the corpse.

He bent Allen over his shoulder and stepped through. He wondered if another thermal face reader awaited them at the top of the stairs; he turned and held the door with his foot before it could close. He leaned through, got a grip on the dead man's foot, and pulled the body into the stairwell. Then he headed for the surface.

ninety-five

AT ONE TIME, THE AIR BASE MUST HAVE HOUSED A GOOD-
sized army, Julia thought. Three rows of Quonset huts were
arranged in a grid, with dirt roads running between the rows.
A large field and the airstrip separated the Quonsets from a
single row of five airplane hangars—now ripped apart and
burning. Whatever function the Quonsets once served—barracks, infirmary, mess hall, armory, chapel, administrative
offices, warehouses—today they were rusty scraps, like half-
buried barrels.

Julia crouched low beside one of the Quonsets, trying to
guess the current position of the three assassins who chased
her. She assumed they had split up, as they had done in Pedro
Juan Caballero. She crept to the edge of the building, peered
around. One of the killers was three Quonsets away, boldly
strolling her direction, his head cocked to look between each

building as he passed. She sprang out, running for the next row. He spotted her, raised his pistol. She squeezed off a round, then another. He didn't dodge away. As far as she could tell, he didn't even flinch. Then she was out of his sight and running full force to the end of the building. Her plan was simple: lead the Atroposes far away from the stairs; then double back, find Stephen, find Allen, and get out of Dodge before the killers caught up with them.

Or before the bombs pounded them all deep into the Paraguayan soil for archeologists to find a hundred years from now.

She hadn't seen a plane or an explosion for a few minutes. The last one she spotted had been an FA-18 with U.S. insignias—her father had built model jets, and she recognized the twin tail fins. It had swooped low without releasing its ordnance. She wondered if the air strike was over. Could its sole intention have been to disable any getaway aircraft? Would the commando team she had hoped Kendrick would send now arrive?

She had reached the opposite corner of the array of Quonsets from the stairs. It was time to circle back around. She had seen only one Atropos since running from them when they first converged on her. That made her more nervous than if they had stayed on her tail. It dawned on her that she had not seen *anyone* in the past five minutes. The people escaping the base had drained through the gate and were gone. What she wouldn't give to be with them, Stephen and Allen at her side.

She clutched her pistol and ran back along the front of the first Quonset. She stopped at the corner to inspect the space between the buildings, then darted across. She tacked around a stack of wooden crates that leaned against the half-moon facade. Bulging burlap sacks squatted beside it like fat trolls. She crossed the next gap and then ran to the back of the building.

Her progress was slow, but finally she found herself at the rear of the Quonset with the stairs. She came around the corner in a strobelike dance of deadly efficiency, swinging her pistol toward the door . . . the arching roofs . . . the crates . . . the corners of the buildings . . . She reached the front, kicked through the door, and moved into the stifling darkness. Her pistol covered the near corners . . . the far corners . . . the overhead beams. She stopped, listening.

A plane approached, followed by explosions—dozens, maybe hundreds of them. They didn't sound like the kind of bombs planes dropped, but smaller, like hand grenades. Still, she heard metal ripping and felt the ground tremble.

So the pause had been a mere respite after all. How could Kendrick Reynolds be so cold? She had told him they were heading here to rescue Allen. Was this his idea of taking care of business—eliminating a threat and cleaning up loose ends all at once? She understood that stopping Karl Litt was more important than three civilian lives, more important than a hundred . . . a thousand. She only wished he'd found another way—sending in a pre-strike ground team, for instance, to pull out the innocent. Or did he think there were no innocents in war? As it was, she felt a bit like Slim Pickens riding an H-bomb to Earth.

Picking up the pace, she moved deeper into the shadows and made out a door at the back of the big room. As she approached, it opened. Her gun snapped up. Stephen stumbled out with Allen over his shoulder. She took her finger off the trigger. Stephen's eyes acknowledged her with compassion, but there was no smile. He fell on his one knee and slid Allen off his shoulder. Allen sat like a rag doll for a moment, then slumped onto his side.

Julia gasped, seeing his battered face, the blood everywhere. "What happened?"

"He's bad," Stephen said dismally. He turned pleading eyes on her. "I think they *infected* him. They . . . Julia, I think he has Ebola." Tears rimmed his eyes, spilled onto his cheeks.

"We'll find help for him," she said, trying to infuse her words with a faith she did not feel. "But we have to go. We have to leave right now."

"I can walk," Allen slurred, pushing himself up. "I can."

Stephen hoisted him by the armpits. Allen struggled to keep his head balanced on his neck, but with an effort Julia took to be equal parts strength and will, he raised his chin, pushed out his chest, and said, "Let's go."

Julia popped her head out the door and looked around. She shuffled out, gun ready. Stephen and Allen sidestepped through the doorway. Allen's foot came out from under him; he overcorrected and fell back into the front wall of the building. A flash of frustration wrinkled his brow. He shook off Stephen's grip, opting to steady himself by keeping only one hand on Stephen's shoulder.

"Same old Allen," Stephen whispered. "Bullheaded as ever."

They started moving south, toward the trash area and the mineshaft. The ground quaked as Navy thunder pealed over the base, reverberating against the buildings' metal skin. Julia and Stephen realized at the same time that a noise at the end of this thunder was caused by something else—a slamming door behind them.

They turned to see a man darting across the road. He stopped and faced them. Julia's mouth went dry. A fleshless skull was glaring at her. Then she realized the black orbs of the eyeholes were a pair of sunglasses, and the face she thought fleshless was merely gaunt—but extremely so, as though it had gone through the Mayan ritual of *tlachaki*, in which dried facial skin was stretched over the skull after everything else had been stripped off. Brittle hair, unnaturally silver in sunlight, exploded back from an overly large forehead, framing the head like the halos of saints in Florentine paintings; to Julia, it heightened the sense of sacrilege this figure radiated.

"Litt," Allen said.

Pressed to his chest with both arms was a silver briefcase.

Julia raised the Sig Sauer, but Litt disappeared behind a building.

Julia reversed for the mine, but Stephen caught her arm.

"He had a case. We can't let him go."

"There's no time."

"We can't let him go," he repeated.

"We can't," Allen agreed. He wiped the back of a hand over his lips. "He won't let this die. He'll be back."

"Allen," Julia said, refusing to believe he would pass up the opportunity to get while the getting was good, "going after Litt may mean the difference between getting out alive . . . and not."

"Doesn't matter."

Stephen again: "We can't let him go."

They were right. Oh God, they were right. With bombs crashing down around his head, the only souvenir Litt could possibly want was whatever would allow him to continue his work in viral terrorism—money or formulae or specimens, probably all three.

Without a word, she took off after him.

ninety-six

THEY CHARGED THROUGH THE ALLEY TOWARD THE LARGE open area that split the base in half. On the other side, in front of one of the hangars, dozens of military vehicles squatted on rubberless rims, rusting. Despite the destruction, Litt had run in this direction.

When they emerged from the alley, Litt was waiting for them. He stood two buildings away, casting a chilling smile. His fingers were massaging the back of the hand that held the briefcase.

She leveled her pistol at him. "Freeze!" she yelled. "Drop the case!"

When he didn't, she repeated the command. Again he ignored her. She wondered if he was concealing a weapon. Slowly, she advanced, Allen and Stephen close behind.

"Shoot him," Allen whispered. His voice was raspy, and he was winded.

They stepped in front of a Quonset door. It burst open, spewing out the Atroposes in a frenzy of gauntleted fists, kicking legs, overwhelming bodies. A black arm lashed out and sent her pistol flying. Julia yelled out in surprise and pain as two of her fingers broke and split open. A hand ensnarled her hair and forced her head back. She swung her arm and hit nothing. She kicked back, felt her captor move away, and struck nothing. She reached behind her head, found the flexing material of the gauntlet, and realized her efforts there would be pointless.

Let a missile hit us now, she prayed. *Just take us all out, whatever good with all this evil.*

She heaved forward, realizing in midfall that someone had planted a foot at the small of her back and kicked her away. She hit the ground hard and tumbled. A body fell on top of her—instinctively, she jabbed a fist into it. The man let out a painful breath of air, too labored to be one of the Atroposes. She pushed him off and found his face: Allen. Snapping her head up, she witnessed Stephen in the impossible task of taking on all three Atroposes. He had one pinned under his massive foot against the building's facade, and another in a stranglehold, gripping the killer's neck despite his captive's pounding fists. He had kicked or punched or shoved the third Atropos—this one was reeling back and falling.

Stephen's eyes found Julia's.

"Go!" he grunted. "Stop him!"

She looked quickly and saw Litt running across the field, toward the smoldering hangars. She scanned the ground for her pistol. It was there, among the scuffling feet of Atropos and Stephen.

The killer who'd fallen was up, moving in on Stephen. She leaped up and kicked him. He spun and planted a heel into her sternum. She flew back. Eyes watering from pain, she rolled toward the battle, reaching, feeling for her gun. A booted foot came down on her arm. She screamed and pulled her arm back. She rolled away, rose, cradling her arm.

The Atropos pinned by Stephen's foot writhed in frustration, not quite understanding yet that the weight of his brothers was anchoring Stephen in place. A spiked fist rose from the headlocked Atropos and came down on Stephen's spine.

His eyes slammed shut against the assault. Tears streamed out. He opened his eyes again, found Julia. "Go! Please!"

Litt was nearly at the hangars.

Beside her, Allen struggled to stand. She sensed the tension coiled in his legs and arms, ready to spring at Stephen's attackers. She reached out and touched him. "No, Allen. They'll kill you with one blow."

"I . . . have . . . to!"

Stephen turned a bloody face toward Allen and shook his head. "No, brother. Go. Stop Litt. Don't let this happen again . . ."

The free Atropos took a step for Allen and Julia. Stephen released the neck he had been gripping and seized the collar of the assassin now interested in Allen and Julia, yanking him back. When the man spun to break the grip, Stephen yelled, "You wimp! Just like your punk *dead* brother!"

Atropos rammed a fist into Stephen's face. The struggling escalated: the movements came faster, the blows harder.

Backing away, Julia saw the Atroposes as something other than individual killers. Though encased in their own skins, they moved in unison, as one creature: one pulling back as another stepped in . . . gripping and releasing like the tentacles of a violently malicious monster. And she realized another thing: they all wanted a piece of Stephen; they all wanted to be part of the kill. In the destruction of their enemies, they were of one mind, one body. They would descend on each of them with a unified, incomprehensible wrath.

She pulled at Allen, aware that she was leaving Stephen to die. They would all perish if they tried to rescue him. And he would die for nothing.

No, she thought. She couldn't leave so easily. She dived for her gun, dodging the kicks, the stomps. Her uninjured hand reached out, grabbed the barrel. She rolled back, back, then up, turning the gun in her hand. She pointed, focused. All three Atroposes stood behind Stephen—a gauntleted arm circling his neck, gloved hands pulling his arms back at horrendous angles, another hand coming from between his legs to grip a thigh. Julia recalled Shiva, the Hindu god of destruction, and Stephen was caught in its many arms. Its necklace of skulls were the faces of the Atroposes, peering wickedly over Stephen's shoulders and around his body. They jostled, shielding themselves.

"Go," Stephen pleaded again, his voice weak and raspy, and her heart ached at the realization that she must obey. It would be crueler not to.

Her fingers, bent grotesquely backward, throbbed and spewed blood. Her forearm felt as though a truck had parked on it, but she pushed the pain down into a black well, where its screams for attention echoed flatly and carried no weight.

She could not get another clear shot. She recognized determination in Stephen's eyes. He wanted everything they'd gone through to matter. Allen's trauma; her efforts and grief; Donnelley's death; the deaths of so many others, ones they knew about and more they didn't; Stephen's own . . . *offering* now—he wanted it all to make a difference, if not to bring good, then to stop evil. She understood. And she knew hesitating would ruin it all, would make futile the blood and tears. She lowered the pistol and gave him a soft nod. She was biting her lip, reopening the wound, tasting the blood. She felt like a small child trying to be brave.

He attempted a smile, but his quivering lips could not hold it. So he held her eyes a moment longer and nodded back, firm, sure.

Again she pulled at Allen. He stood on shaky legs and let her take some of his weight. Then she started backing away.

"No, wait," Allen pleaded.

"We have to stop Litt," she whispered without taking her eyes off Stephen and his captors. The Atroposes stared, knowing they had won.

"I can't leave him," Allen said. "Not like this."

"It's what he wants, Allen. If we don't go now, we won't stop Litt, and Stephen will have—" She restructured the thought. "All of this will be in vain."

"Stephen! I love you!" he cried.

And Stephen did smile, a big ain't-everything-just-dandy grin. It was ecstasy to witness, a cool shower on sweat-soaked skin. Julia thanked him silently for that. Then she tugged again at Allen. He yielded and took a few steps backward with her. He turned away then, apparently wanting to remember the smile, not the aftermath.

One of the Atroposes aimed his pistol at them. Stephen noticed and knocked his forehead into the weapon. He head-slammed the Atropos directly behind him, managed to pull an arm free, then a leg. He grabbed, punched, kicked, and berated the three Atroposes into leaving the other two alone for now. She had the idea. This, after all, was not for pay; this was personal. No one cared whether this "hit" was clean and quick. *They* cared that it was messy and drawn out. And their arrogance, borne of a skill that could do nothing but breed arrogance, would convince them they could take their prey at their leisure. Never mind the air strike; they were here for revenge.

"He's getting away," Allen said, his voice flat.

She turned and saw Litt crossing in front of a hangar. She squeezed off three rapid shots. Small explosions erupted in the dirt around him. He jerked to a stop, turned, and fell. He scooped the case up and disappeared into the space between two hangars.

"Slowed him down," Allen rasped.

"We have to move faster."

"Go on ahead of me. I'll catch up."

But before she could stop herself, she glanced back. Her blood congealed. Stephen was on his knees. An Atropos was holding each of his arms straight out from his body, crosslike. Another Atropos stood behind him, raising a gauntleted fist, focused on the back of Stephen's head. Her heart kicked against her breastbone. She swung the pistol around, but too late. The gauntlet came down, firm and straight as a piston.

Stephen *crumbled.* The two holding him let go, and he fell: no resistance, no spasms, no life.

Julia let loose an animal roar that rubbed her throat raw and rose to the pitch of the siren so that it seemed to go on and on long after she closed her mouth. The Atroposes, standing around their downed foe, rotated their heads to peer at her. It was one thing to accept death, quite another to see it. She tried to steady the heavy weapon it held and pulled the trigger. Again. And again. After five wild shots, she forced her finger to stop. Her shots had not stirred the Atroposes at all; they stood like wax figures, staring.

She spun away from them. She caught up with Allen, who

was stumbling and falling, loping across the field. She was nearly panting, afraid she'd never draw enough air again.

"Is he—?" he asked

"Don't look back." She hitched in a breath. Ten rounds, she thought, her mind flailing for something sturdy. No, eleven. The first took out the light above Atropos's head. Then two as she ran from Atropos, three at Litt, and five more at Stephen's killers. Eleven. The Sig held thirteen rounds, plus one in the chamber. She had three left. Enough to turn Litt inside out.

She bolted for the gap between the hangars.

ninety-seven

KARL LITT LOPED BEHIND THE HANGARS. OFF IN THE JUNGLE, not far from the last hangar, was a shed that housed his Hummer. He could feel the heat of the burning hangars and smell the smoke. Flecks of ash fluttered in his eyes, and he brushed them away. The perimeter fence was a mere thirty yards to his right, and just beyond he could see trees ablaze like pillars of fire. If he had gauged the air strikes correctly, Kendrick's screaming war machine had completed phase two, the tomography bombs. Somewhere overhead, a plane's radar was reading the results and constructing a map of the underground complex. It wouldn't be long before the last and most destructive attack would begin.

He felt the sting before he heard the shot. Then the fire—his ear was on fire! He dropped his briefcase and grabbed his ear. Felt blood and the ragged, tingling edge where the top of his ear was gone.

I SHOT HIS EAR OFF, SHE THOUGHT.

Julia stood watching Litt over the sights of her pistol.
Delicate tendrils of smoke seeped from the barrel and the
notch of the ejection port. He was touching the wound and
probably had no idea what had just happened. She had
aimed for the center of his back, and he was only forty yards
away; she'd won an Academy tournament on a range ten
yards longer. But she was using her injured hand. Extending
out the broken middle and ring fingers instead of wrapping
them around the grip made for shaky shooting. She bent her
elbows and drew the pistol closer to her face. With her left
hand supporting her shooting hand, she centered her sights
between his shoulder blades.

He turned and raised his hands in surrender.

Her finger tightened on the trigger. She imagined the
bullet striking the lapel over his heart. She had the shot.

She let her grip relax, and the barrel dipped. She couldn't
do it. She could not shoot an unarmed man in the act of surrendering. Even soldiers took prisoners on the battlefield,
didn't they? Wasn't it part of the Geneva Convention? But
what would she do with him? If she tied him up or knocked
him out or disabled him somehow, he'd die in the air strike.
That would be no better than shooting him now. If she took
his case and let him escape, would he find a way to continue
killing, to perhaps even duplicate the work he'd done here?
How would she live with herself then? And if she actually
took him in custody, how far would they get—she and the
gravely ill Allen—before he got the upper hand and murdered them both?

"You have no choice. Do it."

At first she thought the words were her own, so persua-
sive as to sound like whispers in her ear. Then she realized

they'd come from Allen, who was slowly, painfully moving up behind her. He came into her peripheral vision on her left, scraping along the wall of the hangar, sucking in wet breaths.

"Julia," he groaned. "Think of . . . the deaths . . . he's responsible for. Think of . . . your partner. Think of Ste . . . Ste . . ."

He sobbed then—or coughed; she couldn't tell. But it didn't matter, because she *was* thinking of Donnelley, she *was* thinking of Stephen. She braced herself, feeling the muscles in her face, especially around her mouth and brow, pinch tight. She brought the barrel back in line with Litt's chest.

"You'd only be killing yourselves!" Litt called.

She held her position. "Meaning?"

"Meaning—"

His left hand moved—he was holding something. How could she not have noticed? In the moment between seeing the movement and deciding to shoot, she heard a machine kick into gear: *clack-clack-clack-clack-clack* . . . Fast, like an anchor chain reeling out to the ocean floor. She shifted her vision to see a contraption on the jungle side of the chain-link fence spin around. A Gatling-style cluster of barrels jutting from its body now pointed not out toward the jungle but inward toward them. When it stopped, she continued hearing the sound for a second longer. She turned to see another of these weapons— Tate had called them Deadeyes— pointing its barrels almost directly at her. She remembered Tate saying soldiers controlled them with remotes, and they could be programmed to monitor certain regions around them. She had just witnessed the redirecting of these two, from outward, where a sniper would fire into the compound, to the compound itself, where she and Allen stood. She had no doubt that either Deadeye was capable of blowing them away, regardless of where along this strip between the hangars and the jungle they were.

"Meaning, if you fire your weapon, my mechanical friends will annihilate you both." He smiled and lowered his arms.

Had Tate not warned them of these antisniper weapons, she probably would have called his bluff.

He continued: "Their response is instantaneous—"

Three seconds, she remembered.

"—and their field of fire is quite broad. You can't elude them. I've seen people try." As he spoke, he squatted and picked up the silver briefcase. Then he took a tentative step back.

"Just . . . *stop!*" she screamed through gritted teeth. He did. She took a step forward. He stepped back. Another step for each of them. Her mind had told her she could not shoot him, and she held to that mandate. But she nearly forgot *why* he was off-limits, and she came within a half pound of trigger pressure of squeezing off a warning round. She pushed the back of her finger against the trigger guard to keep it ready but safe.

"Litt! I said *stop!* I mean it. Don't think I won't end it all right here, right now."

She walked forward, and this time he held his ground. Behind her, Allen pushed himself along the wall of the hangar.

"Allen, stay there. Don't move."

"If you go, I go," he said weakly. She knew he was referring to a longer journey than the distance to Litt. "Besides, he . . . probably killed me anyway." He spat a red glob into the dirt. "Julia, you can get out of this. I know you can."

"Any ideas?"

"No. But I know you. You'll figure something out."

"You're giving me too much credit. I'm stumped."

They reached a gap between hangars. Allen hesitated, and

Julia moved close to him, not taking her eyes or her aim off Litt. "You're not up for this," she said.

"I'm feeling better. Really." He groaned, but she thought he did look stronger. Something inside was fighting hard. "Stephen shot me full of adrenaline. I'm feeling it."

"Take my shoulder, but don't jar me too much. If this is it for us, I want to take him along."

"I believe he's going the other direction." He grabbed hold of her and gently shifted a measure of weight to her.

They crossed the gap, and he let go to continue his sad slide along the wall. They had halved the distance to Litt. This near, she could make out the blood that coated the remainder of his ear and where he had smeared it on his jaw and neck. It was stark against the whiteness of his face. Closer, she noticed that a scarlet trickle had followed his jawbone and formed a bead on his chin like a tiny goatee. An explosion hurled debris against the hangar hard enough to shake the entire wall, but she resisted the temptation to look. Hot air billowed her hair. The air strike had taken a giant step toward them.

A body length from Litt, she stopped. She pointed her gun at the left lens of his black sunglasses.

"You're not going to use that thing," he said, smiling thinly.

"In a heartbeat."

In her peripheral vision, she saw Allen slide down the wall, grunting when he hit the ground. He held one shoulder out at an uncomfortable angle, as if trying not to completely collapse. His head drooped; he appeared to have spotted something fascinating in the dirt. Litt appraised him.

"Well, Dr. Parker. Did you enjoy your stay with us?"

"You're a sick man, Litt," Julia said, not sure what to do next.

"So I've been told. Something about the pointless death of his family will do that to a man."

"That's what this is about? Revenge?"

"When you put it that way, it does sound petty, doesn't it?"

They were both stalling, trying to figure a way out.

"Other people have lost loved ones. They don't kill thousands in retaliation."

"I'm not other people."

Keeping his lenses pointed at her, he placed the remote control device into the breast pocket of his lab coat.

"Don't move. Not even a finger." Julia said, poking the gun at him. Her upper torso leaned into the movement.

"Or what, you'll shoot? Of course, you could pistol-whip me. Would you like that? Maybe this will dissuade you." His hand came out of the pocket with something that looked like a harmonica—

My mind's not working right, she thought. *And if that's true, we're not going to survive.*

Then a fat blade snapped out of the end. He held a stiletto.

ninety-eight

LITT BEGAN CASUALLY STIRRING THE AIR WITH THE KNIFE. It looked utterly ridiculous in his bony fingers, but she wasn't going to bet the farm he didn't know how to use it. That he kept it in motion told her something; a moving weapon was the hardest to take away.

"Don't worry, I have no intention of attacking you. I merely desire the same courtesy."

She raced through her options: Shoot and die . . . Jump him and risk the blade . . . Follow him and hope they moved out of the Deadeyes' sensors. The hangars all had people-sized rear doors. Litt could easily back to a door, then duck in and lock it before she could reach him. By the time she raced around, he'd be gone again. Maybe he had a plane waiting. Or a car. Something with bulletproof windows and bulletproof everything. If she attacked, he might cut her down and get away. The only certain way to stop him was to shoot

But he didn't move; he watched her.

"You're the one, aren't you?" he said. "The information on the chip. You modified it. Hacked it, as they say."

She felt herself smile.

"Oh, you are cunning. The president's family was never targeted. You added them."

"As you said, best not mess with a man's family."

A plane flew over, followed by a tremendous explosion. It had hit well away from them, where the Quonsets were or even farther. Still, the ground shook hard enough to make Julia's feet unsteady for a few moments. Silt and ash drifted down on them. A hot wind blew past.

"Kendrick's final wave," Litt announced. "Annihilation of the base. We'd better resolve this, don't you think?"

"I'm not letting you leave."

"I can help him, you know." He cocked his head at Allen. "All of them."

"What are you talking about?"

"Ebola. I have the cure."

She didn't know whether to believe him. She wanted to see his eyes, but his glasses were too dark.

"It's reversible," he said, "at least in the early stages. Many people have recovered, even after experiencing severe hemorrhagic symptoms. Once the virus is gone, the body repairs itself rather quickly. The cure restores and accelerates intravascular coagulation, which give the endothelial cells time to reform."

She could not risk a glance at Allen, but she knew he looked as if a truck had hit him. *That* was repairable?

Her doubt must have shown on her face. Litt said, "Even

Dr. Parker has a chance. On the scale of heart failure due to the Ebola virus, he is on the early side. His organs have not failed, but his heart is responding to the blood loss and hypotension. He has a chance," he repeated, "with this." He tapped the metal case with his toe.

Then she saw it: movement reflected in his glasses. Silhouettes of legs moving, heads bobbing, a swinging arm. The Atroposes were behind her, approaching slowly.

Litt was stalling, saying, "You can save his life. I'll give you the cure; you let me walk away. Simple as that."

A red light, as small as a paper cut, appeared among the reflected cluster of Atroposes. As it bounced and jiggled, another appeared . . . then another. The laser sites. They were turning on their pistols' lasers, and the smoke was making them visible. She counted three bodies, three lasers.

They won't risk my hearing them. They're going to shoot sooner, not later.

"In fact," Litt said, "I'll get you two out of here, drop you off at the hospital in . . ."

They don't know about the Deadeyes, and Litt isn't going to tell them. Their lives for his . . . what does he have to think about? And they don't care that Litt will go down with me, perhaps killed by the same bullets that kill me. No honor among thieves. Or murderers.

The silhouettes were now indistinguishable from the other shadow-and-light patterns on the lens, but the tiny red beams dancing at their sides were clear as neon. She remembered the shooting styles of the Atroposes she'd seen in action: they didn't pause, they didn't take time to aim. They didn't have to—they were marksmen. When they raised their weapons, they shot. One-second warning. No more.

". . . after that, I started producing antibodies."

"What?"

"It comes from my blood. The cure."

His glasses reflected what she had been waiting for: the lines of lasers rose and shortened as the Atroposes raised their pistols. The short lines of the beams became pinpricks.

"Cure *this*," she said and dropped to the ground.

The silenced weapons spat and popped.

Litt screamed. His blood splashed over her. The knife spiraled out of his hand and clanged against the metal hangar wall—a cymbal clash over the dull tones of bullets plunking into the same wall. As soon as his body hit the ground, she flipped around to face the Atroposes.

They stood in a tight group, their arms straight out in front, clutching pistols that smoked and projected arrows of red light over her head. They shared an expression of vague shock. Then all six eyes flicked to her and the laser beams lowered. The high-pitched whine of motors caught their attention. In unison, they rotated their heads toward the sound.

For the only time since seeing them together, Julia witnessed a disunity in their actions. Two began swinging their pistols toward the nearest Deadeye; the other reeled back, trying to shift his feet into hyperdrive.

The Deadeyes roared and vanished in billows of smoke. The Atroposes disappeared too. In a chunky mist of black and red. Sparks flashed as round after round pinged off their pistols. There were so many sparks, she thought later the gauntlets must have been made of metal as well. The men seemed to blur backward, like inked figures smeared by the artist's hand.

She closed her eyes.

The Deadeyes stopped firing. Their barrels continued to

spin; they sounded like dentist's drills. Something wet smacked against the ground.

She turned away and cautiously ventured into the world of vision. Allen was sitting against the wall, one leg completely off the ground in a posture of defense. His hands gripped his head because they had nothing else to do. His mouth gaped in a silent scream. Moving in miniscule increments, his eyes—too big for his face—settled on her. His mouth closed on a frown; then a bruised tongue poked out and slid over his lips. He swallowed. His hands remained in the air. He started to speak, stopped. Another swallow.

"Did you actually say," he asked, wheezing out a thin chuckle, "'*cure this*'?"

ninety-nine

SHE HAD BEEN GONE NO MORE THAN THREE MINUTES, AND when she returned Allen was still propped against the wall. He bore a numb, dull expression and was staring at the spot where the Atroposes had finally met their match. She had tried to avoid glimpsing any of that particular carnage, but the Deadeyes had done their job so thoroughly, everywhere she looked she saw *something* of the former assassins.

"They're just gone," he said. "They were here, and now they're not. What kind of person creates a thing that can do that?" He looked up at her. "You lost your jacket. You covered him up?"

She nodded. Her eyes were red and swollen, her cheeks still wet. "I had to be sure. What if he was . . . somehow . . . ?"

"I can't imagine those monsters walking away from any adversary who still drew breath."

She picked up Litt's case and sat down beside Allen. The bombs were raining down now, pouring into craters where the Quonsets had been. They had to leave quickly, but an equally pressing need demanded her attention. She squared Litt's case on her lap. There was a single drop of blood near the handle.

She said, "Was he telling the truth, do you think?"

"One way to find out."

She could tell he was in great pain. His breathing sounded sloppy and wet. Still, he displayed more vigor than he had ten minutes before. Eyeing Litt's body, sprawled flat on its back an arm's reach away, she understood how he felt. She hoped he could hold on to the energy awhile longer. She worried about her ability to carry him to safety if he couldn't walk.

She took a deep breath, popped the latches, and opened the case. Mounted to the inside of the lid were two rows of stainless steel vials. Small labels identified their contents: "Ebola Kugel 4212A"; "Ebola Kugel 5211F"; "Ebola Kugel 3294B" . . . The last one on the right was twice the size of the others. "EK Antiserum."

"That's it," Allen said.

"Do you think it's an actual antidote, not just his blood? Doesn't it take years to develop?"

"He told me he had an antidote. Antiserum's the same thing."

The bottom portion of the case contained a square metal box, what appeared to be bankbooks, passports, identification, and other documents. She opened the box. Inside were roughly two dozen memory chips in plastic cases.

"The formula for Ebola Kugel?" she wondered.

"Or digitized DNA records. Blackmail material. Financial transactions. Could be anything."

A jet streaked overhead, low. A thunderous blast shook the hangar. They realized it had emanated from the front of the hangar, much closer than the others.

She slammed the lid closed. "Come on."

"Wait." With some difficulty, he reopened the case, plucked three vials of Ebola from the metal tongs that held them, and tossed them toward Litt's body.

"Don't—" She stopped herself. Of course he was right. Nothing good could ever come from those vials. She reached in, removed the remaining vials—all but the antiserum—and tossed them onto Litt's chest.

"You think they'll be destroyed?" Allen asked.

A missile shrieked into the jungle and exploded. Noises of a million varying pitches and tones collided with each other, forming one bellowing scream.

"Witness the wrath of Kendrick," she said. "If he wanted to take down Litt and get his research, he'd have sent in a platoon of commandos." She thought a moment. "Actually, that's what I expected. No, he wants Litt and his germ destroyed. He won't stop until this entire place is a wasteland. Bet on it."

She removed the memory chips from the case and tossed those too. She pulled out the documents. He stopped her. From the sheaf in her hand, he extracted a stack of hundred-dollar bills. It must have been three inches thick.

"For Stephen's church," he said. He dropped the money back into the case and pushed against the wall to stand.

She closed the case and stood. As she reached for Allen, an explosion rocked the ground and she toppled into him. They hit the dirt hard. Then the neighboring hangar blew apart. Roiling clouds of fire and smoke flung jagged panels of sheet metal and twisted beams into the air. The hangar they leaned against lost a wall and started collapsing.

"Hurry!" She pulled Allen's arm around her shoulder and heaved him forward in a stumbling run.

On the other side of the chain-link fence, a huge tree instantly ignited and crashed down, crushing one of the Deadeyes and a section of fence. Heated air shoved them against the wall. Allen yelled out in pain and dropped to one knee, but he pressed on. She could feel him drawing determination from his physical distress, turning the agony into fuel that powered his fight for survival.

Together, they scrambled behind the hangars, awkward as shackled prisoners not yet attuned to each other's rhythm and gait. They tottered into a wall, pushed off, and stumbled forward another dozen paces before falling into the wall again. Instead of turning into the alley through which she had pursued Litt, she led Allen further south: he did not need to see the body whose head and upper torso she had covered.

The explosions were no longer demarcated in an easily avoided region but seemed to be everywhere, ripping apart the compound's central area, its hangars and Quonsets. She thought the pounding was less severe on the south side of the base near the mineshaft. Or was that just wishful thinking?

She considered escaping through the main gate and along the dirt road where the compound's workers had gone. But she didn't know how far Kendrick would go to eliminate Litt's threat. After pulverizing the compound, might he then start on the road, with the intention of catching up to the fleeing masses? She wouldn't put it past him.

No, she and Allen would leave the way she and Stephen had arrived. If God thought they'd had enough adversity for one day, Tate would be waiting for them with his truck.

At the dilapidated motor pool, they turned west. Across the field, several of the Quonset huts lay smashed and burning. Dense black smoke rose from a crater in the field. Julia had the feeling this opening was intended as a gateway into the underground complex for the kind of building-crushing, concrete-melting, de-atomizing ordnance civilians couldn't even imagine. She stepped up their pace, now pulling him along as well as supporting him. The sight of the Dumpsters spurred her on.

As they passed the guard shacks and entrance gate, a horrendous explosion behind them slammed them to the ground. An army truck sailed over their heads and landed upside down twenty feet away. Its tires were on fire. She rolled over and saw that the motor pool building they had passed—and fallen against—was now a blazing ruin. She rubbed a sudden pain in her shoulder and found her fingers sticky with blood.

Helping Allen to his feet, she steered him around the truck and limped and pulled and hopped the short distance to the trash area. The huge container near the shaft had been knocked over by a blast and partially covered the hole. If Stephen had replaced the lid when they crawled out, she and Allen could never have pried it up again. But he hadn't.

"This is it. Watch your step."

Allen raised his head and peered into the heart of the dying base. "I wish we didn't have to leave Stephen," he said.

"He's not really here, Allen." Through breaks in the smoke, she could make out the growing flyspecks of approaching planes.

"I know," he said.

Putrid slime had oozed from the toppled Dumpster and pooled around the shaft. He lowered his body into this muck, doing so without complaint, and squeezed into the hole. She warned him about the rung that had snapped under Stephen's weight, then lowered herself into the slime and over the rim.

Somewhere she had lost her flashlight, and the other one had fallen to its death. She supposed they could follow the walls to the opening. What was slime, what was darkness next to the things they had gone through?

An explosion shook the shaft. Julia imagined they were in the gullet of a growling beast. Rung after rung they descended, Julia stopping every few moments to let Allen pull ahead. Finally she heard him drop the last few feet to the floor. He groaned.

"You all right?"

"Depends on what you mean." His voice was weak.

"Are you clear—"

The top of the shaft erupted. Concrete chucks punched into Julia's shoulders and head, and she fell. She landed on her back over a boulder, knocking the wind out of her lungs. She gasped, getting a mouthful of dirt. The shaft roared above her. It was breaking up and coming down. She was paralyzed— with fear . . . with pain . . . with the prospect of death. She felt a harsh tug on her arm. She came painfully off the boulder and bounded over smaller rocks. Allen was pulling her, rising up and falling backward, using the momentum of each plunge to drag her away from the cave-in.

"Aaahhg!" he yelled with every tug. "Aaahhg!"

The collapsing earth slowed, then stopped. Silt rained down, hissing against the huge mound of rubble, like the sizzle of molten lava. A gaping chimney as wide as a silo bore up through the earth where the shaft had been. Sunlight pushed through the dust-choked air, casting a weak, murky glow over the place Julia and Allen sprawled.

The opening rumbled once more, the light disappeared,

and something big crashed down, bringing with it grave-sized slabs of earth as it slammed against the sides of the hole. Then the Dumpster struck the rubble and tumbled into the mine. It landed so close to Julia, she could have reached out and touched it. Trash erupted from the container, covering them in the foulest stench ever to lay hold of Julia's nose.

Gagging and coughing, they pulled each other up and stumbled away. Just before daylight completely succumbed to the blackness of the mine, Allen leaned down and picked up a dinged and dust-coated flashlight. He shook it, coaxing a weak light from it.

They shuffled into the mine's inky coolness.

Behind them, someone coughed.

Out of the cloudy air emerged a figure, hazy, blurred. The first thing Julia distinguished was a pistol. Pointed at them. Then the arm that held it. A foot, a leg, stepping forward. The face revealed itself last.

"Gregor," Allen said, nearly choking on the word.

The older man's hair was matted with blood. It flowed past his eye and down the side of his face. But his eyes were clear, his gait strong. He strode directly to them, raised his pistol, and backhanded it into Allen's forehead. Allen crashed against the wall and fell to the ground, motionless.

Julia lashed out, but too fast the gun was in her face, pressed into her temple. Gregor brought his free arm around to the back of her neck, holding her in place. He pressed himself against her. Chest to chest, cheek to cheek, he spoke into her ear.

"In the end, I win."

"What do you want?" she asked.

"What I do *not* want"—the malice in his voice was as plain as the stink of vomit on his breath—"is to chat."

She had recognized his weapon—the popular 1911 Colt .45. Though it was a semiautomatic, it sported a hammer that required cocking. His thumb pulled back on that hammer now.

"We know where Litt's money is . . . and his serum, the Ebola antidote." It was all she could think to say.

Just buy time, she thought.

She didn't know if the words that would save their lives would come to mind. She didn't know if he'd move an inch or look away and grant her a chance to plant an elbow in his throat. What she did know was that once he pulled the trigger, it was over. No more chances. No more hope.

Gregor pushed the barrel harder into her temple. "They're in the briefcase," he said. "I am not a fool."

But he sounded unsure.

Over Gregor's shoulder, she could see Allen. He stirred, then raised his head. He touched his hand to the tunnel wall behind him and pulled it away quickly. He was in front of an oddly flat section of wall, lighter in color from the surrounding rock surfaces. She saw a flicker of light at the floor, smoke streaming out, as if from a volcanic vent.

It was the fire door Tate had described, the abandoned emergency exit. Apparently a blast had taken out the second door Tate had said was at the end of a long corridor beyond this one. If she read Allen's reaction correctly, the door was scalding hot. She thought of the maelstrom of flame and heat that must be on the other side.

"Drop the case," Gregor said.

"The vials might break."

"Just drop it."

She did. It struck her foot and tipped over.

Allen caught her eye. He jerked his head to the side: *Move!* He raised his hand toward the door handle.

She shook her head gently.

He nodded, disagreeing. Of course.

"I already removed the vial," she told Gregor.

"I don't think so."

"Look for yourself. Then I'll take you to it."

He glanced down at the case. His arm came away from her neck.

"Back up slowly," he said. The barrel of his gun never wavered from her face.

She took a step back, then another.

He bent at the knees, keeping his aim and his eyes on her, reaching for the case.

She turned and dived, hit the floor and rolled.

Allen opened the door. Angry flames roared into the tunnel, growling like a beast as they sucked up oxygen, and expanded at lightning speed.

Squinting, squatting, backpedaling away, Julia watched the fire engulf Gregor. It slammed him against the opposite wall and fanned out in both directions. As it lost momentum, flames fell to the floor, burning in a wide swath from the door across the width of the mine and ending at Gregor's burning corpse.

Julia's sneakers and the bottoms of her pant legs were ablaze. She kicked and rolled and finally sat on them to extinguish the flames. She quickly stood, feeling the pain of scorched flesh, and looked around.

"Allen!"

He was thirty feet farther into the mine. His hair was smoking, his shirt was on fire, and he wasn't moving. She threw herself on top of him and ran her hands through his hair.

"Is this your idea of romance?" he whispered.

She gripped his head between her hands, leaned close. "I can't believe you did that."

"I didn't know the door was going to just slam open like that. It batted me like a pinball flipper."

"If it hadn't, you'd have ended up like . . . what's-his-name."

"Gregor. Is he . . . ?"

"Oh yeah." She paused. "Thank you." A tear dropped from her eye and landed on his cheek. It left a white streak on his sooty skin.

"None of that, now," he said. "You'll ruin my image of you."

"Which is what, exactly?"

"Oh, someone who could take my lunch money anytime she wanted to."

"I can."

They laughed, more relieved than humored. It didn't last long. There were too many hurts on too many levels.

She lifted him, and he pretended to help. They made their way to the mouth of the mine leaning against each other, finally in perfect sync. The opening was bright and covered with green leaves. They stumbled to it and did not pause when they reached its lip.

Together, they fell into the cool arms of the jungle.

epilogue

HIS EYES FLUTTERED AGAINST THE STARK SUNLIGHT BREACHing the blinds in his hospital room. As he came awake and his vision adjusted, he saw the blinds were wide Venetians, dated and dusty. The walls were drab brown and unadorned, except for wall-mounted medical instruments. Somewhere, an EKG machine beeped.

Allen took a deep breath. For the first time in as long as he could remember, nothing inside hurt.

He turned his head to examine the room, which looked different outside the veil of pain- and medication-induced grogginess that had enveloped him for . . . for . . . a long time. Perhaps the room seemed changed only because he wasn't only seeing it now but was finally lucid enough to pass judgment on it. He didn't like it much: an empty metal tray on wheels, stained acoustic ceiling tiles, the ugly walls.

He brought his vision around to the other side of the bed and lit on a startlingly beautiful sight among the stale blandness: Julia Matheson's beaming face.

"I thought I'd dreamed you," he said.

"You should be so lucky." She rose from a chair, gripped his hand. "How are you?"

He nodded. "No pain. Or maybe I'm just getting used to it."

"The doctor thinks you'll make a complete recovery. The Ebola was just starting to set in. Everything was reversible and repairable, thanks to Litt's antidote."

"Just thinking about Litt makes me queasy."

"One of the vials in the case we recovered contained his plasma. They think they can make an Ebola vaccine from it."

"How long have I been here?"

"Just over two weeks." She walked to the window and raised the blinds. "A military hospital of some kind, I think we're in Virginia."

He pushed himself up, wincing at sharp pains in his side and back. "You *think?*"

"I guess we're quarantined, but it's more like they don't know what to do with us. They let me call my mom. She had a . . . an episode, but the home health nurse got there pretty quickly. She's in their facility now."

She drew closer, and her voice grew soft. "Do you remember anything? Tate meeting us in the jungle? The U.S. soldiers intercepting his truck outside Pedro Juan Caballero? Getting evacced here?"

He tried to remember. "Vaguely . . . I guess."

She bit her lip. "Do you remember what happened to Stephen?"

He closed his eyes. He didn't move for a long time. Then

a tear broke free and rolled down his cheek. Without looking at her, he said, "He saved my life."

"Both our lives. Many lives. I've had time here to imagine what would have happened if Litt escaped. He would have set up shop somewhere else and terrorized the world with his designer virus. That's what they're calling it, a designer virus, like it was something cool."

"A lot of people died to stop him. Your partner too."

"I wish I could see Goody's wife, the boys. They need to know he died heroically."

"They haven't said when we can leave?"

The door pushed open, letting in a sigh of antisepticized air. With it came an old man, leaning heavily on a cane, with the lax shoulders of a weary traveler. He paused, holding the door, then let it close. Allen felt he'd seen the man before but could not place him.

Julia had one hand resting on Allen's head. He felt it stiffen.

"I should throw you out this window," she said.

"I have no doubt you could, Ms. Matheson." His smile faltered. "I'm sorry for your losses. Both of you."

Allen caught her eye. "I don't understand."

"This is Kendrick Reynolds," she said, keeping a level gaze on the old man. "He promised to help; then he tried to incinerate us with the rest of his problem."

Reynolds shuffled to the end of the bed and rested his long, wrinkled hands over the tubular footboard. He said, "I did what I had to do. There was no time to extricate you and Dr. Parker and his brother."

"So he bombed the base," she continued, talking to Allen, glaring at Reynolds. "With us in it."

"We prevented a holocaust, Ms. Matheson."

"*You* didn't prevent anything. Without us, the antidote would have been destroyed too—the antidote that has saved, what, ten thousand people?"

"Most of them, yes. But if we hadn't eliminated Litt and his virus, we would be living in a very different world right now, one too terrible to think about."

"It was your mess to start with, your Frankenstein monster that got out of hand."

"I accept that indictment," he said with a slight bow of his head. "I can't begin to tell you the kind of second-guessing I've put myself through lately."

"How terrible for you."

Allen felt the coiled tension in Julia's hand. Afraid she might make good on her threat to toss the old guy through the window, he asked, "Why are you here?"

"I stopped by earlier, Dr. Parker, but you were not up to receiving visitors, and Ms. Matheson was busy giving some army officials a hard time."

Allen glanced at her.

"They've been trying to 'debrief' me since we arrived," she explained.

"And she's been trying to debrief *them*," Kendrick said.

"So now they send in the big guns, is that it?"

He sighed. "I need to know only one thing," he told her. "Can you end it here?"

She thought for a moment. "Did you wipe out the virus?"

"We believe so. The compound was completely incinerated—the underground base, the surface, the surrounding areas. We bombed well into the night. Our on-site teams have found no trace of virus or any other biochemical agents. Are you all right?"

Allen was squeezing his eyes shut again, this time tightly. Julia answered for him.

"We had to leave Stephen's body there."

"I know. You told Commander Bransford in Paraguay. I am sorry." He looked at his hands, then again at Julia and Allen. "This country owes you its gratitude. Unfortunately, it cannot publicly recognize that debt. We are prepared, however, to pretend none of this ever happened." His eyes locked on hers. "You understand that you must never speak of Karl Litt or *Ebola Kugel* or the United States' alleged involvement in biological weapons? Where is your laptop, please?"

"It was destroyed on Litt's compound."

Kendrick Reynolds simply stared.

Julia added, "You understand that if anything happens to me or Allen, someone might find it?"

After a moment, Reynolds tilted his head, accepting the arrangement. "When you are ready, you will be given a ticket to Atlanta on a commercial airline."

"I'll wait for Dr. Parker."

"As I said, when you are ready. Dr. Parker, I understand you may be here for another few weeks. We cannot have you treated in a private hospital." He stepped away from the bed. At the door, he turned back. "In my last conversation with him, Karl Litt said something that made me take a closer look at three records on his list of targets."

Julia smiled. "Everyone loves the First Family."

He bowed his head to her. Then he slipped out.

Julia offered Allen a sideways smile. "We're going home."

Allen didn't answer. He was somewhere else.

"What is it?" she asked.

"I don't know. When Stephen gave up on medicine, my family didn't understand. *I* didn't understand. The way we were raised, there was nothing else. It felt like he was turning his back on his family, his destiny." He shook his head. "But I see now that he had *found* his destiny. He chose to look outside my parents' narrow vision for his life. He saw a world that was bigger than himself and our family. He saw something other than patients who could provide him with the wealth and prestige our family expected. He saw *people*."

His voice broke on the last word. He turned his face away, covered it with one hand. He felt Julia's hand on his shoulder, rubbing, comforting.

After a long moment, he continued. "When I was there, in that room in Litt's base . . . when I was . . . *dying*, I thought about the names we found on your computer, the data Vero had smuggled out. Ten thousand names. Ten thousand *people*. I thought about their lives and the people who loved them, who tucked them in at night or called them during the day just to hear their voices. I wondered if they were scared the way I was. If they were in pain. I *felt* for them—not for me, for *them*. For the first time, I understood what had gotten into Stephen. What he did for people—from that little cabin behind the church, with his crummy car—what he did was so much grander than what I did."

"We need doctors, Allen. It's a noble profession."

"Only when your heart's in the right place. Stephen understood that. He went off and did what he *should* have done for the right reason, not what he *could* have done for the wrong reason."

He turned and found her eyes, relieved. She got it. He was making sense.

"Now he's gone," he said. "And I never got the chance to tell him." He paused. "I can't help but believe the wrong brother died."

"That kind of thinking will drive you crazy."

He nodded.

"I mean it. Stephen told me what happened, about killing that man in the bar. He said he felt the same way you do now, that the wrong man had died. Allen, that's not for us to decide. We can only do the best we can with the understanding we have."

Allen smiled. "Didn't I say you were pretty *and* smart?"

"Something like that."

He couldn't hold on to the smile. He felt like weeping, just crying like a baby. "So what am I supposed to do? Fill Stephen's boots? Leave medicine; become a pastor?"

"I can't answer that, but if you follow that course because that's what Stephen did, then it doesn't seem any better than becoming a physician because your dad wanted you to. Why don't you take your time, heal, then see?"

"What are you going to do?"

"Take my time, heal, then see."

She pressed her cheek to his chest and hugged him. He draped an arm across her back and stroked her hair. It felt right. Just two people comforting each other. He smiled again, and this time it stayed.